To my Dad who was everything my heroine's father is not.
Gone from this life, but ever in my heart.

BEYOND THESE

War-torn

LANDS

Wounded Hearts • Book One

Award-winning Author
CYNTHIA ROEMER

Scrivenings
PRESS
Quench your thirst for story.
www.ScriveningsPress.com

©2021 Cynthia Roemer

Published by Scrivenings Press LLC
15 Lucky Lane
Morrilton, Arkansas 72110
https://ScriveningsPress.com

Printed in the United States of America

Paperback ISBN 978-1-64917-141-2

eBook ISBN 978-1-64917-142-9

Library of Congress Control Number: 2021942083

Editors: Elena Hill and Kaci Banks

Cover by Linda Fulkerson, www.bookmarketinggraphics.com

Beyond These War-Torn Lands is a work of fiction. Where real people, events, establishments, organizations, or locales appear, they are used fictitiously. All other elements of the novel are drawn from the author's imagination.

All other scriptures are taken from the KING JAMES VERSION (KJV): KING JAMES VERSION, public domain.

ACKNOWLEDGMENTS

This is now my fourth novel in print. When I consider that, I am overwhelmed with gratitude for all those who have made such a dream-come-true possible. Without the Lord's abundant love and guiding hand, none of this would have been possible. May His name be praised, and may each word I write bring glory to Him.

I'm so grateful to the staff of Scrivenings Press for believing in my stories. Thanks to Publisher, Linda Fulkerson, for her tireless efforts to aid, encourage, guide, and promote my work as well as the numerous other authors she's taken under her wing. Thanks to Content Editor and Virtual Assistant, Elena Hill, who is ever the encourager and diligent to keep things running smoothly behind the scenes. Your spunk and sense of humor keep us smiling! Thanks to editorial and support staff, Shannon Vannetter, Erin Howard, Kaci Banks, and Whitney Bynum, for all their help and assistance. They truly do treat us like family. God bless you all for your commitment to excellence in writing and caring for us as individuals.

I can't say enough about my sweet friends and beta-readers Savanna Kaiser and Cara Grandle. Through thick and thin, you have been there for me. You are both such an encouragement to me as my friends and writing pals. The Lord truly blessed me when He allowed our paths to cross at ACFW all those years ago.

What a huge blessing it was to partner with my dear friend and fellow historical romance author, Kelly Goshorn. I feel I gained a sister when we joined forces to spur each other on in our writing endeavors. You have been such an incredible critique partner for this project and I look forward to sharing in more ventures in years to come.

I'm ever grateful to my husband, Marvin, for enduring my endless hours of research and writing at the computer. Thanks for your understanding and for sticking by me even though writing is so not your thing. Thanks for your patience and enduring love through every project and deadline. I love you!

Lastly, thanks to my parents for buying my first computer, believing in my writing from the start, and backing me each step of the way. God bless you for encouraging this girl of yours to follow her dream!

"You have heard that it was said,
Love your neighbor and hate your enemy.'
But I tell you, Love your enemies
and pray for those who persecute you
that you may be sons of your Father in heaven."
(Matthew 5:43-44)

1

July 9, 1864,
Battle of Monocacy Junction, Maryland

Sergeant Andrew Gallagher drew his bloodied bayonet from yet another gray-clad soldier. All around, the roar of gunfire mingled with the moans of the wounded and dying. The humid air reeked of flesh and gunpowder. Waves of Confederate soldiers continued to pummel him and his men from every side like a swarm of gnats. There was no time to think, only react.

He wheeled around just as another Rebel soldier charged him from behind, rifle and bayonet pointed at his midsection. With a sharp, upward cut of his rifle, Drew tore the weapon from the youth's hands, and it spiraled through the air, breaking as it landed. The young soldier's face blanched, fear mingling with contempt in his eyes.

The defenseless lad gave a shrill cry and leaped at Drew, clawing at him with his bare hands. Rather than gouging him, Drew landed a hard blow to the soldier's jaw. The youth stumbled backward and fell dazed, his inexperienced attempts at warfare temporarily at an end.

Drew's mouth pulled in a sad grin. Lord willing, some mother would have the pleasure of greeting her boy when the war was over.

A shot whizzed past his ear. He flinched and instinctively surveyed his men. They were weary and outnumbered; a good many had fallen.

He clenched his jaw. How many more lives would be lost if they persisted?

A bugle sounded in the distance, and relief washed through Drew. They'd battled nearly non-stop since daybreak, struggling to hold their ground against the Rebs along the Monocacy River. Twice he and his men had sent them scurrying, only to have them come back harder, stronger. There seemed no end to them. General Wallace must have taken note of their plight and realized it was a no-win situation. Raising his arm, Drew signaled his bugler to sound retreat.

He only hoped their efforts had not been for nothing.

As he and his fellow soldiers in blue turned from battle, another volley of shots rang out.

A hot sting seared Drew's shoulder.

Laughter sounded a few yards to his left. "Take that, you ol' blue-belly."

Ignoring the shooting pang in his arm, he fixed his gaze on the jeering Confederate soldier. The Rebel sneered as he lowered his rifle. Drew wavered, knowing he should remain with his men, but the temptation to retaliate beckoned him.

No Johnny Reb mocked him and got away with it.

Vengeance is mine, saith the Lord.

The inner prompting gave Drew pause but wasn't enough to squelch his thirst for revenge. The Confederates owned this day, this battle, but he refused to let this gloating private glory in the victory. Seeing no immediate threats, Drew charged toward him, rifle and bayonet at the ready. The soldier's face paled as he neared. With no time to reload, the man scrambled to unsheathe the bayonet he'd foolishly neglected to attach to his rifle. As Drew threw back his arm to thrust, a flash of silver whirled toward him. Pain sliced through him as the blade lodged deep in his side. At nearly the same instant, his bayonet found its mark in the Rebel soldier's chest. With a loud shriek, the man crumpled to the ground.

A bit faint, Drew loosened his grip on his rifle and turned from the onslaught of Confederate soldiers headed toward him. A riderless horse trotted by several yards to his left. With effort, Drew pulled the knife from his side and pressed a hand to the wound as he limped over to the bay mare. Taking hold of the horse's mane, he heaved himself into the saddle and tapped heels to her flanks. The horse lunged forward as though eager to leave the chaos of battle.

In agony, Drew slumped forward, molding himself to the horse's neck.

His impulsive act had cost him dearly.

The barrage of gunfire followed him along the open field and into the nearby timber to the east. His company had scattered, no doubt having sought refuge among the trees and underbrush. Once out of range, Drew slowed his mount and ventured a first glance at his pierced side. Enough blood had oozed from the wound to leave a sizable dark splotch on his navy wool jacket. Loosening the brass buttons, he cringed at the bright red stain on his shirt. He raised it for a look, the deep gash continuing to spew blood.

At this rate, he'd likely not last long.

He hung his head. "Serves me right for not listening, Lord."

Unbuttoning his shirt, he tied the shirttails together around him in an attempt to stem the flow of blood. He swayed sideways and clasped the saddle horn to steady himself. Sweat trickled down his temples as the sweltering heat and blood loss stole his strength. No telling what would become of him if he fell into enemy hands. More than likely, he'd be imprisoned or hung —neither thought appealing.

Given his rough condition, the Lord might very well claim him first and cheat the Rebs out of having their way with him.

He closed his eyes, melting into the rhythm of the mare's steady gait.

Forgive me, Lord, for being headstrong and thoughtless. I don't deserve your mercy, but if you could see fit to bring me ... through this, I'd ... be ... obliged.

The sound of gunfire faded in the distance. He pried his eyes open. "Stay ... awake."

The trees swirled around him, and he clung tighter to the horse's neck, his breaths growing shallower. Spots marred his vision, then darkness enveloped him.

He sensed himself falling, powerless to stop it.

A TWIG SNAPPED beneath Caroline Dunbar's boot, and she froze. She clutched tighter to her satchel, the quietness almost eerie. The birds stilled as though hiding from the atrocities of war. Not a whiff of breeze stirred in the treetops. She inched forward, wondering if she'd made a mistake in coming.

A soft sigh escaped her. She'd come too far to turn back.

The fighting had sounded so close this time. So near, in fact, their neighbors to the west must have seen the thick of battle. At Caroline's pleading, Mama consented to let her lend help where needed. Long after the guns had ceased, she'd ventured toward the timber that separated their estate from the Thomas Farm. Beyond the trees lay Bush Creek and, further to the west, the Monocacy River.

Somewhere in between, the battle had raged.

No doubt the wounded would be many.

A foreboding plume of dark smoke swirled in the direction of the Thomas farm. Had they suffered harm? Who would have guessed this once-tranquil countryside would become a maelstrom of military tensions?

The afternoon shadows were deepening. If Papa knew she'd strayed into the timber so near the battlegrounds, his anger would prove unsightly. Yet, if she could help even one brave soldier recover from his wounds, it would be worth enduring his wrath. If her brother, Jamison, were lying wounded on some battlefield, wouldn't Papa wish someone to aid him?

Besides, how was she to gain knowledge of nursing without a patient?

A horse's soft nicker startled her, and she ducked behind the trunk of a sturdy oak. She waited, her heart at her throat. Finally venturing a look, she released the breath she'd been holding at the sight of a lone mare munching leaves. The empty saddle across her back indicated the tragic circumstances that had brought her to this desolate place. Had the rider been injured or killed?

Caroline's stomach lurched. Or was he lying in wait somewhere?

She paused to listen but heard only the sound of the bay's nervous chomping.

Convinced she was alone, she eased from her hiding place and stepped toward the animal, hand outstretched. "Easy, girl. I'll not harm you."

The horse reared its head, sidestepping as she neared. Caroline edged closer, letting the jittery mare sniff her fingertips. Speaking in low tones, she touched a gentle hand to the horse's muzzle. "There now. You're safe, girl."

A faint moan sounded several yards up ahead. Caroline sucked in a breath, stifling the urge to flee. She snatched the horse's reins and peered into the underbrush, deliberating. Should she ride away or stay to investigate?

A second groan gave her pause. She'd come to aid the wounded, hadn't she?

With a decided breath, she tugged the mare in the direction of the sound. Hiking her skirt to step over a fallen log, she panned the tangle of foliage stretched out ahead of her.

"Help."

Her gaze darted to the timber floor a few feet to her left.

Though the plea was little more than a raspy whisper, it reached her very core. No longer could she question her need to help, only her abilities.

She lifted her eyes heavenward. *Lord, grant me courage.*

Edging closer, she caught sight of the wounded soldier and clapped a hand over her mouth. Rather than Confederate gray, the injured man wore the navy uniform of a Federal. The sergeant's stripes on his sleeve hinted he would be missed by an entire squad of soldiers.

Her heart drummed in her ears. What now? Did she flee or help this man her family deemed an enemy—one of the very men her older brother sought to kill?

The soldier's eyelids flickered to half-mast. His cap had fallen, revealing a head of unkempt, dark brown hair. Though pale and marred with dirt, his face was pleasant.

One might even dare say handsome.

He cringed, pleading with her through gritted teeth. "Please, miss. I need ... your ... help."

With each breath, his chest heaved as though every word was a struggle. She wavered, torn between loyalty to her southern roots and her God-given duty to aid those in need. With a furtive glance around, she inched closer and knelt beside him. Dark stains soiled the shoulder and left side of his torn uniform.

She cleared her throat, doing her best to appear as though she knew what she was doing. "I'll need to examine your wounds."

His nod did little to bolster her confidence. With quivering hands, she pulled the wool material aside, her stomach lurching at the stench of sweat mingled with blood. Heat singed her cheeks as she reached to loosen the blood-soaked shirt-ends tied around his middle. Never in her nineteen years had she been so near a man, let alone exposed one's bare chest. She kept her attention schooled on the knotted shirt, consoling herself that a nurse was forced to abandon propriety and release fears of indecency.

She could only pray her limited knowledge of nursing would prove adequate.

She fumbled to untie the shirt, her fingers slick from fresh blood. At last, she peeled it back, wincing at the sight of the cavernous gash beneath. It didn't take a seasoned nurse to determine the wound was substantial. With so much loss of blood, it was a wonder he remained conscious.

Or perhaps he had lost consciousness for a time?

No doubt the injury would require stitches—a skill she felt ill-equipped to attempt. "Your wound is quite deep. I'm afraid it will need sewn together, but I—"

"Do it."

His decisive command stilled her words and drained the blood from her cheeks. She'd mended clothing but never attempted to sew flesh. The notion left her a bit queasy. She shook her head. "Under such primitive circumstances, I think it best not to try it. I-I'm not experienced with that sort of thing."

He stared up at her, flecks of blue in his silvery eyes. "Unless you do ... I'll likely ... not ... survive."

Her feeble excuses melted under the sobering words. Though his pain must have been excruciating, he bore it with as much grit as any Southerner could muster. At last, she nodded. "I'll try."

He seemed to relax, mouthing a weak "thank you."

Reluctantly, she reached into her satchel and retrieved her bottle of iodine, along with a wad of cotton. As she doused the fibers with the antiseptic, she did her best not to appear nervous. In her wildest notions, she'd not dreamed her day would include tending the wounds of a Union sergeant.

But pleas for help were not something she could easily ignore.

She sensed the soldier's eyes upon her as she gently dabbed at the wound. Was he equally unnerved by these rather odd circumstances?

"What are you doing ... out here ... alone?" His breathy inquiry surprised her.

She hesitated, keeping her eyes trained on her work. "I-I was on my way to my neighbor's to aid the injured soldiers."

When he gave no reply, she ventured a glance his way. Whether from fatigue or fortitude, he uttered not so much as a groan, though his face pinched from time to time.

His cheeks flinched as he shifted his head toward her. "Confederate soldiers ... I'm guessin' by your ... accent."

She gave a slow nod.

He swallowed, his voice raspy. "Sorry to ... spoil your plans. I'm obliged ... you took notice ... of me."

Setting the iodine aside, she wiped her hands on a cloth and reached in her bag for the needle fastened in its lining. "You needed tending to. I only did what any good Christian would."

He nodded slightly, his eyelids growing heavy. "God ... bless you ... miss."

His head slumped to the side, and for a moment, Caroline thought she might be free of the obligation to aid him. But his chest rose and fell in steady movements. She gnawed at her lip, half-tempted to leave him where he lay, but her conscience, along with the memory of his imploring eyes, held her in place. To desert him now would make her no less than a liar and a murderer.

She'd promised to help, and that she must do.

Having forgotten to pack thread, she stood and strode to the back of his horse, yanking a strand of hair from its tail. Not the most sanitary of materials, but it was all she had. With effort, she worked to thread the coarse hair through the eye of the needle then returned to the soldier's side. With no means to deaden the pain, his unconsciousness proved a blessing. Whispering a prayer, she thrust the needle into his skin and pulled it through.

2

Movement above Drew stirred him to consciousness. A sharp pang shot through his shoulder and side, jolting him back to reality. He forced his eyelids open and stared into the treetops fringed by the dusky-blue of twilight. A shadowy figure loomed over him, his face obscured by the encroaching darkness. The stocky man hadn't the look of a soldier.

More than likely a scavenger out for what he could salvage.

Drew attempted to rise but fell back, every ounce of his strength spent. Whoever it was, he was at his mercy. "Who are you?"

"Name's Cyrus. Miss Caroline sent me t' fetch ya." The hushed voice sounded like that of a slave.

Confusion fogged Drew's senses. "Miss ... Caroline?"

The figure bent lower, his voice a whisper. "The one who found ya and stitched ya up."

Drew slid a hand beneath his unbuttoned uniform and touched his fingertips to his swollen side. Instead of a gaping wound, his fingers met with a jagged line of coarse stitching hemmed in by bulging flesh covered by a thin cloth bandage. Dim recollection washed over him of a dark-haired beauty who'd reluctantly come to his aid. He forced his eyes wider, the intense pain and grogginess making him wish he'd not come to at all.

"How'd you find me?"

"Miss Caroline told me whereabouts you'd be and left your horse tied nearby. I've rigged up a pole sled to tote ya on."

Cyrus moved aside, allowing Drew a glimpse of the bay mare he'd ridden from battle with a crude travois fastened behind. He gave a slight nod, though he couldn't fathom where a slave could safely conceal an injured Union soldier on southern sympathizer land.

Or why he'd risk trying.

Standing, Cyrus shifted to Drew's head and slid quivering hands under his arms. Was he afraid? He had every reason to be. Miss Caroline put her servant in grave danger on Drew's behalf. If found aiding a Union soldier, the man would likely be severely flogged.

Or worse.

A sharp sting pierced Drew's shoulder as Cyrus placed his hands beneath him and lifted. He cringed and held back a groan. Given the raw sensitivity in his shoulder, the minié ball had either lodged deep within or traveled through him completely. With all the loss of blood, it was a wonder he'd not died hours ago. If not for the Lord's saving grace and the kindness of a beautiful stranger, he might well have.

The horse whinnied and pawed at the ground as Cyrus slid Drew onto the makeshift sled. Sweat droplets dampened his forehead and neck at the exertion. His energy sapped, Drew had no choice but to entrust his welfare to this man's benevolence.

And to his Creator.

Stillness blanketed the night, but for the chant of insects and the rustle of feet in the dew-laden grass. Drew felt the travois grow taut beneath him as the horse tugged forward over uneven ground. Each jolting motion pulsed through him like salt in a wound. He stared into the starlit sky, breathless, vulnerable, wondering if he'd ever see the light of day.

As darkness overspread the sky, he sensed himself fading in

and out. His eyelids fluttered closed, and he gave in to the urge to shut out everything around him—the pain, the mistakes, the uncertainties—as a familiar verse drummed through his head. *Yea, though I walk through the valley of the shadow of death, I will fear no evil: for thou art with me.* Thoughts of war and battles faded into the far recesses of Drew's mind as he drifted into unconsciousness, his body teetering between life and death.

CAROLINE SLIPPED into her chair at the dinner table under her father's scrutinizing stare. The red blotches in his cheeks indicated his displeasure. He speared a piece of smoked ham with his fork, mouth taut. "You're late."

"I'm sorry, Papa." She brushed a strand of hair from her cheek, working to still her anxious spirit. If her father knew the reason behind her tardiness, his dour mood would seem mild in comparison to what she would suffer.

"No need to scold, Eugene. Caroline has a fitting excuse for her tardiness. She's been on an errand of benevolence." Her mother's calming voice squeezed some of the tension from the awkward moment.

Papa's brow furrowed. "What sort of benevolence?"

Mama passed Caroline a depleted bowl of mashed potatoes, letting a moment pass before answering as though choosing her words with care. At last, she folded her hands together and met Papa's gaze. "With the battle so near, Caroline thought it fitting to look in on our neighbors and offer aid to the wounded."

Papa paused his chewing, his gaze flicking between Caroline and her mother. "Which neighbors?"

Mama's chin tipped slightly upward. "Mr. and Mrs. Thomas."

He scowled. Papa made no secret of his disdain for their neighbors to the west. Though the Thomas family owned slaves, her father often criticized them for not holding as staunch of allegiance to the Southern way of thinking as he felt they ought. Mr. and Mrs. Thomas's interaction with Union leaders—allowing them to meet in their house on occasion—especially galled him. Rumors claimed they'd welcomed General Ulysses S. Grant himself into their home.

He turned to Caroline, shifting his food to one side of his mouth. "And exactly what was it you did?"

Caroline dropped a small mound of potatoes onto her plate, her mouth turning to cotton. How could she admit she'd not even made it to the neighbors'? By the time she'd finished cleaning and stitching up the Union sergeant's wounds, the sun had set low on the horizon. She'd barely had time to locate Cyrus and inform him of the man's whereabouts before returning home to wash and change her soiled dress.

It was wrong to deceive, but to confess her true whereabouts would be her undoing. "I'm afraid so late in the day I wasn't much help."

"Then why did you bother going?" Her father's condescending tone begged an explanation.

Her throat thickened, and she took a hard swallow. With her brother, Jamison, away at war, it seemed she could never do quite enough to aid the Confederate cause. She squared her shoulders, giving in to the urge to redeem herself in his eyes. "I-I did assist one soldier, though he was in such a sorry state, I'm not certain he'll survive."

Her mother dabbed the edges of her mouth with her napkin and shook her head. "Poor fellow."

Papa's chair creaked as he pushed back from the table. "Let's just hope he took down a heap of blue-bellies with him."

Caroline lowered her gaze to the table, heat rising in her cheeks. Though she'd spoken the truth, she'd neglected to mention the soldier wasn't Confederate. She set the bowl of potatoes aside, her appetite waning. Whether she admitted it or not, she'd aided a man her family deemed an enemy.

In her father's eyes, such an act was unforgivable.

While some in Maryland embraced the Northern way of thinking, her father remained steadfast in his conviction that slavery was every landowner's right and privilege, a cause to fight for to the bitter end. A bullet wound to the leg had ended his time of service. His pronounced limp was a constant reminder of why he despised the Yankees and everything they stood for. Perhaps the injury was also why he remained fixated on news from the battlefront—and why he devoured Jamison's infrequent letters as if experiencing the war through his eyes.

"I hear tell our boys sent the Yankees skedaddling." Her father's words sliced through her thoughts, pride replacing the agitation in his voice.

Caroline's younger brother, Phillip, popped his last bite of biscuit in his mouth, his expression earnest. "Wish I was old enough t' fight. I'd have put some buckshot in more than one of their backsides."

The comment garnered a rare chuckle from their father and a raised brow from Mama. "Phillip Wade Dunbar. Such talk isn't suitable at the dinner table."

The boy's wry grin hinted he was unfazed by the reprimand. He returned his gaze to Papa. "Do you suppose Jamison was with 'em?"

"If he was, I'll wager he was first in line to send them scuttling." His stern mood forgotten, Papa reached to tousle Phillip's hair.

Pricked by the amiable exchange, Caroline finished filling her plate. Though Jamison had ever been her father's pride and joy, Phillip seemed to have taken on the role in his absence. All she ever did was incur her father's wrath. Somehow, in his eyes, she never measured up.

Did he favor sons over daughters? It certainly didn't seem so where her younger sister, Rose, was concerned. Many a time, she'd witnessed him extending her a warm hug and a kiss on the cheek at bedtime. Rarely, if ever, had Caroline received such an endearing gesture from her father. Instead, her earliest memories of him included stern words and an aloofness she didn't comprehend.

She bowed her head, her thoughts veering back to the injured sergeant. When she'd left, he still hadn't awakened. More than likely, he'd not live through the night. A part of her regretted ever lending help to the stranger and convincing Cyrus to join in her deceit. Her stomach churned at having put the dear servant in danger.

What had she been thinking, instructing him to bring a Union officer onto her father's property?

Yet the memory of the sergeant's pleading eyes lingered in her mind. Could it be so wrong to help someone in need, whether he be friend or foe? Jesus commended those who showed kindness to their enemies.

Unfortunately, Papa thought differently.

And she hated to think what would happen should he discover her ruse.

3

Soldiers everywhere. Bleeding. Crying out. Lunging at him. Guns and cannons blaring on every side. Drew reached to unsheathe his bayonet but instead clasped air. "No!"

He thrashed back and forth, his breaths coming in rapid succession.

"Shhh. You're safe now." A woman's soothing voice crooned overhead.

Damp coolness swept over Drew's sweat-drenched brow, pulling him from his nightmarish dream. His eyes shot open, and dim rafters stared back at him. Where was he? He merely remembered fleeing the battlefield on a borrowed horse.

A cotton sheet lay across his bandaged chest, his bloodied shirt and uniform jacket having been stripped away. He shifted his gaze to the woman leaning over him, her honey-colored eyes a blend of softness and alarm. Like a frightened doe, she sat frozen in place, hand suspended in midair, gripping a dampened cloth.

He'd seen that face before. Except now, instead of pinned up, her dark hair cascaded down onto her shoulders, haloing her oval face.

Such loveliness was difficult to forget.

"Who are you?"

She lowered her hand, the slight movement in her lips hinting she was hesitant to divulge the information. At last, she found her voice. "Caroline Dunbar."

Pain sliced through him, and his eyes crimped. "Miss Caroline. I ... remember now. You ... found me and ... stitched my wound. Your slave ... Cyrus ... brought me here."

She nodded, uncertainty marring her expression. "Yes."

Drew wished to put her at ease, to thank her for her selfless efforts, but his voice failed. He was exhausted and so very weak. Like driftwood floating aimlessly downstream, his limbs hung limp, refusing to budge. How he longed to escape the agony and fatigue tormenting his body. His eyes closed, and like an angelic vision, the woman and his surroundings faded.

CAROLINE PRESSED the back of her hand to the sergeant's blistered forehead, thankful he was resting once again. Fever meant his body was fighting infection. That much she knew. Although the minié ball passed through his shoulder, the damage was substantial. She'd pulled several fragments of bone and lead from the wound.

Would her limited knowledge of medicine be enough?

Heat rose in Caroline's cheeks as she pulled the cotton sheet higher on his exposed chest. Too riddled and stained to repair, his bloodied shirt and uniform jacket lay rolled up in the corner to dispose of later. His shoulders looked a bit broader than Jamison's, but perhaps she could sneak into her brother's room and borrow one of his larger shirts for the sergeant to wear once he'd sufficiently healed.

This abandoned slave shack would provide protection for a time, but frequenting it would arouse suspicion. Yet, the sergeant would need daily nourishment and continuous medical care to sustain him. Could she risk asking their house servant, Lily, for help?

She gave a soft sigh. Enemy or not, she hoped the sergeant lived. He'd made it this far. She hated to see her efforts to save him go unrewarded. In the short time he'd been alert, his eyes had displayed the will to live.

Something deep within her longed for him to have that chance.

———

THE DECIDEDLY SOPRANO voices echoed through the half-empty church building as the final note to the hymn rang out. Vacant spots dotted the pews, a sobering reminder that the majority of menfolk were still at war.

Or not coming home at all.

Only a handful of older men and young boys remained alongside the women.

Caroline's stomach hitched at the noticeable absence of both the Worthington and Thomas families. Had something terrible befallen them? Guilt riddled her. By not following through with her intentions to check on the neighbors, she'd not only betrayed her mother's trust but quite possibly missed a crucial opportunity to lend much-needed aid.

Pastor Huddleston plucked off his spectacles and motioned for the congregation to sit. Stepping away from the pulpit, he clamped his hands together behind his back. His wrinkled face drew taut as he waited for the room to quiet. At last, he sighed, his voice solemn and profound. "Yesterday's battle at Monocacy Junction was a costly one for many. I've received word that the Thomas Farm was in the thick of battle. The family's home sustained extensive damage when a cannonball ripped through its front."

An audible gasp swept through the sparse congregation. Caroline recalled the plume of smoke she had seen in the distance. She bit her lip at her parents' puzzled stares from the opposite end of the pew. No doubt they thought her neglectful in sharing their neighbor's misfortunes. But, how could she inform them of something she hadn't known?

The pastor waved the crowd to silence. "Both they and the Worthington family went through a harrowing experience with the constant barrage of fighting outside their homes while they remained hunkered in their cellars. Thankfully no one in either household was injured, but they are in dire need of supplies and assistance. In addition, the Thomas yard is inundated with wounded soldiers in need of care. I spoke early this morning with Mrs. Thomas, who requested all the bedding, food, and willing workers we can muster."

Caroline shifted in her seat. She couldn't undo what had transpired, but she could make every effort to help today.

Pastor Huddleston strode closer to the front pews, gripping his Bible in both hands. "Though this be the Lord's Day, a day for rest and worship, Scripture alludes to the fact we are to do good when it is within our power to do so. Jesus, himself, healed on the Sabbath. I know many of you will want to help. Join me in prayer as we dismiss."

He motioned the congregation to their feet and, with eyes closed, lifted his arms heavenward. "Oh, Lord, we implore You to bring a swift end to this horrific war which has devastated our land. Our nation is divided, and our people perishing. Strengthen our hearts and our hands as we lend aid to our dear friends and the soldiers in their care. May Your grace be upon us all. In Christ's name, amen."

A tear slid down his cheek as his eyes lifted, sadness etched in his long face. Though cautious never to take sides regarding the war, the elderly pastor made clear his contempt for conflict. "May God go with you."

As the somber crowd dispersed, Caroline felt a tug on her sleeve. Turning, she glimpsed hurt in her mother's befuddled expression. "Why didn't you tell us the severity of the Thomases' hardships? Did you not realize the urgency?"

How could she respond? Any attempt to defend herself would be a falsehood. Mama was certain to see right through her … and perhaps pry the true reason from her. Dropping her gaze, she could only plead forgiveness. "I'm sorry, Mama. Forgive me."

Her mother shook her head as she followed Phillip and Rose down the aisle. With a grunt, Papa swept past Caroline and limped his way outside. Her throat tightened. If she'd known the need was so great, she'd have been more inclined to pass the wounded Union sergeant by. And yet, could she have been so callous as to neglect the need before her simply because he wasn't one of their own?

Did a person have the right to pick and choose whom they tended? As much as she regretted not realizing their neighbors' distress, the Lord had placed the sergeant in her path. Ignoring him in his time of need would have made her no better than the priest and Levite who passed the injured man on the roadside in Jesus' parable. She'd done what she felt right, and that was that.

She wound her way through the dispersing crowd, talk of yesterday's battle monopolizing the conversation.

"Mary Worthington said her young son, Glenn, watched the entire battle from their cellar window," she overheard Mrs. Connors whisper to Mrs. Delany.

The elderly Mrs. Delany shook her head. "I'm surprised at Mary allowing such a thing. A boy his tender age shouldn't view such violence."

Caroline skirted around them, certain she would glean no more than hearsay from the two white-haired ladies. As she stepped outside, she adjusted her bonnet to better shade her face from the brightness of the midday sun. Her father and two older gentlemen, Mr. Connors and Mr. Jenkins, loitered at the bottom of the steps, deep in conversation. She made her way toward them, catching bits and pieces of their discussion—

enough to convince her eavesdropping on the exchange would be more worth her time.

Pausing at the opposite side of the bottom step, she feigned looking for someone in the dispersing crowd. She focused on their voices, listening for some tidbit concerning yesterday's battle that would aid the sergeant in his escape. Should he recover, he'd need to know where to reconnect with his men.

"They say Monocacy Junction is in shambles. The bridges burned, the railroad tracks destroyed, and the ground ... with weapons and dead soldiers," Mr. Jenkins's subdued voice made a few of the words hard to distinguish.

Mr. Connors' muffled reply was difficult to catch. Something about another Confederate victory.

Caroline leaned closer, grateful her father's back was to her. While the other men seemed oblivious to her presence, had her father noticed her, he likely would have prodded her on.

Papa let out a chuckle, his voice less restrained than his companions'. "The Yankees took a beatin', that's sure. General Early and his men must've chased 'em halfway to Baltimore."

She cringed, noting a few heads veer in his direction. Not everyone in the congregation shared Papa's sentiments. Some of their neighbors' husbands and sons fought for the Union, which explained why their pastor was careful not to declare sides.

Mr. Jenkins cautioned Caroline's father with a shake of his head and an uneasy look around. He leaned in closer, brow furrowed. "Careful, Eugene. You'll offend."

Unable to see her father's face or read his expression, Caroline breathed easier when he remained silent.

Mr. Connors clapped him on the shoulder. "I'm content the fighting has ended, and the Northerners have left the area."

Caroline gnawed her lip. If the Yankees went northward, no telling where they'd be by the time the sergeant recovered enough to travel. Even in good health, the journey would be treacherous for a Union soldier on enemy soil. How would he manage it in his weakened state?

She strolled toward the line of parked carriages, her thoughts in turmoil. It seemed traitorous to help the sergeant recuperate only to send him back to fight the very men who were protecting her family's livelihood. But if she became a nurse, it would be her duty to help restore a patient's health regardless of his beliefs or status. She could only pray her secret act of benevolence would not prove costly.

For either of them.

4

"I believe I'll walk."

At her mother's nod, Caroline deposited her satchel of medical supplies in the back of the carriage alongside the pile of linens and her father's tools. The mounting stack of materials made it an easy decision to walk rather than ride to the Thomas farm.

As did Papa's furrowed brow.

Despite his contempt for their neighbors' lenience toward the Union, Mama's persistence had paid off. He'd finally succumbed to her pleas for his help with repairs to the Thomas house, citing it as an act of loyalty to the wounded Confederate soldiers.

While Rose and Philip had unleashed an endless barrage of questions, Caroline and her parents had exchanged few words during the ride home from church or their hurried meal. News of their neighbors' misfortunes weighed heavy on her heart. Not that her efforts yesterday evening would have made much of a difference, given the score of adversities the family was facing, but knowing she'd neglected to alert Mama and Papa to their needs left her feeling selfish and irresponsible. However honorable her intentions, she had no plausible excuse.

As she stepped away from the carriage, she noticed Cyrus chopping weeds at the corner of the house. He cut a glance in her direction, then returned to his work, shoulders slumped. How she wished she could speak with him in private about his late-night venture with the sergeant. But the set of his jaw and averted gaze hinted he had nothing to say. She'd put him in a vulnerable position. To further endanger him by bidding him to look in on the wounded soldier would be too much to ask.

Her gaze flicked to Lily, their housemaid, standing at the top of the steps, hands resting on Rose's shoulders. Had Cyrus mentioned the soldier to her? The dubious glint in her eyes suggested he had. Married more than twenty years, the childless couple likely kept no secrets between them.

With Mama and Papa gone, could Lily find an opportunity to slip away to take the sergeant a bit of nourishment? She and Cyrus had been with the family for as long as Caroline could remember and were more trusted employees than slaves or servants. In due time, Papa'd promised them freedom.

No doubt, when they'd outlived their usefulness to the family.

Phillip dropped his load of supplies in the carriage then stood back, arms crossed at his front. "I don't see why I can't go."

Mama pivoted toward him, brows raised. "There's no need for you to view such atrocities of war. You'd best stay and help entertain Rose."

"But couldn't I help Papa with the house repairs?" He kicked the toe of his boot against the rain-deprived sod. At fourteen, her brother was eager to become a man. And by the fluctuating tone in his voice, the time wasn't far off.

Papa exchanged a purposeful look with Mama as he helped her onto the carriage seat. "Phillip has a strong arm and a willing spirit. He might be a welcome asset."

Phillip squinted up at them, his countenance lifting. "Please, Mama? I'm old enough."

Mama seemed to weigh Philip's words. As the youngest son, she tended to pamper him, though his vivacious spirit often called for a firm hand.

At last, she gave a long sigh and pointed to the back of the carriage. "All right. Hop on. But see that you make yourself useful and mind your father."

Phillip's lips spread in a crooked grin. "Yes, ma'am." He hefted himself up onto the cluttered carriage bed, seeming quite satisfied with himself as he shoved supplies aside to make room.

Caroline shook her head and backed toward the house. More times than not, her younger brother weaseled his way into their parents' good graces. At least he wouldn't be around to hinder Lily's chances of slipping away unnoticed.

"Sure you don't want to ride along, Caroline?"

At her mother's inquiry, Caroline paused at the bottom step. "No, thank you. I'll meet you there."

Mama nodded and waved as the carriage pulled forward.

Caroline waited until they were a safe distance away, then climbed the veranda steps. Placing a hand under her sister's chin, she smiled down at her. "Rose, would you be a dear and fetch my bonnet?"

"All right." Without a moment's hesitation, the nine-year-old skipped toward the front door, her dark ringlets bouncing with each stride. Caroline couldn't help but harbor a soft spot for her young sister. Whereas Philip tended toward Papa's solemn disposition the older he got, Rose rarely made a fuss about anything.

Waiting until her sister was out of earshot, Caroline leaned close to Lily, her voice but a whisper. "Did Cyrus mention the old shack has a visitor?"

Lily's fleshy face shifted toward her, white showing in her rounded eyes. She gave a slight nod, her rigid tone laced with angst. "Yes'm."

At the sound of Rose's lively hum inside the house, Caroline's heart leaped to her throat. Time was short. If she were to enlist the maid's help, she had to act quickly. Drawing a breath, she leaned close to Lily's ear. "I saw him early this morning. He survived the night and will need nourishment. I'll have no opportunity to offer him anything. Could you take some broth or ..."

Lily's shaky fingers gripped Caroline's arm, stilling her words. "You knows I'd do 'bout anything for ya, Miss Caroline, but you done put me an' Cyrus in an awful fix. What was you thinkin', bringin' that Yankee fella on your pappy's land?"

Heat flamed in Caroline's cheeks. Lily would never dare such bold speech with Mama and Papa, but the plucky woman took liberties where Caroline and the rest of the family were concerned. Having helped rear them from birth, the maid was known to speak her mind from time to time.

Caroline squared her shoulders. "What else was I to do? I couldn't very well ignore his pleas and leave him to die."

Lily's hold on her arm eased, her chocolaty eyes softening. "No, honeychild. I reckon you done right. You has a heart as golden as the sun. Don't you fret none. Me and Cyrus'll pitch in an' do what we's able, trustin' the Good Lord to watch over our comin' an' a-goin'."

Caroline gave the housemaid's hand a gentle squeeze. "Thank you."

Hurried footsteps padded down the hall to the front door. As Rose burst onto the veranda with the bonnet, Caroline stepped away from Lily and pasted on a smile. With her inquisitive sister to oversee, it might prove a challenge for the dear woman to find the opportunity to slip away. Caroline could only pray she'd find the means.

And that their secret would be kept safe.

———

CAROLINE'S STOMACH wrenched as she topped the rise leading to the Thomas farm. She drew a hand to her mouth, tears

26

welling in her eyes. Never had she witnessed such a horrific sight. Wounded soldiers lay everywhere, scattered about on blankets, beds of straw, and sheaves of wheat, their bodies mangled and bleeding. She looked away. If ever she were to second-guess her desire to become a nurse, now would be the time.

An occasional moan broke the eerie stillness, beckoning her forward. The humid air reeked of body odor and decay. Trudging closer, she scanned the faces of the soldiers, praying none would be familiar—a neighbor or friend. Or worse yet, Jamison. Nearly a month had passed since they'd heard from her brother. He'd been in Virginia then. By now, he could be anywhere.

Several women from church and others she didn't recognize knelt beside the ravaged soldiers, binding their wounds and divvying out rations of food and water to those alert enough to manage it. So intent on their duties, no one seemed to notice her. Two men carrying a stretcher passed, their patient limp and ghostly white. A shiver ran through her as her gaze fell away. The youth's life had been snuffed out before he'd had a chance to live.

She bit back tears, listening to the groans of the surrounding wounded. So much hardship. So many in need. Where should she begin?

"Caroline! Over here."

Relieved at the sound of the familiar voice, she turned to see her mother motioning to her from across the yard, a grim expression marring her usually pleasant face. Hiking her skirt, Caroline wound her way through the tangle of injured soldiers and caregivers. The stench of sweat and filth permeated her senses. She took shallow breaths, doing her best to avoid the pained expressions of the battered soldiers.

As Caroline neared, Mama stood and wiped blood-stained hands on a rag. All the color had fled from her cheeks. "This one has a sizable bullet wound in his thigh. Do you think you can manage it?"

"Yes, Mama." Caroline knelt beside the soldier. His slight

frame gave him a youthful appearance, though his face wore the scars of a man twice his age. Bloody cuts and bruises peppered his dirt-stained face and arms where his shirt had torn away. He stared up at her, eyes bright, and yet his mouth was taut as if holding in agonized cries. Like thousands of others, this young man had witnessed the horrors of battle, given so much of himself in an effort to end this ongoing war. How heartbreaking that he should wind up lying here instead of in the welcoming arms of a wife or sweetheart.

Mama gave Caroline's shoulder a gentle squeeze. "Then take over for me. I'm needed inside." With that, she started toward the house.

Caroline peeled back the torn pant leg and flinched at the ring of redness circling the wound. Infection had set in. Flies swarmed about the exposed area, drawn by the stench of blood and rotting flesh. Caroline swatted them away, only to have them circle back and land once more. Having gone unattended nearly a full day, the soldier appeared almost numb to them.

With trembling hands, Caroline reached for the satchel her mother had left. She pulled a scrap of linen from inside and took up the half-empty bottle of iodine. The man's leg jerked as she touched the iodine-soaked rag to the wound. She pulled back. "I'm sorry."

The tension in his jaw slackened. "It's all right. Do what ya must."

His hands balled into fists as she gave the wound another swab. Shards of bone and shrapnel from the shattered minié ball littered the wound. Her heart sank. More than likely, to spare his life, his leg would need to be taken. Until a doctor arrived, there was little she could do other than cleanse the wound and make him as comfortable as possible.

If only she had some sort of poultice to help draw out the infection or laudanum to deaden the pain. She scanned the plethora of wounded soldiers surrounding her. There was no time or means to treat them all as thoroughly as she had the sergeant.

Setting the iodine aside, she reached in the bag for her tweezers. "What's your name, soldier?"

"Johnson. Daniel Johnson." His voice was wispy, barely audible.

"Where do you hail from, Daniel?" Protocol might not deem it proper to refer to a man she'd just met by his given name. But considering the circumstances, it seemed appropriate.

He cringed as she extracted a bone fragment from the wound. "Marshall, Virginia."

Caroline wiped the tweezers on her rag and gently retrieved another piece of shrapnel. "You're a fair ways from home. Have you a family back in Marshall?"

He gave a slight nod. "Married my sweetheart just over a year ago." A hint of a smile touched the young man's crusted lips. "We're expectin' our first child come fall."

She grinned down at him. "How wonderful. Then you've a great deal to look forward to once the war is over."

The soldier's tinged face lost its shine. "Just hope I'm still in one piece when that time comes."

Caroline's throat hitched. The image of the man hobbling home on one leg to greet his young wife and baby left her cold. Worse yet was the thought that he might not survive to return at all. She squeezed his hand, forcing a smile. "We'll do all we can to see that happens and pray the Lord sees you safely home to your family."

The soldier fell silent, his eyes clouding over as Caroline took up a strip of cloth to bandage his wound. Was he dreaming of the day he would return to his loved ones? Or dreading the uncertainties awaiting him? How many more young soldiers would she encounter with injured bodies and wounded hearts? Each soldier had a story to tell, a life outside the confines of this dreary reality called war.

She was beginning to understand how God cared for each individual life. Why He would leave the ninety-nine to save the one. Her thoughts returned to the injured sergeant. Had she passed him by, he'd likely have died or been taken prisoner. Whether her act of benevolence had saved his life remained to be seen, but Yankee or Confederate, men were men, souls in need. Loved by God. All the atrocities and hostilities of war could not erase that truth.

Neither could her father's bitterness.

5

The he magenta and amber hues of twilight flanked the western sky as Caroline slid from the back of the carriage. She smothered a yawn. *Exhausted* couldn't adequately describe her state of mind or body. Every inch of her begged to slip into bed and escape the fatigue and horrors of the day. But would rest come, or would her sleep be plagued with images of injured soldiers? She'd lost track of how many battle-scarred faces she'd peered into and how many bloody wounds she'd bandaged. So weary and worn, nary a man had complained of the long wait in the heat or the crude medical treatment, though pain shown on their agonized faces.

Cyrus held the horses' bridles while Papa helped Mama from the carriage. Though Caroline longed to speak with their servant regarding the Yankee, now was not the time or place. Clasping her depleted supply satchel, she fell into pace behind her parents.

They trudged up the steps to the house, not a word passing between them. Even Phillip seemed to have lost his zeal. A heavy sigh spilled from his lips as he tromped along beside her. Though he and Papa had merely worked to repair the Thomas house where it'd been damaged by cannon fire rather than tend the wounded, he'd likely witnessed more brutalities than he cared to recall. Twice on the ride home, he'd draped his head over the side of the carriage, looking as though he might heave the contents of his stomach.

As they neared the front door, Rose darted onto the veranda to greet them, her eyes sparkling with energy. She cocked her head to the side and rested her hands on her hips. "What took so long? I thought you'd never get home."

Mama bent to hug her. "There was much to be done, dear. Now we're eager to wash up, enjoy a quiet meal, and retire."

"I'm not hungry." Phillip wedged past them and pushed through the door.

Straightening, Mama stared after him, brows pinched. She cast Papa a worried glance that hinted her regret at having allowed the boy to go. With a shrug and a scratch of his chin, he strode to open the door.

A weak grin touched Mama's lips as she slipped her arm about Rose's shoulders. "Come, dear. Tell me all about your day."

Her enthusiasm returning, Rose chattered away as they headed inside. Caroline slid off her bonnet and followed them in, too exhausted to recall much of what was said. The scent of roast beef and fresh bread roused her appetite. So overwhelmed with her work, she'd taken no time to eat midday.

Lily emerged from the kitchen, wiping her hands on her apron. "You all look mighty tuckered. Supper's still warm on the hearth. I'll fetch it."

Papa swept past Caroline and handed the maid his hat. "We'd like to clean up first. We'll be down directly."

Lily brushed a speck from the straw hat and nodded. "Yes'r."

Caroline set her satchel on the oak floorboards and hung back, doing her best to fade into the backdrop of the plaster wall. Waiting until the others climbed the staircase, she followed Lily into the kitchen. The housemaid stole a sideways glance as she stooped to retrieve the roast beef. A covered tin rested on the hearth, lid askew. Caroline strained to see its contents.

Setting the steamy roast down, Lily raised an eyebrow. "You'll throw your neck out that-a-way."

Caroline rocked back on her heels, voice low. "Did you have a chance to take some broth to ...?"

The maid motioned her to "shush" then peered over her shoulder before whispering, "Miss Rose kept me busy the livelong day. Cyrus went instead, but says he couldn't rouse the fella enough t' eat."

Caroline's chest squeezed. Without nourishment, the sergeant's chances of making it were slim. Nursing the poor soul back to health would take more time and attention than she could manage. But what would she do with a dead Union soldier on her hands? The thought left her squeamish. "Leave the tin of broth on the hearth tonight. I'll see to him."

Worry lines formed at the outer edges of Lily's eyes as she paused from transferring the meat onto a platter. "You, Miss Caroline? You is askin' for a peck o' trouble."

"Well, someone has to—"

A creak of the stairs silenced them. At the sound of footfall in the hall, Lily nervously snatched up the platter of meat, her ample frame moving with uncharacteristic swiftness. Caroline shot her a beseeching glance then turned away, uncertain if her request would be granted. Whatever the outcome, she felt obliged to see the venture through.

With or without Cyrus and Lily's help.

"Sergeant?"

Drew roused to the soft-spoken voice and a gentle shake of his arm. His eyelids bobbed open, revealing the source of the plea. Forcing his eyes wider, he took in the woman's delicate features accentuated by the amber glow of lantern light. The Lord had sent him an angel of mercy.

Her expression softened at his awakening.

He perused the dim interior of the shanty. "Where am I?"

"My family's old slaves' quarters. You'll be safe here while you heal." Her slight southern drawl hung in the air like the sweet scent of honey fresh from the comb.

Drew pulled in a breath, catching a whiff of lavender. "For a moment ... I thought I'd ... gone to Heaven. But death couldn't ... hurt this much."

A faint smile touched her lips then fell away. "I assure you, you're very much alive."

He stared up at her, the fog on his memory lifting. "A fella named Cyrus brought me here. And you're ... Miss Caroline."

She nodded. "That's right."

He smacked his lips, his tongue tasting of bitter dryness. "How long have I been here? I feel as though I've ... slept a week."

"Since yesterday evening."

The darkness hinted more than a full day had passed since the battle and dim reality began to settle in. He'd been left behind—on enemy soil. "My men, I—" Pain ripped through him as he attempted to rise.

The woman pressed a hand to his chest, easing him back down. "Please, you must lie still."

He lay back on the blanket, his breath shallow. Another jolt of pain sliced through him, and he clenched his fists. "It appears ... I've no other choice."

"The minié ball passed through your shoulder without shattering much of the bone. But you've lost a great deal of blood from both wounds. Barring infection, you'll likely be on your feet within a week or two."

He scrubbed a hand over his face, muttering under his breath. "And that much farther behind my regiment."

"I'm sorry."

The kindness in her eyes calmed him. "I didn't mean to sound ... ungrateful."

She touched the back of her hand to his forehead. "Your

fever's down. That's a good sign, but if you don't take nourishment, you'll not regain your strength."

She reached behind her and brought out a small tin. "I brought some broth." Removing the lantern's glass globe with a cloth, she held the tin over the flame. "Not having eaten in so long, I didn't know if your stomach would handle much else."

"Are you a nurse?"

She shook her head. "No, but I intend to be. Someday."

"No doubt you'll make ... a fine one. The Lord was ... smiling on me when you happened by."

Her eyes remained trained on the tin, her cheeks pinking as she gave the broth a gentle stir. "You're a man of faith then, are you, Sergeant?"

He arched a brow. "Does that surprise you?"

"A little."

She stole a glance at him out of the corner of her eye, and he held back a grin. "You regard all us Northerners ... as heathens, I take it?"

Snapping her attention back to the tin, she intensified her stirring. "N-No. Only, I imagine soldier life can be taxing on one's faith."

"That it can. But I also find when one's life is in constant danger, his convictions tend to deepen."

She paused as though considering his response. At last, she nodded. "I suppose that's true. Your faith will take you far in your recovery, Sergeant."

The sincerity of her expression tugged at his heart. Despite her misgivings about him, she was going to great lengths to ensure his survival. He didn't take that lightly. "The name's Andrew Gallagher, and I allot the Lord full credit for sustaining me thus far ... even when I haven't deserved it." His eyes glazed over as he recalled the foolish act of vengeance that nearly cost him his life.

"He has at that." She touched a finger to the broth to test its warmth then set the tin beside her on the floor. "Do you think we might prop you up to eat?"

He gave a slight nod, drinking in the soft contours of her oval face. She had a natural beauty that seemed to radiate from within. With effort, he pushed himself up, and the sheet dropped, exposing his bandaged shoulder and semi-bare chest.

The color in her cheeks deepened, and her gaze trailed away as she reached to support him. "Your uniform jacket and shirt are beyond repair. I'll look for a shirt among my brother's things for you to wear."

Sensing her discomfort, he tugged the sheet higher. "Won't your brother be suspicious of you taking off with his clothing?"

Her head dipped lower. "My brother is away at battle. We've not heard from him in more than a month."

Drew winced, more from the tremor in her voice than his pain. Memories of the foolhardy boy whose life he'd spared seared his thoughts. The lad could have been her brother. Any of the Rebs he was fighting could. And yet, here she was helping him, though he'd been injured likely fighting her kinfolk and neighbors. "I'm sorry. I hope you hear from him soon."

Moisture pooled in her honey eyes, and she blinked it away. "Thank you."

He glanced at his bandaged shoulder, then at her. "You've put yourself and others at risk on my account. I'm obliged for your kindness."

She reached for the tin of broth. "I'll do what I can. The rest is up to you and the Lord."

He met her gaze as she offered him a spoonful of broth. Like the Samaritan tending the man left for dead along the roadside, she'd shown great mercy. Yet, despite her willingness to offer aid, this was no safe haven. He was an enemy to her, her family, and those in the surrounding countryside.

As soon as he was able, he must steal away and journey north.

6

Monday morning, July 11, 1864

Shadowy light filtered through an open window to Drew's left as though dawn was approaching. He'd lost all sense of time and direction. To be laid-up in some Southerner's broken-down slave shanty had never been his plan. But it beat being held prisoner or lying dead in a field of slaughtered soldiers. He had the Lord and his lovely rescuer to thank for at least sparing him that fate.

His stomach rumbled, stirring thoughts of Miss Caroline's late-night visit. The tin of broth had revived him but hadn't been enough to quench his appetite. Would she return with something more substantial? Thus far, she'd come only in cover of darkness. If that were the case, he might have a long wait ahead of him to lay and do nothing.

A man's muffled voice sounded in the distance. He cocked his ear to listen, his palms growing clammy. Another voice echoed back. The commanding tones, though faint, seemed almost militant. Were they soldiers? If so, was he in danger of being found by Rebels in search of carnage? Or were they Union soldiers come to bury their dead?

He pushed himself up onto his elbow and waited to see if the voices would draw nearer. It was difficult to tell how close the men were. On a still morning, one could hear for miles. Ignoring the throbbing pain in his shoulder and side, he struggled to his feet and hobbled to the partially open window.

Unable to see through the dirt-stained glass, Drew strained to lift the windowpane higher. Humid air drifted in at him as he leaned for a look. He squinted into the shadowy landscape, unable to distinguish any sort of movement. A grove of trees in the distance thwarted any chance of determining to whom the voices belonged.

Angling his ear closer to the opening, Drew's efforts to hear the muted, disjointed conversation became obscured by the chortle of robins and Carolina wrens. Though the men's voices were clipped and sharp with a military cadence, none revealed which side of the war they favored. He longed to find out but, uncertain if they were friend or foe, such effort would prove foolhardy, if not deadly.

A surge of light-headedness rippled through him, and he gripped the windowsill. He should've known better than to risk moving about so soon. Sweat trickled down his temples, and the room started to spin.

Sensing himself slipping, he dropped to his knees. The faces of his mother and younger siblings flicked through his mind as the room closed in. Would he die here alone? Would he end up in an unmarked grave with his family never knowing what happened to him?

The pain intensified, and he clamped a hand to his side. "Help me ... Lord."

CAROLINE STARTED awake at the tapping on her bedroom door. She sat up, surprised at the abundant sunlight streaming through the curtained window. It wasn't like her to sleep so late. But then, she wasn't accustomed to being up half the night, either. Threading her fingers through her hair, she swung her legs over the side of the bed. "Come in."

The door eased open, and Lily poked her head in, brows pinched. "You ailin', Miss Caroline?"

Caroline smothered a yawn. "No. Why do you ask?"

Before the maid could answer, Rose bounded in and hopped onto the bed. "Why'd you sleep so long? I thought you'd never get up."

"What time is it?"

"Half-past nine. The others left over an hour ago."

Caroline gnawed at her lip. She must have truly been exhausted. She could almost sense Papa's displeasure and Mama's gentle bidding to overlook her tardiness. Springing to her feet, she reached for her leather boots. "Then I'd best get going."

"Not till you has yer breakfast." Lily ambled over, tray in hand, a determined glint in her eyes.

The maid's commanding tone halted Caroline in place. She dropped back onto the bed, allowing Lily to set the tray of food on her lap. There'd be no arguing with her. Caroline knew the servant well enough to know she was sure to have her way.

Resting her hands on her ample hips, Lily cocked her head to one side. "Did my best t' keep 'em warm, but they's better fresh from the griddle."

"They'll be fine." The buttery scent of johnnycakes and maple syrup wafted at Caroline as she lifted the lid from the plate. She bowed her head in a quick, silent prayer then poured a generous amount of syrup atop the fried corn cakes. Eager to be on her way, she sliced off several bite-sized segments of the cakes and ate them in rapid succession.

Rose stared at her, mouth agape. "Never knew you could eat so fast."

Caroline washed her final bite down with a glass of apple cider, then grinned and wiped her lips. "Neither did I. Now scoot so I can dress."

"Couldn't I go with you this time?"

Recalling the grave injuries of the men she'd treated, Caroline shook her head. "There's nothing there your tender eyes should look upon."

The youngster's shoulders slumped, and her gaze dropped to the quilt beneath her.

Caroline cupped a hand under her sister's chin and waited for Rose's eyes to meet hers. "Trust me. You'll be much better off here pestering Lily."

In her sweet way, Rose responded with an acquiescing grin. "All right."

Winking, Caroline stood and handed Lily the tray. "Thanks for breakfast."

The maid placed her free arm about Rose's shoulders, coaxing her to her feet. "Come, honeychild. Seems Miss Caroline is in an all-fired hurry t' be a-goin'." Lily's tone feigned irritation, though a hint of humor told in her expression.

Caroline followed them to the door and eased it closed behind them. Leaning into it, she rested her forehead against the rough grain of the wood. It wasn't that she was yearning to return to the injured and hurting. On the contrary, she would give anything to be in Rose's place, untarnished by the realities of war.

She donned her day dress, and a glance in the dresser mirror convinced her to pause to pin her hair in a loose chignon. With a frazzled huff, she snatched her satchel from beside the dresser, grateful she'd taken time to replenish her medical supplies the evening before.

Lily's hum drifted upstairs as Caroline opened the bedroom door and stepped into the hallway. Jamison's bedroom door loomed to her right. Thoughts of the sergeant's firm muscles stirred warmth in her cheeks as she recalled her promise to bring him one of her brother's shirts. Now seemed as good a time as any to search for one.

With careful steps, she tiptoed toward his room. Stillness

within greeted her like a January night, numbing and frigid. She hadn't entered Jamison's room since he left for war. Everything remained just as he'd left it—his quilted bed made up lumpy and unkempt, his Sunday shoes protruding from beneath it. His misshapen straw hat and riding crop resting atop his dresser.

Caroline gently tugged the top drawer open, pausing before rifling through the stack of shirts. It seemed intrusive to search through her brother's things. If it had been for one of his Southern comrades she sought to borrow, she'd not hesitate. Jamison would be the first to lend to a fellow soldier in need. But he'd likely feel much different about sharing his clothes with a Yankee.

The thought churned her stomach.

Why must the nation remedy their differences through maiming and killing? Weren't there more civilized ways to settle disputes? Their country seemed to be failing miserably at the command to love their enemies and pray for those who persecuted them.

Her heart grieved over what Jamison must be witnessing. During his infrequent visits, he'd borne the scars of war in his face and stilted demeanor. Would he return home changed when the hostilities finally ended?

Pulling one of his older cotton shirts from the bottom of the stack, she held it up then tucked it inside her satchel. With a final glance around the room, she backed toward the door, praying the garment would not be missed when her brother returned.

"Is ya comin', Miss Caroline?" Lily's voice echoed up the stairs.

"Be right there," she called back, clicking the door shut behind her.

Caroline downed the steps, greeted at the bottom by Lily and Rose, lunch tin and water jar in hand. Lily leaned in close, a slight lilt in her voice as she handed Caroline the goods. "I packed plenty in case ya has need of some *extra*."

Caroline met the housemaid's gaze. Despite Lily's hesitancy to get involved in harboring a Union soldier, her heart of benevolence seemed to have won out. Taking the tin and water jar from her, Caroline mustered a weak grin. "Thank you."

Songbirds greeted her as she slipped outside, the mid-morning sun oppressive as it edged closer to its apex. All at once, the two-mile hike seemed daunting. Her thoughts flicked to the shanty tucked along the timber's edge and to the wounded soldier housed within. His eyes had sparked to life when he'd taken in the broth. A stop-in would prove a welcome oasis from the heat on her way to the Thomas Farm. More than likely, he would be sleeping. But, if not, perhaps she could tempt him to try something more substantial. Late as she was, another short delay couldn't harm.

She arched a brow. Dare she risk approaching the shack in broad daylight? With most of her family away, and the servants in the fields, it didn't seem much of a concern.

With each step, her heartbeat quickened. Her entire life, she'd gone out of her way to please her father. But to no avail. Doing something outside his knowledge or approval seemed rather daring.

Exhilarating, even.

A gentle breeze carried men's voices from the far side of the timber. She slowed her pace and peered into the dense foliage.

No telling who lurked beyond the trees.

Whether the men were Union or Confederate, it seemed in her best interest not to venture farther unchaperoned. Once she'd checked in on the sergeant, she'd have Cyrus accompany her in the carriage.

Easing the cabin door open, she quietly tapped her knuckles on the aged oak timbers. All was quiet within.

Almost too quiet.

"Sergeant Gallagher?" she crooned, her whisper loud against the silence. Opening the door a crack, she ventured a peek inside. A dark form drew her attention to the cabin floor. She sucked in a breath at the sight of the sergeant sprawled in the dirt. The lunch tin and satchel slipped from her grasp as she lunged forward and knelt beside him.

Alarmed by his stillness, she gripped his shoulder, relieved that warmth radiated from his skin. He roused at her touch. "Are you all right, Sergeant?"

7

Mid-morning, July 11, 1864

"I heard voices." The three simple words seemed enough to explain the excursion that landed Drew face down on the hardened dirt.

The woman's brow pinched, her soft features conveying concern more than annoyance. To her credit, she didn't scold but instead helped him to the bed of blankets before hurrying to close the door and collect her things. Upon her return, she knelt beside him, taking a quick peek at his bandaged side before pulling the cover over his chest. The scent of lavender warmed his senses as she leaned in close, as though about to divulge a well-kept secret. "I heard them as well."

"You did? Did you see anyone?" Drew arched his back, struggling to contain his eagerness until her gentle nudge settled him back on the blankets.

She lifted a finger to her lips to silence him, her fawn-like eyes full of caution.

He stared up at her, mindful that each moment there endangered her.

Endangered them both.

A wavy tendril of her hair fell loose about her neck. He resisted the urge to reach up and touch its softness. She was beautiful. Even more so in light of day. He swallowed, lowering his voice. "Were you able to discern if the men were Union soldiers?"

"I couldn't tell. The voices came from beyond the trees and were too faint to distinguish." She raised a brow, surveying the reddish-brown stain on his bandaged shoulder. "But even if they were Union, you're in no condition to go traipsing after them. I just hope you haven't done yourself harm."

"Perhaps they've brought medics and have the means to transport me to a hospital." He didn't mean to sound desperate or ungrateful. After all, she'd shown great prowess in her abilities. In other circumstances, he'd not be so eager to leave her company, but this could be his one chance to reconnect with his fellow soldiers.

She paused, then tugged at his bandages as though ensuring they were in place. "I-I'm on my way to my neighbors. Should I discover the voices belong to Union soldiers, I'll let you know upon my return."

He eyed her, the tremor in her voice unsettling. Was she concerned for her safety or reluctant to have further interaction with those she considered enemies? More than likely, she'd not return until nightfall. The delay could mean he'd miss his opportunity. If the men were Union, would she be willing to alert them to his presence? Or, if Confederate, would she betray him just to be rid of him?

He had no means of knowing how deep her loyalties to the South ran. Still, something bade him trust her. "I'd appreciate it."

She retrieved a garment the color of ripened wheat from her bag. "I've brought one of my brother's shirts, but your wounds need to heal a bit more before you don it. I'll change your bandages when I come tonight."

Drew nodded slowly, a nagging doubt still etched in his mind. "If not the shirt, what brought you here in full daylight?"

"I feared you'd need more than broth to sustain you." Her eyes sparkled. "I hope you can stomach Southern cooking."

His mouth watered, his faith in her renewed. "Anything but hardtack."

"I assure you our maid, Lily, is the best of cooks." She spread a handkerchief on the floor beside him and portioned out two corn muffins, a boiled egg, a slab of smoked ham, a peach, and a jar of water. "Only ingest it in small amounts. Too much too soon will not sit well with you."

He nodded. "Yes, nurse."

A smile edged onto her lips as she lowered her gaze. "I didn't mean to sound forceful."

He touched her arm, a rush of warmth filling his chest. "No, truly. I appreciate your concern. Thank you—for everything."

Her cheeks grew rosy as she slid her arm away. "I-I should go. I'm late, and my family will wonder what's keeping me."

"You're traveling alone?"

She hesitated, then folded the shirt and placed it on the floor beside him. "I intended to, but decided it best to fetch Cyrus to take me."

Relief swept through him. As badly as he wished to be reunited with his comrades, the thought of one of them molesting her turned his stomach. "I'm glad to hear it."

She cast him a sideways glance as if puzzled by his response. Gathering her things, she stood and brushed crumbs from her dress, her full skirt accenting the smallness of her waist. "I trust you'll not do anything so foolish as to attempt to leave your bed again?"

He placed his hand over his heart, a slight grin tugging at his lips. "You have my word."

No sooner had she stepped toward the door than he realized the fullness in his bladder. He called to her. "Then again, if you wish me to stay put, you might consider leaving me some sort of bedpan."

CAROLINE FANNED herself with her hand as the carriage rumbled down the worn path, uncertain if the heat flaming her cheeks was due to the hot day or the sergeant's awkward request. How thoughtless of her not to realize his need to empty his bladder. She scolded herself. A good nurse would never neglect such a thing.

Nor embarrass so easily.

Cyrus had been more than obliging to harness the horse and buggy but had balked at her request to fetch a bedpan when he'd learned it was for their concealed guest. "You is playing with fire, Miss Caroline," he'd muttered as he handed her the contraption, face puckered. She'd taken it anyway, ignoring the warning in his dark eyes.

No one needed to remind her of the risks she'd imposed upon herself. The sooner she was rid of the sergeant, the better. But while in her care, she would do her utmost to see to his comfort and well-being. Yet, if discovered, she hated to think what would become of him—or her, for that matter.

As the buggy cleared the timberline, Caroline tensed at the sight of a handful of blue-coated soldiers in the distance, a slew of bodies spattering the ground. Shovels in hand, the soldiers' dismal task was evident by the numerous mounds of fresh dirt.

A sentry standing guard slapped one of his companions on the arm and nodded in her direction. The soldier paused from digging, a leering grin spilling onto his face. She turned from their ogling, aware of the protective way Cyrus slapped the reins across the horse's back to quicken their pace. Though he'd spoken nary a word since they'd left home, his regard for her welfare seemed to outweigh any grievance he harbored over her lack of judgment.

She ventured another glance at the soldiers, looking for some means of transport. The men continued to gape at her, one letting out a raucous whistle that brought another rush of warmth to her cheeks. Whirling around, she determined it best to stay clear of the brash fellows. If Sergeant Gallagher had been so brazen, she'd be more eager to send him back from whence he'd come. But as he'd given her no cause to doubt his character, she saw no need to rush him away.

A hasty sweep of the area assured her the soldiers had come for one purpose—to bury their dead. She blew out a breath, relieved she could honestly profess the Union soldiers had no means to transport someone in Sergeant Gallagher's condition.

Or would it be best not to admit to seeing them at all?

No. To be dishonest not only went against the Lord's commands but would undermine the element of trust she and the sergeant had established. Instead, she'd pray for the soldiers' quick departure.

As they skirted the Thomas farm, Caroline spied her father and Phillip working outside the house. Papa's head lifted at the sound of the horse and buggy. He straightened, peering at her with furrowed brow, his prominent sideburns showing beneath his wide-brimmed hat. Reaching in his pants pocket, he retrieved his watch and shook his head at her tardiness. She mustered a weak smile and waved, groaning inwardly as he returned to work without so much as acknowledging the gesture.

Cyrus kept his eyes on the path ahead, chin held high as though proud of the passenger he carried. Caroline hung her head, convinced the servant cared more for her than her own father did. While Cyrus's irritation had been prompted by concern for her well-being, her father's annoyance seemed to stem from some deep-seated disapproval she could not fathom.

Within moments, they'd topped the rise to the house. Only a few injured soldiers remained in the yard, along with a handful of doctors and nurses. At the front of the house, four horse-drawn ambulances awaited their allotment of patients. Tracks in the dry grass denoted the numerous trips already made by the sturdily-built wagons.

Cyrus rolled the buggy to a stop a short distance from the

house and offered Caroline a hand down. She squinted up at him from beneath her bonnet, medical supplies clutched in her hand. "Thank you, Cyrus. You may go. I'll ride home with Mama and Papa."

He gave a firm nod. "Yes'm."

She smiled at him, playfulness in her tone. "Not that I don't wish to continue to share your delightful company."

He paused, then tipped his hat to her, a hint of a grin pulling at his full lips. As he tapped the reins across the horse's back, he tossed her a wink, and her smile deepened.

He'd forgiven her—good ol' Cyrus.

Her shoulders sagged as she watched him pull away, joy fading at the memory of her father's rebuff. If only Papa could be so forgiving of whatever grievance he held against her.

Hiking her skirt, she cut the ambulance workers a wide berth and started toward the house. With precision and purpose, they bore the injured on stretchers and aided the walking wounded into awaiting wagons, likely to be transported to the hospital in Frederick.

The canvas coverings had been tied up on the sides of the ambulances to provide for airflow, allowing a glimpse of the weary occupants. The soldiers' distraught expressions and slumped postures showed the devastating losses they'd suffered. The fortunate ones would return home maimed yet alive. Others would succumb to their wounds and meet their end in a hospital bed amid medical staff and fellow soldiers; strangers who'd fought for a common cause.

Caroline couldn't help but wish Sergeant Gallagher could be transported along with these men and receive the care he needed. She'd heard tell the hospital staff at Frederick served men on both sides of the war, without prejudice. If only others could find common ground on which to garner peace and put an end to this appalling war.

The open door of the Thomas house beckoned her. She ascended the steps and crossed the porch, moving aside for yet another patient to be carried out on a stretcher. A rank blend of body odor and chloroform surrounded her as she entered. With shallow breaths, she peeled off her bonnet and searched the parlor for a familiar face amid the flurry of activity. She spotted Mama across the room, bent over one of the remaining patients.

"Miss ... Miss?"

The faint voice called to her from the room to her left, its hoarse tone vaguely familiar. Pausing mid-stride, she peered into the dimly lit sitting room and saw a man lying on a stretcher, a sheet draped over the lower half of his body. She stepped closer, recognizing him as the young man whose leg she'd tended upon her arrival yesterday. "Hello. Daniel, isn't it?"

"Yes, ma'am. I wanted t' thank you for your kindness."

She squatted beside him. "Glad to have helped. Are you being transported to the hospital in Frederick?"

He nodded, his expression solemn. "Soon as I'm able, they'll be sending me home. Now that I'm of no use to my company."

She followed his gaze to the sunken area where his left leg should have been. Her throat thickened, and she struggled for words. Pressing her hand to his arm, she blinked back the moisture in her eyes. "Well then, perhaps you'll be at your wife's side for the birth of your new son or daughter."

A glimmer of hope sparked in his eyes then died away. "What's left of me."

Caroline winced as Daniel shifted his gaze to the plastered wall. What could she say to temper his discouragement? *Lord, grant me the words.*

Her thoughts turned to her father. All her life, she'd measured her worth by his standards, sought to be the daughter he wished, yet he'd shown nothing but disdain towards her. Though she couldn't fully comprehend Daniel's loss, she did understand inadequacy.

Each time she experienced the sting of her father's rejection, she was compelled to draw from strength not her own—strength only the Lord could supply. If Daniel were to accept the hardships that had come his way, he must do the same.

"I have a feeling your wife will be overjoyed just to have you with her."

He shrugged, turning toward her. "I ain't so sure. I'm not the same person as when she married me. I'm scarred and crippled."

Caroline tapped a finger against his chest. "It's who you are deep inside that matters, not how many battles you endure or how many limbs you have. God gave you a unique soul that makes you distinctly you. That's who your wife and child will see when they look at you."

Her heart drummed in her chest at the intensity of his silent stare. Had she overstepped her bounds with this soldier who had been wounded in both body and spirit?

At last, his expression softened, and he blew out a long breath. "I reckon that's so. But, I can't bear the thought of Ellie pitying me or never walking alongside our child."

The honesty of his words pierced Caroline's soul. He was so young, his whole life ahead of him. It didn't seem fair he, like so many other wounded soldiers, would spend the remainder of his life maimed and dependent on others. Yet, often the difficult paths of life led to the greatest faith and fulfillment.

Forcing a breath, she placed a hand on his shoulder. "It's clear you love your wife very much, as I'm certain she does you. Go home, Daniel. Accept what the Lord has entrusted to you. You may be limited in your abilities, but there's no limit to love or contentment."

Moisture pooled in his eyes as he seemed to digest her words. At last, he cupped his hand over hers. "You're right. God bless you, Miss. You've given me a smidgen of hope."

"I'm so glad." Caroline smiled at him, joy washing over her. That the Lord would use her to encourage this soldier who'd sacrificed so much was more reward than she could fathom. *Thank you, Lord.*

Once again, elation fueled her desire to learn nursing. How

many others could benefit if only she were better trained? Could she be unbiased in her work like the hospital doctors and nurses? She'd been reluctant to tend to Sergeant Gallagher's wounds, more out of fear than prejudice. And yet, now, he seemed more like a patient to her than a Union soldier. He'd been kind and gracious to her, never vulgar. In fact, he'd been a near-perfect patient, except for his over-eagerness to leave.

Standing, Caroline extended her well-wishes to Daniel then turned to join her mother. She tipped her head higher as she strode away, more confident than ever that the Lord intended her to use her skills of nursing.

She just prayed her parents would agree.

8

Late night, July 11, 1864

"I'm so sorry."

Drew managed a slow nod, confident Miss Caroline's regrets were genuine. Somehow he'd sensed the voices belonged to Union soldiers, and he'd missed his chance to meet up with them. The tones had ebbed and flowed throughout much of the day, finally tapering off completely by late afternoon. He'd had to summon all his willpower not to attempt to find out for certain, though he knew he hadn't the strength.

With gentle hands, she removed the cloth bandage from his shoulder. "If it's any consolation, I saw no means to transport the wounded. They came only to bury the dead."

He nodded again, still grieving the missed opportunity.

As if guessing his thoughts, she added. "Given more time to heal, you'll be better able to travel."

"That's true." His mouth twisted. They both knew he stood little chance of ever rejoining his company. Letting go of his disappointment, he fixed his gaze on his caregiver. Her compassion overwhelmed him. Though she worked tirelessly all day and tended to him each night, not once had she complained.

Perhaps he should forget his own woes and do what he could to bolster her spirits. He cleared his throat, summoning courage. "Until then, I hope to have your company to enjoy."

She stared at him with widened eyes as though trying to decide if he were in earnest, finally averting her gaze to his injured shoulder. In the lantern light, he glimpsed the flush in her cheeks and the slight upturn of her lips.

He silently chastened himself for causing her embarrassment. At least she hadn't scoffed at him or, worse yet, slapped him for his boldness.

"I'm honored my presence brings you such comfort, Sergeant Gallagher."

For a brief moment, his eyes locked with hers, and he smiled at the mirth in her tone. "Please, call me Drew."

She gave a hesitant nod and leaned closer, holding the lantern over him. "Your bullet wound is red but doesn't seem infected. Given time, I believe it will heal nicely. Now, let's have a look at that stab wound."

The scent of lavender filled Drew's senses as the ringlets of her hair dangled over him. Her nearness vibrated through him like the rush of water from a swollen stream. He turned his head, squelching the urge to touch her soft cheek. He tensed as she tugged at the cloth bandage, dried blood adhering it to his wound.

She drew her hands back. "I'm sorry."

"No. It's all right." He forced himself to relax, deciding a bit of conversation might prove a welcome distraction. "Any word on the whereabouts of your brother?"

Repositioning her hands on the bandage, she shook her head, her expression doleful. "None."

Drew cringed as she tugged the cloth free. "Have you other brothers and sisters?"

"A sister of nine years, Rose, as sweet as she is pretty, and a brother, Phillip, fourteen, who, according to him, could take on the whole Union army single-handedly."

Drew chuckled. "I've a brother, Luke, of much the same mind—eager to be a man and full of advice. Perhaps we'd do well to let the two of them duke it out in a fistfight and be done with the war."

She grinned. "An intriguing idea."

Drew's smile faded as memories of his younger brother flashed through his mind. Months had passed since he'd considered his family back home in New York—his dear mother, brother, and sister. He stared into the dimness of the rafters, his voice softening. "Luke was fifteen when last I saw him. By now, he's well into his sixteenth year. I can only pray he's still at home and not off somewhere toting a gun in battle."

"Or he might find himself wounded and in enemy hands like his big brother?"

The ironic humor in her voice helped to lighten his mood.

He peered up at her, teasing back. "If yours are enemy hands, there are worse fates."

She rewarded him with a shy grin. Glancing sideways, she placed a damp compress over his wound, the strong scent identifying it as some sort of poultice. "Have you ... anyone else awaiting your safe return?"

He arched a brow, curious if her timid inquiry regarding his personal life went deeper than mere small talk. He couldn't resist baiting her to find out. "Well, there is one dear lady who's more than anxious for my return."

Her head dipped, and, offering no response, she focused her attention on his injured side.

Though Drew could only guess her thoughts, he hoped her silence marked disappointment. Such quiet strength he'd not often encountered in a woman. She was so unlike the eligible ladies back home who chattered on about the most frivolous of topics—anything from yesterday's gossip to the latest social fineries. Miss Caroline was controlled and intentional with her actions and words. It was an inward part of her beauty.

He searched her fetching face, wondering how far to pursue

this. Surely one further attempt wouldn't hurt. Clearing his throat, he propped his head up with his good arm. "In fact, she'll be most grateful to learn you've taken such good care of me when she was unable to."

"Will she, now?" The notable influx in her tone, coupled with the tension in her jaw, satisfied him that she at least favored him in some regard.

Feeling slightly guilty that he'd toyed with her sentiments, he put his jesting to an end. "Yes. My mother will likely sing your praises when I tell her how you nursed me back to health."

Her face snapped toward him, the glow in her eyes returning. "Your ... mother?"

Warmth rippled through him at the lilt in her voice and the slight upturn of her rounded lips. Suddenly, getting back to his men didn't seem quite so urgent.

CAROLINE SCOLDED herself as she closed the door to the shack behind her. How addle-headed she was. Why should it matter if the sergeant had a sweetheart awaiting him back home? She'd known him only a matter of days and yet feared she'd given him the impression she fancied him.

Her heart hammered. Did she?

She gave a soft sigh. *Drew Gallagher.* Such a fine name. Handsome and kind as he was, she couldn't imagine becoming entangled with a soldier clad in blue. It was foolhardy. Dangerous, even. And yet, her mind kept dredging up memories of his kind eyes, firm muscles, and infectious smile. Perhaps she should have sent him on his way, regardless of his fragile condition. He was a Northerner. Why did she care what became of him?

But she did care. He was her patient, after all, and a professing believer. Those truths alone compelled her to compassion. Although she had to admit, she was drawn to him in other ways as well. The unsettling thought left her a bit lightheaded.

The bright, three-quarter moon guided her way as she started across the meadow, the swish of her skirt in the tall grass loud against the stillness. Barely a breeze stirred the humid night air. Tucked in a shallow nook of trees, the shanty lay just out of sight of the house—the perfect hideaway.

She curbed a yawn, her late-night visits to the sergeant beginning to take a toll on her. How she disliked the secrecy of sneaking out at night. Deceiving her parents was not something she took lightly, nor was she accustomed to it. But, at this point, she had little choice. Another week should be sufficient time for the sergeant to recover enough to make his journey north. She could only pray until then that he—and her secret—would go undetected.

Coming to the darkened house, she made her way to the side kitchen door and slipped off her boots. With a flip of the latch, she eased the door open and slid inside. Her heart quickened as she wound her way through the kitchen, dining room, and up the staircase. A slight creak of a stair made her cringe and still. When no one appeared, she ventured on, breathing a sigh of relief as she reached the top.

Tension knotted her shoulders as she snugged her boots in the crook of her arm to free her hand to unlatch her bedroom door. A soft thud sounded behind her. She turned for a look, peering into the darkened hallway toward Phillip's room, where the noise had originated. Though there was no visible sign his door had been open, a creak of his bed caused the blood to drain from her cheeks. Had he heard her pass and peeked to see what she was up to? Or was he merely stirring in his sleep?

Slipping into her room, she inched the door closed behind her, praying she hadn't been seen.

9

Tuesday, July 12, 1864

Caroline flinched as her red-faced father slapped the newspaper down on the corner of the table. "Those blasted blue-bellies!"

"Eugene!" Mama's stern rebuke sliced through Papa's rage.

He leaned forward in his chair and jabbed at the newspaper with his finger. "Forgive me, Vivian, but according to this, our boys could have taken Washington and ended the war had it not been for the delay at Monocacy Junction."

Mama dropped a pinch of sugar into her coffee. "But it was my understanding the Confederates won that battle."

"They did, but the day's delay allowed time for Union reinforcements to move into Washington—a costly venture for our side. Now, who knows how long this cursed war will go on."

Caroline's spirits plummeted. The news was disheartening, to say the least. With the dreadful mood her father was in, this wasn't the time to approach him about her desire to learn nursing. She longed to see this awful conflict come to an end and for life to return to normal. Whatever the outcome, likely none of their lives would ever be the same. The nation remained divided in every way.

Even the citizens of Maryland differed in their thinking—some sympathetic toward freeing the slaves, others harboring hatred and bitterness toward the North, including her father and brothers. When the war did finally end, she feared peace and unity would be long in coming.

Her gaze flicked to the folded newspaper. No doubt Sergeant Gallagher would relish reading such news. It pained her to think how many lives hung in the balance between the two opposing sides. How it must grieve the Lord to see them embattled in such a bloody conflict. Surely the prayers of worried parents, wives, and soldiers on both sides of the war continually reached His ears. Which would He honor?

Who was right, and who was wrong?

She sensed eyes upon her and glanced across the table at Phillip. His scrutinizing stare revived last night's fears. She ran her fingertips along the edge of the tablecloth in an attempt to steady her nerves. He must have seen her. Averting her gaze, she prayed he would have the courtesy to ask her privately about the matter rather than arouse suspicions.

"May I see the paper, Papa?"

Caroline tensed at the sound of her brother's voice. Would he let the incident slide then, at least where the family was concerned? Her hopes rose each moment he refrained from addressing her.

Papa slid the newspaper in Phillip's direction and stood. "As if this wretched heat and drought aren't bad enough, I'm exasperated to see no end in sight to this confounded war."

For once, Caroline shared her father's sentiments. What the War Between the States hadn't stripped from them and their land, the drought had. Though more blessed than many households, their supplies were dwindling, and their spirits were waning.

Phillip leafed through the paper then went to join Papa. "Will we help with the Thomas house again today?"

Papa shook his head and donned his hat. "I've my own business to tend to from here on." With that, he started for the door, Phillip at his heels.

"May I be excused too, Mama?" Rose inquired from her seat next to Caroline.

"Yes, dear."

Hopping to her feet, Rose peered over at Caroline. "Since you're no longer needed at the Thomases', can you show me how to bandage a wound? Then maybe someday, I can help too."

The request, though bittersweet, warmed Caroline. "I'd be happy to, just as soon as I finish helping Mama and Lily with dishes."

The youngster trotted off while Caroline helped gather the breakfast plates. She lingered long enough to get a glimpse of the headlines topping the copy of the *Frederick Gazette*.

THE BATTLE THAT SAVED WASHINGTON

Her eyes widened. Had the skirmish at Monocacy Junction truly spared the fall of the Capitol and been detrimental to the South's chance to end the war? She skimmed just enough of the article to get a gist of what had taken place, then hurried on. The paper would be missed should she take it for Sergeant Gallagher, so she put the words to memory to share with him when next she saw him.

Lily's low hum greeted her as she entered the kitchen. The woman was a likable soul. If ever the slaves gained their freedom, she couldn't imagine Lily or Cyrus leaving. They'd become like part of the family. The household wouldn't be the same in their absence.

Caroline set her dishes on the counter and reached for an apron on the peg beside the washbasin. Morning sunlight streamed through the partially open window, ushering in a robin's melodic song. She peered out the dusty windowpane, drawn to movement at the far side of the meadow. A lone Confederate soldier sauntered toward the yard, rifle and haversack strung across his back.

She leaned for a better look, her heart at her throat. Clasping a hand to her mouth, she sucked in a breath. Though the gait was slower than she remembered, there was no mistaking the slant of the man's shoulders or the cadence in his step.

Lily's hum ceased, and Mama stepped up beside Caroline. "What is it?"

A smile broke onto her face as she tossed her apron aside and bolted toward the door. "Jamison's home!"

10

"War is not the glorious thing it's made out to be."
Caroline cupped her hand over Jamison's, stirred to tears by his sorrowed expression. Though not yet twenty-two, he appeared years older than when she'd last seen him. The family's initial joy at his return had melted into solemnness as he'd relayed stories of countless men falling to guns and swords, of bullets whizzing so close he felt their breeze, and of devastating cannon fire followed by the piercing screams of comrades. How he'd anguished over fleeing for his life and leaving them to their fate—to certain imprisonment or death by enemy hands.

Mama hugged Rose tighter in her lap on the parlor settee, a quiver in her voice. "How long is your leave?"

"I'm to report back Saturday."

"Four days? After all this time?" The tremor in Mama's voice deepened. "Why so soon?"

Jamison raked a hand over his face, the dark shadows beneath his eyes hinting of sleepless nights and agonizing days. "Talk is, we're moving out."

Papa edged forward in his upholstered chair, rubbing his hands up and down the decorative, cherry-wood arms. "Where to?"

"Petersburg, Virginia."

Papa's brow creased. "Petersburg? Why, that's more than a hundred miles south of here."

Jamison nodded. "The city's under siege. My regiment is being sent as reinforcements for General Beauregard. Word has it General Lee's Northern Virginians have already joined the defense."

A proud grin spread over Papa's face, and he thumbed his suspenders. "Well, now, ain't that somethin'? Our boy joining ranks with General Lee himself."

Phillip crossed his arms over his chest with a *humph*. "Wish I was older so I could go."

"I'm thankful you're not!" snapped Mama. "One son's sacrifice on behalf of this wretched war is enough."

Caroline's stomach wrenched at the terse exchange. It unnerved her to know Phillip longed to be a part of such violence and devastation. But then, it seemed every man thirsted for battle like it was some sort of rite of manhood. After hearing Jamison's horrific accounts of war, it seemed only by God's grace he'd emerged unscathed. When he'd first enlisted, he'd shared Phillip's eagerness to march into battle. Now, since Jamison had tasted the bitter harshness of war, his enthusiasm seemed to have waned.

He released a long breath. "No more talk of war. I long to be free of it, if only for a short while."

Forcing a smile, Caroline squeezed his hand. "Then we must make the most of every minute."

He returned a weak grin and kissed her hand. "I fully intend to, Linna, starting with some of Lily's johnnycakes, if she can manage some. As well as a few blessed hours of shut-eye on something besides the hard ground."

Mama's face brightened. "Lily set to work making some the moment she saw you coming."

Chuckling, Jamison rubbed his trim belly. "Good ol' Lily. I've looked forward to her victuals. Right now, I don't care to see another ration of hardtack or a Yankee ever again."

Caroline stood along with the others, rejoicing over her brother's return. And yet, uneasiness crept in. His presence here endangered the sergeant and herself; she would need to stay cautious and composed. Jamison's stay would be short-lived. She didn't wish to tarnish the visit with worry.

Neither did she wish to forever taint his opinion of her with the knowledge she was aiding the very enemy he sought to destroy.

Wed. July 13, Pre-dawn hours

THE CREAK of the door startled Drew. More times than not, he was awake when Miss Caroline made her nightly visits, but tonight he'd dozed off. Lantern light filtered into the shanty, casting shadows along the ceiling timbers. The scuff of boots on the dirt floor sounded foreign, so unlike Miss Caroline's tender step. Half asleep, Drew lifted his head, prying his eyes wider. The person held the lantern low at their side, not allowing a clear view of their face.

But the solid frame walking toward him definitely belonged to a man and not Miss Caroline. Certain he'd been discovered, Drew attempted to rise.

"Don't fret, Sergeant. It's me, Cyrus." The slave lifted the lantern enough for Drew to see his dark skin and stubbled jaw.

Drew crumpled back on the mat, his racing heart leaving him breathless. "I thought surely I'd been found out."

Cyrus shuffled closer and squatted beside him. "No sir, Miss Caroline's doin' her best t' see that don't happen. That's why I's here 'stead o' her."

"She's decided it's too risky to come, then. Sensible girl." Drew hoped his disappointment didn't tell in his voice. The moments spent in Miss Caroline's company were all he had to look forward to ... that and the hope of regaining enough strength to rejoin his men.

"For the time bein'. Her brother Jamison has done come home for a visit. I reckon she don't wanna risk him findin' out."

The notion she wished to protect him endeared her to him all the more. "Give her my thanks."

"Yes'r." Cyrus set the lantern on the floor and removed a container from inside a tin. "She had my wife, Lily, bundle up some tater soup and cornbread for ya, along with some biscuits and smoked ham for later."

Leaning on his good arm, Drew pushed himself to a sitting position and took the offered food. "Much obliged."

With a nod, Cyrus sat back and glanced around the run-down shack. "'Tain't much of a hideout." He tugged at his shirt collar. "Kinda close in here, ain't it?"

"So long as no one finds it, I'll not complain." Drew swiped a hand over his four-days growth of stubble and peered at his companion. "You didn't happen to bring a razor, did you?"

"No, sir, but I surely will next time."

"Thanks." Drew ventured a bite of soup. The creamy blend of potatoes, milk, and spices tasted like pure heaven. He emptied the container in a matter of minutes. Noting Cyrus's good-humored smile, he sopped up the remains with a piece of cornbread. "Your wife's a fine cook."

"Yes'r. None better."

Drew shifted his food to one side of his mouth. "Tell me about Miss Caroline. Other than wanting to become a nurse, what's she like?"

Cyrus drew his legs to his chest, wrapping his arms around his knees. "They don't come no finer than Miss Caroline. She's as kind-hearted a person as you'll ever meet. 'Course you already knows that."

Drew nodded, then cleared his throat. "Has she a beau?"

The caretaker arched a brow. "I don't know that Miss

Caroline would take kindly to me sharin' her personal information with no Union soldier." He paused, looking Drew over. "But then, I don't suppose you're likely to do her no harm, so I don't mind tellin' ya so far as I know she ain't partial to no particular feller."

He shook a finger at Drew. "But that don't mean there won't be a pack o' suitors come callin' once this war ends."

Drew cracked a wry smile. "Oh, I don't doubt that a minute."

Cyrus's eyebrows pinched. "Don't you go gettin' any notions, young feller. She ain't about t' take up with some Yank, no matter how nice lookin' and well-mannered ya is."

Hard as it was to admit, he was right. As soon as Drew was well enough, she'd send him on his way and forget she'd ever met him.

The question was, could he forget *her?*

11

C aroline pricked at her green beans with her fork, her appetite waning. She placed a hand on her knee to still it. Time was short. In two days, Jamison would leave.

Anticipation trickled through her. If all went well, so would she.

She ventured a glance at Papa. Not since Jamison's last visit had he been so full of mirth. The notion stung her. Would that she could bring her father even a fraction of the joy and satisfaction her siblings brought him—especially Jamison, his firstborn.

The conversation lulled, and Caroline drew a breath to bolster her courage. She sat straighter, resting her hands in her lap. "I imagine the hospital in Frederick is quite overwhelmed with patients."

The comment garnered a few looks but no comments.

She tried again. "I've heard there is a great need for nurses to aid the sick and wounded. Given the opportunity, I believe I might be useful to them."

Her father wiped his mouth, his glower returning. "Out of the question."

CYNTHIA ROEMER

Caroline's fingernails dug into the backs of her hands. "But why? It would be my way of contributing to the war effort."

Contempt rather than pride saturated her father's face. "What do you know of nursing?"

She swallowed the hurt of his indignant tone. "I-I've always nurtured a desire to learn nursing. I treated and bandaged many a soldier at the Thomas house; surely that counts for something."

"I think you'd make a fine nurse. You bandaged me real good," chimed her sister.

"Thank you, Rose." Caroline's chin tipped higher. She would not be deterred.

Papa seemed not even to hear the comment. "That's different. There's no comparing the two."

"How? How is it different?" Caroline struggled to keep her hands and voice from quivering. Rarely, if ever, had she challenged Papa. In a strange sort of way, it felt satisfying. As well as nauseating.

Mama's calming hand on Papa's arm stilled his certain-to-be heated response. "Your desire to help the injured is commendable, Caroline. But what you experienced at the Thomases' was only a fraction of what takes place in a hospital. Tending half-dressed soldiers day and night, emptying bedpans, assisting with amputations, and worse yet, being exposed to deplorable sicknesses. It would be more than you could tolerate."

Papa glared at Caroline. "Not to mention, the town of Frederick is partial to the Union, which means the hospital there tends Union soldiers as well as Confederate. For that reason alone, I forbid it."

Caroline bit her tongue to keep from revealing she'd already been emptying bedpans and tending a half-dressed Union soldier. But such knowledge would only worsen matters.

Jamison leaned back in his chair, his eyes sympathetic as he stared at her from across the table. "Hospital work isn't for you, Linna. You're much too delicate for such duties. Believe me,

72

you'll aid the war much better by staying home and saving your loveliness for some lucky soldier to savor when he returns from the war."

"Hear, hear." Papa's hearty laughter filled the dining room as Caroline lowered her gaze to the embroidered tablecloth. Tears pooled in her eyes. Attempts to persuade them were useless. With both her parents and Jamison set against her, all hope was lost.

Yet, she still had one patient. Sergeant Gallagher. Her efforts, along with the Lord's mercies, had saved him. She longed to proclaim it to her family, but there was no hope of that. Such a declaration would only bring wrath upon both her and the sergeant.

Jamison's voice cut through the tense silence. "I ... uh ... took a ride over the grounds today on your new bay mare. Wherever did you get such a fine animal when good mounts are so difficult to come by?"

Engrossed in her thoughts, her brother's words barely registered with Caroline.

"Bay mare? I don't recall purchasing a bay. You know I'm partial to chestnuts."

Papa's remark jolted Caroline from her fog. Straightening, she struggled for breath. "Oh. I neglected to mention it, but I found the mare a few days ago wandering the timber. I assumed her rider had been killed or wounded and would have no further need of her."

Jamison grinned. "Shrewd, sis. Very shrewd."

"In the timber? Haven't I warned you to stay clear of there? It's a wonder you didn't find a wayward blue-belly instead of a horse. When will you learn to listen?"

Papa's stern reprimand wounded deep, convincing Caroline once again she could do no right where he was concerned. And yet, how ironic that she *had* met a Union soldier, one that had shown her more kindness and respect in a matter of days than her father had in a lifetime.

Though the Yankees were considered her family's adversaries, Sergeant Gallagher—Drew—seemed more friend to her now than foe.

Unlike her father.

Love thine enemies, Scripture said.

Strange, she thought. It was becoming difficult to tell who her enemy truly was.

Late that evening

THE GENTLE TAP on Caroline's bedroom door brought her to her feet. Her heart drummed in her chest. Who would wish to see her at this late hour? She'd let Lily know she intended to see to the sergeant and instructed her to leave his tin of food in the usual spot. Had something gone awry?

"It's Jamison. Open up," came her brother's hushed command.

Caroline flipped back the covers on her bed to give some semblance she'd been sleeping and moved to open the door. Jamison stepped inside, his gaze flicking from her to her turned-down bed. "You're sleeping in your dress?"

She glanced at herself, having momentarily forgotten she'd not changed to her nightgown. "No, I-I've been reading. I was just getting ready to change." She mentally scolded herself for the fib.

Her brother's face pinched. "Reading? In this meager light?"

Caroline brightened the lantern flame. "I had just lowered it when you knocked."

Another falsehood. God forgive her.

Jamison straddled the chair at her desk and glanced around. "Just as I remember it. Your room hasn't changed a bit. But you have."

She eased onto her mattress. "How do you mean?"

He gestured toward her. "Look at you. While I was away, you've grown from a girl to a beautiful young woman. And the way you took Papa on about your wish to become a nurse. I've not seen you so bold and self-assured."

"Thank you." She returned a shy grin then raised a brow. "But you see where it got me."

Jamison stretched his arms over the back of the chair and rested his chin atop them. "Give Papa time. If it means that much to you, he'll eventually come around."

"I doubt it. He isn't keen on much of anything I suggest." Caroline heaved a soft sigh. "He seems to hold some unknown grievance against me, something that eats at him from within."

"Such nonsense."

"No, truly. There is something. He's always doted on you, Phillip, and Rose. But, with me, he's different, like there's some unseen obstacle between us. No matter what I do or say, I can't please him."

Jamison's gaze drifted to the quilt atop Caroline's bed, his lack of response enough to convince her he knew her words were true. With a mere fourteen months separating their ages, she and her brother had always shared a special bond. In her heart, she knew he could not deny Papa's disdain for her. At last, he reached to pat her hand. "Cheer up, Linna. How about a picnic lunch tomorrow? Just the two of us."

A smile edged out the dreariness inside Caroline. "That sounds wonderful, though it might take some doing to elude Phillip and Rose."

"We'll manage it." He gave her hand a gentle squeeze. "And for what it's worth, if your heart's set on it, I think you'd make a fine nurse ... once this war has ended, of course."

She shook her head at him. "Once a big brother, always a big brother."

He stood and flashed a playful grin. "Gotta look after my Linna ... until someone comes along to do it better."

Caroline shooed him out and closed the door behind him.

Though she'd never admit it, she loved his compulsion to protect her. It made her feel safe, loved amid her father's lack of regard. She listened for Jamison's footsteps to die away and his door to click shut. Then, striding to her bed, she dimmed the lantern once again. She would wait until he was asleep, then make her way to the shack to check on Drew. What a shame the two were on opposing sides of the war. Given opportunity, they might have been friends.

It grieved her to harbor a Yankee behind her brother's back. To do so seemed almost a slap in the face to all he stood for. All her family stood for. But the sergeant was an honorable man, and he deserved the chance to live. God had entrusted him to her care, and she must honor His will above anyone else's.

No matter the cost.

12

1 a.m. Thursday, July 14

Drew couldn't suppress a smile as Miss Caroline sat down beside him. "I thought you'd decided it too risky to come?"

"It is. But I have news."

He pushed himself to a sitting position, pain shooting through his shoulder and side. "Regarding the war?"

"In part." She grew quiet, her eyes downcast, obviously torn.

He leaned his head against the rough, hewn timbers and forced himself to be patient, recalling good news for him meant bad news for her and her family.

She drew a breath, at last finding her voice. "I read an article on the front page of the *Frederick Gazette* regarding the skirmish here. I feared bringing it would arouse suspicions, but I recall most of what was said."

Drew placed a hand on her arm. "It's fine. Take your time."

She tensed under his touch but didn't pull away. "It seems the battle at Monocacy Junction wasn't such a victory for the South after all. The day's delay in their march on Washington allowed time for Northern reinforcements to move into the Capital."

She paused, lifting her gaze to meet his. "They're calling it, 'The Battle that Saved Washington'."

Careful to suppress his elation, Drew rejoiced inwardly. "Thank you for telling me. The news makes my injuries a little more tolerable."

She glanced at his hand on her arm, and even the dim light of the lantern couldn't hide the crimson in her cheeks.

Sensing her discomfort, Drew slid his hand away. "Cyrus tells me your brother has paid a visit. Is he well?"

Her expression brightened. "Yes, though his time at home is short. He leaves early Saturday. It does my heart good to see him again and to know he's safe."

"You think a great deal of him."

"Jamison and I have always been close." Her mouth twisted. "I had hopes of traveling with him as far as Frederick when he left to rejoin his regiment."

"For what reason?" Drew knew he had no right to ask or even to wonder what would become of him if she did leave. He only knew he wished she would stay.

"To offer my services as a nurse in training at the hospital there. I'm certain I could help." She hung her head. "But my parents won't allow it."

The sadness in her voice tugged at Drew. She had such a heart to serve others. What could he say to comfort her? He patted his side. "Well, here's one patient who is more than pleased to have you as his nurse."

Her eyes lifted, glistening in the pale light. "Thank you."

The simple words, spoken so softly, melted his heart. How he wished he could get a better glimpse of her expression, to see her again by the light of day. He scolded himself for allowing her to seep into his affections. Given another time and place, he would savor his regard for her. But not here. Not now. They were on different sides of a war that not only divided their country but their families as well.

Shaking off the urge to stroke her hand, her hair, her face, he cleared his throat and locked his fingers together in his lap. "You implied that news of the war was only part of your reason for coming."

"Yes. Cyrus has your horse stabled and has been tending to her. I was certain she would go undetected since my family rarely visits the stable. But I'm afraid Jamison discovered her and took her on a jaunt around the property. I explained I'd found her in the timber, which was the truth. I merely neglected to mention I'd found you as well."

Drew searched his memory. "My ... horse?"

"Don't tell me you've forgotten that beautiful bay mare? I might have passed you by if not for her."

He scratched at the now five-day growth of whiskers on his chin. "That's right. The bay. I'm afraid she isn't mine."

Caroline blinked. "But she was standing beside you when I found you."

"She appeared from nowhere while I was in the midst of battle. Just stood there as if waiting to spirit me away."

Caroline straightened, a look of wonder in her eyes. "Then the Lord truly *was* looking out for you."

A smile tugged at his lips. "I'll not argue that. Especially where you're concerned."

She remained still so long Drew questioned if he'd somehow insulted her. He was about to apologize for his boldness when she leaned closer, touching a hand to his brow. "You must be someone special indeed."

His eyes locked with hers, and as her delicate fingertips brushed a lock of hair from his brow, he knew she returned his affections.

And that, likely, their lives would never be the same.

13

Thursday, July 14

Caroline followed Jamison into the yard, hugging the blanket they would spread under them on their picnic. She smothered a yawn, tired but still airy from her early morning encounter with Sergeant Gallagher.

Drew.

She'd not slept a wink after leaving him, her mind filled with emotions she had yet to define. How could she allow herself to become attached to a Union soldier? Worse yet, alert him to her feelings?

Jamison turned to her, swinging their basket of fried chicken, biscuits, and boiled eggs. "Did too much reading rob you of sleep last night. sis?"

"That along with a brother's late-night visit." Heat flamed in her cheeks, and she averted her gaze in hopes he wouldn't read the deception in her eyes. Since Drew's arrival, it seemed she'd done nothing but fabricate falsehoods.

Jamison's hearty laughter broke through her thoughts. "That's right. Blame me."

She nudged his shoulder, willing herself to return her focus to the present. This was her time with Jamison. Nothing should interfere. Appraising her feelings for Drew must wait.

Jamison pointed to their left. "What say we spread our picnic over by the old slave shack? That has a pleasant view of the creek and plenty of shade trees to choose from."

"No! Not there."

He stared at her, his furrowed brow implying her words had come too quick and forceful. "Why?"

Softening her tone, Caroline pointed in the opposite direction. "The view is much prettier over there." She pasted on a smile and tugged on his arm. "Come. I know just the place."

As she led him along, her mind churned for someplace grand to settle on. At last, she recalled a fine oak tree on a hill overlooking the meadow. When they came to it, she stretched out her arm. "Here we are. The perfect picnic spot."

Jamison shrugged. "It'll do. But don't blame me if Rose or Phillip come pokin' around. It's in full view of the house. My spot would've been more secluded."

Caroline flashed him a playful grin. "Always did fuss when you didn't have your way."

He shook his head at her. "Just spread the blanket."

With a giggle, she fanned the blanket out and let it settle to the ground. Smoothing her dress out under her, she sat and motioned for Jamison to join her.

He took a glance around and dropped down beside her. "From here, it's hard to imagine there's a war going on."

She followed his gaze to the meadow and the tree-lined creek beyond. "I know. Sometimes it seems nothing has changed. Then, sounds of cannons and gunfire rumble in the distance, and it feels as though nothing will ever be the same, like a bad dream that never ends."

"Nightmare, you mean."

The melancholy in his voice tugged at Caroline's heart. She handed him a plate, troubled by the far-off look in his eyes. "I wish you didn't have to go. I've missed you."

He gave a long sigh. "I've grown weary of fighting, but in due time, we'll reap our reward."

Caroline placed a chicken leg on each plate. "Do you ever wonder if the war is worth the effort? I mean, people like Lily and Cyrus. They're more like faithful employees than slaves. They'd be loyal to our family regardless if they were slaves or free."

Jamison's brows knit. "Of course, it's worth it. I declare, Linna, you sound as though you've stopped believin' in the Southern cause."

Caroline was beginning to wonder herself. Her short acquaintance with Drew had made her view the Union side in a fresh light. "It's just that I hate to see so many lives lost to war. There must be a better way to resolve our differences than fighting and killing."

He pointed his chicken leg at her and grinned. "If you could manage that, I venture to say Abe Lincoln and Jeff Davis would give over their presidencies to you without so much as batting an eye."

She tossed him a boiled egg. "Maybe that's not such a bad idea."

He twirled the egg around in his palm. "So, tell me, as President, how would you resolve the issue of slavery?"

She leaned against the rough bark of the oak. "Well now, let's see. First, I'd send you and all the other soldiers home."

He nodded. "A good start. Then what?"

"Then, I'd set all my top officers and generals down and discuss what needed to be done to find common ground."

"Ah! Therein lies the problem, my dear sister. There *is* no common ground. The blue-bellies are set on freeing the slaves, and we Southerners want the freedom to choose to conduct our lives and property as we see fit."

Caroline brushed a strand of hair from her cheek, squinting at him against the noonday sun. "But don't you think everyone deserves freedom? Is it right for some to gain freedom and others lose it?"

Jamison glared at her. "What are you saying? That you think slaves should be freed?"

She gnawed at her lip, sensing her brother's indignation. "I don't know. I'm just not certain the Lord intended one man to own another."

Dropping the egg to his plate, Jamison stood and paced back and forth. "I'm not certain I even know you anymore, Linna. You may as well spit in my face as to believe as you do. Who's been filling your head with such nonsense?"

"No one." Caroline dropped her gaze and folded quivering hands in her lap.

"Then when did you stop embracing Southern ideas and take on Yankee rhetoric?"

Her stomach reeled. She'd never intended their picnic to turn political. Nor had she anticipated such a transformation of her beliefs. She'd never relished the thought of slavery. Though Papa was not a particularly harsh master to his handful of slaves, Caroline still cringed when she witnessed the field slaves being chastised or pressed beyond their physical limits.

She sighed. "Truly, Jamison, no sister could be more proud of her brother than I am. You're a fine soldier, fighting for a cause you believe in. You're protecting our livelihood and our land, and I love you for it."

Jamison crossed his arms and jutted his jaw but made no reply.

She gave his pant leg a firm tug. "Sit down, Jamison, please? There'll be no more talk of war or politics."

He cut her a sideways glance, his expression softening.

"You have my word." She held a hand up in pledge, her smile returning.

At last, he flopped back down on the blanket and set his filled plate in his lap. "You had me worried. For a minute, I thought I'd lost you."

She nudged his shoulder. "Never. I'm afraid you're stuck with me, dear brother."

Even as she said the words, guilt trickled through her. As much as she loved her brother, she could no longer adhere to his cause. Yet, she pledged never again to say anything to make him feel he was less than a hero in her eyes.

Midnight, Thursday, July 14

DREW SWIPED his fingers over his clean-shaven jaw, grateful Cyrus had remembered to send a razor blade with Caroline. Unable to bend his left arm to fit in the sleeve of the loose-fitting borrowed shirt, he let the empty sleeve dangle at his side. Without a mirror or use of his left hand, he'd nicked himself more than once, but regardless, it felt good to be free of the unwanted whiskers.

Sensing Caroline's eyes upon him, he turned to face her. With a one-shoulder shrug, he flashed a shy grin. "It's nice to feel somewhat myself again. Be sure to thank Cyrus for the blade."

She reached to tie the drawstrings at his neck, her warm smile denoting approval. "I will."

The tenderness in her voice beguiled him. He reached for her hand, and she willingly gave it. Her nearness both invigorated and alarmed him. What could possibly come of their budding affections? Until the fighting ended, any fondness between them was doomed. Even after the war, chances were slim that her family would accept him.

Each day he grew stronger, and his obligations were clear. Within days, he'd leave this place and, Lord willing, make his way north to meet up with his company. Caroline belonged here with her family. Still, he couldn't deny his eagerness to see her again when the war ended.

He gave her fingers a soft kiss. "Is there a chance, once all this fighting is over, I'd be welcome to call on you?"

Long lashes hid her eyes. "I fear my father would never allow it."

"Surely, he wouldn't be so cruel as to deny you your choice of suitors."

She sighed, sliding her hand from his. "You don't know Papa. He'll likely never soften toward a Northerner, no matter what the outcome of the war or how much time passes."

Silence blanketed the small shanty. All seemed hopeless. Now, as well as in the future. But Drew refused to give up. He placed a hand under her chin, and her eyes lifted. "When all seemed impossible, the Lord made a way through the Red Sea for the Israelites. Surely, He can make a way for us."

She managed a weak grin, the curve of her rounded lips inviting. "I'll pray it will be so."

He leaned toward her, brushing a hand against her cheek. She closed her eyes, and her lips parted.

A loud "thud" shattered the stillness, drawing them apart. The rickety door dropped from its hinges. Drew eyed the shadowy figure standing in the doorway, certain his fate was sealed.

Caroline jumped to her feet. "Jamison!"

The click of a revolver was the intruder's only response as he stretched out his arm, closing the gap between them.

14

"Jamison, no! Please, let me explain." Caroline pleaded, wedging herself between him and Drew.

He shoved her aside, angry eyes locked on Drew. "I think the situation pretty well explains itself."

Drew met his gaze, trying to decipher if an attempt to speak on Caroline's behalf would calm or fuel her brother's fury.

Jamison's eyes narrowed. "So, you're the one filling my sister's head with muck. I knew something wasn't right. She seemed too eager to keep me from this place. But I never expected some blue-belly could turn her head."

Drew gestured to his empty sleeve. "Your sister was kind enough to help an injured soldier. That's all."

"From what I heard outside that door and saw in here, there's a lot more to it than that."

Caroline gripped her brother's arm. "Please, Jamison. Drew's a good man. He was injured. I couldn't just leave him there."

He shook her off. "Why not? He's a filthy Yank! Don't you realize he and his kind are out to destroy our way of life and, given the chance, kill the whole lot of us?"

Caroline seemed to waver, her gaze flicking between the two

of them. Her loyalty to her brother left Drew a bit antsy. Would she fight to spare him or allow Jamison to have his way?

Long seconds ticked by, seeming more like hours. When she finally spoke, her voice was breathy, unsteady. "Please, Jamison, I'm asking you to show Christ-like grace and mercy to a man who's done you no personal harm." She focused her gaze on Drew. "A man who's shown me nothing but kindness and gratitude. A man I've come to respect and care for."

Drew's heart melted at her words. Whether her brother heeded her pleas or not, Caroline had given him sentiments he could go to his grave cherishing.

Jamison stood frozen in place, his heavy breaths adding to the tension in the room. Drew waited, feeling like the adulterous woman at the feet of Jesus awaiting condemnation.

But as with her, none came.

Jamison lowered his revolver, his gaze never leaving Drew's face. "Get him out of here. Tonight."

Caroline took a step toward him, a tremor in her voice. "But, he's not well enough. He'll never make it."

Jamison swiped a hand through his hair, plainly agitated. "I don't care. He leaves tonight or not at all. If I find him here come morning, he leaves as my prisoner."

Drew straightened and looked him in the eye. "I'll go. You have my word."

The grimace on his opponent's face told Drew his word meant little, and yet he nodded. "I suppose that bay mare my sister *found* belongs to you?"

Drew's gaze darted to Caroline. "Yes." There was no use explaining how the mare had come into his possession. He only prayed Jamison would allow him to utilize her.

The moment of silence seemed deafening. Jamison took a step closer, his eyes scrutinizing. "I'll leave her saddled and tethered outside. And you'd best light out of here if you know what's good for you."

"I'm obliged to you." The words were heartfelt ones. Drew's

thoughts returned to the lad he'd spared in battle a few days earlier and consoled himself with the notion the Lord was repaying him for the kindness.

Jamison's gaze drifted to Drew's vacant sleeve, then to his chest, turning with a grimace to Caroline. "You gave him my shirt?"

She cringed. "He needed something to wear. His uniform shirt and jacket were beyond repair."

With a shake of his head, Jamison snickered bitterly. "I'm surprised you didn't drag my mattress here for him to sleep on."

Caroline's eyes were pleading. "I'm sorry, Jamison. I never meant to offend you."

"Just see to it I never set eyes on him again." Without a backward glance, he pivoted and trudged toward the gaping doorway.

The tortured expression on Caroline's face as she watched her brother leave made Drew almost sorry she'd ever found him. At this point, nothing he could say would console her. He only prayed someday he'd have the chance to make it up to her.

15

Caroline bit back tears as Drew pulled her into a gentle, one-armed embrace outside the shanty. She would not cry. Though the brother she adored now despised her and the only man she'd ever cared for was lost to her, she refused to give in to self-pity.

Drew's arm slipped from around her shoulders and, despite the warm summer night, a cold emptiness enveloped her. He peered down at her, pale moonlight reflecting in his silvery eyes. "I'd better go."

She moaned softly, heaviness stealing over her. "I'm sorry. It's my fault. Had I not reacted so strongly about the shack, Jamison likely would not have grown suspicious."

Warmth surged through her as he brushed the back of his fingers along her cheek. "You've nothing to be sorry for. I'm indebted to you for my very life—you and the Lord. I only pray no harm will come to you on my account."

Her gaze flicked to the crude sling she'd fashioned to stabilize his injured shoulder. "It's you I worry about, not yet fit to ride and traveling alone by night on Confederate soil. You don't stand a chance."

"With you praying for me, I will." He leaned closer, his voice soothing. "Nothing escapes the Lord's notice. We need only entrust each other to Him."

She nodded, a sense of peace washing over her. He was right. Their lives, their futures rested with the Lord. He alone knew the outcome of the war and if they would ever see each other again.

An owl's rhythmic *hoot* broke the stillness as Drew clasped Caroline's hand and strolled with her to his horse. As promised, Jamison had saddled the mare and brought her with not a word to either of them. Would he keep their secret or expose the deception to the rest of the family?

Caroline's stomach lurched. She hated to think what Papa would do if he found out. He'd certainly never forgive her.

Would Jamison?

Another day and he would have been gone. Caroline gnawed at her lip, inwardly chiding herself. She loved her brother. Wishing him away for her and Drew's sake was selfish. It would be better if she could simply undo it all.

Well, not everything.

She glanced at the man at her side, his strong hand wrapped around hers. She didn't regret meeting Drew. Only Jamison's discovery of him.

Drew paused beside his mare, his eyes locking onto Caroline's then drifting to her lips. Her heart leaped as he ran his fingertips along her jawbone. "I'll not forget you, Caroline Dunbar."

"Nor I you." Her breathing shallowed as he leaned closer and threaded his fingers through her hair. She closed her eyes and tipped her head back to meet his kiss, marveling at the tender way his lips melded to hers. For one exhilarating moment, all their troubles melted away until only she and Drew remained.

All too soon, they parted, and Caroline was grateful the darkness veiled the certain glow in her cheeks. A shy smile tugged at her lips as she met his gaze. Never had she imagined her first kiss would go to a Union soldier.

Yet, she had no regrets, save the hasty way they must say goodbye.

With a sigh, Drew placed his foot in the stirrup, and Caroline helped hoist him onto the mare. A groan escaped him as he landed in the saddle. Tears again threatened to spill from her eyes as she handed him the reins.

He reached out his hand, and she latched onto it. "I'll be back ... when the war is over."

Her pulse quickened at the words, though she dared not let herself believe them. She squeezed his hand, stealing a final glimpse of him in the moonlight. "I'll be waiting. Godspeed. May the Lord guide your way."

He hesitated, his eyes perusing her face but a moment before he released her hand and reined the mare northward.

Caroline backed toward the cabin, watching until the darkness swallowed him. Their time together had been brief, his coming and going unexpected. Though their upbringings differed and their families remained on opposite sides of the war, she and Drew shared what mattered most—faith in God and the hope they would one day see each other again.

A tear dampened her cheek as she gathered her skirt and turned to collect her things. With uncertain steps, she fumbled her way to the dark shanty, wondering what lay ahead when daylight dawned.

And if she'd just seen the last of Drew Gallagher.

THE FAINTEST SLIVER of light fringed the eastern horizon, convincing Drew it was time to halt his travels—that, along with the surge of pain in his side and shoulder. With the North Star as his only compass, he'd made slow progress and passed the night without incident. Daylight's approach would leave him vulnerable to Confederate troops moving through the area. He needed somewhere to hide and rest; a place secluded enough his horse wouldn't draw attention.

Dismounting, he strained to see through the darkness. The moon had dipped below the tree-line, no longer lending its light. A robin's chortle broke the stillness, beckoning the sun to dawn. Time was short. Each passing moment increased his chances of being spotted. He edged forward, eyes searching. To his right, the ground seemed to dip down into a deep gully, and with any luck, a creek bottom. The summer drought ensured any water in the creek would be minimal, but hopefully enough to refill his canteen and water his horse.

Deeming it his best option, he started forward. With careful steps, Drew eased the mare into the ravine. She nickered nervously as the ground became more slanted and unstable, her hooves knocking against sprigs and rocks embedded in the loose soil.

Drew stilled, giving her a soft pat on the neck. Maybe this wasn't such a good idea. The darkness worked both for and against them. With his injuries, the terrain would be difficult enough to maneuver by day. Not being able to see what lay ahead made the gulch near impossible to navigate. It appeared deeper than he'd initially thought. No telling how far down it led. One slip or wrong move, and he'd be in worse shape than he was already.

A horse with a broken leg wouldn't do him any good either.

He leaned against the embankment, staring up at the fading stars. *I could use a bit of help, Lord.*

Almost in answer, a Scripture coursed through his head.

Be still and know that I am God.

Obediently, he paused to listen. In the quietness, he heard a faint trickle of water from no more than a couple feet below—a sign they'd almost reached the bottom. Was the Lord urging him to continue?

He grappled for a solid foothold then, with a tug of the reins, urged the mare forward. The earthy scent of loam filled his nostrils as dirt sprayed down on him from the horse's movement on the steep decline. He shook the soil from his clothes, wishing by some miracle there would be enough water for washing. More than a week had passed since he'd had a decent bath. It was a wonder Caroline had come near him at all.

His foot slid in the powdery dirt, and he caught hold of a tree root with his good arm. Thankful it held, he blew out an unsteady breath. How he yearned to still be under Caroline's watchful care instead of risking life and limb gallivanting all over the countryside in the darkness of night.

Peeks of brightness began to replace the dark as the sun edged nearer the horizon. At last, he could distinguish his surroundings. A wide creek bed stretched out before him, dry but for a shallow pool of water several yards to his left where it narrowed. Lowering himself down, he noticed the waterhole was fed by an underground spring flowing from a crevice in the ravine wall. Here, eight or nine feet below ground level, cool moistness wafted out at him. An overhang of twisted tree roots and undergrowth formed a natural bridge to the opposite side.

He grinned. The perfect hideout. *Thank you, Lord.*

He led his horse onto the hardened clay of the creek bottom, taking it slow to muffle the clop of her hooves. With a glance around to ensure he hadn't been detected, he knelt to fill his canteen while his horse drank.

Drew slid his arm from the shoulder sling and slowly straightened it, stiff from hours of holding it in one position. He reached to splash water in his face and soaked in its coolness. Even traveling at night, the air remained muggy. He rocked back on his heels, taking another look at his surroundings. This place truly was a tiny oasis. He felt a bit like the prophet Elijah being refreshed at a hidden stream.

His throat hitched. The only thing missing was Caroline. The memory of her tender kiss still lingered on his lips. It pained him to think he might never see her again, that he'd promised to return when his future remained so uncertain.

He raked a hand over his face, his strength sapped. A few hours of shuteye was what he needed. The question was, would he be able to sleep without fear of some Reb finding him?

16

July 15, 1864

The clink of silverware rang loud against the quiet. A cloud seemed to have fallen over the family at the reality of Jamison's impending departure. Caroline nudged her dinner plate aside, venturing a glance at him. His slumped posture and furrowed brow hinted he was troubled by much more than leaving. Would he reveal her secret or merely shut her out? Either option made her heart sink.

If only she could talk to him, make him understand. But thus far, he'd not spoken a word nor even looked her in the eyes.

Mama passed Jamison the biscuits, her eyes red from tears she'd tried to hide. At the shake of his head, she set the bowl aside, chin quivering. "When will you leave?"

"After dinner, I reckon." He glared across the table at Caroline. "Gotta get back so I can chase down more Yanks."

She broke into a cold sweat, sensing herself go pale. Worse than the worry of being found out was the ache from vengefulness in her brother's voice. In one swift moment, the closeness between them had shattered. God forgive her if it was never regained.

"I hope you blast the whole lot of 'em." Philip blurted, pretending to aim a rifle at the empty flower vase on the corner cabinet. "Pow! Pow!"

Mama motioned him to lower his arms. "That'll be enough of that."

With a soft snicker, Jamison sat back in his chair, hands locked behind his head. "I'll do my best, li'l brother." He shifted his gaze back to Caroline. "Any Federal within shootin' range of me is asking for a minié ball in his gullet, wouldn't you say, Linna?"

Caroline forced herself to look him in the eyes. She opened her mouth to speak, but there seemed no apt reply.

Papa's gaze oscillated between them. "Somethin' going on with you two?"

Jamison drew himself to his feet. "No, no. Just seems we don't see eye to eye as much as we used to."

"Is that so?"

Out of the corner of her eye, Caroline glimpsed her father's scowl fixed on her, and she seethed inwardly. Why was it he always credited her as the guilty one when situations went awry? Scooting her chair back, she stood and cleared away her tableware. "Excuse me."

With harried breaths, she made her way to the kitchen and set her things in the washbasin. Fighting tears, she leaned her head forward and rubbed her fingertips along her forehead. Whether Jamison chose to expose her or not, she'd never gain her father's favor. All the fret and worry of trying just wasn't worth it.

What troubled her more was her severed relationship with Jamison. Never had she intended to cast a shadow over their friendship. Now, the damage had been done, and there was little or nothing she could do about it.

"What is it, Miss Caroline? Is you feelin' poorly?"

Lily's sympathetic voice from the far side of the kitchen cut through Caroline's angst. "No, Lily. I think I just need a bit of air."

The hefty, dark-skinned housemaid sauntered over and placed a hand on Caroline's back, easing her toward the door. "You go on and drink in some o' that mornin' sunshine. Nothin' soothes the spirit like talkin' things over with the Lord in the open air."

Caroline turned and offered a half-hearted grin. "I'll do that. Thank you." The kind-hearted woman seemed to have a window into Caroline's soul, knowing just the right words to cheer her.

Lily's rounded face lifted, her eyes earnest as she swung open the door. "You go on now, honeychild. Don't you worry none about the dishes. I'll see to 'em."

With a nod of thanks, Caroline strode outside. She squinted against the brightness of the sun, its heat soaking through her cotton day dress. The dry grass crunched beneath her boots. She couldn't recall the last substantial rain they'd had, only an occasional small shower. So much hardship and upheaval—the drought, the war, her father, now her relationship with Jamison.

Her gaze pulled in the direction where the shack lay nestled behind a grove of trees, and her spirits sank lower. Drew and Jamison had been her only bright spots in this otherwise troublesome time. With Drew gone and Jamison leaving, her entire world seemed desolate. Especially knowing how Jamison now perceived her.

She ached to set things right.

Turning, she made her way to the sprawling oak under which she and Jamison had shared lunch. How very long ago that seemed now. With a sigh, she leaned against the rough bark of the tree. She plucked a head of dried grass from its stem and scattered the seeds to the wind, lifting her eyes heavenward. "Lord, forgive my inabilities, my failings. Bring healing where I cannot. Restore this severed land. Bring an end to this horrendous war that shatters lives and sows such hatred and bitterness. You alone know the outcome; what's ahead for me, for my family, for Drew. But whatever the future holds, may I never lose sight of You."

Approaching footsteps broke through her prayer. Her stomach clenched when she saw Jamison tromping toward her, his expression somber. Had he told Papa what she'd done and come to fetch her to receive her punishment?

He came and stood beside her, arms crossed over his chest. "I see your friend is gone."

Despite the churning inside her, Caroline tipped her chin higher, looking him in the eyes. "He gave his word. He left soon after you brought his horse."

Jamison spat on the ground. "I don't take much stock in the word of a Yank."

Caroline turned, fixing her gaze on the distant fields. "If you came to continue your quarrel, I'd rather not hear it."

He caught her by the arm, pivoting her toward him. "I just don't see how you can cotton to some blue-belly."

"Who says I cotton to him?" Even as she spoke the words, she knew the tremor in her voice betrayed her.

He placed a hand under her chin. "It's written all over your face."

Tears welled in her eyes, and she leaned into him. "I'm sorry, Jamison. I admit I do care for him, though nothing can ever come of it. Now that he's gone, I'll likely never see him again. I never dreamed you'd come home while he was here. I'd not intentionally hurt you for anything."

He sighed and placed his hands on her shoulders. "That doesn't change the fact he's a Yank, someone I'm sworn to kill or take prisoner. I could be court-martialed for letting him go."

Caroline pulled back, staring up at him with moist eyes. "I'll not tell a soul. Only we will know." She swallowed, straining against the lump in her throat. "That is, unless you told Papa and Mama."

Time seemed to stop as she awaited his reply. At last, he

shook his head. "Part of me wished to, but I couldn't. After all, I'd be implicating myself as well as you."

An enormous burden rolled from her shoulders as she released the breath she'd been holding. She mustered a weak grin. "Then our secret is safe."

He arched a brow, his green eyes boring into her. "Safe, but not forgotten."

JAMISON'S WORDS haunted Caroline as, hours later, she and her family stood on the veranda waving their goodbyes. She tried to read the depth of his gaze as he turned and gave her a final glance before trekking across the yard to the worn path. Had he forgiven her? To an extent, she knew he had. But deep down, she'd sensed a wall of hurt still lingering between them. She'd broken his trust, and it would take time to regain.

If, by some terrible twist of circumstance, he and Drew should meet in battle, would one strike the other down? She gripped the porch railing, unsettled by the thought. In her heart, she knew the answer. They were soldiers, bent on doing what they were trained to do—kill and defend. They would have no choice. And, Lord help her, she could not bear the outcome.

"HOW'D that fool horse get down there?"

"Beats me. Looks too well-fed t' be one of ours."

The excited male voices snapped Drew from fitful slumber. Though unable to see them on the ledge up above, their southern twang left little doubt the men were Confederate. His heart hammered. Were they soldiers? Deserters? He slunk further into the shadows, relieved he'd thought to conceal his gear.

But where was his horse?

Venturing a look, he cringed to see her standing in plain sight several yards farther along the creek bottom. He leaned back and balled his fists. Somehow the animal had pulled free of the tree root he'd tethered her to and wandered away.

He jerked his head forward, hope swelling in his chest. There was a chance the situation could work to his favor. If the horse were tied, likely the men would scour the area in search of her rider. Free, the mare appeared to have run off.

"Maybe she belonged to some bigwig officer," the second man continued.

"Well, she's ours now. Come on."

At the sound of movement and falling debris, Drew molded himself against the embankment, draping more foliage over him. He dared not breathe as the men maneuvered their way down the slope a mere few yards from him.

A snort sounded further down, followed by the gallop of hooves along the dry creek bed. Drew's lips pulled in a grin. *Good girl. Don't let 'em catch you.*

One of the men uttered a curse and hollered after her. "Get back here, you daft horse!"

The other man chuckled. "You goin' after her?"

"I reckon so. We'll catch up to her eventually. Anyway, this creek shallows a ways up yonder. Be easier climbin' out than the way we came."

Drew breathed easier as their conversation became muffled and the sound of their boot steps faded. Whether the horse knew it or not, she'd provided him a much-needed diversion. Twice she had come to his aid, almost as if the Lord had sent him a guardian angel.

Only now, he'd lost his means of transportation.

———————

DREW YAWNED and rubbed his stiff neck. He wasn't sure when he'd fallen asleep, but last he recalled bright sunlight had shone above him. Now the sky was alive with the amber and crimson hues of sunset. Misty shadows hung in the humid air, spilling down into the creek bottom. After the men had chased off his horse, he'd laid awake for hours snacking on rations of food from his haversack and wondering how he would manage to make his way north on foot.

Travel by night was treacherous enough, and his tender side and shoulder only added to the challenge. Still weak and in need of frequent rests, he hadn't the stamina, in body or spirit, to go far. He'd be fortunate to cover more than a mile or two each night.

His chest tightened. Or did Caroline's plight have him twisted in knots?

It had tormented him to leave her, not knowing what she would encounter. Had her brother berated her for helping him? Had he exposed her to the scorn of her family and community? Drew hung his head. If any harm came to her on his account, he'd never forgive himself. But then, more than likely, he would not know what befell her. The notion soured in his stomach.

Movement drew his attention to the far edge of the pool of water.

His eyes widened at the shadowy object coming toward him.

He blinked. *It couldn't be.*

A grin crept onto his face. It *was* a horse.

But not just any horse. The bay mare.

He'd imagined her miles away by now. Why had she doubled back? Hopefully, the men hadn't trailed her here. He waited, listening for the slightest indication they might be near. But when the horse showed no signs of flightiness, Drew decided there was no cause for alarm. He pulled himself to his feet. Would she run from him as she had the Rebels?

With plodding steps, he started toward her. "Easy girl."

Instead of bolting, she bobbed her head and pawed at the creek bottom much like the first time he'd approached her during battle. Stretching out his hand, he clasped the reins. With a shake of his head, he blew out a breath, conscious of all the abuse his feet had been spared by the horse's unexpected return. "Well, I'll be."

He patted her withers, a surge of relief and awe washing through him. "You and the Lord sure are looking out for me, aren't ya?"

As if in answer, the horse nickered and nuzzled him with her head. Drew rubbed a hand down her face. If she was his for keeps, he needed to call her something besides "horse." A grin tugged at his lips. Only one name suited her.

Angel.

WHAT HAD Jamison meant their secret was safe but not forgotten? Hours after his departure, Caroline still wrestled with the thought. Would they go through life with an unspoken barrier between them?

Sitting at her writing desk, she dipped the quill in the inkwell, intent on penning Jamison a letter. Instead, Drew's name spilled onto the page. Her face warmed. Gone but a day, Sergeant Andrew Gallagher remained at the forefront of her thoughts. Was he faring well? Would the meager supply of food she'd sent be enough to sustain him?

Her throat hitched. Would he be captured?

A thousand questions pummeled her, ones she'd likely never know the answer to. If only Papa would agree to let her go to Frederick to work at the hospital. Not only would her dream of nursing be realized, but if Drew succeeded in finding his way there, at least they'd stand a chance of crossing paths.

She slumped over the desk, resting her chin in her palm. Changing Papa's mind was like trying to bend a dry twig without it snapping.

Impossible.

17

Sunday, July 17, 1864
South of Frederick, Maryland

Drew panned his surroundings as the first peek of sun crested the horizon. Nothing looked familiar. Three nights of travel should have landed him just south of Frederick. And yet, there was no sign of it. Traveling in the dead of night put him at a distinct disadvantage.

Frustrated, he slipped his right foot from the stirrup and dismounted in a slow, arduous motion. He cringed and cut a glance at the dark stain on his shirt. If he didn't find help soon, he'd no longer have to fear being shot or taken prisoner. He'd simply become a casualty of war.

With weighted steps, he led Angel down a vale into a grove of trees, thick with underbrush. Not the most promising of hideouts, but he hadn't the energy to go roaming around in search of a better one. The Lord had aided him every step of the way. But now, it appeared his time for blessing may have run out.

Finding a sizable, flat boulder on which to sit, Drew collapsed onto it and allowed Angel free rein to nibble foliage. He emptied the contents of his haversack on the rock and scratched his stubbled cheek as he realized his food supply had dwindled to one stale biscuit and a sliver of smoked ham. Not enough to sustain him long.

The unmistakable cock of a rifle froze him in place.

"Hands in the air, mister." A nasally voice called from behind.

Heart pounding, Drew obliged by raising his right arm over his head.

"Raise the other one, slow and steady."

His throat hitched. "I can't. I took a gunshot to the shoulder."

Silence. Then, a sharp, "Turn around."

Either the fellow had taken him at his word or noticed the empty sleeve dangling at his side. Drew eased down off the rock and pivoted to face him. Three soldiers clad in blue—two privates and a corporal—stared back at him, and his hopes lifted. He started to lower his arm, but the corporal jutted his rifle at him. "Keep it raised."

Drew lifted his arm. He'd forgotten he wasn't in uniform. In the civilian shirt, it was impossible to determine if he were Confederate or Union.

Angel let out a nervous whinny behind him. If she bolted, likely this time she'd be lost to him. "I'd like to secure my horse, if I may."

The soldier seemed to deliberate then nudged his chin at him. "Go on, but don't try nothin' funny, or it'll be the last thing you do."

The two privates leveled their rifles at him.

Drew gave a brisk nod and, with careful movements, edged over to Angel and gripped her reins.

The corporal motioned to the man on his right. "Get her, Private Benson."

The young, tow-headed soldier lowered his rifle and edged his way forward, looking like a fox about to corner a chicken. Snatching the reins, he flashed Drew a cocky grin. He tugged Angel forward and led her back to his companions.

The corporal relaxed his hold on his rifle, his dark eyes boring a hole through Drew. "Now then, who are ya and what er ya doin' out here?"

Drew pulled himself to full height and tipped his chin forward. "Sergeant Andrew Gallagher of the 112th New York infantry. I'm on my way to the hospital in Frederick for medical treatment. I'm hoping to reconnect with my company once I find out where they've gone."

The soldier who'd retrieved Angel let out a loud snicker. "Sure, ya is. Probably out here scoutin' for the Johnny Rebs."

The corporal nudged him in the forearm. "Shut up." His eyes narrowed as he perused Drew head to toe. "If'n you're a sergeant, why ain't you in uniform?"

"I was injured in the battle at Monocacy Junction. My uniform shirt and jacket were torn and bloodied beyond repair."

"Monocacy Junction? That was over a week ago. You mean t' say you've been wanderin' around all that time with a bullet in ya?"

Drew swallowed, wondering how he would explain his situation without divulging too much detail. He shook his head, thankful the shirt hid his bandages. "I was fortunate the minié ball passed through without much damage."

The third soldier scowled at him through a face full of whiskers. "Where'd ya get that civilian shirt?"

Drew's cheek flinched. More than likely, they'd never believe the truth. He'd keep his answer as vague as possible so as not to incriminate himself or Caroline. "In an abandoned shack a ways back."

The soldiers studied his face as if trying to decipher the truth of his words. The bearded man spat on the ground. "I think he's a spy for the Rebs."

"He don't talk like no Reb," responded the young soldier holding Angel.

The corporal raised a hand to silence them. "I'll settle this." He looked Drew in the eyes. "I know a feller from the 112th by the name of Saunders. If'n you can tell me the nickname he goes by, I'll know you're on the level."

Drew thought a moment; then, a smile edged across his lips. Though he always referred to his men by their last name rather than their given one, he often overheard his men ribbing each other and spouting nicknames. "If you're referring to Private "Buck" Saunders, I know him well. I've had the pleasure of calling him to my quarters on occasion regarding some, shall I say, questionable activities?"

The corporal lowered his rifle, his lips spreading in a wide grin. "That's Buck, all right." He gave the privates a shove forward. "Well, go on. Help the sergeant to his horse. Cain't you see he's injured?"

Drew breathed a sigh of relief as the men started toward him, grateful for the Lord's mercies ... and, for once, that Buck Saunders was a less-than-stellar soldier.

Dear Jamison,

I know you'll soon be moving on, so I pray this letter finds its way to you. It was so good to have you home, even for a short time.

CAROLINE LEANED FORWARD in her desk chair, wrestling with how to express her thoughts on paper. There was so much she wished to say, and yet more than likely, it would sound defensive or jumbled when read by her brother. She touched the freshly-inked tip of her quill to the paper and continued.

I'm truly sorry our time together was tainted by unexpected circumstances. I regret ...

"Who are you writing?"
Caroline startled at her sister's voice near her ear. Heat

burned her cheeks as she rushed to shade the words with her hand. She scowled and glanced over her shoulder. "Jamison. But I wish you'd knock."

"I'm sorry." Rose plopped down on the foot of the bed. "Jamison's only been gone a couple of days. You're writing him already?"

Caroline turned back to her paper, her shoulders sagging at the sight of the blotch left atop the T in *regret*. "Yes. He's moving out shortly. I'm in hopes, if I send a letter quickly, it will reach him before he leaves."

"Oh."

Rose grew quiet, allowing Caroline to concentrate.

I regret if our close friendship has been damaged in any way. It's my wish, and I pray yours as well, that ...

"Who's Drew?"

Caroline tensed at her sister's words, tightness in her chest choking off her air. She pivoted, the blood draining from her cheeks at the sight of her Bible perched on Rose's lap, the letter to Drew in her hands.

Caroline wet her lips, fighting the urge to snatch the note away. How careless of her to keep her letter to Drew in her Bible where it could be found so easily.

She drew a calming breath, determined to keep her wits about her. To react nervously would only convince her sister she had something to hide. Striding over, she eased the letter from Rose's hand, praying she'd read no further than the name. "Just a soldier I once met who seemed lonely. I thought he, too, might appreciate a note."

Rose's gaze flicked from the letter to Caroline, then her eyes widened. "Do you know any other lonely soldiers? Maybe I could write a letter too."

Suppressing the maelstrom of emotions inside her, Caroline forced a smile. "I think that would be nice. Several young men from our community would love a letter. I'll even help you write it once I've finished Jamison's. Why don't you come back in a bit, and we'll choose someone for you to write?"

With an enthusiastic nod, Rose hopped from the bed. "All right. Maybe I'll write Jamison too."

As Rose skipped from the bedroom, Caroline sank back in her chair, pressing the letter to Drew to her chest. As healing as it had been to pen the words to Drew, she should never have written it. It must be destroyed.

Along with her hopes of ever seeing Drew Gallagher again.

CAROLINE STOOPED beside the fireplace in the darkened room and stirred the dying coal embers to life. She slipped the folded letter she'd written to Drew from her pocket, pinching it between her fingertips, unwilling to let go. It was the only reminder she had left, besides the memory of his smile and the warmth of his hand. Brief as it was, he had been her one comfort in this bleak war. But he was gone, and pretending otherwise would not bring him back.

With shallow breaths, she let the paper fall from her grasp. It smoldered but a brief moment before bursting into flames. Heaviness tugged at her chest. In an instant, the heartfelt words she'd penned on the page were but charred ashes. Like the short spurt of fire that soon died away, her acquaintance with Drew had been but a fleeting moment. And yet, he'd left an indelible mark on her heart.

One she could never fully relinquish.

18

Frederick Hospital Complex, Maryland
July 20, 1864

Drew ran his finger along his freshly shaved jaw. Not the neatest of jobs, a few nicks here and there, but better nonetheless. He'd be glad when his arm was of more use to him. He glanced at the young man lying in the cot to his left, a bandaged stub where his right arm should have been. The private's hardened stare remained fixed on the hospital rafters above him.

Drew's stomach lurched. What right did he have to complain? His arm would mend.

The soldier's next to him would not.

"You're looking much improved."

Drew roused at the doctor's voice. "Feeling better, too. Almost well enough to be on my way."

The silver-haired medic chuckled and placed a hand on Drew's shoulder. "I wouldn't be in too big a hurry. You were pretty spent when you arrived. It would be in your best interest to rest a few more days."

Setting his razor blade and cup of water aside, Drew leaned back on his pillow. "Have you learned where my regiment is?"

"Not yet, but we're working on it. As you can see, we're short on staff and supplies, but not patients." The doctor gestured to the long row of occupied cots then returned his attention to Drew. "Though none seem as eager as you to return to battle."

Drew gave a soft sigh. "I have no love of war, doctor, but after all this time, my men will think me dead or captured. I wish to reconnect with them."

The weary doctor stared down at him with bloodshot eyes. "That speaks well of you, Sergeant, but all in good time." He pulled aside Drew's bandages and leaned for a better look at his injuries. "Your wounds are healing nicely. The stitches in your side are crude but well-sewn, just the same. They should be ready for removal within a couple of days. It's plain you received treatment early on. Yet, they tell me you arrived on horseback rather than by ambulance. Why is that?"

Drew's gaze drifted to his socked feet at the end of the bed. It didn't seem fitting to divulge he'd been aided by a beautiful, Southern slave-owner's daughter. He cleared his throat. "A local woman found me near the battlefield and tended me a few days until I was well enough to travel."

The doctor nodded and jutted out his lower lip. "Well, her efforts likely spared you loss of limb. Perhaps even your life."

"I realize that, sir." Caroline's gentle features invaded Drew's thoughts. Not only was he indebted to her for his physical well-being, but his freedom as well.

As he leaned for a closer look at the stitches, the doctor's face pinched. "Is that horsehair?"

"Yes, sir. It was all she had."

A grin crossed the doctor's lips as he replaced the bandage. "It's a pity you didn't bring her with you. I could have utilized such a resourceful woman."

"I'd have liked nothing better, sir." Drew cringed, the words spilling out before he could stop them.

Straightening, the doctor gave a hearty laugh. "A real looker, aye, son?"

Heat singed Drew's cheeks as he held back a grin. "One could say so, sir."

With a wink and a pat on Drew's back, the doctor stepped toward the patient in the adjacent cot then pivoted toward Drew. "I'll have one of the nurses try to locate a newspaper so you can keep abreast of what's happening with the war. Perhaps something in there will help you locate your troops."

Drew gave an appreciative nod. "Thank you, Doctor."

RANSOM PAID - FREDERICK SPARED

DREW READ the front-page headline of the four-day-old newspaper with interest. He'd heard rumors of a substantial ransom being asked of the town of Frederick by General Jubal Early—the same commander who'd led the Confederate attack at Monocacy Junction. But he hadn't known the outcome, or even if the rumor were true.

Skimming the remainder of the article, he learned the citizens paid $200,000 to rid themselves of Early and spare valuable Union supplies. With a shake of his head, he turned the page, hoping to ascertain where his company had been deployed. Midway down page three, a headline snagged his attention.

MORE UNION TROOPS JOIN PETERSBURG SIEGE

That sounded promising. If only it made mention of individual companies.

What began as a simple siege on Petersburg, Virginia, has turned into a strategic stand-off between the armies of General Robert E. Lee and General Ulysses S. Grant. Since mid-June, Grant's forces have surrounded the city but been unable to infiltrate it. The stalled battle has initiated the need for additional Union troops in an effort to end the stalemate.

Drew lowered the newspaper with a sigh. Nothing. No word on which troops had been sent.

"Sergeant?"

The nurse's gentle plea cut through his disappointment. "Yes?"

She stepped closer, a tentative smile on her rounded face. "I hate to disturb you, but I know you've been eager to learn what's become of your company."

Drew set the newspaper aside. "Yes. Have you heard something?"

"Just that a soldier at the far end says he's also with the 112th New York."

His spirits reviving, Drew turned in the direction she indicated. "Who?"

"PRIVATE BROWNING?" The nurse jiggled the young man's shoulder to rouse him.

Drew's stomach lurched at the sight of the stub where the lad's leg had been. Barely eighteen, the youth had once been bursting with vitality. It pained Drew to see him lying motionless and confused in a hospital bed.

"Hmm?" The soldier's eyes bobbed open, his gaunt face a shadow of what it had been only weeks earlier.

"Sergeant Gallagher is here to see you."

The private pried his eyes wider, searching. "The sergeant?"

With a nod of thanks, Drew allowed the nurse to pass, then slipped in between the cots and eased into the chair beside the injured soldier. "How are you, Private?"

A dazed expression stole over the youth's face. "I've seen better days."

Drew scolded himself for even asking the question. He cleared his throat. "What happened?"

Private Browning grimaced as he shifted toward Drew. "Took a minié ball in the upper thigh at Monocacy. It shattered my bone and severed my artery. Jip and Saunders did their best to tie it off, but I'd lost a lot of blood. I tried to tough it out but ended up here in the hands of a sawbones surgeon."

A sense of dread washed through Drew as he glanced at his injured shoulder, his arm in a fresh sling. From all the soldiers with missing limbs he'd passed on his way to the private, amputation seemed the surgeons' first choice of treatment. Would the same fate have awaited him had Caroline not found and treated him?

"What about you?" The private's groggy voice sliced into Drew's thoughts. "We thought certain you'd been captured ... or worse."

"I likely would have been if a local hadn't found me and took me in till I was able to travel."

The soldier offered a weak grin. "The men'll be happy t' see you in one piece."

Drew's throat hitched, not taking the soldier's words lightly. The Lord had spared him the anguish this young private was enduring. He returned a faint smile. "Thanks. I'm hoping to catch up with them once I leave here. Any idea where they headed?"

"After Monocacy, we hightailed it up here to Frederick. Then, those who were able headed for Baltimore. But most likely, they're gone by now."

"Gone? Gone where?"

"Jip sent word they were bein' shipped south down the Chesapeake Bay to the James River."

Drew scrunched his brow. "For what reason?"

"To help with the Petersburg siege." The injured soldier slipped a letter from under his pillow and handed it to Drew.

19

Dunbar Estate, Saturday, July 23, 1864

Caroline leaned against the doorpost of the open stable door, staring into the empty stalls.

Cyrus' pitchfork stilled. "Can I help ya with somethin', Miss Caroline?"

She gave a soft sigh. "No, Cyrus. I just needed to get out of the house a while."

"Yes'm. Does a body good t' get out in the open air now an' then." The metal prongs of the pitchfork scraped against the dirt floor as he returned to mucking stalls.

"That it does." Caroline strolled inside, uncertain what had brought her here. She could think of dozens of better places to spend her time besides a manure-filled stable. Though the horses had been let out in the pasture to graze, their scent lingered in the dusty air. Perhaps it was the peacefulness of the empty stable the drew her.

Her chest squeezed. More likely, it was that Cyrus shared her secret and understood her better than her own family.

Releasing another long sigh, she rested her chin on the stall door, gazing at the straw-covered floor. Cyrus came and stood beside her, his dark eyes studying her. "Appears t' me you've come for more than fresh air, or you'da found a better place t' fritter away your time."

She sagged her shoulders. "I feel so useless. With the war raging and soldiers in constant danger, I should be doing my part to aid them instead of sitting idle."

He scratched the shiny bald spot atop his head and nodded. "You always was one t' look t' others needs ahead of yer own."

Warmed by his words, she mustered a weak grin. "I just hate the waiting, the uncertainty of it all. I worry for Jamison."

Cyrus leaned on his pitchfork, eyebrows raised. "Could it be you're pinin' away for someone else besides Master Jamison?"

Straightening, she looked him in the eyes, his pointed stare penetrating her very soul. Somehow, he'd guessed the truth. Letting go of her pride, she gnawed at her lip. "Do you think he made it?"

With a shake of his head, he pursed his lips. "The Lord alone knows, Miss Caroline. But I figure, him bein' a man of faith and with your prayers b'hind him, he stands a better chance than most."

Footsteps sounded in the open doorway. "Who stands a better chance?"

Startled, Caroline pivoted to face her younger brother. "Phillip. Oh. The Confederates, of course."

"Mmm." Phillip shifted his gaze from Caroline to Cyrus, then back again. "What are you doin' here? Never knew you t' take interest in the stables."

Not daring to look at Cyrus, Caroline scrambled for a reason why she should be in a hot, empty stable. Her gaze fastened on a bundle of straw. "I ... uh ... thought to make Rose a straw doll."

Without waiting for a response, she scooped up a handful of straw and started toward the door. As she passed Phillip, he turned to her. "Where's the bay mare Jamison spoke of? I didn't see her in the pasture."

Caroline stilled, clutching tighter to the bundle of straw in her hand. Her mind raced for an apt reply, yet all she could manage was, "She's ... gone."

Phillip's face scrunched. "What do ya mean gone?"

She ventured a glance at Cyrus and saw he'd returned to his work, leaving her to respond. "I-I let her go."

"What?" Her brother let out an exasperated breath. "Papa sent me to fetch her for auction. Said a horse like that would go for a hefty price and make up for the sparse crop."

Caroline braced herself against the door frame. How would she explain the incident to her father?

As though sympathizing with her predicament, Cyrus called out, "The mare didn't take on with the other horses, Mas'er Phillip. Miss Caroline thought it best to let her roam free."

Grateful for the servant's support, Caroline held her breath and awaited Phillip's response.

The bridle in his hand jingled as he looped it over his shoulder, his eyes shifting between her and Cyrus, finally settling on her. "Is that so?"

The intensity of his gaze stirred a rush of heat in her cheeks, and her stomach knotted.

She hadn't heard the last of this.

"OF ALL THE addle-headed things to do! You had no right to let that horse go."

Caroline winced at her father's harsh tone, disheartened that she'd once again incurred his wrath. Phillip sneered at her from across the table, and she boiled inwardly. To her chagrin, he was becoming more like Papa every day. She dropped her gaze to the embroidered tablecloth. "I meant no harm."

Her father gave a frustrated sigh. "When will you start using your head, girl? That horse would have brought a handsome sum at auction."

"She found the animal. Surely that gives her some right," her mother's gentle voice cut through Papa's irritation.

His tone softened slightly. "Vivian, you know as well as I the crops are withering in this drought and, with the war on, our provisions are limited. That horse would have put food on the table for months."

Mama's tone deepened. "I dare say, the loss of one horse isn't going to ruin us. Caroline's not to blame for our hard times."

The supportive words renewed Caroline's courage, and her head lifted. "I could help with the lack of income if only you'd agree to let me work as a nurse."

Her father raked a hand through his thick, salt and pepper hair and mumbled, "Again with the nursing. I've given my say on that matter. I won't hear any more about it!" He pushed back his chair. "Come, Phillip. There's work to be done."

"Yes, sir." Flashing a smug grin as he stood, Phillip followed Papa from the room.

Caroline worked her tongue over her teeth, fighting the urge to scream. If not for Mama's sake, she'd surely give full vent to her frustration and lash out. Or burst into tears.

A small hand found hers, and she turned to see Rose at her side. "Don't fret, Caroline. I'll help you look for the horse if you like."

The sincerity of the offer melted Caroline's angst. "Thank you, sweetie, but I'm certain some soldier has claimed her by now."

She pulled her sister into an embrace, permeated with thoughts of Drew. Pressing her cheek to the youngster's dark, silky tresses, Caroline closed her eyes, praying he and his horse had found their way to safety.

Washington D.C., Monday, July 25, 1864

HIS SHOULDER still tender and freshly out of its sling, Drew struggled to fasten the brass buttons of his new uniform as Major Daniels rejoined him inside the army tent.

"I've verified your information, Sergeant. Your men are stationed outside Petersburg, down near City Point Depot."

A ripple of excitement worked through Drew. "That's good to hear, sir."

The major took a seat behind his makeshift desk. "There's a supply transport boat headed to City Point early tomorrow morning. I've informed the crew you'll be joining them."

"Thank you, Major."

Major Daniels leaned back in his chair, smoothing his mustache. "You're a lucky man, Sergeant. Few would come through such injuries unscathed."

Straightening, Drew tipped his chin higher, eager to inform the Major luck had nothing to do with it; that it was by God's grace, along with Caroline's willingness to do His bidding, that he'd recovered. Not being at liberty to expound or correct his superior, he instead offered a hearty, "Yes, sir."

"I hear our troops took a beating at Monocacy."

Drew nodded. "The fighting was rather intense."

Folding his hands on the small desk, the major's expression brightened. "Well, the delay allowed time for reinforcements to arrive here. Things were a bit dubious prior to that. We're indebted to you and your men for your efforts."

"Thank you, Major."

The major held out his palm. "Best of luck to you, Sergeant. Feel free to spend the night with the troops or on the transport boat, wherever you're more comfortable."

"Thank you, sir." Drew took the hand offered him, fearful his next request would meet with some resistance. "Would it be too much to ask for my horse to ship out with me?"

The Major's brow furrowed. "Is this horse of yours so special you can't leave without it, Sergeant?"

"You might say so, sir. She's come to my aid more than once."

Major Daniels tapped his forefinger against his lips. At last, he sat back, drawing a deep breath. "I suppose that would be permissible. There are hundreds of horses at City Point Depot. One more won't hurt. I'll have you *and* your horse's commission papers drawn up by this evening."

Drew held back a grin as he gave an open-palm salute. "Thank you, Major."

Returning the salute, the Major refocused his attention to the papers on his desk.

With renewed vigor, Drew backed from the tent. Angel whinnied as he emerged, her large, black eyes fastened on him. Untying her, he leaned closer to her ear. "You bailed me out of a couple of scrapes. The least I can do is let you tag along." As if understanding his words, she bobbed her head up and down.

He led her through the encampment to the water's edge for a drink. The newly completed Capitol dome stood like a beacon of hope in the distance. Drew had caught a glimpse of it once before when it was still under construction. He patted Angel's neck, wishing Caroline were there to enjoy the sight with him.

But then, as a Confederate, she likely wouldn't garner such joy in viewing it.

Thoughts of her pricked him. He needed to let her know he'd made it to safety. Yet, to draw attention to their association in any way could prove costly to them both.

The last thing he wished to do was put her at further risk.

He slid his hand down Angel's neck. There must be some way to get word to her without arousing suspicions.

The question was, how?

CAROLINE LOWERED the book she was reading and eyed her mother from across the room. It was a rare occasion the two of them were alone of an evening. But tonight, Rose had taken to her bed with a stomach ache, and Papa and Phillip barely finished supper when they'd been called away to tend to an issue with the livestock. Uncertain how long they'd be alone, Caroline bolstered courage to ask her mother the question plaguing her.

Days had passed since her father's sharp reprimand, and the two of them had spoken nary a word since. Past skirmishes with Papa had ended in hurt and tears. This time, anger and bitterness had begun to swell within her. Not only had his tone and words been demeaning, but he'd shown utter contempt for her ambition to become a nurse.

He may as well have laughed in her face.

Her mouth twisted. Scripture said children were to obey their parents, but if she recalled, it also said fathers were not to exasperate their children. And at present, she felt quite exasperated.

It was time to learn what fueled her father's disdain.

Her stomach churned as she closed her book and set it aside. She drew in a deep breath to calm her jitters, hopeful she could bear the truth. "Mama?"

"Yes, dear?" Her mother didn't pause her embroidering.

Caroline cleared her throat and laced her fingers together in her lap. There was no delicate way to ask what she longed to know. "What does Papa have against me?"

Her mother's hands stilled. When she met Caroline's gaze, her eyes were stormy. "Your father is merely stressed over this loathsome war. Don't take his rantings to heart."

With a shake of her head, Caroline pursed her lips, eager to learn the truth yet uncertain she could withstand it. "No, Mama. There's much more to it than that. He's treated me differently since I was a young girl. I'm certain you know why. Please tell me."

Mama dropped her sampler to her lap, her face growing taut.

For a long moment, her tawny eyes searched Caroline's then trailed to the hardwood floor. "There are things best left unsaid, events of the past best forgotten."

Her lips trembled as though struggling to form words. "Your father loves each of you in his own way. I know sometimes it's difficult, but try to look past any disparities."

Caroline's breath caught in her throat. "Then there is something."

"Nothing that's any fault of yours." Moisture pooled in Mama's eyes. "I know he can be harsh at times, but deep down, he has a good heart. I pray someday the Lord will heal the hurt that torments him."

Caroline sat forward in her chair. "But, if it's nothing I've done, what is it?"

The kitchen door creaked open, and voices drifted down the hallway into the sitting room. Mama swiped a finger to the corner of her eye and stood, turning her back to Caroline. "There's nothing more to say."

Caroline's heart sank; the answers once again eluded her.

20

City Point Wharf, Virginia, July 28, 1864

Drew stood on the port bow as the transport boat veered along the James River toward the bustling City Point Depot. He breathed in the sultry air, taken aback by the expanse of vessels lining the wharves. The riverfront teemed with wagons and soldiers darting every which way. Drew whistled under his breath. If this flurry of activity was any indication of the stronghold's magnitude, the Confederates were in for a formidable fight.

On the far side of what looked to be a large warehouse, a train clipped along a crude track, a stream of gray smoke trailing behind as it meandered its way to the outskirts of the encampment. A spattering of tents dotted the hillside deeper inland. Anticipation coursed through Drew at the array of soldiers roaming about. Was his squad among them?

A crewman stepped up beside him, propping his foot on a crate. "Quite an operation, ain't it?"

Drew gave a decisive nod. "It looks to be."

"General Grant has made it his temporary headquarters. The president himself spent nearly a fortnight here a few weeks back, along with his son, Tad." The man tipped his stubbled chin higher, an element of pride in his voice.

Impressed, Drew returned his attention to the outpost. "Sounds like a place of growing importance."

"Wasn't much here a couple months ago. The wharves were burnt out, and the railroad unusable. Now, it's all been rebuilt, along with ammunition warehouses and office buildings. Even got a post office."

Drew nodded, fingering the letter to Caroline concealed between the buttons of his uniform jacket. It had taken nearly the entire three-day trip down the Potomac and Chesapeake Bay to decide to pen it. As vaguely as he'd written, no one but her would ever guess he'd authored it. Still, sending it was risky.

As the boat neared the dock, Drew moved to the stall where Angel had ridden out the trip. She raised her head at his approach, nervously munching hay. The vessel lurched to a stop alongside the platform, causing them both to sway. She pawed at the floor, and he patted her neck. "Easy, girl. I'm as eager to leave this boat as you."

He slipped between the stall boards, keeping a hand on her chest to calm her. Careful of his still-tender shoulder and side, he hoisted the saddle onto her back and fastened the cinch. Leading her from the stall, he awaited his chance to unload. As he eased Angel down the ramp, the sounds of the water lapping and hooves clopping were overpowered by the murmur of men's voices, the turn of wagon wheels, and the train chugging in the distance.

Overwhelmed by the flurry of activity, Drew scanned his surroundings for a familiar face. How would he find his men in this jumble? Were they even here?

He arched a brow as the post office came into view. Now seemed as good a time as any to mail the letter—before anyone knew him. With a deep breath, he veered toward the small frame building, praying the letter would find its way to Caroline and wouldn't arouse suspicions.

DREW TUGGED ANGEL FORWARD, venturing closer to the handful of officers outside General Grant's headquarters. As much as he hated to interrupt, the postmaster had informed Drew that, as a newcomer to the outpost, the quickest way to locate his unit would be to report directly to the general. Sweat droplets dampened his brow and temples, yet he dared not wipe them away in view of his superiors.

The men's chatter ceased at his approach, their gazes fixed upon him. There was no mistaking the lean, bearded man seated on the rough bench at their center. General Grant crossed his legs, squinting up at him, cigar in hand. At Drew's open-palm salute, the general nodded. "What can we do for you, Sergeant?"

Drew let his arm fall to his side, struggling to keep his voice steady. "I've just arrived from Washington. I was told my company, the 112th New York, is stationed here."

The general tapped ashes from his cigar, his gray eyes filled with question. "How is it your men are here, but you've just arrived?"

"I was wounded at Monocacy Junction and, until recently, was confined at the hospital in Frederick, Maryland." Drew handed him the note Major Daniels sent explaining the situation.

General Grant took a moment to read it over then returned his attention to Drew. "Your commitment to your men and service to our country are commendable, Sergeant."

Honored, Drew tipped his head higher. "Thank you, General."

"Are you recovered enough to return to full duty?"

"I believe so, sir."

General Grant cocked his head to the side, addressing the officer on his right. "Find out where the 112th New York is and report back to me at once."

"Yes, sir." The man hopped to his feet and started off.

General Grant's gaze flicked to Angel. "That's a fine-looking animal."

"Thank you, sir."

Standing, Grant strode toward her and Drew. He slid a hand down Angel's face, neck and withers. "I know a little about horses, and this mare is fine stock."

"Yes, sir. I agree." Drew tensed, curious if the general had more on his mind than a compliment.

General Grant looked at her teeth and eyes as if inspecting her for purchase. "We're rather short on horses, Sergeant, and those we have are worn out. This horse looks fresher than I've seen for some time. Where did you find her?"

"She more or less found me, sir. Had she not come along when she did, I likely would have been captured or killed." Drew subconsciously tightened his hold on the reins, knowing the general only needed to give the word to claim her as his own. "I'm indebted to her for saving my life on more than one occasion."

"You don't say?" Grant dropped his cigar butt and ground it into the dirt with the toe of his boot. "Then hang on to her, Sergeant. A good horse is worth its hay."

Drew breathed a relieved sigh. "Thank you. I'll do that, sir."

"Come, I'll introduce you to my horse, Cincinnati."

Taken aback by the general's easy-going nature, Drew fell into step beside him.

"Tell me, what do you think of our outpost here, Sergeant?"

Drew took another glance around the bustling encampment. "It looks to be quite an operation."

The general nodded, his face stoic. "We're nearly 100,000 soldiers strong now, with fresh supplies brought in daily. The men have laid over eight miles of new track to within a mile and a half of Petersburg. We're in this siege for the long haul. I believe, in time, not only will Petersburg fall but Richmond as well."

They paused at the sound of boot steps hastening from

behind. The officer who'd gone to inquire of Drew's men turned to face the general and gave a salute. "Pardon me, General, but I've located the 112th New York. They're stationed in the trenches outside Petersburg."

"Thank you, Major." The general pivoted toward Drew, the slightest smile edging onto his lips. "Are you so eager to return to battle you haven't time to meet my horse?"

Drew suppressed a smile of his own at the general's enticing request. "No, sir. I'd be honored."

He'd waited this long to join his men. What was one more short delay, especially when it avoided the trenches of warfare?

———

DREW SHIFTED inside the sweltering supply car, struggling to find a comfortable position. The rickety track, laid in such a short time, made for a jolting ride. And in his case, a painful one. General Grant had warned the eight-mile trip to Pitkin Station would be anything but pleasant.

He was right.

Much more personable than Drew had imagined, Grant had treated him more like an equal than a subordinate. Their shared love of horses might have played a part in that. He'd hated leaving Angel back at the City Point stables, but the trenches were no place for her.

Little conversation passed between him and the dozen other soldiers hitching a ride closer to the trenches outside Petersburg. Fatigue lined the faces of the young privates who'd likely seen more war than they cared to recall.

Guarded anticipation built in Drew as the train rumbled down the track. Though he looked forward to reuniting with his men, the thought of entering battle again unsettled him. Three weeks of convalescence had softened not only his muscles but his thirst for action.

He leaned against the crate of supplies with a sigh. Caroline had ruined him as a soldier. Her efforts to heal rather than harm spoke more commitment to God and country than any forthright soldier could muster. Meeting her and Jamison had made the opposing side more real, put faces and names to those deemed his enemy.

Snuffing out the life of a Rebel in combat in hopes of restoring unity hadn't troubled his conscience before. Now, it haunted him. What if he brought loss or hardship upon Caroline's kinfolk? If he came across Jamison in battle, would he have the resolve to run him through?

He clenched his jaw. The very thought unnerved him. From now on, he'd agonize over every soldier he confronted, fearful he was some relative of hers. If not her brother, a cousin, or neighbor, or acquaintance.

Would his hesitancy be his undoing?

The train whistle sounded and spared him from answering. With a final chug of the engine, the train slowed then lurched to a stop. As the men stirred, Drew stood and brushed off his uniform. A glance out the open boxcar door revealed a long row of army tents: a crude field hospital, no doubt.

While the soldiers unloaded supplies, Drew eased out of the boxcar. It would be weeks before he gained full strength. In his unsettled state of mind, was he even fit for battle? If what he'd heard was true, the siege at Petersburg was more of a stalemated skirmish than a full-fledged battle. But the sounds of gunfire in the distance assured him the war was still very much alive.

21

Outside Petersburg, Virginia July 28, 1864

"Hey, look! Sergeant Gallagher!"

All eyes riveted on Drew as he dropped into the trench next to his men amid a volley of gunfire. A twinge of soreness ripped through his side as he landed. Was he ready for this? The whir of bullets died away as he straightened and brushed dirt from his uniform. Glancing up, his lips pulled in a crooked grin at the soldiers' wide-eyed stares.

Private Jipparo pushed his kepi higher on his forehead. "We thought sure you'd been captured or killed. What happened?"

"I took a minié ball to the shoulder, and a stab wound in the side. Nabbed a horse and rode to safety."

Others gathered around, inundating him with questions.

"Where you been all this time?"

"How'd you get here?"

Unwilling to disclose the full story, Drew kept his answers short and to the point. "The hospital in Frederick, mainly. I met up with Private Browning there. He showed me Jipparo's letter saying you'd come here. As soon as I was able, I headed to Washington and hitched a ride down the Chesapeake."

Private Saunders pushed his way through the men clustered in the narrow trench. "How's Browning, Sergeant?"

"In good spirits, but weak and minus a leg."

Saunders looked down, kicking the toe of his boot in the powdery dirt. "That's tough."

Drew nodded. Private Browning had been well-liked among the men, his vivacious spirit energizing those around him. He'd be missed.

Private Jipparo scratched his stubbled chin. "At least he made it. We lost nearly a third of the men in our company at Monocacy."

A trio of gunshots rang out, and bullets zinged overhead, ending the reunion. Taking up their posts, the soldiers aimed their loaded rifles in the direction of the shots and fired. A few blasts answered back then died away. The men dropped back into the trench and began reloading their rifles as casually as if they were at a turkey shoot with their buddies back home.

Drew bit off the end of his minié ball cartridge and spit it out, the bitter taste of gunpowder spilling onto his tongue. "This all you do? Take potshots at one another whenever the urge strikes?"

"Purty much." Private Jipparo slid his ramrod from its holder and pushed it down his rifle barrel. "One side fires off a volley, and the other answers back. Don't seem either's willin' to take much risk."

Private Saunders smiled a toothy grin. "And with all the fresh troops and supplies bein' hauled in, we can stay holed up indefinitely in these here trenches."

Drew finished loading his Springfield, wondering why Saunders seemed so happy about the situation. He could think of much better ways to spend his days than hunkered in a dirt trench with a bunch of smelly soldiers. Had he traveled all this way for this—a stalemated siege? "Surely there's more to be done than wait them out."

Jipparo nodded. "There is. General Burnside has the

Pennsylvanians diggin' a tunnel 'neath Confederate lines under a fort they call Elliott's Salient."

"Gonna set off explosives soon an' blow 'em all t' kingdom come." Saunders guffawed, his ample stomach jiggling beneath his uniform.

A wave of unease surged through Drew. The gutsy tactic could end the stalled-out siege or backfire and needlessly squander lives on both sides of the conflict. "How soon?"

Private Jipparo shrugged. "Not sure, but word has it within the next day or two."

Another round of bullets whizzed overhead, rousing the men to their posts. Taking up position, Drew set his sights on a Rebel soldier that had just fired his gun. As he cocked his rifle, a knot balled in the pit of his stomach. He hesitated, his finger refusing to pull back the trigger.

An image of Caroline flashed across his mind, her winsome smile and chestnut hair cascading onto her shoulders. The vision faded, replaced by her brother's zealous face. Was Jamison among the Confederates defending Petersburg? Could he perhaps be the very soldier at whom Drew was aiming? Distance prevented him from making that call.

His hands grew clammy. Could he live with himself knowing he might have killed Caroline's brother and caused her anguish? Tortured by the thought, at the last second, he tipped his rifle up slightly—enough to ensure he'd miss his mark—and fired. The soldier he'd targeted ducked out of sight, leaving Drew with both a sense of relief and dread.

No doubt he had lost his ambitions as a soldier. Evidently, the conflict warring within him ran deeper than the one he and his men were fighting.

The question was, would his reluctance cost him his life?

CAROLINE PEELED BACK the corn shucks, noting a number of the kernels hadn't filled out, and a plump worm had eaten its way in, turning the tip to mush. She crinkled her nose as she snapped off the end and tossed it aside. The summer drought had produced a sparse crop. Each day it seemed the family's food supply dwindled. Likely she, rather than the drought, would take the blame for the deficiency.

Much like her life.

For three days, she'd sought opportunity to prod more information from her mother regarding the rift between her and Papa. And yet, Mama's countenance suggested she had nothing more to say.

With a sigh, Caroline finished stripping the silk from the meager ear of corn. If only she and Jamison had parted on better terms. She might at least look forward to his homecoming. But as things were, she had no assurance their relationship would ever fully mend. Each night she prayed he might respond to her letter with words of forgiveness. Until then, her spirits refused to revive.

Lifting the basket, she heaved it onto one hip and wiped the sweat from her brow. She stole a glance in the direction of the abandoned shack where Drew had stayed. Though she held little expectation of him ever returning, for the moment, that sparse hope was all she had to cling to.

A THUNDEROUS EXPLOSION shook the ground at dawn, startling Drew and his men from their fatigued stupor. Horrified screams and a massive spray of dirt clods, broken bits of firearms, and severed limbs accompanied the deafening blast. Drew closed his eyes and turned away from the scene, a crushing weight in his chest.

God forgive us.

The clank of metal and tromp of hurried boot steps sounded

up ahead as the first wave of soldiers rushed toward the breeched Confederate line. Their shouts faded as they disappeared into the fog of dust and debris hovering in the air. Drew and his men scrambled to their feet in stunned silence, awaiting their turn to be sent as reinforcements.

A knot formed in the pit of his stomach. This was madness. Preserving one's life in hand-to-hand combat was one thing, but blowing up hundreds of unsuspecting soldiers in an explosion was flat-out murderous. He had no desire to lead these men into this tumultuous battle. Had he lost his nerve, allowed his injuries to weaken his resolve to fight?

Or had his eyes merely been opened to a larger view of war?

War was fueled by hatred and bitterness. The Lord never intended men to kill each other; He'd commanded them not to. Drew didn't hate the Confederates, especially after experiencing Caroline's kindness and Jamison's mercy. It was war and slavery he despised. When he'd joined up to become a soldier, it seemed enticing to place his life on the line for his country. Now, after seeing so many maimed and killed, he'd lost his zest for battle.

He squelched the urge to flee. He didn't want to be here, but he was no coward. It was his duty to follow orders and lead his men. Like it or not, it was kill or be killed.

At the signal from his superior, Drew raised his arm and motioned his men to advance. They marched as one into the lingering cloud of debris, rifles at the ready. He struggled to breathe against the thick scent of smoldering gunpowder in the humid air. Shots rang out ahead, followed by the piercing cries of men in pain.

The landscape dipped sharply. Drew halted his men, taking in the devastating scene. The former Confederate defense was now a massive cavern into which the Union soldiers ahead of them had blindly marched. Above them, Rebel soldiers laughed and jeered, picking off the trapped Union soldiers with their rifles like cornered rats.

Drew's throat clenched. What had been intended as a break

in the line and a clear path into Petersburg had become a death trap. Hundreds of soldiers were now mired in the thirty-foot crater. Drew called to his men over the roar of battle. "Stay back! Take cover and shoot from here."

Several plunged ahead, either not hearing or giving no heed to instruction. Others ducked and fired upon the taunting Rebs, drawing some of their fire. With only a split-second to weigh his options, Drew wavered. Should he join the skirmish or aid those trapped inside the hole?

Greater love hath no man than this, that he lay down his life for his friends.

His heart pounded in his ears as the familiar verse pulsed through his head. He'd rather go down saving lives than killing them. Jesus had given His life for him. Caroline had sacrificed everything to come to his aid. Should he do any less for his men?

Clasping his rifle, he whispered a prayer and descended into the smoldering pit.

22

Confusion reigned inside the crater. A slew of soldiers lay dead and wounded, the vast majority of them dark-skinned, as if the Rebs had intentionally targeted them. Halfway in, Drew spotted Private Buck Saunders's solid frame slumped in a crevice. He fought for breath against the dense, putrid air as he strode over and knelt beside him. A splotch of blood stained the soldier's trousers. Buck's breaths were heavy as he peered up at Drew. "Sorry, Sergeant. Reckon I'm done for."

Drew strained to let the muffled words sink in amid the spray of gunfire and shouts. He refused to let Saunders give up so easily. With a shake of his head, he clapped him on the shoulder. "Not if I can help it."

A glimmer of hope shone in Buck's eyes, solidifying Drew's determination. He ripped a section from his shirt, weighing his options. Getting the injured, oversized soldier out of the cavern would be no small feat. Even at full strength, it would have been a struggle. It would take more power than he possessed to get the man to safety.

With a silent prayer, Drew tied the rag over the leg wound. Standing, he stretched out his hand and pulled the private to his feet. Drew winced as Saunders slung a heavy arm over his shoulders, brushing tender newly-healed flesh. Shots rang out as they inched their way up the slope. More than once, they lost their footing, struggling to gain ground against the onslaught of panicked Union soldiers.

Drew's senses heightened; every sight and sound intensified as the battle raged around him. Ignoring the stab of pain in his shoulder, he focused on the rim of the hole where soldiers continued to flounder. There seemed a complete lack of leadership, as if all the officers had been killed or deserted their posts.

Glimpsing one of his men hunkered near the top, Drew shouted to him. "Lankford!"

The young private's head jerked toward him.

Drew nodded toward Private Saunders. "Help him up."

With a leery look around, the private clasped his rifle in one hand and slid on his backside until he reached Saunders. While Drew pushed from behind, Lankford pulled the heftier Saunders up, both of them landing flat on the ground before moving out of view. Seconds later, Private Lankford reappeared, calling to Drew. "Give me your hand, Sergeant."

Drew shook his head and shouted, "I'm going for another. Just keep a lookout for when I return."

Seeming to comprehend, Lankford ducked in time to avoid a stray bullet that whizzed overhead.

Drew retreated partway into the crater, overpowered by the stench of sweat and bloodshed. A fog of gnats and flies swarmed about him, drawn by the carnage. He waved them away, uncertain how long he could keep this up. Staying low, he scanned the side of the dip nearest him. There had to be more survivors.

There must be.

There was a moan near his feet, and he dropped to his knees.

The young black private peered up at him, his jaw slackening. "Help me."

Drew nodded. Lord willing, he would help spare several more lives or keep them from being taken prisoner.

Or die trying.

———————

CAROLINE TURNED the envelope over in her hand, examining it front and back. She eased down on the porch chair, swiping a ringlet of hair from her cheek. Though the handwriting was most definitely a man's, it didn't resemble Jamison's. No return address, though the postmark denoted it came from Virginia. Who could have sent it?

"Well, aren't you going to open it?" Mama's voice held a touch of curiosity.

Caroline gave a slow nod, thankful Papa and Phillip had returned to the fields. As she wedged her fingertip under the wax seal, Rose leaned over the wicker chair arm, eyes wide. "Do you s'pose it's from the lonely soldier you wrote?"

Caroline's hand stilled, the blood draining from her cheeks. She'd forgotten her conversation with Rose regarding the letter to Drew. Disposing of the missive hadn't erased the memory from her sister's mind.

Nor hers.

She ventured a glance at her mother, wondering how she would explain away such a comment.

Mama met her gaze, brows raised. "What's this about a letter to a lonely soldier?"

With a disconcerted swallow, Caroline slid her finger from beneath the broken seal. "It's nothing. I merely helped Rose write a letter to one of the neighbor boys to ease his loneliness while away at war."

"And wrote one yourself, too. Don't you remember? To a fellow named Drew."

Caroline jerked her head toward her sister. She'd not

supposed Rose would even remember Drew's name, let alone mention it.

Her mother's brows pinched. "I don't recall any young men around here by that name."

A rush of heat worked its way through Caroline. She gripped the letter tighter, wishing her sister hadn't been so loose-tongued. Fear had compelled her to burn her note to Drew. Had he been more daring?

Her heart stammered at the possibility.

In the one slim chance it could be so, it might prove disastrous to open the note in front of anyone. Tracing her fingertip around its brim, she squeezed out the words, "Please, Mama, might I open it in private?"

The question in her mother's eyes melted into a slight grin. "Come, Rose. I think Lily could use our help in the kitchen."

Rose released a disgruntled "*aaw!*" before complying with her mother's wishes.

Caroline waited until they'd gone inside and then wilted back in the chair, thankful Mama hadn't demanded more of an explanation. Taking a quick glance around to ensure she was alone, she pulled the letter closer. With trembling hands, she unfolded it, her eyes drawn to the scant words at the center of the page.

Unable to wait any longer to learn who'd penned it, her gaze flicked to the signature at the bottom, containing only the initials D.G. Her lips pulled in an irrepressible grin as she hurried to read the contents, just three short lines.

Am safe and eager for an end to the war.
May it come soon.
Highest regards, DG

Thank you, Lord. She breathed a long sigh, grateful for the reassuring words and yet, hungry for more. That the note was brief and ambiguous was evidence of the risk he'd taken in sending it. Just knowing he'd made his way to safety was a comfort and enough to give her hope of his return.

Caroline drank in the cherished words once more, then hugged the note to her breast. Drew had at least been safe when he penned it. She drew a deep breath, feeling this war couldn't end soon enough.

Watch over him, Lord. And if it be Your will, bring him back to me.

LAST NIGHT HAD SEEMED ENDLESS. Each time Drew closed his eyes, he had relived the bloody scenes of yesterday. Never did he wish to endure another such massacre. It was only by God's grace he had not been taken prisoner or killed. He'd lost count of how many injured soldiers he'd assisted from the crater, but according to Private Lankford, twelve men in all had been spared. A minuscule amount compared to the countless casualties. But still, each life saved was a triumph.

As morning dawned, the depleted regiment stood in stunned disbelief. So many lives needlessly lost. Four of their squad were unaccounted for. Saunders had been transported to the City Point hospital, possibly to suffer the same fate with his leg as Private Browning. If the counts were accurate, in all, more than 1,500 soldiers had been injured, killed, or taken prisoner.

Drew could still hear their agonized cries and pleas for mercy as they pled to surrender. But, more times than not, they were gunned down or savagely run through with bayonets. One Reb even bid the Confederate soldiers to let the white men go and kill the black. It grieved Drew to think that might be why his life had been spared.

The entire chaotic attack had proven disastrous and utterly disorganized. No doubt, some of the officers would be reprimanded or demoted. Already it was rumored two of the generals in charge of the operation—Burnside and Ledlie—had been relieved of their duties. If not for the vast resources at the

City Point Depot and the abundant reinforcements, the lengthy siege would have been for naught.

As the troops rallied, stark silence, rather than the usual jesting and small-talk, permeated their ranks. No one seemed eager to resume battle. Too many friends and fellow soldiers weren't there to take up arms. Discouragement had sapped their morale. Though Drew's heart wasn't in it, he felt it his duty to revive their spirits and offer them a reason to fight on.

Stiff and sore from over-exertion, he straightened his forage cap and ordered the men to take up their positions. Amid groans and sluggish replies, he strolled behind them in the trench, encouraging along the way. Coming across one particularly sullen soldier, he placed a hand on his shoulder. "How goes it, Private Gentry?"

The young man hung his head, his tattered blond hair tainted with dirt. "I cain't get what happened yesterday out of my head."

"I don't suppose any of us ever will, Gentry." Drew stared at his dusty trench boots. If he'd been disillusioned with the war before, he was appalled by it now. For more than three years, he'd been fighting the Rebs, never once questioning the methods used. This wretched explosion changed that.

Or perhaps Caroline's benevolence had impacted him more than he cared to admit. Before their paths crossed, he'd not considered the personal lives of the men against whom he was warring. Somehow, she'd opened his eyes, forcing him to look deeper into not only his own men but those they were fighting.

Maybe the Lord was stirring his heart against hatred and bloodshed.

The war had already robbed him of his father. How many countless others—on both sides—had suffered the loss of fathers, husbands, sons, or brothers? Battles like yesterday's were not only senseless but downright brutal. Such warfare turned his stomach. He could only plead for the Lord's mercy and a quick resolution to this seemingly endless conflict.

He gazed down the row of weary, battered soldiers. Most

were mere boys forced into manhood before their time. Their slouched shoulders and hardened expressions made them appear much older than their years. These men needed rest. And this land needed healing.

Lord help them all if the fighting didn't end soon.

23

Wednesday, August 3, 1864

Gunfire exploded from the Confederate trenches as a soldier on horseback approached the Union side. Drew and his men returned fire then eased back to reload and size up the messenger. As the soldier's horse skidded to a stop, the string of men to Drew's right dipped their caps against the spray of dirt.

The soldier tumbled from his mount and flattened himself on the ground. He waited for the gunfire to die away then, with a wary look around, called out. "Is there a Sergeant Andrew Gallagher down there?"

Making his way over, Drew wiped his sweaty brow and squinted up at him. "I'm Sergeant Gallagher."

The corporal thumbed his kepi higher on his forehead. "You're to come with me. General Grant wishes to speak with you."

"Whoa-ho-ho. General Grant?"

"What'd ya do, Sergeant? Insult his horse?"

Ignoring his men's guffaws and good-natured jests, Drew kept his gaze fixed on the soldier. "Right away, Corporal."

A hundred questions gnawed him as he climbed from the trench. Why would the general wish to see him? Had he done something unbefitting his rank?

In the trenches less than a week—though the sweltering heat made it feel more like months—it didn't seem sensible to call him away from his men.

Whatever the reason, he would soon find out.

DREW HELD his open-palmed salute until General Grant acknowledged him. Taking a mental note of the five officers seated outside the oversized tent, Drew stood as erect as his sore body would allow. "You wished to see me, sir?"

"Yes, Gallagher." General Grant stretched his legs out in front of him on the bench, a cigar poised in his hand. "What're your thoughts on the recent events?"

Drew scrambled for a response, wondering why the general would even consider his opinion. He cleared his throat. "If you're referring to the explosion and ensuing battle, I believe they turned out much different than anticipated, sir."

A slight groan escaped the general. "Indeed. I venture to say I've not witnessed a sorrier affair this entire war."

"A terrible loss, sir." Drew struggled to hold his composure, curious where this was leading and why Grant had summoned him. Was he to be reprimanded or stripped of his rank as he'd heard others had been for the disastrous venture? Had his attempts to save wounded soldiers rather than fire upon the Rebels been seen as naive, misguided?

For what seemed a long while, the general's slate-gray eyes remained fastened on Drew. At last, he spoke. "Word reached me of your selfless actions to save those trapped in the crater. While some of your superiors were displaying cowardice, you showed bravery and initiative ... Lieutenant."

"Thank you, General." In his relief, Drew almost missed the general's slip-up of his rank. Should he correct him? It didn't seem proper to draw attention to the general's mistake, especially in the presence of top officers like General Meade.

"Saturday's losses stripped us of valuable leadership, leaving room for advancement. A man of your courage should be rewarded." Grant took a puff of his cigar and nodded to his aide, General Rawlins. "Congratulations, Lieutenant. I've just sent paperwork to Washington requesting your promotion."

Before Drew gathered what was happening, Rawlins approached and handed him the shoulder boards of a 1st Lieutenant. Drew's gaze shifted from Rawlins to Grant. Such a jump in rank was rare, if not unheard-of.

A slight smile edged onto General Grant's face. "Don't look so astounded, Lieutenant Gallagher. A man with a keen eye for horses such as yourself is bound to move up in this war."

Drew gripped the insignias, smothering a smile, and raised his chin. "Thank you, sir."

The unexpected promotion offered more privileges and less chance of being riddled by gunfire—both blessings he was eager to embrace. Had his father known of the advancement, he would have been more than proud.

Drew only hoped his disenchantment with the war wouldn't undermine the general's trust ... or put him back in the trenches.

August 4, 1864, Dunbar Estate

CAROLINE SANK against the parlor doorpost as her father lowered the letter in his hand, his anguished expression more telling than words. Silence fell over the impromptu family gathering. What could have upset him so?

Mama pressed a hand to her chest. "What is it, Eugene?"

Tears gathered in Papa's green eyes as he slowly shook his head.

Caroline held her breath, not recalling him ever having shed a tear. She knew then something terrible had befallen Jamison. Nothing else could render such an effect on Papa. Had her dear brother been wounded, captured ... or worse?

Mama's mouth grew taut as she slumped back in her upholstered chair. "Phillip, take your sister outside." The words spilled off her tongue lifeless, cold.

Phillip's face puckered. "But I wanna hear ..."

"Do as I say."

The tremor in Mama's voice brought tears to Caroline's eyes. *Please, Lord, may it not be as we fear.*

"Come on." Phillip nudged Rose toward the hallway, thrusting his hands into his trouser pockets as he shuffled after her.

Caroline moved to let her siblings pass, fixing her gaze on the floorboards lest they see her angst. The mantel clock ticked loud against the stillness, like a heartbeat drumming a mournful cadence as they waited for the outside door to click shut behind the children.

The moment it did, Mama lifted reddened eyes to Papa. "What has happened to our boy?"

A single tear slid down Papa's cheek as he silently passed her the letter and went to stare out the curtained window. She drew a hand to her lips, a moan escaping her as she scanned the note. With a raspy voice, Mama choked out the words.

"Dear Mr. and Mrs. Dunbar, I feel it my place to inform you your son, Jamison, was ..."

She paused and pursed her lips, emotion stealing over her.

With weighted steps, Caroline went and stood behind her, placing shaky hands on her shoulders. In her heart, she knew what the remainder of the note contained, and yet she yearned to be mistaken. Her breaths shallowed. Try as she may, she could not bring herself to glance at the missive her mother held.

With characteristic strength, Mama steadied herself and continued.

"... your son, Jamison, was ... killed in an explosion on Saturday, June 30th while on guard outside Petersburg, Virginia. He ..."

With a loud wail, Mama buried her face in her hands, letting the paper fall to the floor. Caroline wrapped her arms around her mother, their sobs intermingling. She closed her eyes, memories of her and Jamison's childhood days flooding back like lost treasures. How often they'd wandered the timber together, playing hide and seek, walking across downed trees, and skipping rocks in the creek. So close in age, they'd been inseparable in those days, their world as carefree as leaves drifting on open water.

Before Papa put an end to their merriment.

Before responsibilities crept in to steal away their youth.

Before the war.

A scuffing noise sounded outside the parlor. Caroline raised her head, sucking in a breath at the sight of Phillip standing in the doorway, a ravaged look on his face. No doubt, he'd deceived them and listened from the hallway. Hopefully, in his disobedience, he'd had the sense to send Rose on without him.

His chin quivered as tears streamed down his cheeks. "Those blasted, Yanks! I hate 'em. I hate 'em all!" With that, he turned and fled down the hall.

"Phillip!" Mama called after him, starting to rise.

"Let him go, Vivian." Papa's gruff voice sounded strained, broken as he continued to gaze out the window.

The front door slammed shut, and hurried footsteps crossed the veranda and down the steps. Caroline ached along with her young brother. Phillip idolized Jamison, mimicking the way he walked and spoke, aspiring to be like him. Though she prayed Phillip wouldn't succumb to the hatred fermenting inside him, she understood his anger, his bitterness. In losing Jamison, she'd lost not only her brother but her best friend. What tortured her most was the grim way they'd parted and that they would never have the opportunity to make amends.

With trembling hand, she reached for the note that now rested face down on the rug beside her mother's chair. Skimming to the point where her mother stopped, she read the words silently to herself.

He was a good soldier and friend. I've sent what few possessions remain of his—last month's wages and an unfinished letter addressed to someone named Linna, a sweetheart or sister perhaps? I'm certain you'll know who should receive it. I regret his other possessions were lost in the explosion.

With heartfelt sympathies,
Private William Claxton

Caroline blinked back tears. Had Jamison received her letter and penned her a note in return? But, where was it? With bated breath, she glanced to where the letter had fallen. Nothing. No sign of either the money or the note.

She turned her eyes on her father but observed only the back of his head. Surely he wouldn't be so cruel as to deny her Jamison's final words? She took a step toward him, struggling to find her voice. "Papa? The letter says there's a note meant for me."

"There's nothing."

The mumbled reply rang flat, insincere. Of all times, Caroline dreaded questioning her father, but her need to glimpse her brother's words overshadowed her fear. Bolstering her courage, she ventured to speak. "But the letter says ..."

"I tell you there's nothing for you." Her father whirled toward her, his icy glare chilling her to the bone. Her chest tightened. It was useless to question him further.

Heartsick, she turned away, all hope within her fleeing. She'd sooner ask Mrs. Lincoln to tea than pry the truth from Papa. Either Jamison's note had vanished or, in his anger, her father had seized it. Whatever the case, it devastated her to know her dear brother's final message was lost to her.

As was he.

24

The silence in the house was stifling. Caroline lay on her bed for hours, eyes swollen with tears, mulling over her brother's passing. Midday sunlight streamed through the curtained windowpane, its brightness mocking her shattered heart. She stared at the plastered ceiling, afraid to close her eyes, lest her mind envision the explosion that snatched Jamison from them.

How she ached to erase the bitter news, to see him cross the yard once more, a wry grin on his ruddy face. One moment, she fooled herself into thinking there might have been some mistake. The next, she consoled herself to the fact her brother was gone, likely not knowing what hit him as he passed from this life into the next.

Swiping a tear from her temple, she drew a jagged breath. What message had Jamison penned to her? If only she could read what he'd written. Unfinished or not, the words might have given her some semblance of peace or finality. It infuriated her to think Papa might have kept and read the note.

She tensed. Surely, Jamison hadn't made mention of Drew. *Drew.*

Would something terrible befall him as well? Likely, she'd

never know if it did. The thought left her squeamish. As did the recollection that he was a Northerner.

A Yankee.

A root of bitterness coiled its way around her heart. Jamison died at the hands of Yankees.

I hate Yanks. I hate 'em all! Phillip's harsh words played over in her mind, searing her very soul.

All Yankees included Drew.

Her stomach reeled. She could never hate Drew.

Unless...

Sitting up, she swung her legs over the side of the bed. Unless he'd had some part in her brother's death.

She crossed the room and lifted her Bible from the corner of her desk. Sliding Drew's letter from beneath it, she searched for the postmark. City Point, Virginia, July 28. Drew had been in Virginia, at a place called City Point, just two days before Jamison was killed at Petersburg.

Her mouth twisted. Where was City Point? Saturday's newspaper alluded to additional Union troops being sent to Petersburg as reinforcements. Was it possible both Drew and Jamison were at the siege?

A ripple of unease washed through her. It seemed unlikely, and yet the possibility haunted her.

The slam of the kitchen door startled Caroline from her thoughts. Disgruntled voices emanated from downstairs. Curious, she strode to the bedroom door and cracked it open to listen more intently. Though the words were unintelligible, Phillip sounded distressed about something, his tone bordering on hysteria.

As she stepped into the hall, her father's raised voice bellowed from below. "Caroline! Come here at once."

A sickened feeling permeated her, and she wavered, her head spinning. What could she have done? With the news of Jamison's death still hovering over them, could anything be so important? With a steadying breath, she ventured onto the stairway, each step weighted with unsettled concern. Her entire family met her at the bottom, angered stares lining Papa and Phillip's faces. Rose sniffled and swiped a hand over her tear-stained cheek, evidence she'd received the news about Jamison.

Caroline leaned against the stair rail, her eyes perusing their agitated faces. "What is it?"

"*This* is what." Phillip's eyes narrowed as he held out a filthy, dark cloth, his knuckles white from the tightness of his grip.

With a shake of her head, Caroline scrunched her brows. "I don't understand."

Her father snatched the garment from Phillip and shoved it toward her. "Maybe a closer look will sharpen your memory."

As the riddled garment unfolded and the three bands of a Union sergeant's uniform appeared, Caroline braced herself against the banister, blood rushing from her face. She snapped her eyes shut. Drew's bloodied uniform. How could she have forgotten to dispose of it? Not since the night she'd tossed it aside to bandage Drew had she given it thought.

"See? Look at her. Told ya she'd know about it. I thought somethin' wasn't right when I saw her sneakin' out at night. She was tendin' to some fool Yank!"

Her father's face blazed crimson. "You had the gall to aid a Yankee soldier right under our noses?"

Caroline faltered under his accusing stare. To admit such a thing was certain to incur his unbridled fury.

"Say it isn't so, Caroline."

The hurt in her mother's eyes almost tempted her to lie, yet her conscience, along with her flagrant reaction, compelled her to truthfulness. "That wasn't my intention. I-I came across him in the timber. He pleaded for help. I couldn't ignore him."

Mama's hand flew to her mouth, her head slowly shifting side to side. "Oh, Caroline."

Papa edged closer, his olive eyes laced with hostility. "Jamison knew, didn't he? Didn't he?"

Caroline blinked and took a step back. How could he know that? She swallowed. "I ..."

He drew a paper from his pocket and held it to her face. "That's what he had to forgive you for, isn't it?"

Her breath caught. Jamison's note. It must be.

Papa's shouts sent Rose scurrying to Mama, face buried in her skirt. "Eugene, please."

At Mama's plea, he gave a frustrated growl and crumpled the page in his hand.

Heart pounding, Caroline eyed the wadded paper. Jamison's last words to her were within her reach. How much had he revealed? If only she could have a glimpse. *Lord, please don't let Papa destroy it.*

Tossing the note to the floor, he spoke through gritted teeth. "How does it feel to have helped put your brother in his grave?"

Tears welled in her eyes, the accusation piercing her to the core. To blame Jamison's death on her was more than she could stomach. Mustering her courage, she pulled herself to full height and fixed her gaze on her father. "That's not true. I only tended a wounded soldier. The Lord makes no distinction between people. We haven't the right either."

"You worthless wretch!" He drew his hand back to strike her, hatred flaring in his eyes.

Caroline veered back just as her mother let out a shriek. "Eugene, no!"

He hesitated then lowered his arm, glaring at Caroline. "Get out of my sight. I'll not have a deceitful whelp living under my roof."

Caroline trembled as her mother stepped up beside her. "Oh, no, Eugene. Please. You can't possibly—"

He glowered at her. "I mean it, Vivian. I never want to look upon her traitorous face again. Be certain she's gone when I return."

Turning on his heel, he stomped from the room without a backward glance, leaving devastation in his wake.

HEAVY SILENCE STEELED over Caroline and her mother as they packed her belongings, trading her satchel of medical supplies for a travel bag. Jamison's crumpled note burned in her pocket, begging to be read. She'd snatched it from the floor the moment Papa stormed off, hiding it away to read in private.

Mama folded one of Caroline's nightgowns and hugged it to her chest, her eyes puffy. With a sniffle, she placed it in the bag, her gaze never straying from the quilt atop Caroline's bed. She drew a fragmented breath, her coffee-colored ringlets spilling down over her cheeks, a few flecks of silver mingled in. "I'll wire my sister, Sarah Frances, that you're coming. She and your uncle Samuel won't hesitate to take you in for the duration of the war. By then, all this trouble will have settled, and your father will welcome you back."

Caroline's stomach clenched. "I'm not so sure."

Mama glanced at her, dark circles framing bloodshot eyes. "He will. He has to. I can't bear to lose both you and Jamison."

The anguish in her mother's voice compelled Caroline to lay aside the dress she held and stretch out her arms. Melting into one another's embrace, they shook with uncontrollable sobs. Warm tears dampened Caroline's shoulder, her mother's shattered heart fusing with her own. In a matter of hours, their worlds had been crushed.

Caroline swallowed the hurt churning inside her. Though she would not dispute her mother, deep down, she knew Papa would never relent. She knew him too well. An end to the war would not soften his resolve. He despised her. As did Phillip, it seemed. No wishful thinking could change that.

The Lord alone could soften such a hardened heart. And she would pray each day that, like Saul blinded on the road to Damascus, the Lord would shine light into Papa's darkened soul and consume the anger and bitterness raging within him. Only then could she return.

Only then could she know peace.

"BUT WHY MUST YOU GO?"

Caroline touched a hand to Rose's cheek, brokenhearted at her young sister's pouty expression. Too innocent to comprehend the intricacies of what had transpired, all Rose's mind could fathom was that her eldest brother and sister—whom she admired and loved—would no longer be with her. "It's best I go for now, but I'll write often and tell you how I'm doing. Promise."

In her understanding way, Rose brushed a tear from her cheek and nodded. "I'll write you, too."

Caroline bent to kiss her sister's forehead. "You'd better."

Lily widened her arms for a hug, her doleful expression bringing a round of fresh tears to Caroline's eyes. "Cyrus and I'll sorely miss ya, Miss Caroline. It just don't seem right Mas'er Jamison gone an' you a leavin'. Won't be the same 'round here, that's certain."

Caroline squeezed her ample waist. The caregiver had been like a second mother to her through the years, displaying endless love and support, and on occasion, a well-deserved scolding. "I'll miss you too, Lily."

Turning again to her grief-stricken mother, Caroline attempted to commit every crease and line of her face to memory. "Goodbye, Mama."

Her mother pulled her into a firm embrace and whispered, "May God go with you. I'll not cease to pray that one day you'll return to us."

"As will I." Fighting tears, Caroline kissed Mama's cheek. To be rent apart so soon after Jamison's passing was almost more than she could bear.

Relinquishing her hold, Mama retrieved a coin purse from her pocket and placed it in Caroline's palm. "There's an inn at

Rockville. You should make it there by nightfall. I'll send my sister a telegram and ask her to have Samuel meet you on the road to Piscataway tomorrow morning. You'll recognize him, won't you?"

Caroline slid the cloth pouch into her pocket. "I think so."

Her throat thickened as she numbly turned toward the carriage. She wasn't sure of anything anymore.

"See her safely there, Cyrus, and return home," Mama's quivering voice trailed after her.

"Yes'm." Another slave might have given them cause for worry, but not Cyrus. He was as trustworthy as the foundation of their house. After loading Caroline's trunk and travel bag, he offered her a hand up.

She bit her cheek to stem the flow of tears as the carriage rolled forward. With a soft wave, a devastating thought washed through her. Would she ever look upon their dear faces again? Her father could have wielded no greater punishment for her indiscretion. And yet, had she truly done wrong by helping a soldier in need?

She choked down her angst, gazing at the worn path ahead. Though the unexpected venture was not one she'd chosen, she would deem it the Lord's will. He was almighty God, able to turn heart-wrenching circumstances into blessings. She needed to believe that.

She must believe it.

As they meandered along the trail through the fields, she caught a glimpse of Papa and Phillip chopping weeds in the distance. Phillip straightened and stared at her as the carriage passed, his expression too vague to distinguish. But after a glance in her direction, Papa returned to his work.

Numbness swept through her as she averted her gaze. She meant nothing to him. Papa would work out his grief for Jamison busying himself in the fields. He would not mourn for her. In fact, she wondered if he was relieved at her going. Caroline pulled Jamison's wadded note from her pocket. With shaking fingers, she unfolded it and smoothed it against her black taffeta dress. The handwriting, though less tidy than usual, was familiar, comforting, like a warm cloak on an autumn night.

Dear Linna,

Never fear. All is forgiven.

She paused, tears streaming down her cheeks as she envisioned his baritone voice speaking the words. If he'd written no more, she would be content, but she continued, savoring each word like a fine meal that would end all too soon.

I know now you meant no harm in what you did. You always were one to take in strays. Never could stand to see anything suffer. I suppose soldiers are no different ... no matter what side of the war they're on.

Knowing you as I do, even before your letter arrived, I determined not to hold it against you. How could I, my sweet, compassionate Linna? When I get home, we'll ...

There it ended, the unfinished thought leaving a gaping hole in her heart. She would never know what he'd meant to say, but she could imagine him wishing to share another picnic under the sprawling white oak in the meadow, swapping stories of what had transpired in each other's lives in his absence. How she would miss her dear brother.

She pressed the crinkled paper to her chest, sweet release filtering through her. To know Jamison had forgiven her made Papa's contempt easier to stomach. And yet, overwhelming loneliness welled within her. In one swift blow, life as she'd known it had evaporated like the dew of summer.

How ironic to be banished from home on Drew's account; a man she likely would never see again. Though her thoughts returned to him more often than they should, it was for naught. She couldn't know whether he was alive or dead. If he survived the war and returned as planned, he'd not find her.

She slipped Jamison's note back into her pocket. It pained her to dwell on the past. She needed to embrace a new life with her aunt and uncle—if they would have her.

Situated deep in the largely Confederate Charles County, they were as staunch in their Southern ways as Papa. Would they question why she'd come and learn the reason behind it? Mama had urged her to say as little as possible about the matter.

Lonesomeness consumed her. She had no one, nothing, save her faith. The Lord promised never to leave or forsake her. For the first time in her life, that truth was all she had.

25

August 5, 1864, City Point, Virginia

Drew stooped to fit under the raised tent flap, straightening as he approached the soldier seated inside. "Captain Jacobs?"

The fair-haired captain lifted his head, staring up at Drew with close-set eyes. "Yes?"

"I'm Ser—Lieutenant Andrew Gallagher. I've been assigned to serve under you." Still unaccustomed to the graduated title, Drew handed him the commission notice General Grant had supplied. His unexpected promotion and reassignment proved bittersweet. The parting with his men had been brief yet memorable—something he'd carry with him the remainder of the war.

The captain glanced at the paper, then peered at Drew. "I hope you'll last longer than my previous lieutenants. One was an inefficient buffoon, and the other was killed at the crater."

Drew floundered. "I'm ... uh ... sorry to hear that, sir."

Captain Jacobs leaned forward on his elbow, smoothing his thin mustache. "How long have you been a lieutenant, Gallagher?"

Almost embarrassed to say, Drew cleared his throat. "About forty-eight hours, sir."

"You're referring to 1st Lieutenant, of course."

Drew's throat went dry, and he swallowed. "No, sir. Two days ago, I was an infantry sergeant."

The captain straightened. "So, you've never drilled a company of men?"

The knot in Drew's stomach twisted. This captain thought him inept before he even started. "Just my squad, sir."

A sardonic chuckle sounded from the captain as he sat back in his chair. "Tell me, who made such a stunning recommendation for you, *Lieutenant?*"

The man's taunting glare made Drew's answer somehow more satisfying. He tipped his chin higher. "General Grant, sir."

The captain's eyebrows shot up, and his cheeks grew taut. He wet his lips. "Well, young man. You must have pulled quite a few strings to catch the chief general's attention. I'm eager to learn if his confidence in you is justified."

Something in the captain's tone assured Drew he'd have to prove himself to his new superior officer. That if he didn't watch his step, he and the captain would find themselves at odds.

Standing, Captain Jacobs donned his cap and reached to adjust his weapon belt. "I was just on my way to drill the men. Come. I'll give you your first shot at it."

"Yes, sir." Drew fell into step behind the captain, praying he'd fare better than his predecessors. More accustomed to leading soldiers into the fray than trying to please a superior officer, he felt like an addle-headed schoolboy who'd forgotten to do his homework

Captain Jacobs paused outside the tent, giving Drew's uniform a more thorough glance. "Have you not been issued an officer's uniform? And where's your saber?"

"The appointment happened rather suddenly. I've received only the 1st Lieutenant shoulder boards, nothing else, as yet."

The captain crossed his arms. "Well then, we must get you one. Do you know where the commissary is located?"

Drew hesitated, scouring his memory to recollect if he'd come across the warehouse that would commission uniforms. At last, he shook his head. "No, sir. I don't." He stopped short of explaining he'd been sent directly to the trenches soon after his arrival and had little time to familiarize himself with City Point.

Captain Jacobs' mouth twisted. "It appears I have my work cut out where you're concerned, Lieutenant Gallagher. The commissary is across from the chapel, down from the post office. While I rally the men, see what you can manage, then meet us on the west end of the campgrounds."

"Yes, sir." Drew saluted, breathing easier as the captain tromped away.

The sun's heat bore down on Drew as he started in the opposite direction. The captain's condescending tone left a bad taste in his mouth. He'd not asked for a promotion, but when one presented itself, he'd expected it to bring honor and prestige, not belittlement.

With a glance back at the captain, he breathed a long sigh. Maybe this was the Lord's way of keeping him humble. Then again, with him still weakened from his injuries, perhaps it was God's means of ensuring he'd survive the war in one piece.

And hopefully, reunite with his family ... and Caroline.

———

CAROLINE LOWERED her parasol and sat forward on the carriage seat. "Slow down, Cyrus. I believe that's my uncle coming."

"Yes'm." The servant tugged on the reins, easing the horse into a slow walk.

Caroline squinted against the mid-morning sun at the approaching black, canvas-covered surrey and the man with the goatee at the reins. Though she'd met her Uncle Samuel only twice—seven years ago at his and her aunt's wedding and again at their visit just before the war—she remembered well his thick mustache and pointed beard. Three years had passed since then and, in truth, she had likely changed in appearance more than he.

The driver craned his neck, his carriage slowing as it neared. If not her uncle, this man certainly resembled him. Still uncertain, she resisted raising her hand in greeting. Both carriages rolled to a stop side-by-side on the road. The gentleman tipped his hat, revealing a prominent receding hairline. "Caroline? Caroline Dunbar?"

Relaxing her shoulders, she angled her parasol to better shield herself from the sun. "Yes. Uncle Samuel? I was hoping it was you."

With a shake of his head, he eased back on his seat. "Well, I'm hard-pressed to recognize you. You've changed from a girl to a lovely young lady since last I saw you. What are you now, eighteen? Nineteen?"

She tipped her head higher. "I'm to be twenty next month."

"Where does the time go? Come, your Aunt Frances is eager to see you. And you've a couple of new young cousins to meet as well."

Closing her parasol, she waited for Cyrus to offer her a hand down. For a brief moment, his eyes locked with hers, myriad unspoken thoughts swirling between them. A blend of regret and sorrow mingled in the servant's dark eyes. He and Lily had partnered with her in her deceit regarding Drew. Did he blame himself for her predicament? How she longed to assure him it was no one's fault but her own.

Perhaps even the Lord's plan for her.

She gave his hand a gentle squeeze and mustered a weak grin, resisting the urge to embrace him. How she would miss his comforting presence and undying support. Emptiness gnawed at her at the thought of never seeing her friend again. So many sad goodbyes in such a short time. She drew a sharp breath. "Thank you, Cyrus. For everything."

With a slight nod, his gaze dropped to his tattered boots. "God go with ya, Miss Caroline."

"You as well." Tears stung her eyes as she let loose his hand. Turning, she allowed her uncle to help her onto the seat.

He took up the reins. "Shall we go?"

Tamping down the heaviness locked inside her, she nodded and pasted on a smile. "Yes."

As her uncle turned the rig in the direction from which he'd come, she stole a parting glance at Cyrus. He stared after her as she waved goodbye, his ebony cheeks streaked with tears.

Something within her died as she turned away. She'd not expected such a devastating sense of loss, as if a piece of her life had been stripped from her, never to return. She folded her hands in her lap, blinking back tears.

Her uncle cleared his throat. "Your mother wired us about Jamison. I'm so sorry. This madness needs to stop."

Fearful her voice would fail her, she could only nod in reply.

Her uncle cut a glance in her direction. "Your mother also mentioned how heartbroken you were over the news. You're welcome to stay with your aunt and me as long as you choose."

Caroline melted at his words, relieved her mother had offered an apt reason for her visit. "Thank you."

He gave a soft chuckle. "You may not be so grateful after you've been under a roof with our houseful of rambunctious children. We've four young ones now, you know."

Her face lifted. "It will be a joy, something to occupy my mind." Indeed, she needed something to keep her from dwelling on her hardships.

They fell silent, Caroline taking in the sights as they clipped along the country road, groves of trees decorating both sides mile after mile. When at last they came to a fork in the road, her uncle veered his horse to a lesser worn path on the left. A signpost marked the other road as leading to Bryantown. Caroline shifted on the hard, wooden seat, squelching the urge to ask how soon they would arrive.

Seeming to guess her discomfort, her uncle glanced her way. "Only a few miles to go. Though I did promise one of my patients I'd stop in to check on her. Do you mind?"

"Patients?"

"Yes. Our neighbor to the south, Mrs. Bellamy, is due to have a baby soon. I need to see how she's progressing. Her place is not far out of the way."

For the first time, Caroline noticed the black bag on the floorboards at her uncle's feet, and her mood lifted. She'd forgotten he was a physician. How thrilling to be able to see a doctor at work firsthand. If there was one bright spot in her otherwise dismal world right now, that was it.

Renewed hope swelled within her. Even through all her losses, the Lord had found a way to display his care. She pulled her eyes heavenward. *Thank you, Lord.*

Now, if only Uncle needed a nurse.

DREW DROPPED onto his cot and tugged off his boots. What a miserable, long day, starting with the disastrous drill experience and ending with tedious hours of overseeing the company transport supplies from boat to warehouse. It wasn't so much he'd not understood what was expected of him as it was the lack of instruction. Captain Jacobs threw duties at him without so much as an explanation, almost as if he relished Drew failing.

Drew lay back on his cot and stared at the dim tent canvas, the shadows of twilight seeping in to further darken his mood. Though his new assignment might spare him battle fatigue, he had a feeling it might usher in a whole fresh set of challenges. He'd anticipated the rise in rank to benefit him. Instead, it had quickly soured. Within days, he'd gone from being looked up to by a group of stouthearted soldiers to assisting a conceited captain.

The feeling of incompetence was new to him, as well as

degrading. Up until now, he'd taken pride in his military prowess. Just as he'd begun to rise in rank, the Lord seemed to be pruning away that pride.

He blew out a breath. He shouldn't base the remainder of his military career on his first day as a lieutenant.

Or one arrogant captain.

'Every soldier has his challenges,' his father used to say. Father's chest would have bulged had he known of Drew's advancement.

His throat hitched. In taking his father, this war had stolen more from him than any promotion or ambition could remedy. With a long sigh, he locked his hands behind his head. A twinge of pain sliced through his left shoulder, and his thoughts shifted to Caroline. Had his letter reached her? Was she missing him? More importantly, would he ever see her again?

How quickly they'd turned from enemies to friends. And yet, even before she'd known him, she'd chosen to put personal feelings aside to come to his aid. Such an act was nothing short of Christ-like. To show compassion to a friend was simple, but to aid someone in opposition to her demonstrated true character.

Drew scratched at his cheek. Captain Jacobs might never be someone he enjoyed serving under, but if Caroline could offer kindness to him—her family's enemy—he could overlook his superior's domineering tendencies.

He just wasn't quite sure how yet.

26

"Who's she?" The blond-haired woman on the bed placed a protective hand on her swollen abdomen and nodded toward Caroline.

With a momentary glance her way, her uncle raked a hand over his receding hair and returned his attention to the soon-to-be mother. "That's my niece, Caroline Dunbar. She'll be staying with Frances and myself a while."

Caroline paused just outside the bedroom doorway, not wishing to intrude upon her uncle's wary and bountifully pregnant patient. She offered the young woman a warm smile, receiving a tentative one in return.

The woman's gaze skimmed Caroline's black taffeta dress. Though not much older than Caroline, the shadows of tension and fatigue nipped at the young woman's eyes. "Not sure I want to be around someone who's mournin' while I'm with child."

Uncle Samuel let out a chuckle. "Come now, Myra. Don't tell me you hold to that silly superstition?"

Her gaze returned to Caroline. "I suppose it's all right."

Relieved, Caroline edged closer as her uncle pulled his stethoscope from his black bag and secured the earpieces. He moved the circular endpiece along Mrs. Bellamy's rounded belly, pausing to listen from time to time. She stared at the plastered ceiling of the small bedroom, her vivid blue eyes sated with concern. "Is everything all right, Doctor? I've been awful worn-out of late, and the baby seems as restless as a raincloud."

He finished listening and removed the earpieces, a hint of a grin playing on his lips. "Not to worry, Mrs. Bellamy. You've good cause for fatigue."

The young woman's face blanched. "Why? What is it?"

"Nothing bad, I assure you. Just be sure you and Chester get rest while you're able. Sleep will be hard to come by in a few days."

She cupped her hands around her unborn baby. "Ah, shucks, one little ol' baby ain't much to manage."

He leaned in closer, placing a hand on her shoulder. "One, no, but two could prove a challenge."

Mrs. Bellamy's eyes widened. "Twins?"

"It's sounding that way. I hear two distinct heartbeats."

A broad smile replaced the expectant mother's worrisome frown. "How soon do ya figure they'll come?"

Caroline's Uncle scratched at his chin. "Well, I can't know for certain but, the way you're progressing, I'd say within a week."

With a chuckle, she struggled to push herself into a sitting position and draped her legs over the side of the bed. "Wait'll Chester hears."

Uncle Samuel put a restraining hand on her arm. "Hold up there, Myra. At this point, it's best you stay off your feet as much as possible."

Seizing her opportunity to help, Caroline gestured over her shoulder. "I believe I saw him by your barn. I'll fetch him."

As she turned to leave, a tremendous groan erupted from Mrs. Bellamy. Pivoting, Caroline saw the expectant mother rocking back and forth, hands cradling her womb, a pool of water spreading on the oak floorboards beneath her. "Doc?"

Uncle Samuel hurried to her side. "Looks like these babies are more eager to come than I thought." He eased Mrs. Bellamy back down on the bed. Her breaths came fast and heavy like the cadenced chug of a locomotive.

Caroline stepped to the bedside, a rush of excitement trickling through her. "What can I do?"

Her uncle called over his shoulder. "Tell Chester to bring Frances. I'll need her help."

Caroline's shoulders slumped. He didn't trust her to aid him. "I can help, Uncle. Just tell me what you need."

He hesitated as though weighing his options. A second cry from Mrs. Bellamy seemed to convince him. Nodding, he motioned toward the door. "All right. Have Chester ride to let Frances know we'll be home later than expected, then come help me prepare her for birthing."

Caroline suppressed a grin as she pivoted toward the door. Now was her chance to gain her uncle's confidence ... and hopefully convince him she had the skills to assist in his practice.

THE NUMBING grip on Caroline's hand eased as an infant's squall sounded from the foot of the bed. Mrs. Bellamy collapsed back, releasing an exhausted half-groan, half-giggle. Caroline smiled down at her, dabbing her sweat-drenched face with a damp cloth. "That's one. You're doing fine, Myra."

The new mother smiled back, Caroline's attentiveness during the hours of grueling labor seeming to have dissolved any misgivings the young woman might have had toward her. "Boy or girl?"

"A boy!" Uncle called out.

Myra beamed. "Chester will be so proud. Our little Michael James." Her face pinched, and she groaned softly.

Caroline met her uncle's gaze. He nodded toward the infant in his hands. "Take him, will you? I have a feeling the second isn't far behind."

With a pat of Myra's hand, Caroline released her hold and

hurried to take the whimpering baby. His tiny features crimped then relaxed when she nervously cradled him in the nook of her arm. The awkwardness of inexperience vanished as she cleared the phlegm from his face and body with a dampened cloth. Such a precious miracle of God to behold.

She swaddled him in a blanket and returned to Myra's bedside, holding the child where she could see him. A huge smile lit the young mother's face momentarily, then disappeared, her heightened moans and hurried breaths hinting the second birth was imminent.

Caroline eased onto the bedside chair. Shifting the baby to one arm, she swiped a lock of sweat-drenched hair from the exhausted woman's cheek. "Are you ready?"

Myra nodded, her breaths shallower, weaker. "Just so tired."

"I know you are. You're working so hard. Soon you'll have two sweet babes to cuddle." Caroline dampened a fresh cloth and dabbed at Myra's blistered forehead, praying she would have the strength.

Myra glanced at the baby boy, then turned her gaze on the ceiling above as though trying to focus her energies. A contraction gripped her, and she fastened her hands on the spindles of the headboard above her head. Pressing down hard, she fought for progress, her breaths quickening. The contractions ebbed and flowed, each growing stronger, closer together.

"I see the head." Uncle Samuel's voice pierced through her groans. "Push, Myra."

Her face contorted as she let loose the spindles and curled upward, knees bent, giving it all she had.

"That's it. Once more."

Again, she heaved a breath and bore down hard. This time her efforts were rewarded. When she dropped back on the bed, an exhausted smile edged onto her face. "Is it ... a girl? One of each ... would be ... so nice."

Uncle Samuel turned and strode to the far side of the room, his answer slow in coming. "Yes. A girl."

A smack sounded.

But no cry followed.

A brief silence blanketed the room.

"Caroline? Give Myra the baby and come here, please."

Though spoken in calm, there was an underlying urgency in her uncle's request, one that sent a tremor through Caroline. She laid the little boy beside his mother and flashed her a warm smile. "I'll be right back."

"What is it?" Panic entered the woman's eyes as she cuddled her newborn son. "Why isn't she crying?"

Pressing down her growing unease, Caroline gave Myra's hand a reassuring squeeze. "Rest now. I'm sure it's nothing."

She strode to her uncle and saw the tiniest of babies resting in his open palms. The red-skinned infant displayed little movement, if any. Uncle Samuel met Caroline's concerned gaze with one of his own. He leaned close to her ear, his tenor voice but a faint whisper. "She's alive but very weak. Too weak to nurse or even cry."

Caroline's throat hitched. "What can be done?"

"As weak as she is, she'll likely not make it regardless of what we do."

Tears pricked at Caroline's eyes as she cast a sideways glance back at the baby's mother. "We have to try something."

Her uncle released a long breath. "Have Chester bring fresh milk from a cow, preferably one that has recently given birth. We'll need some way to drop the milk in very slowly."

Caroline gnawed at her lower lip. At last, she leaned in closer. "A hollowed-out quill wrapped in cloth? We could fill the quill with milk and prick a pinhole in the cloth."

The doctor's eyes brightened. "It's worth a try."

"Please. Let me see my baby girl. If something's wrong, I want to know."

At Myra's plea, Caroline noted the look of dread on her

uncle's face. She reached out her hands. "Would you like me to take her?"

His shoulders relaxed. "Would you? I'll gather what we need and return as soon as I'm able."

Nodding, Caroline took the newborn from him, her weight no heavier than a pair of plump tomatoes. Her eyelids flickered as Caroline cradled her in her arm. The infant's thin lips were pale, almost blue; her body warm, yet limber, almost limp.

Uncle clasped Caroline's arm. "The first few days are critical. She'll need constant looking after, more than Chester or Myra will be able to manage."

Caroline read the underlining implications in his tone. "You mean, someone should stay here to care for her?"

He nodded. "I think it would be of great benefit."

"Me?"

A slight grin edged onto his lips. "You do seem to have a knack for this sort of thing."

She glanced at the tiny infant nestled in her arm, so weak, so frail. Was she up to such a challenge? Her uncle's confidence in her was reassuring ... and a stark contrast to Papa's dismal impression of her. The very memory of his constant criticism filled her with doubts.

What if she failed? What if the baby died under her care?

As if guessing her hesitancy, her uncle added, "Your aunt Frances will be sorely disappointed if I come home without you, but if you're willing to stay a few days to ensure the little one gets the nutrients she needs, I think it could make all the difference."

Caroline drew a breath, brushing her thumb against the baby's soft cheek. Better to try and fail than allow her to die for lack of trying. And what better way for Caroline to rid her mind of her troubles than to help someone?

Lifting her eyes, she met her uncle's hopeful gaze. "Tell Aunt Frances I look forward to seeing her in a few days."

27

City Point Depot, August 9, 1864

D rew stacked the crate of supplies in the warehouse and moved to make room for the soldier behind him. Despite the captain's insistence he oversee the transfer of supplies from the ships rather than help unload, Drew just couldn't stand idle while the men worked. Though limited to lighter crates, his shoulder grew stronger each day, more able to handle the loads. At least helping broke the monotony of watching soldiers traipse back and forth.

At times, he suspected General Grant—or the Lord—assigned him the logistics supply detail to spare him while his wounds healed. Though grateful to be away from the thick of battle, he missed the personal interaction with his squad of soldiers. His new rank put unaccustomed distance between him and the men. Here at City Point Depot, the most challenging decision he had to make involved deciphering which crate belonged in what storehouse.

"Lieutenant Gallagher!"

The captain's agitated tone told Drew he'd been caught ... again. Pivoting, he let out a hurried, "Yes, Captain."

177

The disgruntled look in his superior officer's eyes made Drew regret he'd not stayed at his post. This wasn't the first time he'd been reprimanded for not explicitly following the captain's orders. But if he knew what was good for him, it better be the last.

Captain Jacobs stomped over to him, his long, thin nose inches from Drew's chin. "I thought I made myself clear. Stacking crates is for the men. Your job is to oversee."

"Understood, sir. I'll get right on it." Not waiting for a reply, Drew gave a quick salute and headed outside.

He squinted against the bright sunlight, breathing easier in the open air. The captain seemed to have enough qualms about him without Drew giving more reason to fault-find. If standing idle all day in the hot sun pleased the captain, from now on, that's what he'd do.

HOURS LATER, Drew propped his foot on the dock and swiped a hand across his sweaty brow. Standing in the scorching heat was more tedious work than handling crates ever could be.

Something shiny caught his eye on the far side of the bluff. He peered at the tree-lined hillside, trying to decipher what it could be. The light dimmed then brightened before dying away. Moments later, it appeared again, as though catching the sun's reflection. Was someone up there? Who would be in such a remote area of the bluff?

Certainly, no detail from their post.

Deserters, maybe?

Couldn't be. Any deserter with half a brain would high-tail it out of here.

His jaw clenched. More likely Confederate spies.

The thought left him uneasy. City Point Depot would be a treasure store for the Rebs should they infiltrate the post and get their hands on the supplies.

Or worse yet, demolish them.

Certainly worth looking into.

He wavered, shifting his attention between the parade of crate-bearing soldiers and the shiny object. It shouldn't take much to track it down. If he circled his way around, he stood a good chance of finding who or what was up there.

His muscles tensed. He'd promised to stay put. To disobey the captain's direct orders would likely land him with a charge of insubordination. And yet, a possible threat to the military outpost seemed more important.

He blew out a breath. It was a risk he'd have to take.

Maybe he'd merely get demoted. That wouldn't be so bad.

He glanced toward the warehouse for signs of Captain Jacobs. By the time he alerted him or some other superior officer, whoever was up there would likely have moved on. His best bet was to strike out on his own.

Only this time, he'd find someone to cover for him.

He glanced around. "Sergeant Perkins. Take over for me."

"Yes, sir." Pausing in mid-stride, the red-headed sergeant set down his crate and jogged over.

Drew took another look around then slipped away. As he meandered along the riverfront, one thought nettled him—that he might be risking his future on a whim.

Yet something nudged him to continue. If he was right, his actions might just spare them all a great deal of hardship. But if he was wrong ...

He slid a hand down his face. He only hoped he'd find something.

And Lord help him if he wasn't back before Captain Jacobs discovered him missing.

"HERE WE ARE, all cleaned and fed," Caroline whispered as she handed the freshly fed Mary Elizabeth to her mother. Eyes closed in peaceful slumber, the infant's tiny mouth still moved in a slight sucking motion.

Sitting up straighter in bed, Myra flashed a proud smile. "Isn't she beautiful? And doin' well, wouldn't you say?"

Caroline gave an affirming nod. "Right on both counts. She's made great strides these past couple of days. In another week, she'll be as strong as her brother."

The contented mother hugged the infants closer, face beaming. "I never dreamed I'd have two. I truly don't know what I would've done without your help."

"It's been my pleasure. My troubles haven't seemed as burdensome since I've been occupied."

Myra's expression sobered. "I never did ask, who're you mournin'?"

With a deep sigh, Caroline hung her head. "My brother. He died defending Petersburg."

"I'm sorry." The young mother paused, then added, "I thought for a time I'd lost my Chester. He was injured at Chancellorsville and laid up several months before being sent home just over a year ago."

Caroline searched her memory for some sign of injury in Mr. Bellamy, but other than a scar near his left temple and being a bit slow of speech, could recall none. "He seems to have recovered well."

The woman shrugged. "Don't suppose anyone's all right after fightin' a war, but he's as well as can be. He took some shrapnel to the head. The war scarred his mind more than his body, but I love him, just the same."

Don't suppose anyone's all right after fightin' a war. The solemn words played over in Caroline's head.

Her stomach gripped. These many months, she'd prayed for Drew's safekeeping, not once considering he might return altered in mind or body. In the rare instance he did try to locate her, would he be able to?

The uncertainty of it gnawed at her.

A tap on the bedroom door pulled her from her reverie. "Come in."

Chester eased the door open and peeked in, his gaze fixed on his wife. "I thought I'd check if you need anything before I head t' town."

Myra shook her head, a wide grin spilling onto her lips. "I declare, Chester, that's the fourth time this mornin' you've asked that. If I didn't know better, I'd say you were itchin' for excuses to come look in on us."

His cheeks flared a shade darker as he removed his hat and stepped into the room. "Maybe I am. A man's gotta right t' see his wife and young'uns, don't he?"

"'Course he has. Come over here."

The couple's loving gaze warmed Caroline. Would she ever know a love so true? She backed from the room to allow the family privacy. Her efforts as a nurse had been rewarded, and, for that, she was grateful. Amid her loss of home and family, the young lives nestled beside their parents seemed a beacon of hope, as if the Lord were assuring her He was still there and in control.

She could only pray these precious babies would never know the pain of loss or war as she and so many others had.

———

At the sound of hushed voices, Drew peered through the underbrush, resisting the urge to shoo away a pesky mosquito. He caught only a faint glimmer of movement in the small clearing, the foliage too dense to garner anything of substance. Cocking his head to gain a better angle, he listened for some clue to the men's purpose for being here. One of the men seemed to have a foreign accent of some sort. Either Irish or Scottish descent. The other man's voice was deeper and harder to distinguish but held a hint of a southern drawl.

Drew struggled to pick out bits and pieces of the muffled conversation.

"When will it ... ?"

"Soon. Be ... now and le ... me watch," the man with the accent answered.

Drew inched closer, praying the stiff breeze would conceal the crunch of leaves beneath his boots. When he found a better vantage point, he ducked behind the trunk of an oak and ventured another glimpse. Dressed in civilian clothes, the two men took turns peering down at the City Point wharf through a pair of field glasses. Quite possibly the reflection Drew had seen.

His brow pinched. Something definitely wasn't right.

Who were these men? And why were they spying on City Point? He fingered his Springfield rifle. From what he could tell, the men appeared unarmed. If they were the sort of fellows he supposed them to be, it shouldn't take much to convince them to talk.

As he stepped from behind the tree, the ground seemed to rumble beneath his feet, and a tremendous explosion sounded from the wharf area below. On instinct, Drew hunkered down, eyes shut tight. Momentarily deafened by the blast, he remained frozen in place, bits of debris showering down through the trees like massive raindrops.

Faint sounds of rapid gunfire broke through his stifled hearing, and his eyes shot open. Was City Point under attack? Scrambling to his feet, he peered toward the depot. His heart plummeted at sight of the vast cloud of gray smoke billowing from the wharf. Though his view of the riverfront was obscured by timber, the sound of men's agonized cries stood his hair on end.

Something terrible had happened, and he had a feeling these two scoundrels had something to do with it. Leveling his rifle, he shifted his gaze in their direction, and his throat hitched. With an exasperated sigh, he hung his head.

They were gone.

28

D rew's spirit plummeted as he scanned the area. Splintered timbers and wreckage lay everywhere, coating the riverfront with mounds of dirt and debris. The overpowering scent of gunpowder clung in the humid air. He edged closer, dodging dazed soldiers rushing past. The sky had turned gray and heavy like a summer storm. Fragments of shell and splintered wood continued to pelt his forage hat and uniform.

Rifle in hand, he watched for signs of Rebel soldiers but saw only the panicked faces of youths clad in Union blue. This was no full-scale attack. From what he could gather, the shots fired were shells going off from inside the storehouses and ammunition boats. Most likely a result of the explosion he'd heard from the bluff.

He stumbled his way to the wharf area, numbed by the scene before him. The ship he and his men had been unloading was nothing but a shell, the ordnance barge beside it, nearly annihilated.

He clenched his jaw. Two devastating explosions within such a short span of time were too many.

A trail of bodies and severed limbs littered the wrecked pier where he'd stood an hour earlier. He hung his head and raked a hand over his face, fighting to hold down his breakfast. If he hadn't gone after the spies, he likely would have been struck down along with the rest.

Would the Lord's mercies never cease?

Sergeant stripes on the sleeve of a downed soldier glared up at him from several feet away. Bile rose in his throat as he strode over and knelt beside the lifeless form lying face-down in the dirt. Though powdered with debris, the mop of red hair resembled that of Sergeant Perkins.

He hesitated before reaching to turn the man over. One glimpse of the soldier's face confirmed his fears. Cringing, he averted his gaze. It was indeed the sergeant who'd so willingly taken his place supervising the detail. Drew pressed his fingertips to the sergeant's neck, making certain of what he already knew.

He breathed a loud sigh. This should have been him.

And yet, once again, the Lord had spared him.

Why?

He'd done nothing to deserve such grace from the Almighty. Why had he been spared and not this man ... or his father?

His dear mother must be spending a great deal of time in prayer on his behalf.

The thought left him homesick. How many nights had she waited on the porch for his return or some word from him?

Guilt trickled through him. Since his father's passing, he'd neglected to keep in contact with her, except for the occasional money he'd sent. His father's untimely death on the battlefield stunned them all. It grieved Drew to think how grief-stricken Mama would be should he suffer the same fate. Somehow distancing himself made things easier. Yet, was it fair to shut off communication to protect her from sorrow that might never happen?

His shoulders slumped. Or was it himself he was trying to protect?

A full year had passed since he'd seen Mama and his younger brother and sister, and then only for his father's wake. An occasional letter found its way to him, but, to his regret, he'd not taken time to respond.

That needed to change. If his mother was diligently petitioning the Lord on his account, surely he could make an effort to let her know how he was faring.

Warmth permeated his chest. Perhaps Caroline's promised prayers for him had reached Heaven as well. The welcome thought gave him some semblance of purpose—a reason to keep hoping, persevering.

"Help!"

The frail cry pierced through his fog, stirring him to his feet. He scanned the debris for the source of the plea, and a slight movement caught his eye. Half buried beneath the broken timbers of the collapsed warehouse, a soldier sputtered and coughed. Rushing over, Drew lifted the splintered beam from atop the man's legs and pulled him out.

The corporal glanced up at him but made no attempt to move, his lower body twisted at an awkward angle. His soiled face was blank with shock. "I can't feel my legs."

Drew's heart sank. "Hold on. I'll find a medic."

The man gave a raspy cough. "Ain't much a doctor can do for me now."

The corporal's declaration held Drew in place. By the looks of his mangled legs and the blood trickling from the side of his mouth, he was right.

The soldier's pale blue eyes found Drew's, imploring him to stay. "If you're a prayin' man, a plea ... for my soul would be more fitting. I haven't ... led the most ... sinless life, but my mama taught me ... enough t' know ... Jesus ... forgives those who ask."

Placing a hand on the corporal's shoulder, Drew gave a weak nod. "You're right there, soldier. I'll be happy to pray with you."

As he bowed his head, a shout rang out several yards to his left. "Look out! It's gonna blow again!"

A flood of soldiers rushed past. Through the flurry of retreating men, Drew glimpsed the shooting flames of a small fire working its way toward a stack of ammunition. A lone soldier beat at it with his forage hat, those around too intent on fleeing to offer aid. Drew's heart drummed in his ears. The man needed help. If the blaze reached the ammunition, many more lives would be lost.

"What is it?" The corporal stared up at him, his eyes dull.

Drew's jaw flinched. "Let me worry about that. You just keep asking the Lord's forgiveness, and I'll be back." With a reassuring nod, he draped a tent canvas over the corporal to shield him, then ran toward the man battling the flames.

Removing his wool jacket, Drew whacked at the flames edging closer to the ammunition. He shielded his face, the intense heat singeing the hair on his hands. With each strike, the fire tapered off then flared up again. Sweat poured down his neck and chest as he and his companion beat at it harder, faster.

Little by little, they chipped away at the blaze until it began to smolder and die mere inches from the crates of ammunition. A plume of black smoke billowed from it, and Drew coughed and backed away. Breathless and drenched with sweat, he glanced at his cohort, respect passing between them.

The soldier, also a lieutenant, swiped a hand over his sweat-drenched brow. "Thanks. For a minute there, I almost wished I'd run with the rest of them."

A grin tugged at Drew's lips. "I imagine there are an awful lot of fellows who are glad you didn't. Me, for one."

The lanky officer, who looked about Drew's age or younger, slapped soot from his forage cap. "Well, Lieutenant … ?"

"Andrew Gallagher."

The soldier nodded. "I hope our paths cross again, Lieutenant Gallagher."

"Same here."

As they parted, Drew's thoughts returned to the wounded

man he'd pulled from the wreckage. He quickened his pace, knowing the corporal was in a bad way. Coming to the spot where he'd left him, he pulled back the tent canvas. His gut clenched at the sight of the soldier's head lolled to one side, eyes closed, face void of expression.

Downcast, Drew felt the young man's neck then covered him with the canvas. Like so many others, the youth's life had been snuffed out far too soon. Though there was some comfort in knowing the young soldier had left the hardships of war and suffering behind, Drew prayed he'd finished making peace with the Almighty. "Have mercy on him, Lord."

He sat back on his haunches and scrubbed a hand over his face. This conflict had claimed far too many—on both sides. Brushes with death had become commonplace but were something to which he would never grow accustomed.

Memories of Caroline's tender smile and soft touch sliced through his gloom. It was no accident she'd happened by when she did. The Lord sent her at just the right moment to see him through his closest run-in with death. Most likely, he'd never know why he'd been spared and others had fallen. But one thing was certain: if the Lord saw fit to bring him through this war alive, not a day would pass without him giving thanks for His mercies and for the gift of life itself.

His chest squeezed. And, whether or not he saw her again ... he'd give thanks for Caroline as well.

"CAROLINE?" Aunt Frances passed the young child in her arms to the servant girl beside her and crossed the room in three quick strides. Taking Caroline by the hands, she surveyed her with sparkling green eyes, brunette hair pulled into a tight chignon. "Land sakes, child, you're the spitting image of your mother."

Caroline grinned, leaning forward to receive her aunt's welcoming hug. "How are you, Aunt Frances?"

Releasing her hold, her aunt stood back, hands on hips. "More tired than my age should allow, but after you meet our brood, you'll understand why."

A mere ten years older than Caroline, her mother's younger sister, Sarah Frances, retained her youthful figure despite giving birth to four children. She moved to the boy and girl playing five-stones in the corner of the parlor. "You may remember our oldest boy, Andrew, and our girl, Sissie. They were quite young when last you saw them."

She smiled at the pair, the boy's name stirring unwanted thoughts of Drew. "Yes. I remember. Hello."

Her young cousins stared at her a moment before returning to their game.

Aunt Frances shook her head and placed a hand on Caroline's sleeve. "Don't mind them. The only thing that stops their play is meal time."

Caroline chuckled as her aunt scooped up the boy trotting toward her.

"I believe I was carrying Thomas here when we paid you a visit. He's our adventurous one. He'll turn three next month." She cupped a hand under his chin, and he squirmed for freedom. As Aunt Frances stooped to comply, the youngster padded over to his siblings.

Caroline schooled her expression. It was apparent who had the upper hand in the household.

"And this ..." Uncle Samuel took the youngest child from the servant girl and tossed him into the air, "is Samuel Jr."

The boy giggled as his father caught him.

Her uncle's thick mustache and goatee couldn't hide the wide smile that lit his face as he cradled the child in his arms.

Caroline offered a weak grin, a pang of remorse flooding through her. What she wouldn't give to be, just once, her father's pride and joy. Instead, her parting memory of him was his disgust and anger. She clutched her satchel tighter, feeling every bit a stranger in the unfamiliar setting. "You have a fine family."

Her aunt studied her. "Forgive our doting. You must be worn to the nub. Come, sit and rest a while."

She smothered a yawn. "I am a bit fatigued."

"And for good reason," her uncle chimed in. "You should have seen her, Frankie. She took to caring for Myra and those babies like a seasoned nurse."

Aunt Frances beamed. "Is that so?"

Unaccustomed to such flattery, Caroline's cheeks warmed. She lowered her gaze, the corners of her mouth turning up. Her uncle could have bestowed no greater compliment.

Her aunt motioned her over. "How are the little ones doing?"

Setting her satchel down, Caroline joined her on the red velvet settee. "Quite well, I think. The little girl seems to be gaining and nursed for the first time this morning."

"I'm glad." Aunt Frances' forehead crimped. "You do look a mite peaked. I hope you haven't overdone."

With a shake of her head, Caroline met her aunt's gaze. "No, really. The work suits me." She ventured a glance at her uncle. "In fact, I was wondering if Uncle Samuel might allow me to work as his nurse."

Her uncle chuckled. "Never had much call for a nurse."

Determined, Caroline swallowed the nervous lump in her throat. "I'd do whatever you need. Clean instruments, assist you on calls. Anything."

His expression sobered. "I don't know, Caroline. You saw the way Myra responded to you. People around here are wary of newcomers."

She edged forward on the settee, unwilling to give up. "Yes, but you saw how she warmed toward me. I wouldn't press. I'd do only what you ask. Please, Uncle."

Aunt Frances slid an arm around her shoulders and peered at her husband. "Perhaps it wouldn't hurt, Samuel. It might help take her mind off of ..."

The stalled comment sent a rush of emotions coursing through Caroline. She curbed the swelling memories of the troubles that brought her here.

Her aunt tipped her head to one side, sadness and compassion in her emerald eyes. "Terrible about Jamison. Your mother and father must be heartsore over the loss."

Caroline nodded. Her brother's absence left a void that could not be filled. She clasped her hands together in her lap. "We all are."

"I do hope being here can bring you some sort of comfort. In her telegram, your mother said you took the news rather hard."

She swallowed, attempting to edge out the quiver in her voice. "Jamison and I were always rather close."

"Yes, I know. It must have devastated you."

With a nod, Caroline blinked back the tears welling in her eyes.

In the silence, she sensed her uncle's eyes upon her. At last, he sighed. "So, you wish to take up nursing, eh?"

Her head lifted. "Yes. I do."

He scrubbed a hand down his goatee. "Well, I suppose there's no harm in trying."

Caroline sucked in a breath, a smile edging out the sorrow on her face. "Thank you, Uncle."

"I warn you, some of my patients can be quite temperamental at times ... as can I." He winked.

"I'll take that risk."

He propped his foot on the fireplace hearth and bounced his namesake on his knee. "I heard about that explosion at Petersburg. What you may not know is the Union's brutal attack backfired. Word has it, the blast they set off created a huge hole that entrapped a vast number of their own men. Hundreds, if not thousands, were picked off by our boys like spring turkeys. So, to an extent, Jamison's death was revenged."

Caroline's stomach lurched. Had she not only lost Jamison in the battle but Drew as well? The possibility existed. The uncertainty of it was nearly as taxing as knowing the truth.

Her only hope was to put her worries and heartaches behind her and pursue the opportunity the Lord had placed in her path.

Becoming a nurse.

29

August 10, 1864
General Rawlins's quarters, City Point

"The man's a coward."

Drew flinched against Captain Jacobs's assessment of him. Standing at attention, Drew kept his gaze fixed on the canvas of General Rawlins's spacious tent. Somehow, the captain had gained the ear of General Grant's top aide. Drew only hoped he was as fair and even-tempered as he appeared.

The general sat back in his chair, raking a hand over his thick beard. "That's a strong accusation, Captain, after having him under you such a short time. What leads you to such a harsh conclusion?"

Taking a step forward, the captain gestured toward Drew. "After explicit orders not to, he left his post just prior to the explosion. The sergeant who took his place died in the blast. It seems mighty suspicious to me. Almost as if he knew something was going to happen."

Drew clamped his jaw tighter. To defend himself would only further agitate the captain as well as make him appear guilty. In time, he would have his say, but until then, he'd be wise to hold his tongue.

General Rawlins's chocolate-brown eyes skittered to Drew. "So, you're saying your lieutenant here is a spy?"

Jacobs tipped his chin higher. "At the least, he's insubordinate. He's been with my company a mere week, and in that time, I've found him inept in his duties and unwilling to follow orders."

"Such as?"

The captain stammered, seeming to fumble for words. "Such as having no experience drilling the men and leaving his post to carry crates instead of overseeing the unloading operation as directed."

Drew sensed the general's eyes upon him but did his best not to exhibit a response. He'd be the first to admit he wasn't suited to this sort of position. Yet, the captain's lack of patience and instruction had made matters far worse.

"What have you to say on the matter, Lieutenant? Are you a spy?"

The touch of sarcasm in the general's voice hinted he was aware of the captain's questionable nature. Perhaps Captain Jacobs had brought similar charges against his previous officers. Hadn't he called one of his lieutenants a buffoon?

Drew sucked in a breath. He could do no less than look his superior in the eye and speak the truth. "No, sir, I'm not."

General Rawlins's chair creaked as he leaned forward and met Drew's gaze. "Then, how do you counter these charges against you?"

Relaxing his stance, Drew clutched tighter to his forage cap. "I admit I'm not well equipped for this sort of duty. Since the war began, I've done nothing but fight alongside my men. I'm not accustomed to standing idle while others work."

"You're saying your recent promotion to lieutenant doesn't suit you?"

Drew weighed his response. To agree to such a statement

would seem critical of General Grant's decision to promote him. But to admit he was content in his present circumstances wouldn't be honest. He stood taller. "I'm honored by General Grant's confidence and willing to serve in whatever capacity he chooses."

Though General Rawlins made no comment, the slight glint in his eyes hinted he was pleased with Drew's response. He locked his fingers together on his makeshift desk, his gaze intent on Drew. "And what of the accusation of you being a spy? What reason have you for disobeying your captain's order and abandoning your post?"

Drew cleared his throat, eager to have his say, though he wasn't sure his answer would justify his actions. "I saw a reflection on the far side of the bluff and suspected something was amiss."

The general scrunched his eyebrows. "What sort of reflection?"

"I feared it might be field glasses or a telescope reflecting the sun."

With a loud "*humph,*" Captain Jacobs edged forward. "So, you took it upon yourself to disobey my orders and strike out on your—"

"I'll do the questioning, Captain." General Rawlins's raised voice silenced Jacobs.

He slunk back. "Yes, sir."

The general's voice leveled as he returned his attention to Drew. "Why did you not alert someone to the incident, Lieutenant?"

Drew hesitated, aware he'd not followed protocol and that his answer might incriminate him. "I feared the delay would allow whoever it was time to escape, so I asked Sergeant Perkins to take over for me while I investigated."

"And what did you find?"

Relieved the general was at least giving him an ear, Drew continued more confidently. "Two men, sir. Though I couldn't overhear their full conversation from where I was concealed, I heard and saw enough to conclude they were indeed spying on City Point."

"And where are these men? What prevented you from apprehending them?"

Drew stared down at his boots, the memory of that devastating moment etched in his mind like a nightmarish dream that refused to end. "The explosion, sir. It happened just as I was about to approach the men. By the time I'd recovered from the shock of the blast, they'd disappeared."

The general fell silent, his gaze moving between Drew and the captain. At last, he stood. "You two are free to go. I'll brief General Grant and let you know the outcome."

With a quick salute, Drew followed Captain Jacobs from the tent, wondering if his integrity would be rewarded.

Or if he'd crossed the captain one too many times.

AUNT FRANCES CLASPED the handle of Caroline's satchel and motioned her to follow. "You look plum worn out. Come on up, and we'll get you settled in your room."

With a tired nod, Caroline hiked her skirt and started up the stairs after her, sliding her palm along the smooth mahogany banister. Unaccustomed to the shorter steps, she kept her eyes trained on each successive one. The shadows of twilight began to filter into the dim stairway, and she smothered a yawn. It had been a long week. She'd not anticipated news of Jamison's death initiating such drastic changes in her life. How her heart ached to undo all the sorrow weighing on her. Instead, she could only pray for the Lord to ease her burden of loss.

As they reached the top, Aunt Frances gestured toward the first of two rooms situated just to the left of the stairway. "That's Samuel's medical office."

Caroline stole a glance inside, unable to distinguish more

than a small table and chair tucked in front of a curtained window. She longed to gain a better look by light of day.

"And this," her aunt paused, peeking through the cracked door of the adjacent room, "is the children's bedroom." She spoke in hushed tones so as not to disturb the sleeping brood of youngsters. Caroline couldn't blame her. The mother of four had worked long and hard to coax them all to bed.

Aunt Frances motioned her forward. "Your room is just down the hall."

Caroline followed her to a third room, eager to rest her weary muscles and catch a glimpse of the section of the house she could temporarily call her own. A contented sigh escaped her at the sight of a spacious room with a bed on either side of the doorway and a washbasin nestled between two curtained windows. "This is lovely. Thank you."

After setting Caroline's satchel on the nearest bed, her aunt lit the lantern. "It's yours for as long as you're here; however, Samuel sometimes has patients who require overnight stays. So, I'm afraid there may be times we'll need to move you in with the children for a short stint."

Though the thought of sharing a room with four rambunctious children didn't appeal to her, Caroline merely mustered a smile and nodded. "Of course. That's quite understandable."

Aunt Frances rested her hands on her hips. "Well, if there's anything you need, don't be afraid to ask. We're pleased to have you and want you to feel at home."

"Thank you. You've been more than gracious."

Her aunt stepped toward her and placed a hand under her chin. "It's the least we can do. Having you here brings back memories of your mother when she was your age. You're so like her."

Caroline smiled, grateful she'd been compared to her mother and not Papa. She was nothing like him, nor did she wish to be. "Were you and Mama close growing up?"

Her aunt grinned, a far-off gleam in her eyes. "Oh yes. Despite our difference in age, we got along splendidly. I suppose she seemed more a mother figure to me than a sister. How I looked up to her and longed to be like her."

She paused, her face pinching in feigned anger. "Then your dashing father came along and stole her from us."

"Papa, dashing?" Caroline smirked at the idea.

Aunt Frances arched a brow. "Indeed, he was. At least your mother and I thought so. Vivian was barely eighteen when they wed, and I was seven. How I missed her when she moved away."

Caroline eased onto the bed, seizing the opportunity to inquire more of her parents' courtship days. "It's hard to imagine my parents young and in love. Especially Papa. It's not often he shows a tender side."

Especially to her.

Aunt Frances chuckled. "Time has a way of adding pounds and wrinkles, pilfering away our youthful fancies, but underneath, I'll wager your father hasn't lost all his endearing qualities."

Caroline ached to delve deeper, curious if her aunt knew the reason behind Papa's hidden resentment. She swallowed, hesitant and yet eager to find out. "Were you around my parents often in their early years of marriage?"

"On occasion, over holidays and such. Why?"

Caroline gnawed at her lip. "I just wondered if they seemed as happy once we children came along?"

Her aunt pushed the satchel aside and took a seat beside her. "I suppose so. Children can be taxing on a relationship at times, as I well know. But I've never seen a prouder father than your Papa when they came to show off Jamison after he was born. My, how he doted on that little boy."

Dropping her gaze to her lap, Caroline blinked back the moisture gathering in her eyes. Her mouth quivered, not only at the thought of Jamison but from the question her lips burned to ask. "And when I was born?"

The delay in response prompted her to venture a glance at her aunt, deep in thought. "I don't recall them coming after you were born. If memory serves me, Vivian fell silent for a time. I believe you were well over a year old before we laid eyes on you."

Caroline's stomach clenched, her hands clasped so tightly her fingernails dug into her skin. "Do you know the reason for the lapse in visits?"

Aunt Frances shook her head. "I'm not sure. Busyness, I suppose. Once or twice I sensed your mother wished to confide in me about something, but I never could pry it from her. I only know a change seemed to have overtaken them during that gap of time. Your father especially."

"How so?"

"They were more guarded, distant. Almost as if a shadow had fallen over them."

Caroline tensed, locking her ankles together to keep her legs from trembling. She was sure now. Something dreadful had happened to her parents. Something that involved her.

But what?

A smile edged out her aunt's unsettled expression. "Enough gloom. I only meant to say how pleased we are to have you here."

Caroline mustered a grin. "Thank you."

Aunt Frances gave her hand a gentle squeeze then stood. "If there's anything you need, don't hesitate to ask."

With a nod, Caroline accompanied her to the door. "I won't."

The room grew quiet as she closed the door behind her aunt. A sigh escaped her as Caroline opened her meager luggage and pulled out her nightgown. Too weary to unpack the rest, she lowered the bag to the floor, her mind awhirl. Though Aunt Frances seemed oblivious to the reason behind her questions, she'd only confirmed Caroline's suspicions.

Slipping out of her black taffeta dress, she donned the cottony nightgown. As she pulled back the covers and doused the lantern, a gentle breeze drifted through the open windows, ushering in a chorus of cicadas and katydids. She settled down on the mattress and allowed her eyes time to adjust to the darkness. Moonglow filtered into the unfamiliar room—a room that would likely be her home for quite some time.

Hollowness gnawed at her chest. Despite her aunt and uncle's warm welcome, she found it difficult to think of this place as home. A real home was where your family dwelt. Here, she would merely be a guest.

Her thoughts traveled over the miles to where she truly belonged. About now, Mama would be tucking Rose in bed for the night and, if she were there, Caroline would have peeked in to wish her good night. She longed for the familiar nightly routine and for her dear mother and sister.

Were they missing her as well?

She missed Cyrus and Lily, too. But, most of all, Jamison. A tear slid down her temple, dampening her ear. She wiped it away, imagining him free of pain and the trauma of war, sitting at the feet of Jesus. The image initiated more tears but also a sense of peace. How grateful she was for her brother's forgiveness and for the note he'd left. Without it, she might never have known peace.

A twinge of bitterness pierced through her moment of contentment. How cruel of Papa to attempt to deny her that blessing. Such an act was heartless, spiteful. Whatever he held against her couldn't warrant that much resentment.

She closed her eyes, trying to block out the unpleasant memories. Thoughts of Drew drifted in to take their place. She could still feel his firm muscles draw her near and his lips pressed against hers. Where was he now? Wounded? Imprisoned?

Dead?

For a brief time, she'd known what it was to feel favored by a man. Why had the Lord allowed Drew to come into her life only to snatch him away? Since childhood, she'd heard about the love of God and that He had a plan for her life. And yet, nothing made sense now. In a matter of days, her entire world had been uprooted. How could she believe in His plan for her when everything had gone awry?

Help me trust you, Lord, even though I don't understand.

She snapped her eyes open, the prayer spawning recollections of a verse of Scripture she'd once taken to memory. Proverbs 3:5-6 What did it say? Something about leaning on the Lord's understanding.

Reaching over the side of the bed for her satchel, she rummaged through it until her hand gripped the rough-grained leather of her Bible. She moved to the foot of the bed, where the glow of the moon shone brightest through the windowpane, and opened her Bible. When she came to the verses, she slanted the page closer to the window and read softly, "Trust in the Lord with all thine heart; and lean not unto thine own understanding. In all thy ways acknowledge Him, and He shall direct thy paths."

She closed the Bible and hugged it to her chest, peering into the heavens. "Lord, I *don't* understand what's happened. Grant me strength and patience to trust You even when I lack wisdom to see the outcome. You work in ways we cannot see. Please, Lord, help me to lean on You."

With a deep breath, she lay back on the bed, a new sense of peace stealing over her. She would give the Lord time to work His will for her life, time to make things right amid all the hurt and regrets.

Though she had no idea what it might bring.

30

August 13, 1864, Grant's Headquarters

Drew trudged alongside his men back to camp, utterly worn. Four days after the explosion at City Point, the massive clean-up effort was still underway. The company had done everything from shoveling dirt to hauling debris to burying the dead. As of today, the tally of lives lost topped two hundred. The sweltering heat only heightened the stench of decay.

"Lieutenant," a high-pitched voice hailed from behind.

Drew turned toward the approaching messenger boy. "Yes?"

"You're to report to General Grant's quarters at once."

His stomach knotted. Days had passed without a word from General Rawlins regarding the outcome of his inquiry. Now, it seemed, he'd have his answer.

The boy peered across the yard at Captain Jacobs, raising his voice a notch. "You too, Captain."

"Be right there." Captain Jacobs answered back. He locked eyes with Drew, a slow smirk creeping onto his lips, leaving little doubt as to his assumptions.

Drew averted his gaze, brushing dust from his uniform. Any attempt to make peace with the captain had proved futile. All he could do now was pray his reprimand wouldn't be too severe and that, whatever his punishment, he'd no longer have to endure the captain's disrespect.

The trek to General Grant's quarters seemed all too short amid Drew's ponderings. He caught the scent of pork roasting over an open fire, and his stomach rumbled. He wished he were joining the rest of the officers and soldiers headed for evening rations instead of on his way to a reprimand. He was eager for a quiet evening with nothing to do but sit under the stars and listen to the soft trill of insects and the low murmur of voices.

Coming to General Grant's tent, Drew slowed his pace. The wooden bench his superior often occupied at the front of his quarters lay vacant, his staff's chairs empty. He choked down the bile in his throat. His first two encounters with General Grant had been agreeable ones. This third meeting was setting up to be different.

How disappointed the general must be after bestowing such a solid promotion on him. Drew had let him down.

Something the General-in-Chief wasn't likely to let him forget.

As he neared the tent opening, hurried boot steps approached from behind. He paused for a look, stepping aside when he saw Captain Jacobs on his heels. Without so much as a glance his way, the captain veered in front of Drew and, upon entering the general's quarters, offered a crisp salute. Drew took a cleansing breath, then ducked inside the tent. His open-palm salute received a straight-faced acknowledgment from both General Grant and General Rawlins.

Grant crossed his legs, his uniform sagging against his slight frame. What he lacked in size, he made up for in presence. He tapped his cigar, sending a flurry of ashes to the parched ground below. His dark gray eyes shifted from Drew to Captain Jacobs and back again. "Tell me, Lieutenant, what was your occupation before the war?"

Taken aback by the unexpected question, Drew floundered a moment before answering. "I was a surveyor and a farmer, sir."

Grant nodded, then addressed the captain. "And you?"

The tow-headed captain tipped his chin higher. "A lawyer from New York City, sir."

The general took a draw on his cigar and released a puff of smoke, filling the tent with the strong scent of tobacco. "General Rawlins informs me there's bad blood between the two of you."

The captain's face paled. "I-It's this fellow, General. He's not suited to be my lieutenant."

Without a moment's hesitation, General Grant gave a consenting nod. "I quite agree."

Drew swallowed, the blood draining from his face. He'd hoped the General-in-Chief would see past Captain Jacobs' conceited accusations, but it appeared he concurred.

The general rose to his feet and paced the length of the tent. "I believe you referred to him as an insubordinate coward, did you not, Captain?"

Drew's insides crumbled. To endure such a degrading accusation from the captain was one thing, but to hear General Grant utter the words pierced him like a dozen bullets in his chest.

Though Drew did his best to keep unflinching eyes fastened straight ahead, he couldn't miss the captain expanding his chest as he responded. "Yes, sir. I did."

General Grant locked his hands together behind his back, brows raised. "Then there's something I'd like you to hear." He cast a glance toward his aide. "General Rawlins, please read the note I received earlier today from Lieutenant Morris Schaff."

Drew didn't recall the name. His brow pinched, curious what bearing the letter could have on his impending punishment.

Rawlins retrieved a paper from between the brass buttons of his uniform jacket and cleared his throat. "I wish to acknowledge a certain officer who, with no regard to his own welfare, showed great bravery in the face of danger during the City Point explosion."

He paused, inadvertently casting a glance in Drew's direction, before continuing. "While others fled the threat of further blasts, this officer took it upon himself to rush to my aid in extinguishing a fire that otherwise would have reached a pile of ammunition and caused dozens, if not hundreds more deaths, including his and mine."

Drew's heart pumped harder, his mind racing back to the incident near the pier. Morris Schaff. Was that the name of the man he'd helped douse the flames? He'd never thought to ask.

He recalled the lieutenant inquiring his name but never imagined he'd remember it, let alone alert General Grant of his actions.

General Rawlins's tone deepened in intensity. "Therefore, I wish to thank Lieutenant Andrew Gallagher for his selfless service and honor him for his bravery. Signed, Lieutenant Morris Schaff." Lowering the paper, Rawlins lifted his gaze to Drew. "Well done, Lieutenant."

Though eager to sag his shoulders in a relieved sigh, Drew bridled his emotions, meeting General Rawlins's pleased expression with a stoic nod. "Thank you, sir."

General Grant clutched a hand to his unbuttoned uniform jacket and pivoted toward Jacobs. "I ask you, Captain, does that sound like a coward or a spy?"

Jacobs shot Drew a desperate glance then returned his gaze to the general. "N-No, sir. But you did admit his insubordination makes him unfit to be a lieutenant."

The general stepped toward the captain with characteristic composure. "I'm afraid you misinterpreted. I said he was not suited to be *your* lieutenant. Lieutenant Gallagher is a man of action who places his own well-being aside for the sake of others. You may consider that insubordination. I do not."

"Yes, of course, sir." The captain's face blanched, and, for a moment, Drew almost felt sorry for him.

Almost.

Grant dropped his cigar butt and trampled it into the dirt with the toe of his boot. "Lieutenant Gallagher will be commended for his actions and reassigned where his abilities will be better utilized. You may go now, Captain."

"Yes, sir." All the fight had fled from his voice and demeanor, but as he turned to go, he narrowed his eyes at Drew.

"Oh, and Captain?"

At the general's summons, Jacobs paused and swiveled to face him. "Yes, sir?"

"If you wish to remain a captain, I suggest you stop nitpicking your men and work to earn their respect."

Tempted to revel in the captain's reproof, Drew averted his gaze as he passed, chastising himself for wishing the man ill. He couldn't say he was sorry to be free of him, but it was wrong to be spiteful. As a follower of Christ, he was called to love those who hated him and pray for those who mistreated him.

"Now, Lieutenant." General Grant's voice curtailed his thoughts. "Tell us more about your encounter with the men on the bluff."

CAROLINE SLID her fingers over the instruments in the cloth medical kit atop her uncle's desk. How she could have utilized these in tending Drew's and the other soldiers' wounds. Though uncertain of the appropriate use of some, the delicate picks and tweezers would have done well at fishing out shell fragments.

The sound of hurried footsteps coming up the stairwell startled her. Pulling her hand back, she turned toward the doorway of her uncle's small office. Would he be angry with her?

He peeked in, a puzzled expression spilling onto his face. "Why, Caroline. Whatever are you doing in here? I thought you'd be settling in or downstairs getting more acquainted with Frankie and the children."

She struggled to find her voice. Here less than a full day, and already she was disrupting things. "I-I'm sorry, Uncle. I didn't mean to intrude. I simply wish to learn all I can about becoming a nurse."

He stepped into the room, his expression softening. "I applaud your enthusiasm."

His gaze flicked to the kit of medical tools left open on his desk, and he arched a brow. "However, these are a doctor's instruments."

Caroline's cheeks warmed as she swiveled toward the array of surgeon tools exposed on the desk. "I'm sorry. I-I should have asked."

Striding over, he folded the cloth covering and put it in its place, his expression difficult to read. He turned toward her, a weak smile edging out the seriousness on his face. "No harm done. I'm glad you feel at home. Feel free to look around."

Relieved, she laced her hands together behind her back, peering at the array of medical books housed behind the twin glass doors of her uncle's desk hutch. "Such large textbooks. You must have to study very hard."

"Not really. I just keep them there to impress my patients and refer to when I don't know what I'm doing."

He tossed her a wink, and she chuckled lightly in return.

"Would you like to see one?" He reached a hand to the latch.

Caroline's heart leaped. "Very much so."

Opening the glass doors, he ran his fingers along the spines then paused. "Ah! Here's an intriguing one. *The Science and Art of Surgery* by John Erichsen."

Caroline took it from him and flipped through its pages. A host of sketched illustrations, displaying everything from how to remove an appendix to amputation, stared back at her. Crinkling her nose, she finished glancing through it then handed it to her uncle. "I'd best stick to nursing and leave the doctoring to you."

With a hearty laugh, he replaced the book on its shelf.

In the silence that followed, Caroline drew a breath to

bolster her courage. Now seemed an apt time to pose her question. "Uncle Samuel?"

He closed the hutch doors then turned to face her. "Yes?"

"I was wondering when I might accompany you to visit patients?"

He arched a brow. "You are eager, aren't you?"

Caroline smiled shyly. "I'm sorry. It's just ... I've never had the opportunity to learn nursing skills before."

"Not to worry. We'll get to patients." He tugged at his trousers. "But, I'm a tobacco farmer as well as a doctor and, as you can see, today I'm dressed for field work. Barring some emergency, I see patients on Tuesdays and Fridays."

He motioned over his shoulder. "I came to let you know dinner's ready." Edging toward the door, he sniffed appreciatively. "I can smell the chicken and dumplin's from here."

"Coming." Caroline followed him from the room, the elation she'd expected to feel hampered by memories of her father. He'd mocked her nursing ambitions. And yet her Heavenly Father, in His goodness, had allowed her the opportunity.

What her father meant as punishment, the Lord had turned for good.

As she started down the stairs, she sighed. Somehow, someday, she would prove to Papa—and herself—that she could be the person he never thought she could.

31

August 20, 1864
Globe Tavern, Weldon Railroad

Drew squinted against the rising sun, keeping watch for Rebel soldiers. Yesterday's pounding rain had held them at bay, offering a welcome reprieve for the weary unit of soldiers. Today would likely prove different. He tensed at the thought of his first combat since the crater. There, he'd fought to save lives. Here, he'd have no choice but to fight to stay alive.

Was he ready?

Still haunted by images of Caroline and Jamison, he could only pray for the Lord's spirit to guide and spare him an encounter with her kinfolk. He shifted his feet, boots bogged down in several inches of mud. Back on the farm, he might have welcomed the relief from the long summer of drought. But, here, the heavy rain only succeeded in turning the parched ground and trenches to sludge, hindering their efforts to expand the Union stronghold over Petersburg.

Captain Lansing, Drew's new commanding officer, stepped up beside him, staring over the desolate landscape, his dense beard and mustache concealing much of his expression. "Any sign of the Rebs?"

Drew turned his gaze to the vacant fields and timber. "Nothing yet, sir."

"Well, keep your eyes peeled, Lieutenant. They're coming. You can bank on it."

"Yes, sir." Drew didn't doubt that a minute. Not only was his hair standing on end but, in their short stint together, Drew had come to trust the seasoned officer's instincts.

The captain made his way along the company of soldiers, his stately poise evoking respect from both Drew and the men. In the week since he'd been reassigned to Captain Lansing, he'd learned more about being a lieutenant than he ever could have from Captain Jacobs. Under Lansing's tutelage, Drew felt ready when the company had been commissioned to assist General Warren's Fifth Corps in holding their position along the Weldon Railroad near Globe Tavern. Though they'd helped regain some lost ground, the losses earlier in the day had been substantial— nearly an entire Brigade taken prisoner.

Now that the rains of yesterday had ended, the Confederates were certain to counter-attack in an attempt to regain control of the all-important railroad. Destruction of the tracks meant the Rebels' access to much-needed supplies into Petersburg would be cut off. A crucial victory for the Union.

If they could accomplish it.

A mist hung in the inclines and valleys, lending an eerie appearance to the desecrated land. Still damp from the rain, the iron railroad tracks glistened in the early morning sunlight. Already the clang of metal echoed in the distance as the Fifth Corps resumed their work heating the rails and bending the iron in the shape of their insignia, a Maltese Cross—an added jab at the Rebs.

Drew continued to scan the sullied landscape, rifle and bayonet ready. Though he didn't relish the idea of another hand-to-hand combat, he knew if ever one side were to emerge as winner in this miserable war, more bloody battles must be fought.

He exhaled, longing for the day all this would end. Surely, there must be a better life awaiting him beyond these war-torn lands.

One he hoped included Caroline.

Shadowy images appeared on the horizon, setting Drew's heart to pounding. He raised his voice to sound the alert. "Rebels, Captain!"

A shot rang out as Captain Lansing ordered the company to advance. Drew gripped his loaded Springfield and whispered a prayer as he followed the soldiers into the fray.

August 20, 1864
Dear Mama and Rose,

> *How I miss you. The two and a half weeks since we've parted seem more like years. My heart aches for home and to be near you during such a sorrowful time. And yet, for the time being, I feel as though I'm where the Lord intends me to be.*

> *Uncle Samuel and Aunt Frances have welcomed me with open arms and have made my stay here a pleasant one. The children are beginning to warm to me, though it is quite different being in a household with four spirited youngsters.*

> *At my request, Uncle Samuel has graciously allowed me to accompany him on his medical rounds. What a joy to work alongside a real doctor and be allowed to learn skills of nursing. The Lord must have had this in mind when He sent me here.*

> *Write very soon. I long for word from you and trust I am in your*

thoughts as you are ever in mine. The Lord bless and keep you in His care.

All my love,
Caroline

CAROLINE TOOK a final glance over the missive and folded it to post at her first opportunity. Though it did her heart good to imagine she was conversing with her family, deep down, she wondered if the heartfelt note would ever reach them. Or if her father would confiscate it the way he had Jamison's letter. Could he be so hateful?

A burning sensation balled in her chest as she dripped candle wax on the crease to seal the letter. If Papa did destroy the note, she hoped he would at least read it first and learn of her opportunity to assist as a nurse. Spiteful as it seemed, she longed for him to regret his harsh words and realize her banishment hadn't been her undoing. Lord forgive her, she hated him for sending her away and would not rest until he displayed some semblance of remorse for his cruelty.

DREW TOOK a cautious glance around then squatted beside the injured soldier nearest him, the putrid scent of blood and gunpowder hovering over him. The young private's breaths were heavy, his gaze fixed on the sky above, the luster in his eyes all but extinguished. Oily stains darkened the midsection of his uniform. He coughed and sputtered. "We ... whooped 'em ... didn't we?"

Drew forced a smile, feeling anything but cheerful. "We sure did."

Though the soldier made no further effort to move or speak, a sliver of hope glistened in his dark eyes. A raspy sound accompanied the youth's every breath, hinting his time was short. Not much older than Drew's younger brother, Luke, the boy would die a man's death, having served his country to the bitter end.

When the labored breaths ceased, Drew pressed his fingers to the soldier's neck then under his nose. Lowering the young man's eyelids, Drew hung his head, heartsick from yet another life snuffed out too soon. He'd seen his fill of death and dying.

When would it end?

Drew's chest squeezed as he stood and ventured another look around. Today's victory came at a high price. Countless men had been taken prisoner. Many lay wounded and bleeding amid cries for help. Others remained so still it was impossible to tell if they were dead or alive.

A moan sounded from a downed soldier a few yards ahead. Drew glanced in his direction and then regretted it, his jaw clenching. Of all the injured men to come across, must it be Captain Jacobs?

For an instant, Drew felt tempted to turn away and let the captain suffer. After all, there were scores of others more worthy than him to tend to. But the words of Jesus pulled at him like an unalterable force he couldn't ignore.

Love your enemies and do good to them which hate ye.

If ye love them which love you, what thanks have ye?

And if ye do good to them which do good to you, what thanks have ye?

Be ye therefore merciful, as your Father also is merciful.

With a sigh, Drew bowed his head. *I hear You, Father. Forgive me.*

Striding over, he dropped down beside Jacobs. The captain grimaced and gripped his upper right arm, blood oozing between his fingers. He stared up at Drew, his crusted lips parting slightly. "Well, well. Lieutenant Gallagher. Come to gloat, have you?"

Drew suppressed the urge to roll his eyes at the snide remark. Instead, he blew out a long breath. "No. I've come to help. Now, let's have a look at that bullet wound."

The captain's eyes flickered, and some of the challenge fled from his expression. Slowly, he slid his bloodied fingers from atop the wound, revealing a mass of severed flesh and bone fragments.

Drew winced. What he wouldn't give to have Caroline at his side right about now.

Or any time, for that matter.

He ripped a section from the captain's tattered shirt and tied it around the wound. With no means to alleviate the pain or remove the fragments, all he could do was stem the flow of blood and get him to the field hospital. He eased back on his haunches. "I'm no medic, but that oughta help with the bleeding."

Jacobs flinched as Drew tightened the cloth over the wound. His eyes narrowed. "Tell me, Lieutenant. Why would *you* wanna help *me*?"

The question was enough to convince Drew that if he were the one injured, the captain would not have extended the same kindness. He wiped bloody hands on the grass and shrugged. "Because it's the right thing and because my faith compels me to."

The captain's lips lifted in a half-sneer. "Your faith, huh?"

Drew squared his shoulders and looked him in the eyes. "That's right. Jesus asks us to show love when others hate and compassion when treated with contempt."

Though Jacobs gave no reply, his face lost all expression, his pale, blue eyes locking on Drew for an instant before drifting away.

Drew cleared his throat. "Can you stand?"

Jacobs swallowed hard and nodded. "I think so." With effort, he heaved himself to a sitting position and Drew helped him to his feet. The captain teetered. "On second thought, I'm not sure I have the strength."

Drew placed a steadying hand on his arm. "I'll help. You'll be fine once we get you to the hospital."

The captain shook his head as he draped his good arm around Drew's shoulders. "I won't pretend to understand you, Gallagher, but ... thank you."

Drew nodded, content he and the Lord were winning a battle no earthly weapons could attain. One of love over hatred.

If only the North and South could do the same.

Together, they staggered their way through the muddy, open field, besieged with the wounded and dying. Though it was too soon to tell the long-term outcome of the day's events, today's victory dealt a hard blow to the Rebels. For the time being, the Union's hold on this section of Weldon Railroad appeared secure. Control of it left the Confederates with no way to replenish supplies. All the Union need do is pray ...

And wait.

32

Six weeks later, October 1, 1864

"Thanks for stitchin' me up, Doc."

Uncle Samuel clapped the injured man on the shoulder. "Next time, Ned, use that ax to chop the tree instead of your leg."

Caroline held back a grin as she wiped off the suture needle and placed it in her uncle's surgery kit. Ned Maynard seemed to have a knack for getting into predicaments. This wasn't the first time she'd assisted her uncle in treating his injuries. In the little over two months she'd been here, Mr. Maynard had required medical attention for an injured hand, a broken nose, and now a gash in his leg.

He let out a chuckle and then a groan. "I'll do my best."

"Humph." Fixing her gaze on her husband, Mrs. Maynard crossed her arms over her chest, her thin, upper lip growing taut. "Last time you said that you came in last place at the turkey shoot."

Caroline cringed at the willowy woman's criticism. Though her husband passed the comment off without a word, its sting was evidenced by his tightly knit brows. Around her father's age, with tufts of gray highlighting his thinning red hair, the man had a good hundred pounds on his scant wife. Even so, she seemed to have the upper hand in the relationship.

Caroline handed her uncle the bottle of iodine, noting how smooth and even his stitches appeared, so unlike the jagged sewing job she'd performed on Drew. Her mind drifted to that fateful afternoon when she'd found him lying helpless and bleeding on the timber floor.

By now, his wounds must have healed over. Her chest squeezed.

If he were still alive.

She yearned to know what had become of him just as she ached to undo the telegram that brought the dreaded news of Jamison. Two long months had passed since she'd bid them both farewell.

An eternity.

She brushed a speck of dirt from her dark sleeve. Four months of grieving remained. When the time came to shed her mourning clothes, would she be ready to don something colorful and cheery? Or would her heart forever cling to the now too familiar black taffeta?

"Caroline?" Her uncle's brisk summons roused her from her thoughts. "Bring the pair of crutches from my office."

With a nod, she stood and strode toward the door. Rather than force Mr. Maynard to make the arduous climb upstairs to the medical office, Uncle Samuel opted to stitch his leg on the parlor settee, laying a blanket down to protect it from stain.

By the time she returned with the crutches, her uncle had the patient's pantleg back in place and was gently lowering his foot to the rug beneath. "Here you are, Mr. Maynard."

The bulky man reached for the wooden crutches, his smile cut short by an obvious stab of pain. "Thank ya, miss. You're right kind."

Mrs. Maynard pursed her lips, casting Caroline a sideways glance. "A mite too kind to an ol' fool like you."

Caroline burned inwardly as Mr. Maynard hung his head. Why did people have to be so cruel? Individuals like Papa and Mrs. Maynard seemed to have no regard for others' feelings, speaking their minds without giving thought to their words.

"Come along, Ned." The woman nudged her husband on the arm then stalked toward the door, a nettling tempo in her voice. "You've taken up enough of the doctor's time."

Uncle Samuel shook his head, assuring Caroline she wasn't the only one who found the woman thoughtless and rude. He motioned her over, and the two of them helped Mr. Maynard to his feet.

Leaning in close, their patient kept his voice at a whisper. "Don't mind Emma. She gets a mite cross when I do somethin' clumsy."

Caroline nodded. She knew all too well how it felt to be the recipient of someone's constant ire—a feeling that knotted her stomach just to recall.

Her uncle brandished a grin. "Easy does it, now."

Tightening her hold on Mr. Maynard's arm, Caroline helped her uncle ease him outside and down the steps. She snugged her shawl higher on her neck, the October breeze holding a chill as they crossed the yard to the awaiting wagon.

Rather than attempt to hoist himself onto the wagon seat beside his wife, Mr. Maynard eased into the strawed wagon bed. "Thanks again, Doc. What do we owe for yer trouble?"

"Whatever you can manage. I know times are tough with the war on."

Releasing the brake, Mrs. Maynard craned her neck and looked back at them. "Money's a bit sparse. I'll have Ned bring over some firewood and a bushel of garden potatoes for payment, soon as he's able."

"No hurry. It'll take a few weeks for that leg to heal." Uncle Samuel lowered his voice and leaned closer to his patient. "You keep off that leg a few days. I'll stop by to check on you at the end of the week."

Mr. Maynard nodded, gripping the side of the wagon as it jerked into motion.

Caroline shook her head as she turned and strolled with her uncle toward the house. "She doesn't coddle him much, does she?"

With a glance over his shoulder at the departing wagon, he gave a soft snicker. "Poor ol' Ned. He's about as prone to calamity as they come ... and even more henpecked."

Hiking her skirt, Caroline upped the porch steps. "He seems like a nice man. I feel sorry for him."

"The man's had a rough go of it, all right, in more ways than one." Her uncle stooped to retrieve his medical kit. "You were good with him. In fact, you're good with all my patients."

"Thank you." Caroline brightened; the welcome compliment was balm for her unsettled spirit. At least in her uncle's eyes, she'd proven herself capable. Would that she could do so with her father.

Despite all the upheaval in her life, she sensed the Lord's guiding hand upon her. Through all the heartache, He'd not forgotten her.

"I will never leave thee, nor forsake thee." The familiar verse scrolled through her mind, and a sense of peace washed over her.

No matter what lay ahead, she was not alone.

33

City Point Depot, November 2, 1864

Drew sank onto his cot and looped his hands behind his head, a movement he'd only recently been able to complete without discomfort. Only scars remained where his wounds had once been, yet his stomach reminded him his bout with dysentery was not quite over.

He'd fared better than most, a few doses of quinine—and a heavier dose of prayer—sparing him severe symptoms. Though he'd grown tired of being confined to his quarters, at least he hadn't had to stay in the City Point hospital for long. It was dismal enough enduring his own misery, let alone a roomful of groaning, nauseated soldiers.

He stared into the log rafters of the newly fashioned hut. As autumn chilled the air, he was grateful to have a roof over his head instead of thin tent canvas. Following their successful campaign to gain control of much of the Weldon Railroad, his company, along with others, had been commissioned to erect log huts in preparation for winter. The bout with dysentery cropped up soon afterward.

A rap on the cabin door roused him. He cleared his throat. "Come in."

Captain Lansing peeked his head in, his thick mustache and beard concealing much of his face. "Feeling better?"

Drew exhaled a long breath. "Some. Though the thought of food still isn't enticing."

The captain stepped inside and held out a tin. "Then I don't suppose you'll want the bean soup and cornbread I brought."

Drew grimaced and shook his head. "Not a chance. It wasn't any good when I *had* an appetite."

With a shrug, Captain Lansing swirled the tin under his nose. "I've smelled worse."

"It's all yours." Drew waved a hand at him. Somehow, thus far, his superior had escaped the dreaded illness.

Captain Lansing grinned and set the soup aside. "Here's something that might sit better with you. Word has it Petersburg is short on provisions. The Rebs will be fortunate to last the winter."

Drew gave a slow nod. "Then maybe we can finally put an end to this siege."

"If things continue as they're going, it's only a matter of time."

"I hope you're right." Drew arched a brow. "But, if I know the Rebs, they won't give up without a fight."

"Never do." Captain Lansing snatched up the tin of soup. "Say, if I can't interest you in some supper, maybe I can your horse."

Drew scoffed. "I wouldn't bet on it. But, thanks for looking after her while I'm laid up."

The captain chuckled and backed toward the door. "Take care, Gallagher."

When the cabin was again quiet, Drew reached under his thin, lumpy mattress and retrieved the stack of letters from his mother. Since he'd written to let her know where he was stationed, she'd been faithful to correspond once or twice a week. Unfolding the letters in turn—oldest to most recent—he reread each one. The unwelcome news that his brother, Luke, had entered the fight still left a raw ache inside him. At seventeen, his younger brother was brash and unafraid—qualities that made a gutsy soldier.

But also ones that got a person killed.

With each consecutive letter, he could sense his mother's concern growing. Several weeks had passed since she'd heard from Luke. At last report, his company had been stationed near Winchester, Virginia, under General Sheridan.

No telling where he was now.

A pang of remorse rent Drew's middle as he envisioned his mother waiting on the porch rocker watching, hoping, yearning for word from them. But, though certain her heart was overflowing with concern, he knew she would be continually praying for their safe return. She'd already lost a husband. To lose a son as well would devastate her.

With both Luke and him away at war, Mama and Drew's young sister, Lydia, were left to fend for themselves. Would they have what they needed for winter? Firewood? Coal? Food?

He turned on his side, concern growing. As long as her letters kept coming, he at least had some inkling as to how they were managing. That is, if his mother would confide in him. Not one to complain, she would likely not mention if they lacked anything, regardless of how bad things got.

His gut clenched. The South had endured even more hardship and devastation, both from drought and combat. Were Caroline and her family in want? Had they endured more battles near their property?

How he'd come to despise all the bloodshed.

Being laid up had given him plenty of time to pray and think. The extra prayer time proved an asset. It was the idle moments spent worrying that had him tied in knots. As eager as he was to return home to attend to his mother and sister, he was equally concerned for Caroline's welfare.

A nervous pang rippled through him. Foolhardy as it may seem, his promise to return was one he intended to keep.

"Caroline? Would you come down a moment?"

"Coming." Heeding her uncle's summons, Caroline set her quill in the inkwell and strode toward the staircase.

As she started down, Uncle Samuel peered up at her from the hall below, a curious grin lining his lips.

Tilting her head, she edged closer. "What is it?"

"A letter came for you."

With a gleeful gasp, she clutched a hand to her chest and bounded down the stairs. She'd waited so long for news from home. Months had passed with nary a word. "From Mama?"

"No." He patted his vest pocket and slid a hand in to retrieve the envelope. With dancing eyes, he held it out to her. "Does the name Rose Dunbar sound familiar?"

Her lips spread in a wide grin as she clasped the long-awaited letter between her fingertips. Her young sister's familiar, large letters stared up at her, filling her with unbridled joy. "At last."

Uncle Samuel scrubbed a hand over his thick goatee. "Just when I'd become accustomed to having a nurse, I suppose they're going to steal you from me."

A nervous tingle rippled through her. Not likely. It would take more than a mere few months to appease her father's wrath. "You needn't worry about that. So long as the war is on, and I'm welcome, I'd like to continue to stay and work with you."

He gave a brisk nod. "Fine. Then I'll leave you to learn what word young Rose sends of home."

As he made his way outside, Caroline dropped down on the next-to-bottom step and pried open the wax seal. Unfolding the letter, she savored each imperfect stroke of ink.

Dear Caroline,

Why haven't you returned my letters? You promised to write.

CAROLINE WILTED. The heart-wrenching words were not ones she'd hoped to hear. She *had* written. Every week since she'd left home. Though it occurred to her Papa might confiscate her letters, she'd not considered he would attempt to intercept Rose and Mama's correspondences as well.

She clenched her jaw. How could anyone be so heartless?

By some miracle, one had slipped through. Perhaps their mother had grown wise to Papa's tactics and mailed the letter personally. If only there were some way to squelch his interference on her end as well.

With bated breath, she continued.

It's lonely here without you and Jamison. Phillip is always with Papa and calls me a pest if I try to tag along. Nothing is the same since you left. Papa is out of sorts much of the time. Mama tries to hide her tears, but I hear her cry in the night. Some mornings her eyes are puffy and red. It makes me sad that she's unhappy. Even Lily is no longer cheerful.

I miss you. Will you be home for Christmas? Mama and I pray every night this war will end, and Papa will allow you to return. Please write soon.

Your loving sister,
Rose

Tears stung Caroline's eyes as she pressed the disheartening letter to her chest. How she ached to hold her dear sister and assure her she hadn't forgotten her. Despite the failed attempts, she would keep writing. In time, maybe Mama would find a way to thwart Papa's vicious attempt to keep them apart.

Her stomach knotted. Even here, far from the confines of her father's harsh presence, he was controlling her, squeezing the very life from her. Not only had he exiled her from her home and loved ones, but he had also stolen the last means of contact she had with them. And with it, her last remnants of joy.

"Why, Lord? Why?"

She balled her fists, fuming inwardly. She'd tried to forgive Papa as she knew the Lord would want her to, but this was too much. Try as she might to fight it, the seed of bitterness she'd harbored toward her father swelled into loathing. His vindictive ways had crushed her aspirations of one day returning home.

He would never allow it.

Never.

Hollowness nipped at her as thoughts of Drew coiled their way inside her heart. There was no hope for them now. Even if he survived the war, he would have no means of finding her.

She stifled a cry. He, too, was lost to her.

A tear slid down her cheek, and she swiped it away. She had but one choice—forget the life she once knew and make a fresh start. Until the war ended, she would remain with her aunt and uncle. Afterward, she would seek a position as a nurse.

Someplace far away from the father who despised her.

Though her future remained uncertain, one thing she did know.

She never wished to see or have anything to do with her father again.

34

Saturday, November 5, 1864

"I don't believe it." Uncle Samuel slumped back in his chair and lowered the newspaper, his exasperated words echoing through the crowded dining room.

Caroline craned her neck in an attempt to see what had her uncle so riled, to no avail.

Aunt Frances finished feeding Samuel Jr. a spoonful of potatoes and glanced at her husband, brows knit. "What is it, Samuel?"

He snapped his fingers against the newspaper. "It says here Maryland voted to free the slaves."

With a shake of her head, Aunt Frances wiped a glob of potatoes from the youngster's mouth. "I suppose it was inevitable. We held out longer than most."

Uncle Samuel smacked the paper down with uncharacteristic angst. "It's a travesty! As long as Lincoln is president, this nation will remain in shambles."

Caroline winced at his sharp tone, so reminiscent of her father's.

Young Samuel Jr.'s face puckered, and tears welled in his eyes as he released a loud wail. The other children stared at their father with widened eyes.

Aunt Frances glowered at him and bounced his namesake on her knee. "No need to shout, dear. Perhaps he'll be voted out this term."

Uncle scowled but lowered his voice. "Regardless if Lincoln or McClellan wins the election, the slaves will likely remain free."

Caroline slid her hand along the frayed edge of the table cloth, her mind traveling over the miles to home. No doubt her father would take the news as bitterly as her uncle. Would Cyrus and Lily's loyalty to her family hold them in place? Whether she was allowed to return home or not, she couldn't bear the thought of them leaving or being sent away.

"What about Lettie and Lousia?" Her aunt cast a sideways glance at the servant girls as they cleared away the supper dishes. "Ours is the only home they've ever known."

The young black girls of no more than ten and twelve years of age kept their eyes lowered, displaying no sign they were taking in the conversation.

Expelling a long breath, Uncle Samuel crossed his arms over his chest. "They'll remain with us. If necessary, we'll pay them a small allowance, though I feel room and board are quite sufficient for ones so young."

He smoothed his mustache and goatee. "It's the farm laborers that concern me. Some have already deserted us. Now that they've been declared free, the others will likely follow. How am I supposed to put in a crop next spring without slaves to work the fields?"

"If they choose not to remain with us, perhaps we can hire some workers."

"Who? Most able-bodied men have joined the war effort."

When Aunt Frances gave no reply, he shook his head

defiantly. "No. If we wish to live as we please, we must win this war!" With that, he smacked his fist down on the table, rattling the remaining dishes. The commotion intensified young Samuel Jr.'s sobs.

Caroline shuddered. She'd never seen her uncle so agitated. The fire in his eyes almost frightened her. Though she, too, longed for the war to end, its consequences would be long-lasting. If the South emerged the victor, what would become of Union soldiers like Drew? Would they be allowed to return to their homes, or would they be punished or imprisoned?

Her chest squeezed. Either way, the chances of ever seeing him again were slim. Any hopes of future happiness taunted her like a peek of moonglow on a cloudy night.

The war had stripped this land of something precious, something God alone could restore—wholeness and unity. If every man held such strong convictions, an end to the fighting would likely not appease their bitterness. Jamison was one of thousands who'd died as a result of the nation's animosity.

When would it end?

And, even more elusive, what would follow?

St. Mary's Church
Sunday, November 13, 1864

A SNOWFLAKE DAMPENED Caroline's cheek as the carriage rolled to a stop outside St. Mary's church. She slid the blanket from across her and the older children's laps, shivering as cold air replaced the warmth. She took in the cathedral-style building, awaiting her turn to exit the carriage. Though different from the church she was accustomed to, she'd agreed to attend with her aunt and uncle while she stayed with them.

Uncle Samuel lifted Thomas from the front seat of the

carriage then reached to help her aunt. "Go on in and find a seat. I'll join you shortly."

Aunt Frances's face pinched as she clutched Samuel Jr. tighter and accepted her husband's hand down. "I don't understand. Who are these men you must meet with?"

He cast an uneasy glance around, his eyes settling on two gentlemen at the far side of the churchyard, one elderly and the other young. "No one of importance. I won't be long. Now, take the children inside before they catch a chill."

The slight edginess in his voice hinted to Caroline that he either didn't wish to be questioned or wasn't being entirely truthful.

Shaking her head, Aunt Frances shifted her hold on the rosy-cheeked youngster and reached out her other hand for Thomas to grasp. "Come, children."

Taking Sissy's tiny hand in hers, Caroline followed her aunt toward the church building. Six-year-old Andrew ambled along beside them with his hands tucked in his pockets, evidently thinking himself too mature for hand-holding.

As they walked, Caroline peered back at the fellow shaking hands with her uncle. Though she couldn't place him, his face looked strangely familiar. Who could forget that pasty complexion, wavy brown hair, and coal-black eyes? Catching her aunt by the elbow, she nodded in his direction. "Do you recognize that young man Uncle Samuel is speaking with?"

Aunt Frances shifted the squirmy Samuel Jr. from one arm to the other, her eyes crimping as she studied the fellow. She shook her head. "I can't say I do." With a sideways glance at Caroline, she arched a brow, her thin lips lifting. "He's not a bad-looking sort. Perhaps we should have Samuel introduce you."

Caroline's cheeks warmed. An introduction was the furthest thing from her mind. "That won't be necessary. I just have the feeling I've seen him somewhere."

Her aunt returned her attention to the dark-haired stranger.

"Now that you mention it, he does look vaguely familiar." She shrugged. "We must have seen him in town at some point."

Though she didn't wish to dispute her aunt, Caroline knew that was impossible. In her three months at her relatives' home, she'd met only her uncle's patients and those at church. The man in question seemed more like someone whose picture she'd seen rather than met in person.

As others thronged toward the church building, the trio of men slipped farther into the background. While huddled together, they cast frequent glances over their shoulders as though intent on keeping their conversation private.

Shrugging off the unsettled feeling, Caroline turned away. Her uncle hadn't been himself of late. He'd been on edge and withdrawn. It wasn't like him to alter plans or exclude Aunt Frances from decisions.

Something wasn't right.

A gust of cold wind tugged at Caroline's bonnet, and she held it in place as she followed her aunt up the church steps. She cast a final glance over her shoulder, and a chill ran through her. She was meddling in affairs not her own.

She only hoped her uncle wasn't doing the same.

November 24, 1864, City Point Depot

"I NEVER TOOK you for such a glutton, Gallagher."

"Neither did I. But after what my stomach has been through, it's a mite greedy." Drew grinned at Captain Lansing and shoveled in his final bite of pumpkin pie. Though the ample meal couldn't compare to his mother's fine cooking, it had been tasty enough to tempt him to overindulge.

The blithe sounds of harmonicas and raucous singing drifted from deeper within the encampment. Drew stretched his legs closer to the fire, nodding toward the array of pup tents. "Sounds like the men are enjoying their night of leisure."

"They'd better. It won't last long." The captain leaned back in his chair, locking his hands together behind his head. "A well-deserved reprieve."

While some units remained on guard, the bulk of the soldiers had been granted the evening to celebrate Thanksgiving, a privilege decreed by President Lincoln, whose solid victory over General McClellan had earned him a second term.

Drew's stomach gurgled, and he began to regret downing that second piece of pie. He glanced toward Petersburg, encircled by countless campfires. Likely, the siege had put a damper on their Thanksgiving. "Doesn't appear our Confederate friends have joined the festivities."

Lansing's chair creaked as he craned his neck for a look. "I doubt they've much to celebrate."

Drew rubbed a hand over his full belly, feeling almost guilty. What the Rebs wouldn't give to have even a portion of the meal they'd just been served. "How much longer do you think they can hold out?"

With a shrug, Captain Lansing raked a hand down his wiry, brown beard. "Unless something unforeseen happens, a few months at best. As resilient as they seem, they can't continue fighting without food and ammunition. They won't keep us out forever."

A breeze stirred the November air and Drew tugged his coat tighter around him. As the last remnants of sunlight faded from the western sky, a spattering of stars shone overhead. For the first time in a long while, an end to the war seemed a fair possibility. If Petersburg fell, Richmond would likely soon follow.

Right now, returning to his mother and siblings and the lush, green countryside of home seemed a distant dream. But one he longed to realize.

Another hopeful image burned in his chest—one of Caroline waiting on the veranda for his return.

He tensed. Or would their brief time together be but a forgotten memory?

If the Captain was right, only a short time remained before Drew learned the answer. That is, if he could finagle his way past her over-protective father and brother who'd sooner see him at the end of a rifle barrel than courting Caroline.

35

Sunday, December 18, 1864

"I don't understand why Samuel insisted on going to mass alone."

Caroline finished setting the porcelain plates around the dining room table, uncertain how to respond. "It's rather cold out. He must have been considering the children's well-being."

Aunt Frances nodded. "I suppose. With Thomas and Samuel Jr.'s sniffles, it was probably for the best."

The clop of hooves and whir of carriage wheels drew her to the dining room window. She moved the sheer, white curtain aside, straining to see out the frosty pane. "There he is now. Lettie, Lousia, let's get dinner on. Frigid as it is, he'll be eager for some nourishment."

"Yes'm." The two young girls scurried to the kitchen to take up the platter of roast beef, mashed potatoes, and a basket of fresh-baked bread warming on the hearth. Though freed of the title of slaves, there'd been no change to the girls' duties other than receiving a pittance for their services in addition to their room in the kitchen loft.

"I'll help." Caroline maneuvered past the string of children in her path. Hardly seeming to notice, they continued to bicker and squabble over their game.

A blast of cold air, accompanied by the sound of men's jovial voices, stopped Caroline in her tracks. Turning toward the open door, she was taken aback at the sight of the dark-haired man she'd seen talking with her uncle last month at St. Mary's. His ebony eyes met hers, and, once again, she was struck with the thought she somehow knew who he was.

Uncle Samuel followed close behind, securing the door shut after them. He flashed her aunt an apologetic grin as she gaped at him. Removing his overcoat, he cleared his throat. "I hope you don't mind, Frankie, but I've brought a guest for dinner."

Aunt Frances's face pinched as she looked the man over. "You were at St. Mary's a few weeks back."

The visitor slipped off his coat, making his small frame seem even slighter. "Indeed I was, ma'am. I'm so taken with the area I've decided to purchase some real estate here."

Uncle Samuel reached for the man's coat. "He's also in need of a horse. I'll take him by George Gardiner's place after dinner to see if he can find a suitable mount."

Aunt Frances's gaze shifted from her husband to the visitor, her scowl transforming into an accepting smile. "We're quite partial to this region ourselves. Welcome, mister ... "

"Booth. But, please, call me John."

Caroline gnawed at her lip. Like the face, the name seemed so familiar.

He glanced her way, his dark eyes trailing down her black taffeta before returning to her face. "And who's this?"

Uncle Samuel passed their coats off to Lousia to hang in the hall. "My niece, Caroline."

The stranger reached for her hand and gave a courteous bow. "A pleasure."

"Thank you." She squirmed under his scrutinizing stare, his cold fingers sending a shiver through her.

His thick eyebrows lowered. Loosening his grip on her hand,

he stood erect, the top of his head a mere three or four inches above her own. "My condolences for your loss. May I inquire for whom you grieve? A father or husband, perhaps?"

"My brother." The confession left a sour taste in her mouth. It still pained her to think of Jamison as truly gone.

Mr. Booth tipped his chin higher. "My deepest regards and sympathies. To lose someone for the sake of the Confederate cause is truly a noble sacrifice."

Caroline stared at him, his poignant words hanging in the stillness. She'd seen that expression, that pose.

She lifted a brow. Now, she remembered. His photo had appeared in *Harper's Weekly* on numerous occasions. He'd been on stage at some of the theatres in Washington.

John ... Booth.

Her breath caught.

The man before her was none other than the acclaimed actor ... John Wilkes Booth.

Christmas Eve, 1864

"Dismissed."

At Drew's command, the company of men disbanded from morning drill, scurrying for someplace warmer. He rubbed his hands together to ward off the chill as he started for his cabin. Thick, gray clouds loomed overhead, holding the promise of snow. Winter had arrived just in time for Christmas.

Up ahead, he caught sight of General Grant, his wife Julia and son Jesse strolling alongside. The recent appearance of some of the officers' wives on the post stirred unsettled feelings within Drew. Though the fighting had quieted, it just didn't seem right to allow womenfolk so near the battlefront. The Rebs weren't licked yet, and until they were, anything could happen.

And yet, the ladies' presence here at City Point had

undoubtedly boosted morale. Their lilting laughter and feminine charms bolstered many a soldier's spirit. Part of him longed to glimpse Caroline's delicate frame striding toward him, a tender smile gracing her lips, her honey eyes dancing as she neared.

But it could never be.

Not until peace ruled where now only discord reigned.

He tugged his coat tighter around him against the frigid air, homesickness washing through him. Three Christmases away from home in as many years. He'd almost forgotten how festive and inviting the holiday could be. Before the war, he, Luke, and Father would comb the countryside for just the right tree to please Mama and Lydia. Even now, he could envision his mother and young sister popping corn over the fireplace, singing carols as they threaded a needle through the fluffy kernels.

His chest squeezed. With the menfolk gone, would they even have a tree this year? In his next letter home, he'd ask. This being their first year without Luke and Papa, it likely would not be a cheerful one. Hopefully, his package containing the dress material he'd purchased for Mama and Lydia had arrived in time. It wasn't much, but all he could manage.

As he rounded the corner of his cabin, Captain Lansing stopped talking and peered at him around the shoulders of a lean corporal. There was something familiar about the young man's stance and the blond curls protruding from beneath his kepi.

Nodding toward Drew, the captain's lips lifted in a sideways grin. "Here he is now. I'll leave the two of you to catch up."

Drew's eyes widened as the corporal swiveled toward him and recognition washed over him. "Luke?"

A broad smile split his brother's face, his boyish features having thinned and matured since last Drew saw him. With a loud chuckle, Luke traipsed over and threw his arms around him. "Merry Christmas, big brother."

Drew clapped him on the back then held him at arm's length. "How'd you know I was here?"

Luke thumbed his kepi higher on his forehead. "One of my

buddies heard there was a bigwig Lieutenant here named Gallagher. So, first chance I got, I started nosing around."

Drew gave his brother's shoulder a nudge. "Still tagging along after me, aye?"

"I reckon so. I promised Mama I'd do my best to look you up. I'd about given up hope."

"From Mama's last few letters, it seems she's ceased to worry about me and grown anxious over you."

Luke kicked the toe of his brogan in the dirt. "Yeah. I know. Things got rough, and I slacked off."

Drew took another sweep of his younger brother's face. Seeing him again was like a breath of springtime. Yet, the pale, blue eyes and ruddy complexion staring back at him were no longer those of a boy but a man. "How long you been here?"

"About a month."

Drew arched a brow. "It took you a whole month to find me? You must be slippin'."

Luke gave a lopsided grin. "Didn't see you combin' the trenches to find me neither."

Chuckling, Drew crossed his arms. "How goes the fight?"

Luke shrugged. "Haven't seen much action the past few weeks. I reckon the Rebs don't relish fightin' in cold weather any more than we do."

"I'll not complain." Drew smiled and gripped Luke's shoulder. "How soon are you due back?"

"Day after tomorrow."

A cold wind nipped at Drew's exposed face and neck. "Then, let's get inside. We've all of Christmas to get caught up."

"Sounds good."

"Hold up." Pausing, Drew caught him by the arm. "First, we'd better send a telegram to let Mama and Lydia know we're okay and together for Christmas."

A wide smile lit Luke's face. "Lead the way, big brother."

Despite the cold, warmth surged through Drew as he strode shoulder to shoulder with Luke. He breathed a silent prayer of thanksgiving. For one bright moment in this neverending war, the family could take comfort in knowing they were together in spirit.

Who knew when such a blessing would come again?

He could only pray for an equally joyous reunion for Caroline and her family.

CAROLINE PEERED out the frosty windowpane as the mantel clock chimed seven. Darkness had settled in, and still no sign of her uncle.

What could be keeping him?

A layer of new-fallen snow glistened in the pale moonlight, bringing a faint smile to her lips. If the snow had reached home, Rose would be ecstatic. Come morning light, she would be fashioning snow angels and rolling snowballs.

"How much longer?" Sissy's tender tone broke into Caroline's thoughts.

Aunt Frances brushed a wayward strand of hair from her cheek. "Soon, dear. Be patient."

Caroline glanced at the four eager youngsters seated in a half-circle around the evergreen tree at the corner of the parlor, its branches void of decoration. Afternoon and evening had trickled by while they awaited their father's return.

Now, they were growing restless.

With a discontented sigh, Sissy glanced over her shoulder at the string of popcorn and pile of candles stretched across the parlor rug. "It's nearly bedtime. Can't we decorate the tree without Papa?"

Andrew yanked on her pigtail. "'Course not, you ninny."

She squealed and batted at him with her hand. "Stop, Andrew!"

Aunt Frances' brow furrowed. "Children, please." She cast a

longing look out the darkened window, her voice trailing. "He'll be along. He promised."

Caroline placed a hand on her aunt's shoulder, the strong scent of pine tickling her nose. "I'm sure he'll be home soon. The snow must have delayed him."

The comment garnered a nod and a faint smile from Aunt Frances, though the muscles in her shoulders remained knotted beneath Caroline's fingertips.

Her aunt's uneasiness was understandable, seeing as Uncle Samuel had offered no explanation for the unexpected trip to Washington. His odd behavior began about the time Mr. Booth made his first appearance at St. Mary's. Despite the man's amiable personality, there was something unsettling about him. After he'd purchased a horse from Mr. Gardiner, Mr. Booth spent the night and departed the next morning. Uncle Samuel had left shortly afterward, assuring them he'd be home in time to decorate the tree on Christmas Eve.

That time was fast disappearing.

The hall door opened and closed, and all four children scrambled to their feet. Footsteps sounded in the hall, and Caroline rubbed her arms against the draft of frigid air filtering into the room. With a sudden intake of breath, Aunt Frances rose from the settee and strode toward the parlor entrance. Uncle Samuel appeared in the doorway, his winning smile putting them all at ease. Placing his hands on Aunt Frances's forearms, he leaned to kiss her cheek. "Sorry I'm late. The trip took longer than I anticipated."

Her brow creased. "I'm grateful you're home. Perhaps now you can explain what this trip to Washington was all about?"

"All in good time, my dear Frankie." He twirled her around. "But, if all goes well, our beloved South will soon gain the advantage it needs to win this wretched war."

The response left an uneasy feeling in the pit of Caroline's stomach. How could her uncle help provide the Confederates an advantage that would influence the outcome of the war—a feat

General Lee and his entire army had been unable to accomplish in years? Was Uncle Samuel involved in something deceitful? That was difficult to believe.

Recovering her footing, Aunt Frances giggled at his antics. "What kind of advantage?"

He arched a brow, a devious grin on his lips. "You'll know soon enough."

The children crowded in, tugging at his pant legs and pulling on his arms. "Can we decorate the tree now, Papa? We've waited so long."

He waved a hand in the air. "By all means. It's a night to celebrate." With that, he scooped Thomas up in one arm and Samuel Jr. in the other, whistling as he followed the older two children to the Christmas tree.

Caroline shared her aunt's puzzled expression. She'd never seen her uncle so carefree and elated. Perhaps, in time, he'd disclose the meaning behind his alarming statement and his cheerful mood. But for now, she tried to convince herself he was merely overflowing with Christmas cheer and not plotting some diabolical scheme that would endanger him and his family.

Or, more likely ... Drew.

36

"Charity. Unity. Bah!"

Caroline cringed at her uncle's assessment of Mr. Lincoln's inaugural speech, grateful the noise of the crowd around them swallowed up his words. She'd thought the president's message eloquent and brimming with hope for a nation divided.

Aunt Frances shook her head, adjusting her voice to counter the chatter of patrons. "I'll never understand why you wished to attend the inauguration of a president you despise. It's not like you, Samuel."

Uncle Samuel seemed not to hear amid the dispersing crowd. He peered in every direction, scanning the array of people as if in search of someone.

Intrigued, Caroline followed his gaze. "Who is it you're looking for, Uncle?"

"No one." He sank his fist in his palm, mumbling under his breath. "It wasn't supposed to be this way. Something must have happened."

Aunt Frances leaned in closer. "What wasn't supposed to be this way? You're not making sense, Samuel."

Though Caroline couldn't agree with her aunt more, she held her tongue. Nothing made sense where her uncle was concerned anymore. Over the winter, his jubilant mood had deteriorated into a tense, almost disgruntled state. He seemed shrouded in mystery. Even his doctoring had suffered, his efforts to aid patients half-hearted at best.

He breathed a loud sigh. "I needed to come, in case ... "

Aunt Frances's eyes were pleading as she stared up at him. "In case what?"

He clamped his jaw, shutting off his words. With eyes downcast, he shook his head. "Nothing."

Frances huffed with frustration, her hazel eyes dulling. "Then let's leave this wretched city with its muck and mire." She turned her gaze on her muddied skirt. "Honestly, Samuel. This entire affair has accomplished little more than the ruination of my dress and to rouse my temper."

Caroline shared her aunt's sentiments. Since their arrival yesterday, it had rained ceaselessly until giving way to warm sunshine just as President Lincoln began his address.

Uncle took Aunt Frances's arm, guiding her from the thick of the gathering. "Forgive me, Frankie. This has all been for naught. Believe me, I'm as eager to leave this dreadful city as you."

Hiking her soiled skirt, Caroline fell into step behind them, pulled along by the flood of dispersing onlookers. She cast a final glance to where the President stood. He smiled, shaking hands as he made his way from the platform, his expression warm, kind. Caroline had listened carefully to his words, taken aback by their simple wisdom.

With malice toward none.

The concept, though referring to the North and South, returned Caroline's thoughts to her father.

Could she let go of her malice toward him?

What sounded simple in words seemed much more challenging to put into practice.

The phrase sounded like something Jesus might have uttered. Having been rejected, beaten, and killed, He'd suffered far more than she could fathom. How could He forgive such hatred and injustice?

Caroline breathed a soft sigh. He was perfect.

She was not.

Weaving her way around a group of men who'd paused to chat, Caroline tried to ignore the knot in her chest. If only Papa would show even a glimmer of his heart softening. Yet, a second letter from Rose and Mama had given her no more hope than the first. It galled her that after all these months, he refused to allow her any contact with the family.

Her gaze drifted to the crowded platform above the President. One face stood out in the swarm of onlookers, one that sent a chill down her spine.

Mr. Booth?

A passerby bumped her shoulder, the distraction causing her to lose sight of the man she suspected was John Wilkes Booth. She knit her brows, her mind awhirl. Why would two staunch defenders of the South—Booth and her uncle—want to witness the president's inauguration?

Perhaps she was mistaken. Perhaps it wasn't Mr. Booth at all.

Shielding her eyes against the midday sun, she perused the spot where the pasty-complexioned man once stood.

But like a bird taken flight, he was gone.

37

City Point Depot, March 28, 1865

T he morning breeze held a chill as Drew sauntered toward the cluster of soldiers peering down into the wharf area from the bluff. His mouth twisted. Ogling one of the officer's wives, no doubt, by the way they were clamoring for a better view. The long, uneventful winter had taken its toll on the lot of them. The recent battle at Fort Stedman had awakened them from their stupor. Though they'd won the skirmish and taken scores of prisoners, the unexpected Confederate attack had them all a bit antsy to end this war and return home.

Visions of Caroline's ready smile and pleasant features invaded his thoughts. No one was more eager for this conflict to end than he was. Drew tugged at the sleeves of his new captain's uniform. News of the promotion came just after Christmas, a result of Lieutenant Schaff's commendation after extinguishing the wharf fire. Though honored, he'd almost been disappointed to leave Captain Lansing. Between Lansing and Jacobs, he'd witnessed the best and worst of what an officer should be.

He was still getting used to the thought of being in charge of an entire company of men.

Edging up beside the soldiers, Drew clasped his hands together behind his back. "Find something of interest, Private Knolls?"

"Sure did. Look who's standing on the pier alongside the River Queen." The curly-headed private eased back, his animated expression sobering as his gaze fell on Drew. "Sorry, Captain."

Snapping to attention, he nudged the private next to him. Upon seeing Drew, the second soldier alerted his buddies, who, each in turn, stepped away from the bluff. The group of soldiers stood erect, arms at their sides, chins tipped high.

Drew arched a brow. "And who might that be, Private?"

"The President, sir."

Drew's jaw slackened at the unexpected response. He craned his neck for a look. He'd heard rumors President Lincoln had arrived at City Point, but none that had been substantiated.

Private Knolls held out his field glasses. "See for yourself, sir."

Taking the glasses, Drew sought out the River Queen docked at the pier. His eyes widened as the lanky man in black came into focus. There was no mistaking the bearded gent in the felt top hat. Engaged in conversation, the President nodded to his companions, General Grant and General Sherman. An admiral approached, and after a glance around the wharf, ushered the three aboard the River Queen.

Drew watched until the foursome disappeared inside the riverboat then lowered the field glasses. Obviously, some sort of important meeting. What he wouldn't give to listen in on the conversation.

The private took back his field glasses, his expression earnest. "Do ya think they're plotting how to finish off the Rebs, sir?"

Not wishing to give the soldier false hope, Drew responded with caution. "I imagine ending the war is never far from their thoughts."

The gangly private next to him tugged at his sagging

trousers. "If the hoard of prisoners we took at Fort Stedman is any indicator, the Rebs have about had it. The way I see it, we'll have this war wrapped up in no time."

Though Drew gave no response, he prayed the private was right. Countless lives had been shattered by injury and death, and the land itself was ravaged and scarred. Even after the war ended, it would likely take years for the country to lick its wounds. Hatred and bitterness had ruled far too long. But like a bad omen, the knot in his stomach hinted there was more to come.

March 29, 1865

CAROLINE TURNED the page of her uncle's medical book, studying the diagrams more than the words. Over the months, she'd grown less squeamish at the sight of them. She still couldn't decipher all the complicated medical terminology, but what she *had* gleaned fascinated her.

Uncle Samuel strode into the room and shook his head, arms crossed over his chest. "It seems you never tire of poring over these books."

Pressing a finger to hold her place, she grinned up at him. "There's so much to learn. How do you remember it all?"

"I don't." He wagged his finger at her. "A good doctor or nurse never stops learning. New procedures are being developed even as we speak. Much of the information you're reading there is more than likely outdated."

"In fact ... " He arched a brow. "You may as well have one."

Caroline searched his face for signs of jesting. "You don't mean it?"

He chuckled. "Why not? It will give me an excuse to update my library." He ran his fingers over the row of books. "Ah, here's a good one. My very first one. *A Manual of General Anatomy.*"

He pulled it from the shelf and held it out to her. "Here you are."

"Oh, but I couldn't."

"You'd be doing me a favor." He leaned in closer, cupping a hand to whisper. "Frankie will never let me spend money on a new edition so long as I have the old one."

A smile crossed Caroline's lips as she took it from him. "Then I accept. Thank you."

With a nod, he closed the desk hutch doors. "Now, if you'll excuse me. I have some business to attend to."

"Certainly." Closing the book she'd been reading, she stood and clutched the one he'd given her to her chest.

He turned his back to her and worked to straighten the cluttered desk. "Shut the door behind you, please."

"Yes, Uncle." With a tug on the door, Caroline pursed her lips. Her uncle's recent behaviors puzzled her—his bouts of secrecy, his unexplained outings, his connection to John Wilkes Booth, and his attendance at the inauguration.

He seemed especially fixated on the whereabouts of the President, becoming agitated whenever Lincoln received too much notoriety. Perhaps he'd simply become disgruntled at President Lincoln winning another term. Whatever advantage her uncle believed might tip the war in the South's favor never materialized. She longed to inquire about it but refrained lest he become angry with her.

Caroline crossed to her bedroom and eased onto the mattress, an unsettled feeling in her stomach. According to *Harper's Weekly*, starvation and disease were claiming more Confederate lives than warfare. Each week, newspaper headlines grew grimmer, reporting numerous lost battles and dwindling provisions.

She traced her fingers along the frayed edges of the medical book. If the South succumbed to the North, what would happen? Would the two sides continue to be at odds?

Her stomach lurched. Men like Papa and Uncle Samuel

would not surrender their ways lightly. How many others would offer resistance? Would violence and unrest continue even after the fighting ceased?

Over recent weeks, she'd pushed thoughts of Drew aside, not allowing her heart to hope. By now, he'd likely forgotten their brief encounter, the tender moments they'd shared in the shanty.

Her throat caught. If he still lived.

She blinked back the moisture brimming her eyes. Their abrupt parting left little opportunity to voice what was in their hearts. Jamison's angry threat had severed their budding relationship. Papa sending her away had snuffed out any hope of it altogether.

Closing her eyes, she bowed her head, a tear dampening her cheek. *Lord, my heart is grieved over this war, as I know Yours must be as well. May You bring a swift resolution to the conflict and bring peace and healing to our nation, whoever emerges the victor. Please watch over Drew. May You grant him health and safety.*

She squeezed her eyes tighter.

And, if it be Your will, allow him to find his way to me.

38

Midnight, Sunday, April 2, 1865
SW of Petersburg

"Well, goodbye boys. This means death." The foreboding whisper cut through the stillness as Drew's company, along with the rest of General Wright's Sixth Corps, stumbled their way into no-man's land with only a half-moon and stars to ease the thick darkness.

Drew bristled. Such talk was pure poison. Didn't the soldier have any regard for his comrades?

Word of the daring mission to infiltrate the Confederate stronghold surrounding Petersburg came on the heels of yesterday's victory at Five Forks. He could still hear the whoops and hollers of the men celebrating. In contrast, General Grant had responded with signature calmness. Yet, the much-needed triumph seemed a vague memory in light of the daunting task that lay before them.

A solemn mood settled over the men as they moved into position to strike. Prior attempts to break through the Rebel boundaries had ended in retreat and severe casualties.

Apparently, some of the men feared this maneuver would end much the same.

Drew and his company hunkered in a grove of trees, awaiting the signal to press forward. They kept their rifles loaded but not capped, lest one go off accidentally and expose their position. At their head, a team of "pioneer" soldiers with axes waited poised to cut through the hedge of abatis and the wooden *chevaux-de-frise*. The string of sharpened timbers and bent trees were all that stood between them and the Rebs.

He shifted his feet, the heel of his right boot sinking in the mud. Recent heavy rain left the earth saturated, the cool, damp air making his shoulder ache. A chorus of spring peepers called from a distant creek bed, momentarily transporting him back to better days—when he, Luke, and Papa had hunted frogs by lantern light in the shallows of Sutter's Pond. He'd not realized how carefree life had been in his youth. Despite the chores and rigors of farm life, he'd had time for leisure that now seemed a luxury he would never regain.

The snap of a twig brought him back to the present. He tightened his grip on his rifle and glanced around. When no one stirred, he again fixed his gaze on the flickering campfires of the Rebel forts that taunted him from a distance. The waiting seemed endless. Even in the silence, he could feel the tension in the air, sense the eagerness of the men to pounce upon the unsuspecting Rebs.

He rolled a kink from his shoulders. It must be nearing midnight—the designated time to advance. While other corps were positioning for a frontal attack and Fort Mahone to the east, General Wright's Sixth Corps had been commissioned to infiltrate the southwest region of the Confederate defenses along the Boydton Plank Road. If successful, they would breach the Rebel lines and put an end to this ongoing siege. Without Petersburg, Richmond would be defenseless.

Drew's heart pumped faster. If the Confederate capital fell, the war could end within a fortnight. The very thought revitalized him.

One side of his mouth lifted. He had a promise to keep.

He drew a prayerful breath. *Bring an end to it, Lord.*

A barrage of rapid gunfire ricocheted through the vale, setting his hair on end.

This was it.

Though the signal to advance became lost in the volley of blasts, the raucous noise was enough to spur the company to action. Doing his best to block out the barrage of cannon fire and guns flaring about him, Drew was grateful for the steady glow of muzzle flashes to light the way. Up ahead, the pioneer soldiers wielded their axes, clearing a path. A chorus of shouts rang out from the men, mingling with the constant roar of gunfire; commotion enough to drive a man mad.

Hours of grueling forward movement brought them ever closer to the Confederate trenches. Return fire intensified, and a soldier to Drew's left let out a shrill cry and dropped to the ground. Others fell around him. The troops slowed their advance, faces distorted with fear and fatigue. Drew urged them on—they were too close to falter now.

Too much was at stake.

As the first hint of color spilled onto the horizon, Boydton Plank Road came into view. On the opposite side, the flash of guns revealed chaotic scrambling in and around the Rebel earthworks, reminiscent of a colony of ants that had veered off course. The Confederate defense appeared sparse in comparison to the onslaught of approaching Union forces.

Drew's boot kicked against something soft, almost tripping him. Glancing down, his heart sank at the outline of a body on the ground. With the horde of men around him, he had no choice but to step over the fallen soldier and press forward. Those ahead of him weaved in and out as if the ground were littered with the dead and dying. Sorrow tore at Drew. The daring mission came at a high price for many.

His mouth turned cottony. Would he be the next to fall?

Caroline's honey eyes and chestnut hair flashed through his mind. He couldn't die now. Not when the war's end seemed so near. He'd promised to return, and Lord willing, he intended to keep that vow.

Excited shouts filled the early dawn air, and the pace of those in front of Drew quickened. Reaching in his belt for a cap, he strained to see beyond the rows of infantry. Though darkness still overshadowed the landscape, he caught a glimpse of the downed Confederate pickets up ahead. A surge of adrenaline flooded through him at the realization that a breach in Petersburg's defenses was imminent.

His rifle and bayonet ready, Drew plunged ahead, alongside the sea of soldiers. Blue and gray intermingled, gouging and slashing at each other, desperately fighting for their lives. Drew stared into the faces of the Rebels, keeping watch for Jamison and praying their paths wouldn't cross. At last, he and his men overpowered the Confederates. The ground fairly shook as the band of Union soldiers rushed forward. Wave after wave of blue-clad infantrymen poured across the lines onto Rebel sod.

Something foreign stirred within Drew as he raced after them. A sensation he'd not felt in a long while.

Hope.

39

April 3, 1865
Outskirts of Richmond, Virginia

Exhaustion tore at Drew's limbs. As if the fight to infiltrate Petersburg hadn't been enough, the twenty-five-mile trek to Richmond had taken every last ounce of his strength. Breaking for a few hours of sleep did little to relieve the fatigue in his feet and lower back. And yet, as the Confederate capital came into view, his spirit revived.

"Look at that, Captain," whispered Private Knolls. "The Rebs must've heard we was comin' and lit out of here."

Plumes of smoke billowed over the Confederate capital, tainting the brightness of the midday sun. Fire shot up from buildings and warehouses throughout the city, amber flames reflecting off the darkened surface of the James River.

Optimism stirred within him, and he nodded. "It looks that way."

The private released a long sigh. "Good. 'Cause I'm too bushed t' fight any more Rebs."

Drew smothered a grin. "I think that speaks for us all."

He stared in amazement at the shattered ruins of the former

Confederate stronghold and Union cavalry soldiers patrolling Richmond's streets. His heart hammered. Had they taken the capital city without so much as a shot fired?

A sense of pride and relief stole over him at the sight of the United States flag flying at the front of the Capitol building, a stiff south breeze whipping it side to side. Four long years of bitter fighting finally paid off.

His stomach clenched. But at what price?

An explosion split the air, and the troops fell back. Drew flinched as black smoke poured from a warehouse near the ironworks.

Private Knolls raised his gun, the whites of his eyes showing.

Drew motioned him to calm. "Most likely ammunition going off."

The private nodded and slowly lowered his rifle, visibly shaken.

Drew understood the young man's jitters. They'd been through so much. Boys forced into manhood, fighting to stay alive long enough to return to their kin. He could only pray this conquest would ensure a quick end to the war.

Drew signaled his men to proceed across the river. Their field boots clicked in unison along the pontoon bridge, sharp and steady. Confederate bills littered the ground beneath them, a sure sign the Rebels had lost their will to fight. The once-treasured currency now seemed a forgotten remnant of a cause nearing its demise.

In silent reverence, they infiltrated the ruined city. Drew stared into the embittered faces of the convalescent soldiers and black-garbed women and children lining the rubble-filled streets, their hardened expressions chiseling a cavern in his soul. Taking Richmond was no small matter. Years of hatred and bitterness had scarred this land, these people. How many months or years would it take to heal the damage?

More blasts sounded from the ironworks. Obviously, the Rebs had no intention of allowing the Union to gain control of anything of value. Bucket brigades attempted to douse the many fires peppering the city. A steady wind fueled the flames, showering the sultry air with hot embers. The scent of smoke and soot stung Drew's eyes as he glanced around.

A curly-headed corporal crossed the street, his gait and stance familiar. Drew craned his neck for a better look, and his lips lifted. For months, he'd kept watch for his kid brother but hadn't set eyes on him since Christmas. He'd prayed on Luke's behalf, never knowing if his prayers had been answered. Seeing him now—alive and in one piece—was like a breath of spring. *Thank you, Lord.*

He stepped over to his lieutenant, an over-eager yet likable fellow. "Take over here for me, Lieutenant Gibbons."

The lanky officer jutted his chin higher. "Yes, Captain."

Sauntering up behind Luke as he doused a fire, Drew nudged him on the arm. "I see you finally made it out of the trenches."

His brother whirled to face him, a huge grin covering his smudged face. Abandoning protocol, Luke flung his arms around him in a tight squeeze and gave him a firm pat on the back. "Hey, big brother. Never expected to meet up with you again."

Drew released his hold and took in his brother's ruddy complexion and sparkly blue eyes. "I was hoping our paths would cross. Just never dreamed it would be here in Richmond."

Luke's gaze settled on Drew's new uniform, and his mouth flew open. He brushed a hand over Drew's shoulder boards. "Look at you! A full-fledged captain. I believe if the war weren't about over, you'd make colonel by summer's end."

With a shake of his head, Drew tugged Luke's kepi down over his face. "Your head's always been full of fancies."

Luke chuckled and pushed the cap back on his head. He glanced around the charred city. "Isn't this great? We've finally got General Lee and the Johnny Rebs on the run. Won't be long till we're headed home."

Drew arched a brow, curious how his brother could so easily

overlook the devastation that had initiated the evacuation. "You sound pretty sure of that."

"Sure, I'm sure." He stuck his nose in the air and took a long sniff. "I can almost smell Mama's fried chicken."

A smile edged out Drew's uncertainty. He gave his brother a good-natured punch on the arm. "You've been in the trenches too long. All I smell is smoke."

"That's the trouble, big brother. You only see what's in front of you. No imagination."

He was right. No one would ever guess the two of them were brothers. They were as different as summer and winter, not only in appearance but temperament. While Drew analyzed everything, Luke leaped into life with both feet. Whether from pure pluck or unwavering faith, his little brother had never known a challenge too great.

A lesson he himself could stand to learn.

Drew cast a glance back at his men interspersed with other soldiers passing buckets of water. "I'd better get back." He took a step backward, then paused. "But if it turns out you're right, when you get home, tell Mama I'm coming but that I have something I need to do first."

Luke swiped a hand over his sweaty brow and squinted over at him. "You on some sort of secret mission or somethin'?"

Drew cleared his throat. "Something like that."

His face warmed under Luke's penetrating stare. A lopsided grin tugged at his brother's lips. "By the way your face is glowing, I'd say you've got yourself a lady friend."

Suppressing a grin, Drew shifted his gaze to his field boots and took a step back. "Just tell her I'll be home when I can."

"Will do, big brother."

A hearty laugh trailed after Drew as he turned and strode back to his men. He clasped his hands together behind him. Maybe Luke was right. Maybe the end of the war was within their grasp.

He swallowed. Just the possibility of seeing Caroline again

after all these months made him weak in the knees. Would she still wish to see him, or had the months eroded the memory of their short time together?

He took his place in the long line of soldiers, his stomach knotting. If his kid brother could so easily undo him, how would he face Caroline's outraged father and brother?

40

April 10, 1865

The gallop of hooves pulled Caroline's attention to the worn path leading to her aunt and uncle's yard. She leaned on her broom handle, attempting to distinguish the rider, his bulky frame bent over the sturdy chestnut's neck. The speed of his approach made her wonder if her uncle would need to be summoned from the fields. Propping her broom against the door frame, she downed the front steps, finally identifying the rider as Ned Maynard.

Her spirit plummeted. What had he done to injure himself now?

She strode to the yard fence to greet him, casting a glance toward the barren tobacco fields. Her shoulders dipped. Where was Uncle when she needed him? Returning her attention to the approaching visitor, she did her best to assess his well-being. Though his expression remained shadowed by his tattered, wide-brimmed hat, his demeanor seemed marked with great urgency. By all appearances, he looked coherent, with no visible signs of injury. Perhaps his wound would be minor enough she could tend to it herself.

Or, heaven forbid, was it his wife that required attention?

Caroline paused outside the yard gate, intent on looking the part of a capable nurse. As Mr. Maynard reined his horse to an abrupt halt in front of her, she took a step back to avoid the spray of dirt from the horse's hooves. Shielding her eyes against the mid-morning sun, she squinted up at the harried neighbor. "Good day, Mr. Maynard. Are you and the missus well?"

He struggled for breath, his full cheeks spreading in a curious scowl. "Have you heard the news?"

She blinked, probing her mind for some critical, forgotten tidbit. "What news?"

His stubbled jaw twitched. "The war. It's over."

Caroline drew a hand to her chest and rocked back on her heels. Though she had no reason to doubt Ned Maynard's word, the news seemed too incredible to believe. "You—you're certain?"

"Yes'm. Got the word this mornin'. Lee surrendered down at the Appomattox Courthouse just yesterday."

She wavered, uncertain how to respond or react. The news, though welcome, teemed with uncertainties. What would it mean for the South and the thousands upon thousands of men who'd fought four long years to preserve their way of life? What would it mean for her family? For her?

For Drew?

Her mind reeled. And what of Jamison? Had he died in vain?

Moisture stung her eyes, and her heart drummed at the swarm of emotions the news kindled. With a hard swallow, she gathered her wits. "I thank you for informing us, Mr. Maynard."

He shook his head. "It's a sorry day for us all." Tightening the reins, he wheeled his horse to the left. "Be sure to pass the news on t' Doc and his missus."

Still a bit dazed, Caroline strained to find her voice. "I will."

With a brisk nod and a tip of his worn hat, he clicked his cheek and tapped his heels in his horse's flanks. The animal lurched forward, jolting him back in the saddle.

The creak of the door behind her startled Caroline. She turned to see her aunt peering after Mr. Maynard from the house steps, young Samuel Jr. perched on her hip. "Was that Ned?"

Nodding, Caroline took a tentative step toward her. "Yes."

She tugged her son's roving fingers from her hair and gestured toward the fleeing neighbor. "He left in a rush. What did he want?"

Struggling to rein in her frayed emotions, Caroline took a steadying breath. "To share news the war has ended."

Her aunt's eyes widened, the slack in her jaw causing her face to appear gaunt. "In favor of the South?"

With a slight shake of her head, Caroline strode closer. "I'm afraid not. General Lee has surrendered."

Aunt Frances slumped against the door frame, sending the propped-up broom toppling to the ground, her face blanching. "Lee? Surrender? It can't be." Her eyes glossed over and trailed to the sprigs of new spring grass below her. "I hate to think how Samuel will take the news."

Caroline's chest squeezed, certain her uncle's response would be tame compared to her father's. In a way, she was thankful not to be home to witness the tirade, but most of her yearned for her mother's arms and Rose's sweet, comforting presence.

Aunt Frances shrugged, her lips flattening in a thin line. "Well, I'm relieved it's over. Perhaps now, at least, the ravaging and killing will end." At Samuel Jr.'s soft whine, she retreated inside the house.

As the door clicked shut, an ominous sensation pulsed through Caroline. It would take more than a mere surrender to extinguish the flames of hatred that plagued their land. This nation had a rough road ahead to establish peace. Only the Lord could restore the severed ties between North and South.

With a deflated sigh, she stooped to retrieve her fallen broom. Until hatred was banished, there could be no room for healing.

Nor was there hope for her and Drew.

April 11, 1865

DREW RELEASED A LONG BREATH. The trek to Monocacy Junction seemed endless. Two days had passed since word came of Lee's surrender at Appomattox Courthouse. He'd spent half of that time trying to wrap his mind around the fact that the war had all but ended and the other half thinking of a way to keep his promise to Caroline. Fortunately, he'd finagled a week's leave. It wasn't much time, but hopefully enough to convince Caroline he intended to keep his word.

He reached to pat Angel's neck. Though a bit saddlesore from lack of riding, it felt good to be astride her again. Once he reached Monocacy Junction, he'd retrace his way to the section of timber where Caroline found him. The rest would be guesswork since he'd been unconscious.

Having tucked his captain's jacket and hat in his knapsack to avoid unwanted suspicion, he kept a sharp eye out for signs of hostile Confederates. More than likely, some hadn't yet received word of Lee's surrender. Come to think of it, it probably wasn't smart to be roaming about Rebel territory so soon.

But he couldn't help it. This time his heart had overruled his head.

41

April 12, 1865

Caroline flattened her boots on the floor of the carriage and shifted on the hard seat. She glanced at her uncle, his sober expression betraying a troubled spirit. Since learning the outcome of the war, he'd become more withdrawn, his mood touchy at best. She stared at the passing scenery, seeking a way to engage him in conversation. At last, she cleared her throat. "Did Myra say what ailed the twins?"

Uncle Samuel tapped the reins on the horse's rump, keeping his gaze fixed on the path ahead. "From her description, it sounds very much like the croup." He again fell silent, with only the rhythmic turn of the carriage wheels to fill the void.

In those quiet moments, Caroline's mind stirred up memories better forgotten, thoughts of Drew, Jamison, and her father. Tightness pulled at her chest. Jamison's absence still haunted her like a recurring nightmare ... as did her father's rage. Recalling his harsh words still made her shudder. In contrast, Drew's tender goodbye lingered in her heart, warming her very core. Every inch of her longed to know if he would hold true to his promise to return. The hope was almost enough to convince her to go against her father's decree and plead for another chance.

But she couldn't. No, she *wouldn't* give him that satisfaction.

Pain shot through the back of her hand where her fingernails cut into the skin. Forcing herself to relax, she eased back on the carriage seat and rubbed the throbbing indentations with her fingertips. Clearly, her anger at him hadn't relinquished its hold.

"Now that the war is over, have you given any more thought to your pursuit of nursing?"

She startled at her uncle's abrupt question—one she'd sought an answer to many times, to no avail. But this was the first time her uncle had inquired of her plans, which made her wonder if she was in danger of outstaying her welcome. "Yes. I have."

"And what did you decide?"

Lacing her hands together, she considered how to respond. With the war ended, there was no reason she couldn't leave. But, where would she go? Certainly not home. Did she have enough skill to seek a position as a nurse? Helping her uncle tend patients was one thing, but working in a hospital would be much more taxing.

She released an unsteady breath. "I'd like to pursue nursing. I'm just uncertain how to go about it."

He jutted out his lower lip, glancing her way for the first time. "Assuming you plan to return home, I would suggest the hospital in Frederick a suitable place to start. I'd be happy to write you a reference."

"Thank you, Uncle." Though her heart plummeted, she mustered a weak grin. Her aunt and uncle's home had provided an apt setting to suppress her troubles. Now, it seemed, her time with them was coming to an end. Yet, with no funds to live on, how would she manage until she secured a position? Mama would see she had what she needed if she could only contact her.

She swallowed the lump in her throat. Would she be forced

to beg for her father's mercy after all? The very thought made her ill. As far as she knew, she'd done nothing to warrant his rancor but received nothing else.

A sigh escaped her. There must be another way.

Monocacy Junction area
April 13, 1865

DREW PERUSED the countryside with his field glasses. Three houses dotted the landscape. Was one of them Caroline's? His cheeks flinched. If only he could spot the shanty where he'd stayed. From there, he'd likely be able to decipher which manor belonged to her family.

Tapping his heels to Angel's flanks, he reined her in the direction of the closest homestead.

His stomach tightened. He only hoped her father or brother wouldn't shoot him on sight. The sound of a hoe scraping loose soil pulled his attention to the far left. As he rounded a grove of hickory trees, he spied a spindly fellow thinning a row of tobacco seedlings.

At his approach, the farmer paused and leaned on his hoe, a look of wariness overtaking his gaunt features.

Drew hoped his blue trousers were worn and faded enough not to draw attention. Yet, there'd be no disguising his Northern dialect. With a friendly nod, he tugged Angel to a stop at the edge of the field and rested his arm on his saddle horn. "Good day, sir."

The man continued to peer at him with narrowed eyes but gave no reply.

Undeterred by the man's silence, Drew cleared his throat and proceeded. "Could you tell me how to find the Dunbar residence?"

The farmer lifted his wide-brimmed hat and raked a soiled sleeve over his blistered forehead, his pinched features marred by suspicion. "Who wants to know?"

Drew waffled, uncertain how to provide an honest answer. "I'm an acquaintance of Jamison and Miss Caroline's." It was a stretch, but true nonetheless.

The man stared at him long and hard, one eye scrunched as though trying to decipher if he spoke the truth. "I've not seen hide nor hair of Miss Caroline for months, but I hear tell Jamison was killed in an explosion a while back."

The news hit Drew like a minié ball to the chest. Surely not the explosion at Petersburg. His shoulders dipped. Caroline must be devastated. He gave a low sigh. "I'm sorry to hear that." He cast a pleading glance at the fellow. "Please. Then it's even more important I find Miss Caroline."

With a scratch of his chin, the man finally gestured to the rolling hills beyond. "Their place is a couple miles east of here. Second house."

"Thank you." Heavy-hearted, Drew reined Angel in that direction. Knowing Caroline's close attachment to Jamison, his untimely death must have shattered her. Drew grappled with unwelcome fear, wondering if she would somehow hold the loss against him. How thankful he was not to have taken any lives there.

With each stride, the ground beneath him seemed to lengthen. He prodded Angel faster, eager to see Caroline face to face and learn the truth of her feelings. At last, he came to the house amid sprawling, freshly worked fields. He perused the area for signs of life, but the midday sun and the rumble in his belly assured him the reason the fields were empty.

As he dismounted, his heart drummed faster. Interrupting the family's noontime meal would ensure an audience but might not work in his favor. Nothing in the landscape looked familiar, yet Drew trusted the neighbor had steered him correctly. The shanty was nowhere in sight; Caroline had been wise to choose such a secluded place to tend to him.

With a deep breath, he approached the front door. The brick house, though elegant with its white, ivy-coated pillars and painted window sills, looked a bit weathered, as if the years of war had snuffed the life and soul from it. Clasping the door knocker, he hesitated but a moment before giving three solid taps.

He tugged at his shirt collar, his sweat-drenched neck and brow more from nerves than the heat. Taking a step back, he clutched his hands together at his front and whispered a silent prayer—one of many he'd lifted heavenward in the past few days. After what seemed an eternity, heavy footsteps lumbered closer. His breaths shallowed as the door eased open, exposing a heavyset servant, her dark skin contrasting with the whites of her widened eyes. "May I helps ya, sir?"

Drew cleared his throat, doing his best to ward off the unsteadiness in his voice. He'd waited months for this moment— months that seemed like years. "I wish to speak with Miss Caroline, if I may."

At his request, moisture pooled in the servant's eyes. She cut a glance over her shoulder and, with a forlorn shake of her head, her eyes dipped downward. Her sorrowful expression sliced its way to Drew's very core. In a voice so small he had to lean in to hear, she said, "Miss Caroline's gone."

Following her lead, he responded in hushed tones. "Gone? Where?"

The scoot of a chair stilled the maid's reply. Hurried footsteps sounded down the hall toward them. Averting her gaze, the servant inched back to allow a middle-aged man to approach. Though the man's sour features and stocky frame bore no resemblance to Caroline, without a doubt, he was her father.

Drew met his piercing glare with a steady gaze of his own. "Mr. Dunbar?"

The man's upper lip lifted in a snarl. "Who are you?"

He gave a slight tip of his head, careful not to include his rank in his answer. "Andrew Gallagher. I've come to inquire about your daughter, Caroline."

Contempt streamed from Mr. Dunbar's eyes. "I have no daughter by that name."

With that, he attempted to wedge the door shut, only to have Drew slip his boot in to prevent it. "Please, sir. If you could only tell me what's become of her."

Widening the door, Mr. Dunbar leaned forward and spat in Drew's face. "Git out of here, you blasted Yank, before I fetch my gun and pump you full of buckshot."

Drew tensed and wiped the warm spittle from his face, struggling to compose himself. "I understand your resentment, Mr. Dunbar, but if you could only tell me where to find her, I'll be on my way."

Without a word, he left his post at the door and marched down the hall, most likely to make good on his threat. A woman and young girl clung to each other at the end of the hall as he passed, distress and sorrow intermingling in their expressions. The maid stepped closer, her rounded face scarred by worry. "You best skedaddle, mis'er, if'n ya wanna see nightfall."

"Go!" The frantic plea blared from the woman down the hall, the pitch in her voice and shape of her eyes identifying her as Caroline's mother.

Drew wavered until heavy boot steps and the cock of a rifle from a side room convinced him he had no choice. He turned and sprinted to Angel, hopping onto the saddle and reining her around in one smooth motion. Kicking his heels in her side, he bent low and clung to her neck as she galloped away. A shot rang out behind and zinged past just inches above Angel's left ear.

Too close for comfort.

Drew molded himself to her neck, urging her faster with another knock of his heels. He wasn't about to stick around to see whether Mr. Dunbar had merely fired a warning shot or missed unintentionally. By the time he reloaded, Drew intended to be well out of reach.

With each stride, his heart sank deeper. Worse than being shot at was the thought he'd missed his chance to find Caroline.

42

Outskirts of Washington
April 14, 1865, 11:00 pm

D rew shifted in his saddle. The last thing he'd figured on was backtracking forty miles to Washington. Had his hopes all been for nothing? The request for leave. The lengthy trip. Months of hoping and dreaming of a reunion with Caroline had melted like spring snow. He hated to give up so easily, but the servant plainly said Caroline was gone. And her father claimed not even to know her.

It made no sense.

One thing was certain: he would gain nothing by going back. The hostile greeting didn't bode well for a second attempt. His only option was to cut his leave short and head back. If he had his bearings, he ought to reach Washington in time to secure a room for the night.

He raked a hand over his face, tortured by the unknown. What had become of Caroline? Had she been so grieved by her brother's death that she'd felt compelled to leave? Or, worse yet, had her benevolence towards him been found out, and she suffered the consequences? The very idea tore him up inside.

The yearning to find her gnawed at him. He'd thought of little else since his abrupt departure yesterday noon. Yet, he felt helpless to do so. He could only pray the Lord would keep her well and safe and that if they were meant to be together, the Lord would find a way.

At last, he reached the outskirts of Washington. Fatigue tore at his limbs. All he could think about was finding a hotel bed to collapse into and sleep.

If his restless mind would allow it.

He guided Angel along the cobblestone street, a string of gaslights brightening his way. For such a late hour, the city seemed astir with activity. His path was congested with horse-drawn rigs, men on horseback, and pedestrians dashing about, their excited voices filling the air with unwanted clamor. Heavy military presence hemmed the bustling street, the soldiers' expressions guarded as if some unwelcome threat had them on edge.

Eager to learn the cause of the commotion, Drew halted Angel beside one of the soldiers. The young corporal stared up at him expectantly, his expression haggard. Drew leaned toward him, raising his voice above the ruckus. "What goes on here, Corporal? The entire city seems in an uproar."

The young man's face pinched. "It's the President, sir. He's been shot."

Drew slumped back in his saddle, his jaw slackening. It couldn't be. Just days ago, he'd witnessed Lincoln walking the streets of Richmond, surrounded by crowds of newly-freed men and women, cheering.

He hung his head. *Lord help us; this conflict isn't over yet.*

43

April 15, 1865, 4 a.m.

Caroline started at the pounding on the downstairs door. She blinked her eyes wider, shaking off sleepiness in the darkened room. She stilled, listening, her heart ticking loud against the silence. Who would be calling at such a time of night? A patient, perhaps? Someone sick or injured?

Murmurs and the creak of her aunt and uncle's bed assured her they'd heard the knock as well. Footsteps dragged down the hall to the door. Hushed men's voices wound their way through her closed bedroom door. She strained unsuccessfully to make out the words. Should she see if she could be of help?

When shuffling feet and the men's voices shifted to the parlor, she sat up and groped for her robe. If nothing more, she should at least find out what it was about. She slid out of bed and made her way toward the door. As she clicked it open, she could distinguish her uncle's voice conversing with the other men in low tones.

Tiptoeing into the hall, she was relieved the children seemed undisturbed by the disruption. Quietly, she ventured halfway down the stairs until she glimpsed the glow of dim lantern light in the parlor below.

"Your ankle is swollen. I'll need to cut your boot off to determine if the leg is broken." She heard her uncle declare.

"We're in a hurry, Doc. Do what you need to." The voice was unfamiliar to Caroline, but its urgency spoke of desperation.

The sound of ripping leather split the quiet.

Assured the man was a patient in need of care, Caroline descended the remaining stairs and edged closer to the parlor entrance. In the dim light, she glimpsed her uncle bent beside a man reclining on the settee, his leg exposed and outstretched. His features were shadowed, his face tilted downward.

Her uncle sighed deeply. "It's fractured and will need to be splinted."

The other man paced back and forth behind the settee like a caged dog. "Can you fix him up where he can ride?"

"Possibly. But I have no splint. I'll have to make one."

As Caroline stepped into the room, the pacing man paused, a flash of distrust in his eyes.

Uncle Samuel glanced her way, and she spoke quickly. "I thought you might need some help."

He hesitated but a moment before nodding. "Yes. I think Frankie has a bandbox around here somewhere. Fetch it for me. We can use it to fashion a splint."

Caroline recalled seeing the box in the hall closet. Making her way to it, she fumbled in the dark to unlatch the door. She reached toward the upper shelf, grateful when her hands fastened on the thin, wooden, cylinder-shaped hatbox.

With careful strides, she returned to the parlor and handed the box to her uncle. For the first time, she caught a glimpse of the injured man and sucked in a breath. "Mr. Booth! What happened?"

His agonized features squeezed tighter, his dark eyes momentarily shifting toward the young man behind him. "I— came off my horse."

Caroline refrained from questioning him further and stooped to help her uncle dismantle the bandbox. Forty-five minutes later, the split was intact, and Mr. Booth and his friend were eager to be on their way. Mr. Booth grimaced as Uncle Samuel helped him to his feet. Her uncle swiped a hand down his goatee. "Don't you think it wise to stay the remainder of the night and get a fresh start in the morning? We've a couple of beds in the upstairs guest room." He turned to Caroline. "That is, if my niece doesn't mind moving to the children's room."

She shook her head. "Not at all."

The two men locked eyes, seeming to deliberate silently with each other. Mr. Booth tested his leg on the floorboards once more and cringed. "Perhaps it would be best. A bed sounds much more inviting at the moment."

Uncle Samuel gave a curt nod. "Come. I'll get you situated."

Taking up the lantern and the discarded riding boot, Caroline lit the way for them. As she started up the stairs, one question troubled her—what was a famed actor like Booth doing roaming the countryside on horseback in the middle of the night?

Washington, April 15, 10 a.m.

"I'm glad you're here, Captain Gallagher. With your tracking skills, General Grant wants you on this."

Drew stared at General Rawlins, taken aback by the unexpected request. "Yes, sir."

Still reeling from news of President Lincoln's death, Drew was as eager as anyone to locate the killer. But, General Grant's confidence in him was a bit unnerving. He glanced around the impressive stateroom with its ornate chandeliers and lush curtained windows. When he'd chosen the Willard Hotel to stay the night, he never imagined he'd happen across General Rawlins—or a new assignment.

Rawlins motioned to the plush, upholstered chair across from him and held out a copy of *The Daily Morning Chronicle*. "For the most part, Booth seems to have escaped unnoticed. The few leads we have indicate he and another unknown man headed south toward Piscataway. General Dix has already dispatched a Cavalry patrol down that way."

Drew's brows pinched as he skimmed some of the headlines. "Sounds like some sort of conspiracy."

"It appears so. Besides the President, Vice President Johnson and Secretary Seward were also sought out. Both Secretary Seward and his son were injured." General Rawlins raked a hand over his long beard. Fresh in from Lee's surrender at Appomattox Courthouse, his bloodshot eyes relayed weariness. "There are even suspicions that if General Grant hadn't left town, he, too, might have been targeted."

Drew flinched. Such a conspiracy, along with President Lincoln's passing, on the heels of what seemed a great victory, dealt a terrible blow to the finality of the war. He took another glance at the newspaper. "It says here Booth was injured."

Rawlins nodded. "He hurt his leg jumping onto the stage from the President's box. The injury wasn't severe enough to keep him from escaping."

"But it might slow him or cause him to seek refuge among those he knows are loyal to the Confederacy."

The general arched a brow and assented, "It might at that." He shot Drew an expectant gaze. "How soon can you leave?"

Thoughts of Caroline pricked at Drew. How he wished he was at liberty to seek out her whereabouts instead of being commissioned to pursue the President's assassin. In time, perhaps he could. But for now, his duty was clear.

His chin lifted. "I'll head out at once."

MR. BOOTH'S companion leaned back in his chair and rubbed a hand over his belly. "That was a mighty fine meal, ma'am."

Caroline eyed the young man whom they'd learned went by the name Davey Herold, his casual demeanor far different from the harried fellow she'd witnessed the night before.

Aunt Frances wiped the corners of her mouth. "Thank you. It's a shame Mr. Booth didn't feel up to joining us."

Mr. Herold snickered. "He won't know what he's missin'. Hasn't moved since he hit the bed."

Caroline set her fork on her plate. Mr. Herold himself had risen only long enough to eat breakfast and return to bed, reemerging just in time for the noon meal. What had tired them so?

Uncle Samuel sipped his tea. "Are you from around here, Mr. Herold?"

"Please, call me Davey." With a shake of his head, a mischievous grin spread across his full lips. "Nope, but I've been galavantin' about Charles County for months now."

"In search of property for Mr. Booth, no doubt."

Aunt Frances's innocent remark was interrupted by a loud guffaw from Davey. "Joy ridin', more like it."

Caroline shared her aunt's puzzled gaze. The young man seemed oblivious to Mr. Booth's earlier claim of seeking real estate in the area. Had he fabricated the story? Equally troubling, why had two able-bodied young men chosen to aimlessly chase around the countryside rather than join the war effort?

Leaning forward, Davey propped his elbows on the table and peered at Uncle Samuel. "I've been thinkin'. Even with the splint, John may not be up to ridin' horseback. Would you know where we could find ourselves a buggy?"

Uncle Samuel scrubbed a hand down his goatee. "Let's see. Tomorrow being Easter Sunday, one may be difficult to find." His eyes widened. "Why don't we ride over to my father's place? He might be able to scrape one up."

With a brisk nod, Davey was on his feet. "Well, all right then. Let's go."

Unsettled feelings plagued Caroline as the two donned their hats and made their way toward the door. Good-natured though he seemed, there was something disconcerting about young Davey Herold. In fact, the whole incident seemed rather peculiar. Try as she might, she couldn't shake the suspicion that he and Mr. Booth were up to no good.

44

April 15, 1865, 1 p.m.

Drew shifted in his saddle and cast a glance at the Potomac to the west. Even here, miles from Washington, pockets of soldiers roamed its banks, some standing guard, others milling haphazardly about, all keeping watch for one man. It was unlikely Booth would attempt to cross the river with it so heavily guarded. By now, he must be miles away.

But where? The possibilities seemed endless.

There was no way of knowing how intricately Booth planned his escape, but he couldn't have reckoned on being injured. That single detail could prove his undoing. If Drew could only deduce what the assassin's next step might have been.

He had to *think* like Booth. If he were in his place, what would he do?

Deep in thought, Drew curled his fingers tighter around the reins, rolling with the rhythm of Angel's smooth stride. A man like Booth would likely seek relief from pain in a bottle of whiskey. Maybe stop at a tavern; an out-of-the-way one, where he wouldn't stand out. More than likely, he'd passed through the area before news of the shooting spread. Taking no chances if he were smart. But maybe he had formed acquaintances.

Drew slid the photo General Rawlins had given him of Booth from his pocket. The actor's dark eyes stared back at him, a slight smirk on his thin lips. What would possess such a well-known public figure to commit such a heinous act? Despite Lee's surrender or Lincoln's 'malice towards none' speech, it seemed animosity between the North and South was still very much alive.

He returned his attention to the wide open countryside and the distant timber to the southeast. Booth could easily become swallowed up by the vastness of the landscape and reemerge where no one would ever find him. Word had it the South had its own underground network to aid southern sympathizers.

His mouth twisted. If so, finding Booth might prove more complicated than anyone dared imagine.

There was no way of knowing which direction Booth chose to take. Would he hang close to the river or head toward the wooded regions? Already, Drew could be miles off course. All he could do was go with his instincts and pray the Lord would guide his way.

April 15, 1865, 3 p.m.

RAPID HOOFBEATS APPROACHED, pulling Caroline's attention to the kitchen window.

Aunt Frances paused from kneading her mound of bread dough. "Who is it?"

"Mr. Herold." Caroline watched him dismount and dash toward the house. What was his hurry?

He tapped on the windowpane and motioned for her to let him in. Setting her chopping knife aside, she unbolted the side door. He entered a bit breathless, his stout frame making the kitchen seem smaller.

Aunt Frances looked past him to the yard beyond. "Did you find a rig?"

The young man shook his head. "No, ma'am. Doc's father said they need it for the Easter church service tomorrow. I came back with thoughts of tryin' our horses."

Aunt Frances brushed flour from her hands and took another glance outside. "Where's Samuel?"

Davey searched for an out-of-the-way place to stand, struggling with what to do with his arms. "He ... uh ... had some things t' do over at Bryantown. He'll be along after a while." The nervous tic in his voice made his attempt to appear casual unconvincing.

Caroline closed the door and returned to her dicing. Out of the corner of her eye, she could see him fidgeting with a knob on the corner china cabinet. No longer was he the calm young man she'd witnessed at noontime. Instead, he'd transitioned back into the jittery individual from the previous night.

He backed toward the dining room and bumped into the cutting table. "I reckon I'll go see if John's up."

With a handful of quick strides, he was to the hall and mounting the stairs. A moment later, the bedroom door hinged open and shut.

Aunt Frances shot Caroline a bewildered glance. "He seems a bit frazzled."

"He certainly does." She resumed her chopping, resisting the urge to voice her misgivings about both visitors. Something didn't sit right where they were concerned. And she feared her uncle was somehow a part of it.

Soft chatter drifted from the upstairs room, and Caroline longed to hear what was being said. A short time later, the door opened. Numerous moans and painstaking movements on the stairway pulled her and Aunt Frances from their duties. Her aunt's face scrunched as she wiped dough-crusted hands on her apron. "What on earth?"

Caroline followed her through the dining room and into the hall. The two men stood halfway down the stairs, Mr. Booth slumped against the railing. His pasty complexion bore a look of agony, his breaths coming rapid and shallow. With a gasp, Aunt Frances skittered up beside him. "Mr. Booth. You have no business moving about. Go back to bed. If you're hungry, I'll have one of the servant girls bring up a tray of food."

He shook his head. "We need to be on our way."

"You're in no condition to ride. At least wait until Samuel returns."

Booth seemed to waver and then nodded. "All right. But we'll saddle the horses and wait outside." The obstinate tone in his voice assured he'd accept no further arguments.

With slow, arduous steps, he downed the remaining stairs, a riding boot on one foot, the other bare, but for the splint on his leg. As he rounded the bottom step, Caroline's eyes jolted to the pistols strapped around his waist, and her heartbeat quickened. Why would an actor need such weapons? Nothing about this man seemed ordinary or rational.

She chose not to question him about the disturbing display but instead opened the hall door for them to exit. Using the crutches her uncle fashioned for him, Booth ambled outside and down the steps.

Two hours later, when Caroline was out back of the house emptying a dishpan of water, her uncle rode in almost as frantically as Mr. Herold had. She was about to round the corner of the house to greet him when she noticed the intensity of his scowl as he approached the duo of men outside the barn.

Retreating into the shadows at the side of the house, Caroline strained to hear the heated conversation.

"How dare you come here and endanger my family," her uncle's tenor voice carried in the night air, hushed yet clear.

Booth snickered. "Don't sound so high and mighty, Doc. You were willing enough to put in with us."

Uncle Samuel's tone bristled. "I agreed to kidnapping, not assassination. If I'd known last night what you'd done, I'd have sent you on your way then."

Caroline's hand flew to her mouth, stilling her sudden intake of breath. Kidnapping? Assassination? What had her uncle gotten himself mixed up in?

She cocked her ear, her heart pounding faster as her uncle continued. "Bryantown is crawling with soldiers. You must leave at once."

"Told ya," Davey's voice cut in. "We should've high-tailed it out of here hours ago."

"We will. Soon as the doc here tells us where to head and who to contact." Booth countered.

Samuel's response was immediate. "Head down that way toward Zekiah swamp and cut a wide berth several miles south and east through the timber until you're below Bryantown. You'll find safe refuge at the home of either William Burtles or Samuel Cox. Now, go!"

Groans sounded as Booth struggled to mount. Moments later, the canter of horses pulled Caroline's attention eastward. As dusk fell over the landscape, two figures moved along the worn path, heading toward the thick timber beyond.

Caroline clutched the empty dishpan to her chest and retraced her steps to the back of the house, her spirit shattered. She'd not thought her uncle capable of such a diabolical plot. Who had he wished to kidnap? And who'd been assassinated?

Her mind fled back to Christmas Eve and his jovial declaration that the war might soon tip in the South's favor. Were the two incidents somehow connected? If so, something must have gone terribly wrong. Someone of importance had been killed, and her uncle was privy to the knowledge.

Her hands quivered. And now, Lord help her, so was she.

April 15, 6 p.m. Surratt Tavern

DREW REINED Angel to the front of the two-story building, bearing the sign *Surratt Tavern, John Lloyd, Manager* at its front. This looked to be among one of the better-kept establishments in the string of taverns he'd investigated. Already he'd tired of the smell of whiskey and the less-than-virtuous atmosphere each possessed.

Dismounting, he breathed a weary sigh and fingered the newspaper clipping in his pocket. Most of the places he'd stopped had either shuffled him aside as a nuisance or told him to buy some whiskey or get out. Likely, this one would prove no different. Bolstering his resolve, he sauntered toward the tavern.

The scent of cigar smoke wafted out as he opened the door and stepped inside. Sectioned into various rooms, the building appeared to have at one time been a fine home. A burly man emerged from the room on the left, a half-filled whiskey bottle in one hand, an empty glass in the other. His bloodshot eyes narrowed as he took in Drew's uniform, finally meeting his gaze. "We're closed."

The slight slur of the man's words hinted that, despite the earliness of the evening, he'd already succeeded in taking the contents of the whiskey bottle down a few notches. Drew forced a grin. "I'm not here for a drink. Are you Mr. Lloyd?"

"What if I am?"

Ignoring his uncouth manner, Drew pulled the newspaper clipping with Booth's photo from his pocket. "I need to know if this man paid a visit here sometime late last night?"

Something akin to panic flashed in the man's eyes as Drew held out the clipping. Lloyd's mouth twitched slightly, and he cleared his throat, sobering. "No. No one like that came here." His words sounded forced, strained.

Hope stirred within Drew. The tavern manager seemed to know more than he was saying. "You're certain?"

The man lowered his gaze, his bulbous nose glowing red. "Yeah. I'm sure."

Withdrawing the clipping, Drew slipped it back in his pocket. "Thanks for your time, Mr. Lloyd. If he should happen by, please alert the nearest authorities."

Lloyd's eyes lifted to meet his briefly before he turned away. After two steps, he paused and pivoted toward Drew. "What'd he do?"

"Assassinated President Lincoln."

The man's face paled, and he gave a slight nod as he walked away.

Drew let himself out, a burning in his chest. Booth had been here. He could feel it. Lloyd may not be talking now, but at his first opportunity Drew intended to send a telegram to Washington suggesting the tavern manager be taken in for questioning. He might not know much, but he knew something.

Drew took a glance around. He had no idea where to go from here. But, for the first time, there was one thing he did know.

He was on the right track.

45

April 17, 1865, Late night

PRESIDENT LINCOLN ASSASSINATED BY
JOHN WILKES BOOTH

The newspaper heading churned in Caroline's mind like a bad dream. She stared at the darkened bedroom ceiling, unable to sleep. Had her uncle indeed been involved in a plot to kidnap the President? It didn't seem possible. And yet, she'd as much as heard it from his own lips.

At least she could console herself that he had nothing to do with the assassination. He'd sounded genuinely angry with Booth for his actions. She drummed her fingers on the mattress. Still, he'd let them go without alerting the authorities. Would his sin find him out?

For two days now, she'd deliberated whether to confide to her uncle she knew the truth. But each time she approached him, she lost courage. What concerned her most was that he displayed no sign of guilt or alarm. Instead, since Booth and Herold departed, he'd returned to his normal activities as if nothing was amiss.

While she was as restless as a frog on a creekbank.

With a sigh, she turned on her side and punched her pillow. Mere days ago, the man who'd killed President Lincoln had slept in this very bed. She tugged the covers tighter to her neck to ward off a chill. It seemed beyond belief. Her heart pulsed in her ears as she recalled her glimpse of Mr. Booth on inauguration day and the secretive meeting outside St. Mary's Church. Her suspicions about the man had proven true.

It was Uncle Samuel who'd disappointed. And now, she was in a quandary of what to do.

To confront him about the incident seemed futile. His intentions had not panned out, and to accuse him of wrongdoing would simply foster resentment. As far as she knew, he'd done nothing wrong save aiding fugitives. The question was, did she have the moral responsibility to pass on that information?

Or would her silence somehow convict her as well?

April 18, 1865, Bryantown, Maryland

DREW REINED Angel toward the Bryantown Tavern. Despite numerous attempts to pick up Booth's trail, he'd no fresh leads since his encounter with Lloyd three days ago. The heavy military presence here hinted this might be a good place to concentrate his efforts.

Tying Angel to the hitching post, he nodded to the elderly man seated on a wicker chair at the front of the building. The Southern gentleman sneered and turned his head, a clear reminder that Union officers weren't welcome here in the South. From what he'd heard, one would be hard-pressed to find a Union loyalist in Charles County.

Ignoring the snub, Drew made his way inside. His attention settled on a group of men gathered around a table and poring over a map. Unlike the man out front, their expressions livened as their heads veered toward him. Though only a couple wore uniforms, they looked military. One of the men strode over and greeted him with a salute. "Lieutenant David Dana of the 13th New York Cavalry, sir."

Returning the gesture, Drew scrunched his brow. "Why aren't you in uniform, Lieutenant?"

"My men and I are on assignment to locate the assassin, John Wilkes Booth, and find people more willing to talk when we're dressed as civilians."

Drew gave a brisk nod. "Clever. How goes the search? Any leads?"

The young lieutenant shook his head. "Nothing substantial. Our trail seems to have run cold. The only lead we have is from a Dr. George Mudd, a rare Union loyalist who mentioned two strangers having stopped by his cousin's place the night of the assassination."

The news sparked renewed hope in Drew. "What else does he know?"

"Detective Lovett is upstairs questioning him now."

Just then, two men ambled down the stairs, the first a burly fellow with a thick mustache, the other a well-dressed, distinguish-looking gentleman. The larger man gestured to the other fellow. "This man knows nothing, only that his cousin, a Dr. Samuel Mudd, treated a man for an injury the night of the assassination."

"Doctor, huh? What sort of injury?"

Drew's question garnered a curious stare from the man Lieutenant Dana referred to as Detective Lovett. "A broken leg."

Drew locked eyes with Lieutenant Dana. "Booth injured his leg jumping onto the stage. If he were in enough pain, it makes sense he would seek medical attention."

Nodding, Lieutenant Dana scratched at his chin. "It does at that." He cut a glance at the doctor. "What can you tell us about your cousin? Is he sympathetic toward the Union or the Confederacy?"

The doctor's gaze trailed downward. "I believe he favors the Confederacy."

Dana propped his foot on a chair. "And how did you come by this knowledge of the strangers' visit?"

Mudd's head lifted. "Samuel confided in me and asked that I pass the information on to the proper authorities."

"Why didn't he inform us himself?"

The doctor shrugged. "I'm not sure. Perhaps he thought, as someone with ties to the Union, it would be easier for me."

Lieutenant Dana glanced at Drew. "What do you think, Captain?"

Drew stepped up beside him. "As our only lead, I say it warrants checking into."

"I agree." The lieutenant turned to the doctor. "How far to your cousin's place?"

"About three miles. I'll take you there if you like."

He gave a curt nod and glanced at Drew. "You're welcome to ride along, Captain."

"Thank you, Lieutenant."

Dana pivoted toward the civilian-dressed soldiers at the table behind him. "Mount up, men, and let's be on our way."

"THAT'S my cousin's place, up ahead."

Drew took in the well-kept white frame house, trimmed in green. It seemed Dr. Samuel Mudd had done well for himself. Hemmed in by a white fence and several outbuildings, the spacious yard and home looked like an ideal place to rear a family.

The place appeared peaceful, with no sign of activity. Having removed his wool captain's jacket and hat to better blend in with the plain-clothed soldiers, Drew hung toward the back of the group of cavalrymen, allowing Lieutenant Dana, George Mudd, and the four detectives with them to take the lead. Despite

Drew's superior rank, he didn't wish to interfere with the ongoing investigation. If there were anything of substance to glean from the information Dr. Mudd provided, they would all benefit.

In response to George Mudd's knock, a woman, presumably Mrs. Mudd, appeared at the door and greeted him, a young boy in tow. From his position outside the yard fence, Drew saw her expression change from recognition to confusion as she took in the array of visitors.

"Good day, Frances. Is Samuel at home?"

Mrs. Mudd shook her head. "He's in the fields. What's this all about, George?"

"These men have some questions to ask him regarding the two strangers who came here the other night. I'll go fetch him."

Her cheeks went taut as she joggled the fussy child in her arms.

Another woman appeared in the doorway and took the boy from her. Drew strained to see past the soldier in front of him, but she'd disappeared before he'd barely caught a glimpse. His heart hammered. Maybe it was only wishful thinking, but something about her reminded him of Caroline. Same trim figure. Same chestnut hair. He shook off the thought. There must be dozens of women who fit that description.

As George Mudd made his way to his horse, Detective Lovett stepped forward to question Mrs. Mudd. "When did the strangers arrive, Ma'am?"

She brushed a wisp of hair from her forehead. "I'm not sure. Sometime in the night or early Saturday morning."

He nodded. "And how would you describe them?"

"I-I don't know. Average, I suppose. Brown hair. Medium height."

Her answers were vague, as if she were afraid to give much detail.

The detective shifted his feet, his baritone voice raising a notch. "How long were they here?"

Even from the yard fence, Drew could sense the woman growing more flustered with each inquiry.

"Your husband said one of the men was injured. What did he do to treat him?"

She gave an exasperated sigh. "I don't know. My niece was the one who assisted him. She could answer better than I. Caroline?"

Drew straightened, his pulse quickening at the name. Surely there couldn't be two Carolines so similar in appearance. He craned his neck for a better look, eagerly awaiting the woman's reemergence. As she stepped into view, a rush of warmth swelled in his chest. It *was* her. He could have searched for months on end and not found her. And yet, there she stood, beautiful as ever, as though the Lord had plucked her from hiding and placed her in his path.

A tender smile edged out the shock of seeing her. *The Lord doth work in mysterious ways.*

Deep longing enveloped him, and he fought the urge to push through to her side. But, how would it look for a Union officer to go falling all over himself after a Southern beauty? He'd do better to lay low and find out what had brought her here.

And even more importantly, what she knew about Booth.

CAROLINE PROPPED her boot on the yard fence and embraced the final amber hues of twilight, attempting to push away the unpleasantness of the day. How thankful she was that her uncle had come to deflect the questions away from her. And yet, she burned inwardly each time she recalled his half-truths and, at times, outright lies in regards to Mr. Booth. How could he deny knowing the man when he'd met with him on more than one occasion and even housed him under his roof?

She clutched the fence with her hands and leaned into it, her conscience pricked. Though she'd not been asked any direct questions regarding her knowledge of the fugitives, she couldn't get past the feeling that her silence rendered her just as guilty. Aunt Frances, too, had held her tongue as if afraid something she said might incriminate her husband.

Lord, forgive our deception.

"Hello, Caroline."

She startled, the soft-spoken words coming from behind a shrub to her left. The gentle male voice, though vaguely familiar, eluded her. "Who's there?"

A broad-shouldered figure stepped from behind the scrub, his face shadowed by the dim light of evening. "Forgive me. I didn't mean to frighten you, but I doubt your aunt and uncle would take kindly to a Union officer calling on their niece."

Caroline's eyes widened, and her heart fluttered like a hummingbird in flight. "Drew?"

He stepped opposite her, with only the fence between them. "I couldn't believe it when I saw you today. It was as if the Lord led me right to you."

Caroline glanced toward the house, her voice hushed yet animated. "However did you find me?"

"I didn't. I came with the cavalry patrol this afternoon, and there you were."

Her eyelids flickered downward, her joy diminishing. He was here out of duty, not for her sake. "I suppose you've come to further your investigation."

He cupped a hand to her cheek, and her eyes lifted. "It's you I've come to see. I've dreamed of this moment for months."

Relieved, she leaned into his warm touch. "I thought I'd never see you again. You don't know how many times I prayed and longed to know what became of you."

"And I you. When I went to your house and found you weren't there, I thought I'd lost you."

Her throat hitched. "You ... you went to my home?"

He lowered his hand, his soft chuckle leaving her weak in the knees. "Yes, and I didn't receive the warmest of welcomes."

She cringed. "I can imagine. No doubt you tasted Papa's fury."

"And nearly his bullet."

Caroline sucked in a breath. "He didn't shoot at you?"

A gentle smile spread over his handsome face. "It isn't the first time I've dodged a bullet. Though I must say, I'd hoped to make a better first impression on your father."

She held back a grin. "I'm afraid you have your work cut out for you there. I warned you winning Papa over would be a challenge." The sting of that truth washed over her, stealing her moment of joy. How would Drew win him over when she hadn't succeeded in doing so herself?

Drew's expression sobered. "Tell me. What are you doing here? Were you sent away on my account?"

Caroline considered trying to convince him it was her idea to leave, but the sincerity in his eyes compelled her to speak the truth. "I neglected to dispose of your bloodied uniform jacket in the shanty, and my younger brother found it. Papa was furious when he learned I'd aided a Union soldier. My mother sent me here until his anger subsided."

Which it clearly hadn't.

Drew gave a soft sigh. "I feared as much." His hands enveloped hers, their warmth permeating her very core. Moonlight shimmered on his hair, fringing the tips in light as he gazed down at her. "I'm sorry."

She entwined her fingers with his, losing herself in his dark eyes. With a shake of her head, she struggled to find her voice. "I'd do it all again. Yours was a life worth saving."

Raising her hand to his lips, he gave it a gentle kiss. "And you're worth waiting for."

Whether at her own boldness or Drew's tender words, heat rushed to her cheeks. For the first time in her life, she felt loved, cherished.

Lantern light streamed through the dining room window, and

Drew glanced toward the house. "I should go, but I'll be back as soon as I complete this assignment."

She swallowed, almost afraid to ask. "And what is that?"

Even in near darkness, she sensed his reluctance to answer. He shifted his feet. "To find Lincoln's assassin."

Caroline tensed. Though she suspected he'd wanted to, Drew had made no attempt to prod her for information about Booth. Should she tell him what she knew?

She peered up at him, his eyes shimmering. "How long do you think it will take?"

He blew out a breath. "Longer than I'd hoped, the way things are going."

In the lingering silence, Caroline deliberated within herself. For days now, she'd kept quiet about her encounter with Mr. Booth for her uncle's sake. The information she'd overheard could help Drew. But would sharing what she knew somehow betray Jamison's memory? He'd given his life for the Confederate cause. What Mr. Booth did was wrong, but to disclose what she knew of his whereabouts seemed a traitorous act.

She wet her lips. Her loyalty should be to God, not some cause or individual. Her conscience had remained burdened long enough. It was time to ease the crushing weight. Drew was an honorable man, a God-fearing man. She could trust him. Drawing a deep breath, she met his gaze.

"I may have some information that will help you."

46

Friday, April 21, 1865
Dr. Samuel Mudd home

Detective Lovett leaned over and scrutinized Uncle Samuel, suspicion marring his dark eyes. "The men were armed? The wounded man had a beard? Why did you not tell us this earlier, Dr. Mudd?"

With shallow breaths, Caroline awaited her uncle's response. His face was pale from sleepless nights pacing the floors. He'd been a bundle of nerves since Detective Lovett's first visit three days earlier.

Her uncle rubbed his palms on his knees. "I-I didn't think of it. I didn't get a good look at the man's face. I'm not certain if the beard was real or fake."

"It was fake. I saw it pull away from his cheek."

Caroline turned in astonishment to her aunt. The claim was utter falsehood. Booth had worn no beard. What had come over her aunt and uncle? Why were they so frightened of the truth?

She clamped her mouth tighter to still her tongue. To dispute them would be disastrous for them both.

With a sigh, Detective Lovett straightened and motioned to the soldiers on his left. "Search the house."

Uncle Samuel's hand shot up. "Wait! I just remembered. The injured man's boot is upstairs. I cut it off his swollen foot to tend his wound."

Lovett's brows pinched. "I'd like to see it."

Caroline's heart leaped to her throat at the first bit of truth her uncle had spoken.

"I'll get it." Aunt Frances dropped her gaze as she edged past the soldiers. It took but a moment to ascend the stairs and retrieve the slit boot. With quivering hands, she gave it to the detective.

He peeled back the leather to examine it. "There's writing inside."

"I wasn't aware of that." Uncle Samuel blurted, a bit too insistently.

Lovett arched a brow. "It seems there's much you aren't aware of, Doctor." He peered at the lettering. "It's the name of a boot factory in New York. No, wait. There's something else."

He lifted the riding boot closer to his face, then glanced up, eyes wide. "J. Wilkes. I knew it!"

Uncle Samuel slumped back in his chair, face blanched.

Standing, Detective Lovett studied Caroline's uncle. "I think it's time you go with us to Bryantown for further questioning, Doctor."

Aunt Frances gasped, and Caroline moved to place an arm around her waist. All the lies and misconstrued details were certain to fall back on him.

He turned to Aunt Frances, a look of despair in his eyes. She whimpered, gripping Caroline's hand with an intensity that numbed her fingers.

As the soldiers escorted her uncle out, Caroline's heart sank. She'd had a feeling something was amiss the moment Mr. Booth came into the house. Her uncle's loyalties to the South had overshadowed his good judgment.

Leaning into her aunt, she voiced a silent prayer. Only God could spare her uncle now.

47

Port Conway Ferry
Tuesday a.m., April 25, 1865

D rew stepped onto the ferry, the log platform shifting under his and Angel's weight. He stroked her neck and breathed a low sigh. Wandering the Zekiah Swamp region for days was enough to tire any man. He'd found no sign of Booth other than possibly an abandoned campfire. Nor had Cox or Burtles been very cooperative when questioned. But while the information Caroline provided hadn't proven very helpful, it had set him on the right path ... as well as cleared her of any wrongdoing.

He could still see the anguish in her eyes when she'd relayed her knowledge of Booth. She'd risked much in telling him, both to her welfare and her uncle's. While neither of them had mentioned Jamison, Drew knew well her devotion to her brother and that he and the cause he'd died for were never far from her thoughts. To set aside her personal allegiances to do what was right endeared her to him all the more.

Thankfully, he'd stumbled across a couple of other weak leads that led him here to Port Conway. His eyes surveyed the opposite shore of the Rappahannock River. If the tip he'd been given was correct, Booth and Herold had crossed on this same ferry, not more than a day ago.

He eyed the muscled men stationed at each corner manning the poles, their gruff exteriors making him wonder how approachable they'd be. He'd hate to get on their bad sides by asking too many questions, but how else would he find out what he needed to know?

Leading Angel closer to the ferryman on his left, he nodded and offered a faint grin. "You must make quite a few trips across a day."

The bearded fellow glanced at Drew, then turned to gaze at the flowing current. "Mmm."

Drew scratched his cheek. At least he'd answered.

A commotion behind alerted him to a horse and wagon being loaded onto the ferry. Edging closer to the poleman, he took the newspaper clipping from his pocket. "Do you recall seeing this man in the past couple of days?"

The burly fellow took a quick glimpse then stared at Drew with close-set eyes. "Cain't rightly remember. Lots of folks cross on this ferry."

Drew returned a slow nod. He had a feeling a coin or two would improve his memory. He reached in his pocket and brought out a half-dollar. "Will this help you recall?"

A lopsided grin edged onto the man's thick lips. "It might."

Tossing him the coin, Drew glared at him expectantly.

The fellow pushed the currency in his pocket. "Yeah. I saw him. Walked with a limp. He and the fellow he was with were chummin' around with three Confederate soldiers."

Drew straightened, his hopes lifting. "Do you know the soldiers' names?"

"Only one. Willie Jett. He crosses quite a bit. I figure he's got himself a lady friend or somethin'."

"Any notion where I might find him?"

The ferryman jutted out his lower lip and nodded toward the

far riverbank. "Cain't say I do. But people over at Port Royal know each other's business right well. Someone there might be able t' tell ya."

"Much obliged."

Drew's nod of thanks went unnoticed as the man turned and lowered his pole deep in the murky water. He gave a powerful shove in unison with the other ferrymen, setting the loaded ferry in motion.

The forward jolt almost knocked Drew off balance. Angel swayed and snorted nervously. He gave her a reassuring pat on the neck. "Easy, girl."

As the raft drifted onto open water, Drew perused the small settlement on the far side of the river. Booth and Herold were out there somewhere.

And he intended to find them.

CAROLINE SHOOK off her melancholy as she finished clearing away the dinner dishes. She must be strong for Aunt Frances and the children's sake. Her aunt had spoken nary a word since Uncle Samuel's startling arrest. After being questioned in Bryantown, he'd returned, only to be taken into custody two days later. The whole encounter left them all a bit numb.

A twinge of guilt riddled her each time she recalled her confession to Drew that Booth and Herold had been there. And yet, she didn't regret it. She'd spoken the truth and hopefully, in doing so, given Drew a better chance of fulfilling his mission.

And returning to her.

At a sob across the room, Caroline glanced at her red-eyed, swollen-faced aunt. How she ached to see her hurting. The children, too, had become solemn, reserved, their usual squabbles silenced. Her uncle's indiscretions had all but sealed his fate. Already he'd been confined at the Old Capital Prison awaiting trial, leaving them all in a quandary.

A firm knock pulled her attention to the dining-room door. Aunt Frances pressed a hand to her chest, fresh tears welling in her eyes as the children huddled around her with long faces. Caroline mustered a weak smile and edged toward the door. "I'll get it."

Easing the door open, she peeked out, relieved to find the young man from the Bryantown post office. "Afternoon, Miss." He tipped his hat and handed her a telegram. "This came over the wire for you."

"Thank you." An amalgam of emotions frothed inside her as she took it from him and closed the door. A smile edged out her worry when she saw it bore her mother's name. "It's from home!"

Breaking free of her youngsters, Aunt Frances stepped closer. "I could do with some good news. What does it say?"

Hope surged within Caroline as she eagerly unfolded the telegram. Surely, this must be her long-awaited invitation to return home. Every fiber of her being rejoiced. She'd waited so long. Had Papa finally softened toward her?

With bated breath, she skimmed over the words, and her smile faded.

DEAR CAROLINE
YOUR FATHER HAD A BOUT OF APOPLEXY
BEDRIDDEN. NEEDS YOUR HELP
PLEASE COME HOME
MUCH LOVE, MAMA

Dazed, Caroline slumped against the doorframe. It was an invitation home, all right. Just not the sort she'd wanted or anticipated.

She boiled inwardly. How could Mama summon her to care for Papa when he'd mocked her nursing and ordered her sent away like a stray cat? Why should she rush home to tend him? He'd shown no sign of remorse. Instead, he'd banished her, detained her letters, and even shot at Drew.

No. She wouldn't do it.

"What is it?" Her aunt's voice sliced through Caroline's agitation. "Not bad news, I hope."

Collecting herself, Caroline shook her head and folded the paper. "Just news of how things are going."

As though too burdened to inquire more, her aunt simply nodded and kissed each child on the head before heading to the kitchen.

Regret weighed on Caroline as she gathered the last of the dinner dishes. Though she yearned to see Mama and Rose, she refused to tend a man who'd disowned her.

She set her jaw. Perhaps the ailment was Papa's comeuppance for his cruelty.

And she would not interfere.

48

Late night, April 25, 1865
Garrett Farm, Virginia

Drew strained to see past the underbrush to the two-story farmhouse. Men's low voices bantered back and forth from the porch, their words indistinguishable. Darkness had settled in, rendering it impossible to decipher their faces, but lantern light shone from the farmhouse windows. If this were the Garrett farm, it was a good bet he'd found who he was looking for.

After making several stops in Port Royal, Drew happened upon two sisters by the name of Peyton who claimed to have encountered Booth and Herold. After denying the two a place to stay the night, the women had overheard another man direct them to the Garrett farm. Following the sisters' directions, Drew made the three-and-a-half-mile trek to what he hoped was the right place. He'd tied Angel several hundred yards back so as not to alert them to his presence.

He edged closer, hoping to get a glimpse of one of them or catch a few words. The sound of galloping horses stilled him.

From his hiding place, he caught sight of two horsemen approaching at a frantic pace. They hollered to the men on the porch. "You two best light outa here. There's a pack of Union soldiers headed this way."

Like cornered rats, the men on the porch scrambled down the steps. Drew's heartbeat quickened when he detected a notable limp from one of the men. Uncertain whether they were armed, he hesitated. Such desperate fellows were likely to shoot at anything that moved. With the cavalry on its way, he'd be wise to wait.

While the horsemen cantered off, the two men trekked toward the barn and into the timber beyond. The sound of their movement gradually died away, leaving only the rasp of frogs and nightlife to break the stillness. Drew leaned against a tree trunk listening, waiting. More than a quarter-hour ticked by before the faint clank of metal and rumble of horse hooves sounded in the distance.

Drew rallied, his senses heightening. But the procession passed to the west without so much as pausing. He wavered, torn between keeping an eye on Booth and backtracking to Angel and going after the cavalry patrol. If he had Booth pegged right, he suspected he'd take his chances in the comfort of the farmhouse rather than sleeping on the timber floor.

So, he waited.

Moments after the hoofbeats died away, he heard shuffling noises from the timber behind the barn. Hushed murmurs and a slight chuckle assured Drew the men sensed the threat had passed. As they ambled closer, the door to the farmhouse swung open, and the glow of lantern light flooded onto the porch. The silhouette of a man appeared in the doorway, blocking the two men's approach. "You won't be staying in the house."

A curse erupted from one of the men. "Then, where do you expect us to sleep?"

"There's plenty of straw in the barn. You can sleep there."

"Can we at least have a lantern and some blankets?"

The man Drew supposed was Mr. Garrett disappeared only to return moments later with the requested items. As the disgruntled pair turned on their heels and headed back toward the barn, Drew craned his neck for a look at their faces. Though the light was dim, the glimpse was enough to convince him he had indeed found the fugitive assassin.

It seemed Mr. Garrett had lost trust in the twosome, for the moment they were inside, he slipped out of the house and quietly bolted the barn door, trapping them in.

With a lopsided grin, Drew backed from his hiding place. Time to fetch Angel and retrieve the misguided calvary.

CAROLINE DRIED her silent tears and slid the folded telegram back in her pocket, wishing it had never come. She dropped down on her bed, spent in body and spirit. Tireless months of waiting and hoping had rendered her defenseless against the myriad emotions bubbling inside her. How she'd yearned for her father to relent. Instead, the war had ended, and nothing had changed.

His treatment toward Drew was proof of that.

The wound Papa had inflicted ran deep, its scar still evident in the bitterness that surfaced each time she recalled the atrocious way he'd treated her. What sort of father turned his back on his daughter, claiming not even to know her? It wasn't right, and—Lord forgive her—she loathed him for it.

She rubbed her temples, feeling strangely at odds with herself. Her mind swirled with anxious thoughts. Mama would expect her to come, or at least offer a reply. But, right now, she couldn't think. Between Drew's sudden appearance, her uncle's arrest, and news of her father's ailment, she needed time to pray and sort things through.

2 a.m. April 26, 1865
Garrett Farm, 3 miles from Port Royal, Virginia

THICK DARKNESS BLANKETED the Garrett farm as Drew and the men of the 16th New York Cavalry surrounded the tobacco barn that housed Booth and Herold. Dim lantern light filtered through wide openings in the boards from within.

The cavalry commander, Lieutenant Doherty, slipped up to the barn, peeked through one of the cracks, then doubled back to the locust tree Drew was concealed behind. "It's them, all right." Excitement flared in the lieutenant's hushed voice.

Drew's heart hammered. Twelve days had passed since the manhunt had begun, and there wasn't a soldier out there who wasn't eager to see it come to an end—no one more than Drew.

The lieutenant raised his voice. "Booth! Herold! We know you're in there. Come on out. We have you surrounded!"

Murmurs and scrambled boot steps sounded inside the barn. "Who are you?"

"U.S. Cavalry. Now, come out, or we'll burn you out!"

The command was met by panicked curses and, moments later, a pounding at the front of the barn. "Wait! I don't wanna burn to death. I'm coming out!"

Drew edged up to the barn and peered through one of the gaps in the boards. Booth stood hunched near the center, looking defeated as he leaned on his crutch, while Davey Herold banged again on the door, eager to get out. Drew nodded to Lieutenant Doherty, who motioned one of his men to open it. The soldier snatched Herold from inside, slammed the door shut behind him, and then tied him to a nearby tree.

"Are you coming out, Booth?" inquired the lieutenant.

"Never!"

At Booth's ardent response, Doherty ordered two of his men

to set fire to the shed. The dry wood of the tobacco barn crackled as the soldiers set it ablaze. The fire spread quickly, sending billows of smoke inside the barn. Drew watched through the crack long enough to see Booth attempt to stomp out the flames, then backed away. Whether the man was reaping his just retribution or not, Drew didn't wish to witness his demise.

A gun cocked.

Seconds later, a shot rang out.

Drew locked eyes with Doherty then peered inside the barn. Through a haze of smoke and flames, he caught a glimpse of Booth lying on the barn floor. "He's down!"

Following Doherty inside, Drew covered his face with his bandana, squinting against the dense smoke. The lieutenant knelt for a closer look at Booth. "He's alive. Get him out of here."

Gripping him under the arms, one of his men drug him outside beneath one of the nearby locust trees. Though Booth's dark eyes perused the crowd of soldiers encircling him, he did not move. In the firelight, blood oozed from a wound in his neck. Lieutenant Doherty bent over him and peered up at his men. "Did he shoot himself?"

"No, sir." A young sergeant wormed his way to the front. "I was watching from a crack in the barn wall. I saw him level his carbine as if to shoot his way out, so I shot him with my pistol."

"Finish me off." The actor's slight frame sagged against the ground, his body limp and lifeless. Fear and anger mingled in his coal-black eyes. His breaths were shallow, stilted. Twelve days on the run had taken its toll.

Booth coughed and licked his quivering lips. Closing his eyes, he spewed the words, "Useless. Useless."

Moments later, his head fell to one side, and his breaths stilled.

Drew shook his head. What a waste. The man's life had been cut short by hatred and bitterness. If he'd learned anything over these strife-filled years of war, it was that a life ruled by animosity and resentment brought only misery.

His cheek flinched. From now on, he intended to do what he could to foster healing in this broken land.

Starting with a certain disgruntled father of a very special lady.

49

Mudd Farm, April 27, 1865

Caroline read over the missive a final time then folded it. Her reasons for not returning home were flimsy ones, she knew, but hopefully Mama and Rose would understand. Most likely, Mama would read between the lines and realize she was making excuses, but Aunt Frances truly could use her help with Uncle Samuel away.

She bit her lip. Was she a coward? The nagging knot in her chest made her wonder. Yet, even Jesus had condemned the hypocritical Pharisees. Surely, her father's ill-treatment of her was no better.

With a sigh, she sealed the letter with a drop of wax. It was unfair of Mama to ask her to tend to someone who'd treated her so harshly.

She asked too much.

The canter of hooves pulled her attention to the open bedroom window. Striding over, she saw a lone horseman approaching at a hurried pace. The waning sun cast a golden hue over the rolling landscape, illuminating the broad-shouldered figure.

Her heartbeat quickened, and a smile spread over her face. Even at a distance, she recognized Drew's masculine silhouette atop his bay mare.

He'd come back.

Gathering her skirts, she hurried toward the door, her letter forgotten. One chapter in her life might be closing, but a new one was about to begin.

DREW TUGGED Angel to a halt outside the Mudd home and dismounted, the sight of Caroline hurrying to greet him flooding him with renewed vigor. Looping the reins around the yard fence, he rushed to meet her.

As she neared, she slowed her pace and locked her hands together behind her, smiling shyly. "Have you found him?"

He moved as close as he dared without wrapping her in his arms and claiming her ruby lips. "Yes." He would spare her the details of the tragic, drawn-out affair.

"Your mission is accomplished, then?"

He nodded. "I have only to return to Washington to report to General Grant and resign my commission." He clasped her hand, the crimson hues of the setting sun catching the flush in her cheeks. "If you like, I can escort you home before I go and join you there afterward."

Her smile faded. "I-I've decided not to return home."

He could think of but one reason she would choose not to go back. "Is the loss of Jamison so painful for you?"

Her hand stiffened, and she slid it from his grasp. "How could you know ... "

"In my search for you, your neighbor mentioned he'd been killed. I'm truly sorry."

Her eyelids fluttered downward, and the color drained from her face. "Thank you, but no. I don't wish to return because of my father."

The raw honesty of her words both touched and saddened him. He'd witnessed firsthand her father's unforgiving nature. It was plain he'd hurt her deeply and Drew intended to learn just how.

He offered her his elbow. "Walk with me?"

Hesitantly, she slipped her arm through his. The tip of her bonnet barely topped his shoulder, her delicate frame feeling so natural alongside him. As they strolled in the twilight, she shared her heart with him, how her father had repeatedly rejected her, scoffed at her desire to pursue nursing, and disowned her, calling her a traitor and a deceitful whelp.

The grip on his arm intensified. "Then yesterday, Mama sent a telegram telling me Papa is bedridden. She wants me to care for him." Caroline paused and turned toward Drew, hurt and bitterness flaring in her honey eyes. "For months, I've longed to be welcomed home, to know Papa has changed his heart towards me. But he hasn't. And I want no part in him."

Pierced by the anguish her father had imposed on her, Drew's chest constricted. If only he could erase the sting of her emotional wounds the way her kindness had eased his physical ones.

Yet only Christ's love wielded such power.

He placed his hands on her shoulders, praying for words of wisdom. A meadowlark's sweet song broke the stillness as he drank in every contour of her face. "Don't take your father's words to heart. You're a kind, compassionate, gracious woman who deserves to be treated with the utmost care and respect."

A gentle smile touched her lips as she gazed up at him, eyes moist. "Then you see why I can't go back. Why Papa deserves none of my sympathies?"

Drew's mind returned to Captain Jacobs and John Wilkes Booth. Both allowed hatred to rule their lives and the effects were devastating. He couldn't bear to watch Caroline suffer a similar fate. "That's why you *must* go back."

Her face contorted. "What? Why?"

He gave her shoulders a gentle squeeze. "I've seen what a life of hostility and bitterness can do to a person. Left unchecked, such emotions will destroy you."

She averted her gaze, the tremor in her voice deepening. "So, you're saying I should forgive him and forget all the anguish he's inflicted on me?"

He cradled her chin in his hand, pulling her attention back to him. "I'm saying don't allow your father's mistakes to dictate how you respond. We can't control the hardships others force upon us, but we can refuse to allow them to eat away at us."

Though she made no reply, her eyes softened. A tear trickled down her cheek, and he swiped it away with his thumb. "It wouldn't seem right to start a new life together without at least attempting to make amends with your father."

Her eyes brightened, then dimmed. "It won't work. Even if he recovers, he'll never change towards me ... or you."

He brushed the back of his fingers along her cheek. "What's impossible for us is possible with God."

Her mouth twisted. "The Lord has His work cut out for Him where Papa and I are concerned. For some unknown reason, he hates me."

Drew arched a brow. "Funny. At the end of his rifle barrel, I rather thought I was the one he loathed."

She shook her head, a hint of a smile touching her lips.

Drew chuckled and pulled her into a tender embrace. "Pray about it. I'll swing by in the morning, and if you decide to go home, I'll be happy to escort you."

She leaned into him, her slight nod assuring him she'd give the offer consideration.

To forgive a grudge was no simple task, but Drew had witnessed first-hand the freedom that came from compassion. He could only pray Caroline would experience that same release.

THE BRIGHT, three-quarter moon shone in Caroline's bedroom window, beaming a steady stream of light across the foot of her bed. Hours had passed since Drew left, and she could still feel the warmth of his embrace. With a sigh, she tucked her hands behind her head. He'd given her plenty to ponder and pray over. She hadn't anticipated his response. After experiencing her father's wrath, Drew was the last person she'd expected to encourage her to make amends—a testament to his honorable nature.

In her attempts at prayer, her mind kept wandering back to all the reasons she had to spurn her father in his time of need. She'd finally confided the news to Aunt Frances, who, despite her own dire circumstances, had encouraged Caroline to return home.

She brushed a wayward strand of hair from her cheek. Even if she did go, she wasn't confident she'd know what to do. Unless there was something regarding apoplexy in the medical book Uncle Samuel had given her. She started to retrieve it, then stopped with a huff. It didn't matter. He would refuse her help, and she did not wish to fight him.

Wide awake, Caroline sat up and lit the bedside lantern. The golden glow of the flame danced with shadows on the walls and ceiling. She blinked tired eyes and reached for her Bible. Flipping through its pages, she sought out a Scripture to still her mind and reassure her heart.

When she happened upon Romans chapter twelve, she paused and read with careful resolve.

Recompense to no man evil for evil.

If it be possible, as much as lieth in you, live peaceably with all men.

Dearly beloved, avenge not yourselves, but rather give place unto wrath: for it is written, Vengeance is mine; I will repay, saith the Lord.

Therefore, if thine enemy hunger, feed him; if he thirst, give him drink: for in so doing thou shalt heap coals of fire on his head.

Be not overcome of evil, but overcome evil with good.

Tears welled in her eyes. The words nearly leaped off the

page to coil around her heart. Drew was right. She was responding to Papa's hostility with resentment of her own. Convicted, she leaned her head against the wall. She'd become no different than her father.

Closing her eyes, she clutched the Bible to her chest. *Forgive me, Lord. Papa acted evilly toward me. Please give me strength to overcome that evil by returning good. Whether he clings to his animosity toward me or softens, give me the courage to show him Christ-like love.*

With a ragged breath, she closed her Bible and placed it on the nightstand. Dousing the lantern, she slipped back under the covers, the heaviness on her heart lifting. Perhaps now she could sleep.

Come morning, she would have a long journey ahead.

50

Dunbar Estate, April 28, 1865

"There it is."

Drew detected a hint of excitement in Caroline's voice as he steered Angel and the borrowed rig in the direction of the pillared house in the distance. Out of the corner of his eye, he saw her slip an arm around her slender waist as though fighting nerves. He clasped her free hand and squeezed it. "Glad you came?"

She blew out a long breath. "I'll let you know when you return from Washington."

He laughed softly. "Then I'll be certain to hurry back."

Averting her gaze, she fingered the brass buttons of his captain's uniform on the seat beside her. "Are you certain you wish to resign your commission?"

He hesitated. The decision to give up a promotion to Major and the prestige of working under General Grant hadn't been an easy one. But if doing so helped span the chasm between him and Caroline's family, it was worth it. The Lord had brought them together in unexpected ways, not once but twice, and he intended to make the most of it. "General Grant doesn't stand a chance against you."

She smiled that alluring smile of hers, her gentle features melting his heart all over again.

He pressed her gloved fingers to his lips. The many miles had flown by in her pleasant company. He hated to leave her again, but then, given his last encounter here, he likely wouldn't be welcomed into her home regardless. Caroline only had to win over her father. Drew had the entire family to sway in his favor.

Patches of green dotted the moist fields surrounding the estate so that it was difficult to ascertain the seedling tobacco plants from the weeds. Caroline shook her head. "I can tell Papa's laid up. He'd be appalled to see the fields so unkempt and overtaken with weeds."

"Has he no field hands?"

"My younger brother, Phillip, and perhaps a couple more workers. Evidently, not enough. He suffered quite a setback with the loss of his slaves ... and Jamison."

The pain in her eyes told Drew she still felt the sting of Jamison's absence. "Jamison was a good man. I wish I'd had the opportunity to get to know him."

Meeting his gaze, Caroline laced her fingers through his. "I have a feeling you and he would have gotten on quite well."

As they neared the manor, she sat taller and slipped her hand from his to adjust her bonnet. A smile lit her face at sight of a black man at the side of the house. She waved to him. "Cyrus!"

He strode toward them, mouth agape and eyes wide. "Be it you, Miss Caroline?"

Drew pulled Angel to a halt beside him.

"Yes, Cyrus. I'm home." Caroline giggled like a schoolgirl, barely letting the buggy roll to a stop before descending.

The two embraced, tears of joy streaming down Cyrus's cheeks as he wrapped her in his arms and swung her around. "Glory be. This ol' house ain't been the same since you left."

His gaze shifted to Drew and his brows furrowed. "Ain't that the feller ... "

Caroline tugged on his arm, her eyes dancing. "The very same."

The door to the house burst open, and Drew recognized the woman and young girl he'd seen huddled in the hall against Mr. Dunbar's rampage, along with the woman who'd opened the door to him. Jubilant shouts poured from them as they scurried to greet Caroline, their faces gleaming with joy.

Drew took up the reins, a sense of peace washing through him. Now that Caroline was in good hands, he could be on his way to Washington. As if sensing his departure, she glanced over her shoulder and offered him a gentle smile. The others gawked at him, a hint of recognition on their faces. With a nod and a tip of his hat, he flicked the reins and pulled away, praying Caroline would be received half as well by her father.

"WHO WAS THAT?" Mama's voice tingled in Caroline's ear.

She kept her eyes trained on Drew until he was but a speck on the worn path. "His name's Andrew Gallagher."

"But who is he? I feel I've seen him somewhere."

Try as she may, Caroline couldn't keep the corners of her lips from tipping upward. She must be cautious. To reveal the whole truth about Drew could jeopardize their chances. Given time, and a great deal of prayer, her family would warm to Drew. At least, that was her hope. "He's ... a dear friend."

The answer seemed to appease Mama's curiosity for her questions stilled, and she gave Caroline another hug. "I'm so glad you're here. How are Samuel, Sarah Frances, and the children?"

Caroline hesitated. It seemed her mother had no knowledge of the challenges facing her aunt and uncle and now was not the time to expose them. "They send their love."

Her mother's smile deepened. "Come inside. Are you hungry?"

"A little."

Lily leaned in close, hands on hips. "Don't you fret, honeychild. I'll warm a pot of stew up quicker than you can say Sweet Dixie." She patted Caroline on the arm. "Seein' you again is like sunshine after rain."

"Thank you, Lily."

Small arms encircled Caroline's waist, and she looked to see Rose's big brown eyes staring up at her. "I missed you, Linna."

The endearment often used by Jamison tugged at her heart, and she bent to hug her sister. "I missed you, too, sweetpea."

"Then why didn't you write?"

Caroline blinked moisture from her eyes. "I wrote every week. I'm sorry you never received my letters."

She locked eyes with her mother, who seemed to read her implications. Caroline suspected Mama knew the truth behind the missing letters but refused to taint Rose's opinion of her father. "How's Papa?"

Mama shook her head then slipped a hand under Rose's chin. "Rose, dear. Could you help Lily in the kitchen while Caroline and I chat?"

The girl started to protest, but when Mama raised a brow, she scrunched her face and nodded. "Yes, ma'am."

As Rose scampered away, Mama turned to Caroline. "He's not well. It's been a couple of weeks now, and no change. The doctor indicated the longer he remains in this condition, the less likely he is to recover."

"Did he offer any suggestions on his care?"

Weariness brimmed in her mother's eyes. "Only to keep him as comfortable as possible and to give him broth for nourishment. I thought, having worked with Samuel, you might know of some technique to try. Come. I'll take you to him."

Unable to find her voice, Caroline nodded slowly. Mama's faith in her was heartening, but she doubted there was much she could do if the doctor himself suggested only quiet rest. Time and prayer seemed their greatest asset. Her breaths shallowed as she followed her mother inside and down the hall to the guest bedroom. After so many months away, the house seemed familiar and yet, in a way, foreign.

Pausing outside the bedroom door, her mother spoke in quiet tones. "He can't move or speak, but I'm convinced he knows what's taking place around him."

Silence blanketed the room as they entered. Caroline swallowed her angst at the sight of her father lying motionless on the bed. The drawn curtains gave a gloomy feel to the dimly lit room. Stepping to the side of the bed, her mother brushed a wavy lock of hair from Papa's brow. The simple gesture hinted of a fondness that she'd not witnessed in years. "Eugene? Look who's come."

His eyes remained fixed on the ceiling above, his swollen face and heavy breaths making him appear beyond hope. One side of his mouth was drawn taut, higher than the other. His paled skin lacked its usual vibrancy and color.

Edging closer, Caroline fought for breath, almost afraid to step into his line of sight. He'd ordered her never to return. Would he be angered she's come? Or would he even recognize her?

Strength, Lord.

"Hello, Papa."

The words squeaked out barely above a whisper, but their effect was immediate. His brow furrowed, and though his throat was silent, the fire of disdain burned in his green eyes.

Her heart plummeted. Even in his depleted state, he found a way to convey his displeasure. Just as she'd supposed. Her presence here would bring nothing but grief—to herself and her father.

Washington D.C., April 29, 1865

GENERAL GRANT FINISHED glancing over Drew's report and gave a satisfied nod. "You did a fine job, Captain Gallagher. The 16th New York Cavalry may have received the credit, but you played an important role in tracking down Booth and Herold."

"Thank you, sir." Drew held his composure but thrilled inwardly. He didn't deserve all the credit, either. Though he couldn't divulge Caroline as a source, she'd given him valuable information and set him in the right direction.

Grant took a puff of his cigar and blew out a trail of smoke. "Sure you won't change your mind and stay on another stint?"

Drew hesitated but a moment before shaking his head. "I'd like to, sir, but I-I've other plans for the near future."

"I see." A hint of a smile edged across Grant's face as he reached to snuff out his cigar butt. "Is she pretty?"

Drew met his gaze, trying unsuccessfully to hold back a grin. "Very."

Rising, Grant laughed heartily and reached his arm across his desk. "Well, if you ever change your mind, come see me. There'll be a position waiting for you."

He stood and clasped the general's outstretched hand. "Thank you, sir. I'm honored."

Drew offered a heartfelt salute, then pivoted toward the door. Though part of him would miss the adventure of the military, he felt at peace with his decision. Four years was a long time to serve his country. The Lord had spared him again and again, blessing him each step of the way.

It was time to learn why.

51

Monday, May 1, 1865

Caroline closed the medical book and glanced at her bedridden father, his face less swollen than when she'd first arrived. For days now, she'd scoured the book for ways to treat apoplexy and come up short. The doctor's suggestion of bloodletting seemed futile. *I need your help, Lord. Show me what to do.*

"How's it going?"

Caroline startled at her mother's voice inside the bedroom door. "Getting nowhere, I'm afraid. There doesn't seem to be an effective treatment for severe apoplexy."

Mama moved closer, a tremor in her voice. "Is there nothing that can be done? I can't bear to watch him just lie there day after day."

Caroline slipped an arm around her mother's waist and walked with her to the bedside. Papa's eyes flickered open and fastened on them. He looked so weak and helpless, so unlike his usual domineering self. Despite her initial misgivings about coming, she truly longed for his recovery—if not for his sake, for Mama's.

331

"From what I read, he needs his mind and body engaged. We should talk to him, read to him, and exercise his limbs."

Mama's eyes brightened. "It's worth a try, much better than just watching him deteriorate."

Caroline sat on the edge of the bed and gently lifted her father's arm. "I'm going to move your arm, Papa, to see if we can get your circulation flowing again."

A weak growl sounded in his throat, his only way to express his disdain. Setting his arm down, Caroline turned to her mother. "Perhaps you should do it."

Mama shook her head. "No. You go ahead. I'll speak to him." She moved to his head, stroking his thick salt-and-pepper hair. "Caroline is here to help, Eugene. Please be agreeable and let her do what needs done."

His eyes crimped like a child who hadn't gotten his way. Mama gave Caroline a reassuring rub on the back. "Go ahead. I'll bring the paper to read and warm some broth for his dinner."

An hour later, Caroline emerged, her muscles fatigued from all the lifting. Not once had Papa glanced her way. Instead, he'd squeezed his eyes shut or stared at the ceiling or wall.

Be not overcome of evil, but overcome evil with good.

Over and over, Caroline recited the verse, reminding herself why she needed to persevere. But she also needed answers. What made his resentment so deep that he would rather waste away than receive her help?

"PLEASE, MAMA." Caroline shook off the tremor in her voice. "I've come home to a father that would sooner die than let me tend him. I have a right to know what he holds against me."

Her mother's russet eyes filled with tears as she dropped onto the settee. Lowering her gaze, she finally nodded. "You're right. You deserve the truth, though I wished to spare you."

Caroline drew a shallow breath. Would she, at last, learn the truth? Easing down beside her, Caroline placed a trembling hand atop her mother's. "I don't know that anything you say could hurt me worse than the pain I've already suffered."

Her mother's eyes lifted. "I suppose I should have told you sooner. I'm just so ashamed—" Her words trailed off as tears spilled down her cheeks.

Leaning closer, Caroline gave her mother's hand a gentle squeeze. "It's all right, Mama. Whatever it is, it's time we faced it together."

Reaching in her pocket for a handkerchief, her mother drew a shaky breath. "I've kept it locked up so long, I'm not certain how to relay it."

Caroline brushed a tear from Mama's cheek. "We've nothing but time."

Her mother sniffled and dabbed her nose. Then, expelling a long breath, she lifted reddened eyes to meet Caroline's gaze. "When Jamison was but a baby, your father went to Baltimore for a time to help his brother—your Uncle Charles—set up his shipping business. Since he was going to be gone several weeks, he felt it necessary to ... hire someone to oversee the farm while he was away."

She swallowed, a shadow cloaking her face. "A Mr. Banthom."

The loathing in her mother's tone as she spoke the name sent a shiver down Caroline's spine. "Did this man rob or harm you in some way?"

Her mother's eyes glazed over, her face void of expression. "Everything seemed fine for a time. Mr. Banthom performed his duties well and gave no cause for concern, even shared an evening meal with Jamison and me on occasion."

She searched her mother's face, resisting the urge to ask what all this had to do with her and her father. "Then what?"

Her mother's ice-cold fingers entwined with hers, the tightened grip draining the color from Caroline's hand. "One afternoon, I was alone gathering vegetables from the garden, and he ..." The word caught in her throat, fresh tears spilling down her cheeks.

Caroline shivered, and her throat constricted. There was no need for her mother to say the words. Her expression spoke for her. "He ... accosted you?"

Mama nodded, a whimper in her voice. "He came from behind and covered my mouth. I didn't hear a sound. It happened so fast, if only I ..." She fell into Caroline's arms, years of pent-up emotions pouring out in anguished sobs.

Caroline held her close, her own eyes blurred with tears. How her heart ached for this woman who'd always been so strong and able, her mainstay in time of need. Now it was her time to offer strength and comfort, to ease this burden she'd carried silently for decades.

Lord, give me words to comfort.

She rested her cheek against her mother's head, stroking a hand through her soft, brunette waves. "It's all right, Mama. It wasn't your fault. There's nothing you could have done."

Her mother's sobs gradually tapered off then stilled. At last, she sat back, and Caroline loosened her hold. She blew her nose on her handkerchief, her eyes glossing over once more. "The news liked to have killed Eugene. He was never quite the same afterward."

Caroline kept her voice soft, tentative, not wishing to press. "You told him what happened?"

Her mother shook her head. "I didn't intend to, but when he noticed the bruises on my arms and ... elsewhere ... I could no longer conceal it."

The agony in Mama's voice tore at Caroline. "Was the man caught?"

Her mother dropped her gaze, fingering the handkerchief in her hand. "No. Eugene searched for him but never found him. It's just as well he didn't. If he had, he likely would have killed him, and where would that have left me?"

A moment of silence blanketed the room. Though the

appalling incident explained the change in her father and the time of seclusion her aunt had spoken of, it still didn't account for his ill-feelings toward her. She bit her lower lip, trying to find her voice. "How does all this tie in with his grievance against me?"

Mama released a long sigh. "When Eugene returned from his search empty-handed, he was outraged. Rather than comfort me, he withdrew, taking up residence in our guest bedroom for a time."

She paused and swallowed hard, the memory obviously still raw. Finally, she continued. "It was during this time of estrangement that I learned I was ... with child."

Caroline tensed, the full impact of her mother's words taking root in her mind and weaving a stranglehold around her heart. She slumped back on the settee. Everything was starting to make sense now. She was not Papa's child. Each time he looked at her, he was reminded of the despicable act that resulted in her birth. "So that's it."

Her mother placed a hand on her arm. "I'm sorry, dear. You've suffered all these years for no fault of your own."

Caroline wrinkled her brow. "But why blame me? I was but an innocent child."

"With no one else to lash out at, Eugene took his hurt out on me for a time. Once you were born, he seemed to funnel all his bitterness at you. The more I sought to defend you, the worse his resentment became. After a while, I grew resigned to the fact he would never fully accept you. Forgive me."

Blinking back tears, Caroline mustered a weak grin. "I'm glad you told me. Somehow, knowing the reason behind Papa's rejection makes it a bit easier to bear."

Mama touched a hand to her cheek. "I'm so glad you're here. I know it hasn't been easy, but despite the way he's treated you, I'm certain that he regrets his actions. Deep down."

Caroline hung her head. "I wish I could believe that."

Her mother's hand moved to her chin, forcing Caroline to

meet her gaze. "He may not realize it himself, but in his own way, I believe he does love you."

Caroline's lips quivered. It certainly didn't seem so, though she didn't wish to argue. With a soft sigh, she laced her hands together in her lap. "Well, regardless of how he feels toward me, I've come to help. He may not be my true father, but he's the only one I have. And like it or not, I mean to do what I can for him."

Hope streamed in her mother's eyes. "Do you think there's a chance he'll recover?"

Caroline's brow furrowed. "That depends on him and the Lord."

Her stomach knotted. The Lord had asked her to show unconditional love, expecting nothing in return. It was time to relinquish not only Papa's future but her yearning to earn his love and respect.

She glanced at her mother. Now seemed as good a time as any to share the other matter weighing heavy on her heart. She drew in a long breath. "I'm afraid I have some rather disturbing news for you as well. News that involves Uncle Samuel and Aunt Frances."

"STUPID, MEASLY, NO-GOOD TOBACCO PLANTS." The boy tossed his hoe and plopped down cross-legged at the edge of the field, elbows on his knees, palms cradling his cheeks.

Drew halted Angel beside him, curious what had the young man so distraught. Though his hair was a shade darker and his build stockier, the boy's facial features resembled Jamison's enough to convince Drew he must be Caroline's younger brother, Phillip. "Having troubles?"

"Had nothin' but trouble since Papa fell ill."

"Anything I can do to help?"

The boy sat up straighter and scrutinized Drew more closely.

His eyes narrowed. "You're a filthy Yank! Don't need help from no mangy blue-belly."

Ignoring the slurs, Drew cocked his head and clicked his tongue in his cheek. "That's an awfully big field to tackle alone. Even filthy Yanks know how to lend a hand."

Phillip spat on the ground. "I'd sooner take help from a thievin' coyote."

Drew held back a grimace. Plainly, the boy took after his father. It would require some cunning to override his biased defenses. With a shrug of his shoulders, Drew took up the reins. "Well then, I guess you don't care to learn how to cut your transplant time in half."

Phillip shot him a curious glance then tossed a clod of dirt into the field. "You're bluffin'. There ain't no fast way."

Dismounting, Drew squinted over at him. "Give me ten seconds, and I'll prove it."

Before the boy could argue, Drew tromped his way to the discarded hoe and returned to the spot where Phillip had left off. He dug the heel of his boot in the soil and hoed a cone of dirt around it. Lifting his foot, he pointed to the hole it left behind. "Stick your plant in, and you're set. That's how we do it up my way."

Though the boy said nothing, his eyebrows shot up.

Drew snatched up a plant and gathered the dirt around it, securing it in place. "'Course it goes even faster when one person hoes and another plants." He intentionally avoided looking Phillip's way. Instead, he moved along the row, making more holes with his boot. If he were a betting man, he'd wager the lad would choose help over hatred.

A rustling noise sounded to his left. Out of the corner of his eye, he caught a glimpse of Phillip setting a plant in place, and his lips lifted.

He'd bet right.

CAROLINE STOOD at the foot of her father's bed, praying for words. All this time, she'd thought she'd unknowingly done something to warrant his animosity when in reality, it was deep hurt that fueled his resentment. His eyes flickered open, and she forced herself not to pull back into the shadows. It was time to face him, put an end to the bitterness and strife.

Moving to his bedside, she eased down onto the mattress. "Hello, Papa."

The same guttural growl and pointed stare greeted her. She took a deep breath and pushed down the hurt welling within her. For once, she was thankful he was incapacitated so he would have to hear her out without interruption. Bolstering her courage, she cleared her throat and began to gently massage his arm. "Mama told me what happened before I was born. I understand now the hurt you've harbored all these years."

His eyes narrowed, then widened.

She dropped her gaze to his arm, bending it at the shoulder first and then the elbow. "I know we've not gotten on well in the past, but I pray, given time, that will change. What happened wasn't my fault, or Mama's, or yours."

Still unable to meet his gaze, she swallowed hard. "Just as Jamison's death wasn't anyone's fault." She paused, uncertain how he was responding to the one-sided conversation. "The war took him from us, and I miss him as terribly as you."

Holding her father's thick fingers in her hand, she flexed each one, relieved he hadn't grumbled at her. Tears filled her eyes, and her voice hitched as raw emotions bubbled to the surface. "It's true I'm not your flesh and blood like the others, but you're still my father, and I'd like to be your daughter if you'll allow me."

When she ventured a glance, his olive eyes did not look away. His lips moved slightly, and a noise sounded in his throat. Not a growl this time, but more an attempt at words. Leaning over, she put her ear to his lips but gleaned only indistinguishable whispers.

Frustration edged out the softness in Papa's voice. Sitting up, Caroline marshaled a weak grin, all her bitterness melting into genuine concern and desire to help. "It's all right, Papa. Be patient. Give yourself time. We'll keep working and praying every day. The Lord will restore you to health, you'll see."

She moved to his leg, massaging then bending it. His eyes followed her as she shifted from limb to limb. At last, she stood and covered him with the quilt. "Get some rest. I'll check in on you later."

As she turned to leave, she paused for a look, and her spirit lightened. No longer did Papa seem the fearsome man she'd come to dread, but a helpless figure who'd been held captive to anger and misery. Bowing her head, she closed her eyes.

Lord, help him see past the hurt. Enable him to let go of the pain of the past and learn to love rather than hate. May he come to accept that being a father is more about choosing to give of oneself instead of being blood-related.

She squeezed her eyes tighter, her heartfelt prayer penetrating her very core. *Soften his heart, Lord. May he come to accept me ...*

And, in time, Drew.

52

"Mama, this is Andrew Gallagher."

The tremor in Caroline's voice as she introduced him to her family did little to still his nerves. Drew offered a friendly nod to the comely woman who, with her brunette hair and trim figure, was an older version of Caroline. "Nice to meet you, Mrs. Dunbar."

Though she returned his smile, her brown eyes were tentative as she perused his dusty trousers and smudged boots, making Drew wish he'd had an opportunity to clean up after working with Phillip in the field much of the afternoon. "And you, Mr. Gallagher."

After so long in the military, the term "mister" sounded stiff, foreign.

Caroline strode over and placed her hands on her sister's shoulders. "And this is Rose."

Drew gave a slight bow, the child's ringleted hair and youthful face reminding him of his sister, Lydia. "A pleasure, Miss Rose."

The youngster grinned, her eyes dancing.

Caroline gestured to her brother leaned against the parlor entry. "I believe you're already acquainted with Phillip."

"Yes." Drew's smile met with a solemn stare from the boy. At least, he wasn't spouting foul names at him or threatening to fill him with buckshot like his father.

Mrs. Dunbar studied Drew then wagged a finger in the air. "Now I know where I've seen you. You came to our door looking for Caroline a few weeks back."

Drew swallowed, twisting his hat in his hands. "Yes, ma'am."

Her gaze flicked to Caroline and back to Drew. "You are a Northerner, are you not?"

With a sideways glance at Caroline, Drew cleared his throat. "Yes, ma'am."

Mrs. Dunbar's brow creased. "I see. And, how did you become acquainted with my daughter?"

"We ... uh ... that is, I was under her care for a short time during the war."

"That seems rather odd, given our families were on opposite sides of the conflict."

Caroline took a rapid step toward her. "Not so, Mama. Doctors and nurses are duty-bound to treat anyone in need."

Her mother nodded. "I suppose that's true."

"Betcha he's the Union soldier she had hidden away in the shanty." Phillip's voice, though laced with sass, wasn't as hostile as she might have expected.

At her brother's words, Caroline's face blanched.

Her mother turned to her, her jaw slackening. "Is that true, Caroline?"

In defense, Drew stepped to her side. "Mrs. Dunbar, your daughter is a kind, compassionate woman for whom I care deeply. Whatever grievances the North and South have had, I pray that animosity will not live on in us. I hold no grudge against your family for being from the South, and I ask you offer me the same grace."

Mrs. Dunbar blinked, scrutinizing him in a long silence. Her softened expression spoke to her being a fair-minded person. At last, she arched a brow. "Well said, Mr. Gallagher. I take it you intend to present yourself on a regular basis around here?"

Drew released the breath he'd been holding and shot a glance at Caroline. Hope shone in her eyes, giving him courage. "Yes, ma'am, I would, if you'll permit me. I'd be pleased to help Phillip with the crops until your husband is up and about."

Mrs. Dunbar hesitated then turned her eyes on her son. "Is that agreeable to you, Phillip?"

The pointed question pulled everyone's eyes to the boy. Drew's heart drummed in his ears as he waited. So much depended on the youth's response. Finally, Phillip shrugged and dropped his gaze. "I reckon Yankee help is better than none."

Drew shared a humored grin with Caroline until her mother's voice snagged their attention. "Well then, I have no objection. I'll have Cyrus fix up the old slave shack for you to stay in, and you may take your meals with us."

"Thank you, ma'am."

Mrs. Dunbar fixed her gaze on him, her voice deepening. "But understand, I can't speak for my husband. This arrangement all changes if Eugene rallies and wishes you to leave."

Drew's grin faded. "Understood."

His gaze flicked to Caroline. A blend of emotions lined her eyes as though she knew his stay would likely be short-lived. She was doing her utmost to help her father, and Drew couldn't ask her to do anything less. They would simply have to make the most of what time they had.

CYRUS PAUSED OUTSIDE THE SHANTY. "Ain't much of a place, but I've done what I can t' tidy it up. Put new hinges on the door an' patched some holes in the roof."

"It'll do fine." Drew followed him inside, pleased to see a cot, nightstand, and lantern now filled some of the void.

Cyrus scratched at his chin. "You must've done some awful fancy talkin' to convince young mas'er Phillip and the missus t' let you stay on, even in this ol' run-down shack. Never heard tell of a Yankee bein' *allowed* t' set foot on Dunbar land."

Chuckling, Drew set his things on the thin mattress. "I'd say it was more convincing Phillip I could ease his workload. But I won't be staying long if Mr. Dunbar recovers and has his say."

With a shake of his head, Cyrus crossed his arms. "Poor mas'er Dunbar. He's in an awful state, body and mind. Sendin' Miss Caroline away like he done—weren't no call for it."

A knock stilled their conversation. The door eased open, and Caroline smiled in at them, her gaze resting on Drew. "Are you getting settled?"

He gestured to the furnishings. "Thanks to Cyrus, it's a palace compared to the last time I was here." Striding over, he brushed a wisp of hair from her cheek. "You look tired. How's your father?"

Her shoulders sagged. "Very little change."

With a pat of her arm, Cyrus ambled toward the door. "Don't lose heart now, Miss Caroline. Between you an' the Good Lord, he's bound t' improve in time."

The comment brought a tender smile to her lips. "Thank you, Cyrus."

He nodded and headed outside, his cheery whistle gradually fading away.

Drew cupped Caroline's cheek. "He's right, you know."

Her eyes drifted to his shirt. "It's terrible to say, but I'm almost afraid he will recover and send you away."

Touched by her honesty, he leaned to kiss her forehead. "I'll admit I've had the same thought. But we can't live in fear of what may happen and miss out on the Lord's blessings today." Taking her hands, he rubbed his thumbs along their soft surface. "The best way I know to combat fear is to pray."

She stared up at him, her lips lifting in a gentle grin. "I agree."

Together they bowed their heads, choosing faith over fear and God's will over their own.

CAROLINE SHADED her eyes against the midday sun, staring into the distance where Drew and Phillip worked side by side to transplant the seedling tobacco plants. Joy bubbled inside her at the sight. Though, not half as much as at the feel of Drew's warm hands clasping hers as they'd prayed together. In that moment, when she'd gazed into his silvery eyes and they'd bowed their heads to pray, her heart had flooded with love for him.

His prayer had been so simple and yet so powerful, asking the Lord to shroud her family with love and blessing and her father with healing and grace toward her, to love and accept her as his daughter. Not once had he prayed selfishly that her father would show him approval or that she and he could remain together always. His humility had entwined her heart with his all the more.

With a satisfied sigh, she tore herself away and headed inside. She'd worked with Papa twice a day for well over a week now with little change. Discouraging though it was, she refused to lose heart.

She would not give up.

With a light tap on his door, she stepped inside. His eyes opened at her approach. To her relief, they no longer held contempt when he looked at her but instead an eager awareness of her presence. "How are you this morning, Papa?"

His mouth opened slightly as if in answer, his slurred attempt to speak almost recognizable. Caroline's eyes widened. "Did you say 'better'?"

He managed a slight nod.

A smile tugged at her lips, and she brushed the hair from his forehead. "That's wonderful, Papa. Keep trying. Your words will come."

Starting with his arm, she worked from shoulder to hand, massaging and bending. As she laid his hand atop hers, his fingers flexed slightly. Caroline pulled in a breath and stared

345

down at her father. "They moved! Your fingers moved. Can you do it again?"

She returned her gaze to his fingers, waiting, hoping. The fingers curved over her hand, giving a slight squeeze. A smile erupted onto her face. "You did it, Papa. You're going to get well, I know it."

Moisture glistened in his eyes, and tears spilled down onto his temples. Fighting tears of her own, Caroline dried his face with a kerchief. Never had she witnessed her father so humbled and broken.

He attempted to speak, and she leaned in closer. "What, Papa? What did you say?"

"Thak ou."

Her throat thickened. Had she heard him right? *Thank you?* She'd never dreamed her father's first words would be ones of gratitude toward her. Uncontrollable sobs welled inside her, and she laid her head in his lap, crying tears of thanksgiving and healing.

And as she felt his hand move in an attempt to embrace her, her heart grew full. She'd chosen love over hate, and oh, how grateful she was.

May 12, 1865 (Two weeks later)

THE SMELL of roast beef and potatoes filled Drew's senses as he washed up in the basin for dinner. He grinned to himself at the sound of Phillip's excited voice echoing from the dining room. "We did it, Mama. We finished transplanting all the fields and thinned out most of the weeds. I'm gonna go tell Papa."

The pride in the young man's voice warmed Drew. In the short time he'd been there, he'd witnessed Phillip grow from a spoiled, headstrong boy to a responsible, hardworking young man. Though Drew didn't claim credit for the transformation, being out from under his father's biases and overbearing ways hadn't done him any harm.

"Don't be long, young'un. We's about t' take up dinner." Lily's voice rang after him.

Drew dried his arms with the towel, a bit guilt-ridden about his duties at home. In helping out here, he'd sacrificed putting in his own crop. He only hoped Luke was taking care of the place for Mama and Lydia. Yet, it wasn't right to leave Luke to shoulder the load indefinitely.

His chest clenched. If Caroline's father continued to make progress, it was likely he'd be sent away soon regardless. It would break his heart to leave her, but what choice would he have?

Making his way into the dining room, he took his place at the table—Jamison's place. Though no one made mention of it, he wondered if his sitting there bothered them. And yet, he'd felt honored to have his chair.

Caroline brought a plate of bread and a bowl of potatoes to the table then took a seat beside him. He smiled at her, never tiring of her soft, oval eyes and the gentle upturn of her lips.

Hurried footsteps pounded down the hall.

Mrs. Dunbar placed the platter of meat on the table then swiveled around, pressing a hand to her chest. "What on earth?"

A breathless Phillip appeared in the doorway, a frenzied expression on his face. "Come see. Papa's sitting up in bed."

"Glory be!" Lily declared amid the excited chatter.

In a matter of seconds, the room emptied, leaving Drew alone to ponder what the news meant for him and Caroline.

53

May 24, 1865

Caroline helped her father out to the veranda and eased him into the wicker chair. "There now, you did it."

He slumped back, breathless from the exertion. "And nearly ... died ... trying."

She smothered a grin and leaned his cane against the brick. He was growing feistier with each passing day. A good sign. "The fresh air will do you good."

His breathing slowed, and he squinted out to the field where Drew and Phillip were working. "Who's this fellow Phillip keeps talking about? Drew Gallagher?"

Caroline laced her hands together behind her to stem their trembling. She'd known the question would come, but that didn't make fronting it any easier. Since Papa had been up and about, Drew had made himself scarce, washing up and taking his meals in the shanty instead of the house. For weeks, she'd dreaded the confrontation. Now there was no getting around it.

"He's a good man, Papa. Without his help, Phillip never could have gotten the fields planted."

Papa kept his eyes fixed on the pair in the field. "But who is

349

he? Where did he come from? And how did he happen to show up here?"

She hesitated, weighing how to respond. "H-he's an acquaintance of mine who ... has a background in farming."

"Not from around here, or I'd know of him."

"No." She bit her lip, bracing herself as she squeaked out the words. "From ... New York."

His head jerked toward her, his green eyes wide. "A Yankee?"

Her heart plummeted. "Please don't send him away, Papa. I'm ... quite fond of him."

"Quite fo—?" His mouth clamped, and his eyes narrowed as his gaze returned to the field. "Go fetch him. I wanna speak to him."

With a heavy heart, Caroline hiked her skirt and downed the veranda steps. Her breaths shallowed as she tromped across the yard to the field where Drew was busy cutting the heads from the plants. She suppressed a moan as he paused and peered toward her. They'd fretted and prayed over this moment. Now, they could only trust their petitions had been heard.

Sheathing his knife, Drew made his way over, his somber expression evidence he guessed her reason for coming.

Tears blurred her vision as she stopped beside him. Choking down the emotion in her voice, she forced herself to meet his gaze, lips atremble. "Papa wishes to speak with you."

He nodded and brushed a reassuring hand along her arm. "It'll be all right."

She turned to walk with him, wishing she could believe that. Papa had changed immensely toward her over recent weeks, but it was too much to hope he'd accept a Yankee.

To her relief, she saw her mother join Papa on the veranda. Perhaps her presence would help temper his response. Papa's eyes never left them as they strode toward the house. His brow furrowed when Drew neared. "You!"

Mama squeezed his shoulder. "Now, Eugene. Don't judge the

man without giving him a chance. He's been a great asset to us in your absence."

Papa eased back in his chair, gaze still fixed on Drew. "I'm surprised you had the gumption to return after being run off."

Drew looked him in the eyes, his voice calm and steady. "I came for Caroline's sake and to lend a hand where needed while you're recuperating."

Grunting, Papa pursed his lips. "Caroline tells me you have a farm of your own to tend."

"Yes, sir. My father was killed in the war, so it's only my brother and me left to manage it."

"Then why aren't you there?" Papa's tone seemed more laced with curiosity than accusation.

Drew's lack of response compelled Caroline to glance his way. A swirl of emotions streamed in his eyes, the meaning of which she couldn't quite decipher. At last, he turned to her father. "I love your daughter, sir. Being here seemed more important."

Caroline's throat hitched, and it was all she could do not to throw herself around him and smother him with kisses. Instead, she looped her arm through his and fixed her eyes on her father. "I love him too, Papa."

Warmth and peace enveloped her as Drew cupped his hand over hers. As much as she longed for her father's blessing, knowing a godly man like Drew loved her somehow eased the burden to gain her father's favor. Whatever his response, she would stand by this man who'd taught her so much about grace and forgiveness.

Papa scrubbed a hand down his face, his eyes flicking back and forth between them. "So, it's like that, is it?" With a sigh, he fastened his hands on the chair arms. After a moment of silence, his gaze latched onto Drew. "Well, all I can say is, my daughter's a good nurse. See that she has opportunity to use her skills."

Caroline's breath caught. *His daughter? A good nurse?*

He wagged his finger at them. "And don't be filling my grandchildren's heads with a lot of Yankee nonsense."

Her mind was still reeling when Drew's strong hands lifted her and twirled her around amid joyful shouts. She giggled, the essence of her father's words finally soaking in. As Drew set her down, she held him fast and flashed her father a wide grin. He winked at her, his wry smile like a sweet melody in her soul.

Her mother leaned to hug him, her eyes filled with tears of joy. Papa lifted a hand to her cheek, and for a moment, Caroline glimpsed a tenderness between them reminiscent of what their love must have once been.

Grateful, her heart rejoiced. For, like light shining in the darkness, Christ-like love had changed her father.

And extending it had changed her.

THE END

EPILOGUE

June 19, 1865, Rural New York

The soothing turn of the carriage wheels brought Drew added solace as he sat with Caroline on the buggy seat, her head propped against him. The Lord had done some wondrous things over recent weeks, but none so incredible as allowing Drew to marry the woman he loved and softening her father's stony heart.

Caroline glanced up at him, her felt bonnet clipping his chin in the movement. "Do you think your family will like me?"

Chuckling, Drew shifted the reins to one hand and wrapped his arm around her shoulders with the other. "Of course, they will. How could they not?"

She snuggled closer, twirling the gold band on her ring finger. "Mmm. I hope you're right. I do so want to make a good impression."

He gave her shoulders a gentle squeeze. "If I know Mama, she'll spot a fine wife when she sees one, whether from the North or South."

Caroline stretched to kiss his cheek. "She sounds like a very gracious lady. If she's anything like her son, I'll adore her."

"Actually, she's a lot like *you*. It was your heart of compassion to tend my wounds that brought us together."

Her breath tickled his ear as she spoke in soft tones. "And it was your encouragement to extend grace to Papa that allowed me to experience both your loves."

He leaned down to give her a tender kiss, then gazed out at the sunlit landscape. "If only our nation could learn kindness instead of hatred and mercy rather than strife. Then the Lord would heal this war-torn land."

"Perhaps, in time, He'll turn our small efforts into something bigger."

"He might at that." Drew breathed deeply, satisfied. The nation may not have escaped the atrocities of war, but, with the Lord's help, it could win the battle waging within—good over evil, one heart and soul at a time.

A familiar homestead appeared up ahead, and his lips lifted. "We're home."

Caroline straightened, peering at the white frame house and fenced-in yard in the distance. "Is that your mother?"

"It sure is." Drew tapped the reins on Angel's rump, spurring her faster. His telegram must have arrived for, like the prodigal's father awaiting his son's return, Drew's mother sat on the porch, eyes searching. As they neared, she rose from her chair and flew down the porch steps to greet them, her smile radiant. The door to the house banged open, and, with a squeal, Lydia rushed from within, looking more like a young lady than the child he remembered. Though Luke was nowhere about, his handiwork showed in the freshly-plowed fields dotted with seedling plants.

Drew could almost imagine his father alongside his mother and sister, lifting a hand in greeting. Even more, he sensed his Heavenly Father's presence. In all Drew had endured, the Lord had never left his side, lending strength and guidance for each new day.

Clasping Caroline's hand, he gave thanks for his many blessings ... and for new beginnings.

AUTHOR'S NOTE

When it comes to writing, I'm a stickler for authenticity. But, when I decided to write a Civil War novel, I never dreamed the extent of research it would entail. I often became so engrossed in the details that writing slowed to almost a standstill at times. Coupled by the fact that I was diagnosed with cancer and undergoing treatment through much of the writing of this novel, it truly proved a challenge.

And yet, I loved every minute of it. The writing and research ... not the cancer. =(

Though my Prairie Sky Series required attention to period detail and some historical background, *Beyond These War-Torn Lands* is steeped in actual historical events and people. That alone demanded I delve deeper into every detail—from the color of General Grant's eyes to the time of day the Union soldiers stormed Richmond.

Rather than more notable battles, I chose to include some lesser-known conflicts such as The Battle of Monocacy, The Battle of the Crater, and the City Point Depot explosion. Only true history buffs will catch all the historical elements woven within the pages of the novel.

Though my hero (Drew) and heroine (Caroline) are both

fictional, many individuals they encounter along the way are real. Caroline's neighbors—the Thomas and Worthington families—were actual witnesses to the Battle of Monocacy, hunkering in their cellar while the fighting raged outside their homes.

Also real was the incident in which Lieutenant Morris Schaff risked his life to snuff out flames following the explosion at City Point Depot. Inserting Drew into the scene seemed the perfect way to earn him credibility in light of Captain Jacobs' criticisms.

The President's visit to City Point on the River Queen and General Grant's presence there were also true to history—down to Grant's favored horse, Cincinnati, and the wooden bench he often sat on outside his summer quarters.

Probably my favorite aspect of blending history with fiction was placing Caroline in the home of Dr. Samuel Mudd. I purposely withheld his name early on to allow readers the thrill of discovery, leaving a trail of clues along the way as to his identity. I hope you enjoyed an "ah-ha" moment when the truth came to light and you figured out just who he was and his association with John Wilkes Booth.

Dr. Mudd is truly a fascinating personality. The Mudd family welcomed numerous people into their home which I didn't include in the story, other than their four children and the two young servant girls. Making Caroline Dr. and Mrs. Mudd's niece provided a natural entrance into their home as well as an eye-witness account to his encounter with J.W. Booth.

If you're unfamiliar with Dr. Mudd's story, I invite you to visit the website: https://drmudd.org/. I had hoped to make a trip out to his house and museum, and then Covid hit, followed by my cancer. The information and virtual tour at this site proved invaluable to me in lieu of viewing it in person.

I also couldn't resist mentioning the completion of the Capitol dome, a tidbit of history I previously didn't know took place during the Civil War. The original dome was much smaller, and became dwarfed by the expanding Capitol building. The time and detail that went into the upgraded dome is truly amazing.

I hope you enjoyed *Beyond These War-Torn Lands*. I'm currently writing Book Two in the series, tentatively entitled, *Beyond Wounded Hearts*. This second novel is due to release in late 2022 and will be the story of Drew's younger brother, Luke, whom we meet briefly in this first book. I look forward to introducing you to my heroine, Adelaide Hanover, a rather feisty Southerner with a vengeance toward Yankees.

Following is a list of some of my main resources in writing *Beyond These War-Torn Lands*.

Book Sources:

Manhunt: The 12 Day Chase for Lincoln's Killer by James L. Swanson, Harper Collins, New York, NY, 2006.

Pursuit to Appomattox: The Last Battles by Jerry Korn, Alexandria, VA, Time-Life books, 1987.

Web Sources:

https://www.battlefields.org/learn/maps/battle-monocacy-july-9-1864

https://drmudd.org/

https://www.battlefields.org/learn/articles/richmond-flames-and-rubble

https://www.gettysburgdaily.com/john-wilkes-booths-escape-3-with-gettysburg-lbg-mike-kanazawich/

https://www.gettysburgdaily.com/john-wilkes-booths-escape-8-with-gettysburg-lbg-mike-kanazawich/

DISCUSSION QUESTIONS FOR BOOK CLUBS & GROUPS

1. When Sergeant Drew Gallagher chooses to avenge himself against the gloating Confederate soldier who shot him instead of heeding the inner promptings of the Holy Spirit, his decision costs him dearly. Why is revenge a poor choice? Recall a time you had the choice to either seek revenge or let a wrong slide. Do you feel good about your response? How could you have handled the situation differently?

2. Caroline makes the difficult decision to aid a man her family deems as an enemy. What sacrifices does she make in order to do this? Why do you think she chooses to take such a risk? Have you ever been faced with a dilemma that pits your faith against your loyalties?

3. Hurt by her father's obvious prejudice against her, Caroline struggles to understand his embittered feelings. Have you ever had someone single you out and treat you unkind or unjustly? How did you respond? Did you secretly let it eat at you? Ignore them? Treat them coldly in return? How does Scripture say to treat our enemies or those who are unkind to us? Take a few

minutes to read and discuss verses that address this topic such as: Matthew 5:43-44, Romans 12: 14-21 and Colossians 3:12-14.

4. At the Battle of the Crater, Drew struggles with the horrors of war and the thought of taking the life of someone Caroline is acquainted with. How does he remedy this? How can we honor God by choosing to help people rather than harm them?

5. When Caroline discovers her father is withholding her letters to her mother and sister, she becomes further embittered toward him. How does letting hard feelings fester inside us make grudges worse? What can we do to safe-guard ourselves against seeds of bitterness?

6. When Drew stumbles across an injured Captain Jacobs, he sets aside hard feelings and makes the conscious choice to aid him (his enemy). What effect does this have on Captain Jacobs? What effect does the action have on Drew?

7. After Caroline discovers her uncle has been less than honest with authorities about his association with Booth and Herold, she debates whether to share what she knows or conceal it to protect her relatives. What finally convinced Caroline to relay the truth to Drew? Is it ever right to withhold information to protect ourselves or someone close to us? Have you ever felt prompted by the Holy Spirit to do or say something outside of your comfort zone?

8. Drew has the opportunity to share his faith with a dying soldier as well as Captain Jacobs. Why is it important for us to look for opportunities to speak words of life and encouragement to others? Even though Captain Jacobs seemed to scoff at Drew's faith, do you think deep down he respected him for it? The story is open-ended about what happens to Captain Jacobs once he's taken to the hospital. Do you feel Drew's faith and act of

kindness made enough impression on Jacobs to plant a seed of change in his heart?

9. Caroline's desire to learn nursing is a source of strain between her and her father, and though her dream of becoming a nurse isn't actualized in the story, she uses her gift of aiding others to nurse Drew and her father back to health. Have you ever had a dream that didn't fully come to fruition in the way you'd hoped or anticipated? Did God have a better plan?

10. Both Drew and Caroline deal with difficult people in their lives, ultimately choosing to forgive and overcome evil with good. With all the animosity and bitterness prevalent in today's society, what can we learn from their example? How does responding in kindness to those who mistreat us help defuse volatile situations? What would our world be like if more people chose to love their enemies rather than respond in hatred and revenge?

ABOUT THE AUTHOR

Cynthia Roemer is an inspirational, bestselling author with a heart for scattering seeds of hope into the hearts of readers. Raised in the cornfields of rural Illinois, Cynthia enjoys spinning tales set in the backdrop of the mid-1800's prairie and Civil War era. Her Prairie Sky Series consists of Amazon bestseller, *Under This Same Sky*, *Under Prairie Skies*, and *Under Moonlit Skies*, a 2020 Selah Award winning novel.

Cynthia writes from her family farm in central Illinois where she resides with her husband, Marvin. They have two grown sons and a daughter-in-love. When she isn't writing or researching, Cynthia can be found hiking, biking, gardening, reading, or riding sidesaddle with her husband in the combine or on their motorcycle. She is a member of American Christian Fiction Writers. Visit Cynthia online at: www.cynthiaroemer.com and sign up for her newsletter list here: https://mailchi.mp/2aod03dfaa50/newslettersignup.

ALSO BY CYNTHIA ROEMER

Becky Hollister wants nothing more than to live out her days on the prairie, building a life for herself alongside her future husband. But when a tornado rips through her parents' farm, killing her mother and sister, she must leave the only home she's ever known and the man she's begun to love to accompany her injured father to St. Louis.

Catapulted into a world of unknowns, Becky finds solace in corresponding with Matthew Brody, the handsome pastor back home. But when word comes that he is all but engaged to someone else, she must call upon her faith to decipher her future.

Unsettled by the news that her estranged cousin and uncle are
returning home after a year away, Charlotte Stanton goes to ready their
cabin and finds a handsome stranger has taken up residence. Convinced
he's a squatter, she throws him off the property before learning his full
identity. Little does she know, their paths were destined to cross again.

Quiet and ruggedly handsome, Chad Avery's uncanny ability to see
through Charlotte's feisty exterior and expose her inner weaknesses
both infuriates and intrigues her. When a tragic accident incites her
family to move east, Charlotte stays behind in hopes of becoming
better acquainted with the elusive cattleman. Yet Chad's unwillingness
to divulge his hidden past, along with his vow not to love again,
threatens to keep them apart forever.

She had her life planned out - until he rode in

Illinois prairie - 1859

After four long years away, Esther Stanton returns to the prairie to care
for her sister Charlotte's family following the birth of her second child.
The month-long stay seems much too short as Esther becomes
acquainted with her brother-in-law's new ranch hand, Stewart Brant.
When obligations compel her to return to Cincinnati and to the man
her overbearing mother intends her to wed, she loses hope of ever
knowing true happiness.

Still reeling from a hurtful relationship, Stew is reluctant to open his
heart to Esther. But when he faces a life-threatening injury with Esther
tending him, their bond deepens. Heartbroken when she leaves, he sets
out after her and inadvertently stumbles across an illegal slave-trade
operation, the knowledge of which puts him, as well as Esther and her
family, in jeopardy.

Under Moonlit Skies won first-place in the Western Fiction category of
the 2020 Selah Awards.

MORE HISTORICAL ROMANCE FROM SCRIVENINGS PRESS

Love's Kindling

by Award-winning Author Elaine Marie Cooper

Book One of the Dawn of America Series

This title includes *War's Respite*, prequel to the

Dawn of America series.

During the American Revolution, Aurinda Whitney lives with her cold and calloused father, an embittered veteran of the previous war. Aurinda's life changed forever when her father returned for her after that war, taking her away from the only place she'd ever experienced affection. Since her father blamed Aurinda for the death of his wife in childbirth, Aurinda is convinced she is unworthy of love.

Zadok Wooding believes he is a failure as he tends the smithy at home while others go to battle against the British. Just when he has an opportunity to become a hero, he is blinded in an accident. Now he fears he will never live up to the Biblical "mighty man of valor" for whom he was named.

When the couple meet, they are both challenged to overcome adversity as well as their inadequacies. Unexpected secrets of their past emerge that can change their lives forever. But can they look past their present circumstances to heal—and find love?

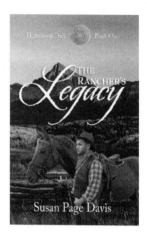

The Rancher's Legacy

Homeward Trails

Book One

Matthew Anderson and his father try to help neighbor Bill Maxwell when his ranch is attacked. On the day his daughter Rachel is to return from school back East, outlaws target the Maxwell ranch. After Rachel's world is shattered, she won't even consider the plan her father and Matt's cooked up—to see their two children marry and combine the ranches.

Meanwhile in Maine, sea captain's widow Edith Rose hires a private investigator to locate her three missing grandchildren. The children were abandoned by their father nearly twenty years ago. They've been adopted into very different families, and they're scattered across the country. Can investigator Ryland Atkins find them all while the elderly woman still lives? His first attempt is to find the boy now called

Matthew Anderson. Can Ryland survive his trip into the wild Colorado Territory and find Matt before the outlaws finish destroying a legacy?

Scrivenings
PRESS
Quench your thirst for story.
www.ScriveningsPress.com

Stay up-to-date on your favorite books and authors with our free e-newsletters.

ScriveningsPress.com

Made in the USA
Las Vegas, NV
09 December 2021

36889220R00210